Born in Belfast, Mary Larkin is a housewife. She moved to Darlington with her husband and three sons in 1974 and has lived there ever since.

When not writing, she divides her time between Darlington, where her youngest grandchildren, Declan, Joseph and Thomas live, and Pickering, North Yorkshire, where her eldest son and his wife live: the main attraction there being her two granddaughters Louise and Coleen. She also manages to visit Belfast twice a year to meet old friends and relatives and to research her novels.

Also by Mary A. Larkin

THE WASTED YEARS
TIES OF LOVE AND HATE
FOR BETTER, FOR WORSE

Playing With Fire

MARY A. LARKIN

A *Time Warner* Paperback

First published in Great Britain in 2001 by Little, Brown and Company
This edition published by Time Warner Paperbacks in 2002

All characters in this publication are fictitious and any resemblance to real persons, living or dead, is purely coincidental.

A CIP catalogue record for this book
is available from the British Library.

ISBN 0 7515 3221 5

Typeset by Palimpsest Book Production Limited,
Polmont, Stirlingshire
Printed and bound in Great Britain by
Clays Ltd, St Ives plc

Time Warner Paperbacks
An imprint of
Time Warner Books UK
Brettenham House
Lancaster Place
London WC2E 7EN

www.TimeWarnerBooks.co.uk

I dedicate this book to my daughters-in-law,
Debbie and Helen, and my sons,
Con, Paul and Edan.

Acknowledgements

I would like to express my sincere gratitude to Shelagh Peacock of Darlington, Cath Holden, also of Darlington, and Sue & Billy McDowell from Belfast, whose special assistance was invaluable.

Author's Note

The geographical areas portrayed in *Playing With Fire* actually exist and historic events referred to in the course of the story are, to the best of my knowledge, authentic. However, I would like to emphasise that the story is fictional, all characters fictitious and any resemblance to real persons, living or dead, purely coincidental.

Chapter One

Nervously Susan Cummings followed her friend up the stairs that led to the Club Orchid dance hall. Each Sunday night saw them outside the Club Orchid on the corner of King Street where they met for their weekly venture into modern ballroom dancing. In the small cloakroom Ruth Vernon met Susan's eyes in the mirror and asked excitedly, 'Well? Did he turn up?' Receiving a brief nod, she hurried on. 'Well, what happened? Was he nice? Are you going out with him again?'

'Yes, he was very nice. A perfect gentleman, if you must know. But . . . I don't think I'll be seeing him again.'

Ruth's eyes went round with surprise and her mouth gaped slightly as she probed. 'Why on earth not?' Bewildered, she cried, 'I don't understand. Did you not fancy him after all?'

Oh, if only that were the case, Susan lamented inwardly. But the simple truth was he hadn't asked her for another date. They had gone to the Ritz Cinema but she couldn't remember much about the film; just that it was a western and Jim seemed to have enjoyed it. He had held her hand throughout the film and she had been so aware of the pressure of his arm against hers, sending tingles through her body, that she lost all interest in the film and sat in a well of happiness. He had been a perfect gentleman all evening. After the film they had walked up to Johnny Long's and each had one of his famous fish suppers. Sitting in one of the booths they had talked for ages. She had been enchanted. No long pauses punctuated the conversation, like they usually did when she was talking to the opposite sex.

At the corner of the street where she lived, Jim had seemed taken aback as he eyed the wide avenue with its opulent houses. He made no attempt to find out which of these houses was her home. He had already realised his mistake and was content to make his good night at the corner of the street. 'Posh, eh?' he said and a wry smile twisted his lips. Her heart had turned a somersault when he placed his hands on her shoulders and looked down into her eyes. With all her might she willed him to kiss her, but in vain.

'Susan, I've really enjoyed myself tonight. You're wonderful company. Thanks for coming out with me.' His voice was full of emotion and the back of his hand sensually trailed her cheek, but as she moved her lips towards it, it was quickly withdrawn. 'Good night, Susan.' To her amazement, with a light peck on the cheek he had turned tail and was gone before she could voice her concern.

Tears pricked her eyes as abruptly she answered Ruth's question. 'He didn't ask for another date.'

'Didn't ask? You're having me on! It's obvious he fancies you. Good heavens, he never takes his eyes off you. Even when you're both dancing with different partners.'

'Well, he didn't ask me, so there!' Susan cried, her frustration showing. 'He was a perfect gentleman, so he was. He gave me a peck on the cheek and thanked me for going out with him. And that was that! He must just like dancing with me,' she added forlornly. 'Or perhaps he found me too boring.'

'Don't be silly! It's obvious that he cares for you. He was probably afraid of you turning him down.' Ruth shot a concerned look at her. 'Were you snooty with him? You can sometimes be very snooty, you know, Susan. You take after your mam in that respect. Still, he will be here tonight, you'll see. The minute we enter the ballroom he'll be there like a flash, asking for a dance.'

Susan fervently hoped her friend was right. She certainly hadn't been uppish with him. She saved that for people she didn't like. And she liked Jim. More than liked him. In fact, to her great consternation, she thought she was in love with him. Could these feelings possibly be love? They had danced often these past six weeks ever since they first met. She had been thrilled to bits when he had at last asked her for a date. And this was the outcome: sadness and despair.

Fluffing her soft, dark-brown hair loose around her face, she renewed her lipstick and eyed her reflection in the mirror. Big, dark, grey eyes, set in long thick lashes, gazed mournfully back at her.

'Don't look so glum,' her friend advised. Then, seeing the big eyes cloud with tears, Ruth added more gently, 'You really do like him, don't you? Never mind. Let's hand in our coats and go and give tonight's talent the once-over.'

Inside the ballroom they made their way over to the side of the dance floor where all the girls gathered. A quick glance across the floor to where the men stood and Susan felt her heart drop. Jim Brady was tall, easily identified in a crowd, and it was obvious that he was not present. Ruth squeezed her hand in sympathy. 'It's early yet. He'll come,' she whispered. 'Don't worry about it.'

The music started up and two young men who had been eyeing the girls up, and slowly edging closer, approached and asked them to dance. The evening entertainment had begun. The girls were extremely good dancers and popular with the regulars. New patrons soon noticed and the girls seldom sat out a dance. The time flew past and, in spite of Jim's non-appearance, Susan enjoyed dancing to her favourite records.

At the intermission, while their current partners were in the pub below the dance hall getting them drinks, the girls climbed the stairs to the cloakroom to powder their noses.

'For heaven's sake cheer up, Susan. I don't know how you're managing to get any partners tonight! You've a face as long as a Lurgan spade.'

Susan rounded on her in anger. 'Don't exaggerate, for goodness sake!'

Then, catching sight of herself in the mirror, she had to agree with her friend and giggled ruefully.

'That's better. Forget Jim Brady and enjoy yourself. Maybe it's just as well he's not here if you care so much for him. He's probably got more sense than you and doesn't want to start something that can only end in tears.'

'What do you mean?'

'He's a Catholic, isn't he? Imagine your dad's reaction if you dared bring a Catholic home. Eh? Why can't you be like me and love them and leave them? Enjoy yourself! You wouldn't catch me getting involved with a Catholic.'

They were descending the stairs to the dance hall when Susan saw Jim cross the lower landing and enter the hall. Seeing the joy on her companion's face, Ruth followed the direction of her gaze and sighed. 'Really, Susan, you would be better off without him,' she warned. 'I didn't realise that you were so keen on him.'

'Oh, don't be daft. I just like him.'

Dismayed that she had allowed her current dance partner to monopolise her time, Susan trailed reluctantly behind Ruth to join the two lads. Jim's swift glance quickly found her and their eyes locked. He nodded in acknowledgement. His glance also noted that she and Ruth had obviously paired off with the two young men. He eyed the unattached girls still gathered in a group to one side of the dance floor and, when the music started up again, he had already chosen his partner: a tall, willowy blonde, who entered his arms obviously delighted at the chance to dance with him.

They passed each other often on the crowded floor, but Jim studiously avoided looking her way. Susan was annoyed with herself. She should not have allowed this stranger to stake a claim to all her dances. She might have guessed that Jim could possibly arrive late. Still, he had never been late before, so how was she to think otherwise? As the evening wore on Susan tried to think of a way to get rid of her partner without offending him, but he just would not take the hint.

Meanwhile Jim danced all the dances with the blonde and Susan noted that the tall girl hung on his every word. Was he not going to ask her to dance with him at all? But how could he, when her partner never left her side? As the last dance was announced, and knowing that Jim would never encroach on another man's territory, Susan was tempted to excuse herself and, leaving her partner, ask Jim for the last dance. She was saved from the embarrassment this would undoubtedly have caused by seeing Jim leading the blonde on to the dance floor at the first bar of the final waltz. Blinded by tears and seeking comfort, Susan let her partner hold her closer than was necessary. Jim made her aware of the wantonness of this action by the disdainful sneer he directed at their bodies.

Bewildered, she pressed closer still. How dare he! How dare he look at her like that, after ignoring her all evening. To her great shame she suddenly realised the effect her actions were having on her partner. Gazing up into his dazed eyes, she pushed him away. 'I'm sorry. Very sorry.'

'No, it's me who should be sorry. I apologise. I couldn't help myself.'

Breaking from his grasp she pushed through the dancers and left the ballroom. In the cloakroom she powdered her flushed face and, retrieving her coat and Ruth's, waited impatiently for her friend. She was one of the last to arrive and, pushing through the other girls, confronted Susan.

Edging her into a corner for some privacy, Ruth whispered furiously, 'Just what do you think you're playing at? Leaving that poor sod standing on the dance floor.'

'Oh, I'm so sorry, I didn't mean to offend or embarrass him.'

'I don't know how you manage it, but in spite of everything he still wants to see you home.'

'Oh, no!' Susan was aghast. 'I don't want him to see me home. I just want to be alone.'

'Catch yourself on! Jim Brady will probably be seeing that blonde home. Show him you couldn't care less. Anyway, I'm afraid you have no choice. I accepted for you. And I think it's the least you can do, after the way you behaved. They will both be waiting outside for us.'

Ruth started back in amazement when her friend gripped her arm. 'Tell him I've already gone. Please, Ruth. Here, I've got your coat for you. You go on now and I'll stay here as long as I can. Give you all a chance to get on your way.'

Ruth looked at her friend's flushed, distressed face. Heavens above, she was actually trembling. 'What's got into you, Susan? You've been leading him on all evening. It's not like you to deliberately hurt someone.'

'I don't want to hurt him, but I will not be pressurised into his company. Not in the state I'm in at the moment.'

'Oh, all right then! I'll give you a ring tomorrow afternoon.' Ruth peered intently into her friend's eyes. 'Will you be okay on your own?'

'Of course. Just get me off the hook, please.'

Oblivious to the curious looks and whispers of the other girls, Susan waited patiently until the cloakroom emptied and she was alone. Then, stretching her limbs to relieve some of the tension from her body, she slowly left the cloakroom, knowing the staff would want to lock up as quickly as possible.

Downstairs, she cautiously stepped on to the pavement and breathed a deep sigh of relief. The crowds had thinned out and there was no one she knew in sight. It was a beautiful evening; a time for lovers, and she felt sad as she made her way down to the bus stop. As she hurried along she became aware that someone was close behind her and glanced anxiously over her shoulder. Jim lengthened his stride and quickly joined her.

'Is it all right if I see you home, Susan?'

A quick disdainful lift of the head accompanied the derisive retort. 'Huh! What happened to the beautiful blonde you danced with all night?'

'Janet? She is attractive, isn't she?' He grinned and glanced sideways at Susan's glum face. 'However, I had no desire to see her home. I hung about outside in the hope that you wouldn't let that big ape you were dancing with take you home.'

'He's a very nice person, so he is,' she defended her absent partner. Turning a suspicious look on him, she frowned. 'I didn't see you outside.'

'Well, I saw Ruth and the two lads head towards Castle Junction, but I stayed out of sight in case someone else was with you.'

She stopped and rounded on him in anger. 'What do you take me for? Eh? Do you really think I would dance all evening with someone and then go home with another man?'

Gripping her by the elbows, he shook her slightly.

'Then why isn't he here with you now? The way you were dancing together I could see he thought he was on to a good thing.'

'How dare you! If you followed me just to hurl insults, please leave me alone.' With these words she wrenched herself free of his hold and stormed down Castle Street.

Jim gazed after her for a few seconds, then with an exasperated sigh set off in pursuit.

When he reached her, he was dismayed to see tears rolling down her cheeks. Drawing her into the doorway of the Bank Buildings, he thrust a handkerchief into her hand and gathered her close.

'Here now, don't go on like that,' he said gently. 'I didn't mean to upset you. It was just my jealousy getting out of hand.'

Surprise stopped the tears and she gaped up at him in disbelief. 'You were jealous?'

He frowned. 'You sound surprised.' A quick glance at his watch caused him to exclaim. 'Look, if we don't hurry we'll miss the last bus. I'll explain later.'

Taking her hand, he pulled her arm through his and hurried her down into the town centre and towards her bus stop. Ashamed at her outburst and thinking that she must look a sight, Susan stood in the bus queue, head bent, wishing Jim would explain what he meant. Had he really been jealous? It was hard to believe. He had appeared to be enjoying the blonde's company. Still, the girl had looked as if she would gladly have let him escort her home, but obviously he hadn't asked. Janet! Even her name was different – sophisticated.

The bus arrived and the queue moved forward. At the entrance she turned sadly to wish Jim good night.

To her amazement he hustled her aboard, asked for two fares and guided her upstairs to the upper deck. They sat on the back seat and he put his arm around her.

Aware that he lived on the Upper Falls, the opposite end of town from her, she reminded him, 'You won't get another bus back into town at this time of night.'

'I'm well aware of that,' he said resignedly. 'Still, it's a beautiful night and the walk back will do me good. I can go to a late Mass in the morning. You do realise that I'm a Catholic? Don't you?'

She nodded and the silence lengthened. She willed him to speak, but he remained deep in thought throughout the journey. They had left the bus and were making their way to the top of her street before he spoke again.

'I didn't intend going to the Club Orchid tonight, you know.'

'Oh?' Her eyes searched his face. She sensed that she wouldn't like what he was about to say.

He continued slowly, as if choosing his words carefully. 'But then, I couldn't help myself. I'm vain enough not to want you to think too badly of me, so I came to explain.' He grimaced. 'I didn't expect the jealousy that overwhelmed me when I saw you stuck against that guy like a sticking plaster. Was there any need for that?' She writhed with shame and he smiled and assured her, 'I didn't really think him a big ape. You could probably do a lot worse. He seemed a nice enough lad, but that didn't make any difference. I still didn't like it one wee bit.'

They had arrived at the corner of her street and he threw his arms wide as his eyes roamed over the detached houses set in their own grounds. 'Believe me,

Susan, I was gobsmacked when I saw all this opulence the other night. I hadn't realised you were so well off. I nearly died when I saw all this.'

'What difference does it make?'

'Are you kidding? Of course it makes a big difference. Had I known, I wouldn't have asked you out in the first place. Can't you see? We don't move in the same circles. I'm surprised that your parents allow you to frequent the Club Orchid.'

'They don't know! Anyhow, I don't honestly see what difference it makes. After a few dates we would probably be bored stiff with each other. Do you know what? I think you're a coward, Jim Brady. That's what I think.'

His arms circled her waist and a smile softened his features. 'You don't really think that,' he disagreed. 'Or you wouldn't be attracted to me. You *are* attracted to me, aren't you, Susan? I'm not wrong about that, am I?'

His lips were tantalisingly close and she trembled in his arms. 'A little,' she confessed with a slight smile and pressed closer. 'It can't do any harm to see each other now and again. Can it?' she added persuasively.

Framing her face with his hands, he whispered against her lips, 'Do you really believe that? You won't be disappointed when we have to part? Because we will have to part, there's no doubt about that. You won't say that I led you on? You see, there really is no future for us to share, Susan.'

'No, I won't hold it against you. Let's give it a try and see what happens. Mm?' Her lips parted in invitation and all his good intentions went out the window as he claimed his first kiss.

* * *

Rachel Cummings sat at the breakfast table after her husband had left for work and eyed her two daughters in concern. They were out every night of the week and her husband had insisted that she find out just what they were up to. She hated to pry into their affairs, but Trevor was right. They were both young and impressionable, Susan having just passed her twenty-first birthday and Alison nineteen. It was their duty as parents to keep a close eye on them and make sure they didn't get into any trouble.

Why did Trevor leave everything up to her? she lamented inwardly. On the other hand, he could be so forthright that the girls would probably take offence and there would be one hell of a row. So, determined to keep the conversation amicable, Rachel said in a teasing voice, 'Your father and I were just saying last night that we don't see much of you two lately.'

The look of amusement that the sisters shared and then bestowed on her showed her plainly that they were not fooled.

It was Alison who spoke first. 'Ah, me dad has asked you to find out what we're up to. Is that right, Mam?'

An embarrassed flush crept up Rachel's face. 'If you could be a wee bit more open about your affairs we wouldn't have to pry,' she declared. 'But no, you disappear every evening dressed to kill and we don't know where you are or who you're with. When I ask where you've been, all I get is "Out!" You can't blame us for being worried. We do right to worry about your welfare. Some of the young ones are so permissive these days.'

'Well, since you put it that way, if you must know,

I'm seeing a very nice bloke. Shall I bring him home for you and Dad to run your beady over?' Alison asked and laughed as alarm registered in her mother's eyes.

'It must be serious if you're willing to bring him home,' she cried. 'Do be careful, Alison. You're young and have your whole life ahead of you.'

'You can't have it both ways, Mam! Do you want to meet him or not? It's not serious. At least not as far as I'm concerned. I had no intention of inviting him to tea, but if it sets your mind at rest I'll bring him home on Saturday. I know you'll like him. I just hope it doesn't give him any ideas.'

Rachel looked more alarmed than ever. 'Ideas? What kind of ideas?'

'He might think I'm keen on him since I'm bringing him home to meet the family. You know, getting his feet under the table, you might say.'

Susan rose to her feet and, to avoid any awkward questions being directed at her, said, 'Do bring him to tea, Alison. Let's have a look at him.'

Alison looked sternly at her mother. 'I'll invite him to tea as long as you promise he won't be given the third degree. All right?'

'I can't speak for your father, Alison, but I will have a quiet word of warning in his ear before the lad arrives.' Rachel turned to her other daughter before she could escape. 'What about you, Susan? Would you like to bring your young man home on Saturday, as well? Make a night of it?'

Trying to appear nonchalant, Susan asked, 'What makes you think I've got a young man?'

'Haven't you? Where do you go every night, then?'

'I'm with Ruth a lot of the time, and now and again I go out with a boy. Nothing serious.' She wept inwardly. Four months of dating had not lessened her feelings where Jim Brady was concerned and she was sure he felt the same. It was serious; very serious. She just had to persuade him that they were meant for each other.

'Will you be here to meet Alison's young man on Saturday night, then?'

'Yes, I'll be here to tea, but I'll be going out shortly afterwards,' she warned.

'So will I!' Alison cried in alarm. There was no way she was going to sit in on a Saturday night. 'I'll bring Graham to tea, Mam, but I'm not staying in all evening. Do you hear that?' She emphasised, 'I'll be going out as well.'

No matter what her mother said to try to convince her otherwise, Alison made it clear that she had no intention of sitting in the company of her mother and father on Saturday night, and Rachel had to give in gracefully.

Trevor straightened his tie and patted his thinning hair into place before turning to his wife. 'Well, will I do? Although why we have to dress up to meet some lad we don't even know, I'll never understand.'

'We want to make a good first impression, just in case he turns out to be Mr Right.' Rachel smoothed her hands over her hips and wiggled the material of the pale-grey crêpe dress she was wearing into position. It was a long time since she had worn this dress and she was dismayed to find that she had put on a little weight. She hoped Trevor wouldn't notice.

He did, and in his usual blunt manner remarked on it, running a critical eye over her body and exclaiming, 'You've put on a bit of weight, girl. Don't let it get out of control. You know I can't stand fat women.'

Rachel smiled wryly as she watched him pull his tummy in. He was so conceited he would never admit to being overweight. 'I could say the same about you, Trevor, if I was as tactless as you, that is.'

He buttoned his jacket, patted his stomach and smiled smugly. 'There you are. Look at that.'

'I advise you to keep your jacket open or that button will pop the minute you sit down,' Rachel warned. 'Let's go downstairs. He'll be here any minute now.'

Graham was already standing on the doorstep gathering the courage to ring the bell. It had come as a great surprise to him when Alison had invited him to tea. He cared deeply for her. Did this mean she cared for him? It was up to him to make a good impression. Straightening his shoulders and fidgeting with his tie, he reached for the bell.

It was Alison herself who opened the door. She looked good enough to eat, dressed in a short white dress of clinging material that left little to the imagination. Her hands reached for his and drew him inside. 'Hello, Graham. I might have guessed you'd be on time.' As she spoke she was slowly leading him towards the lounge. 'Don't look so scared,' she whispered. 'They won't bite.'

Her parents rose to their feet when Alison pushed him gently ahead of her into the lounge. 'Mam, Dad, this is Graham Robson.'

Her father eyed him and apparently liked what he saw. But then Alison had expected him to, hadn't she?

Graham was every parent's idea of a suitable suitor for their daughter. Grasping his hand, Trevor said, 'Welcome, son. What would you like to drink before the meal? Sherry? Whiskey?'

'A small whiskey please, with plenty of lemonade.'

Rachel's mouth gaped slightly. She couldn't believe her ears. Imagine Trevor offering Alison's boyfriend alcohol. But then this was no young lad, this was a mature young man. A frown furrowed her brow. Surely he was much too old for Alison?

Aware of her surprise, Graham cleared his throat and turned to her. 'I'm very pleased to meet you, Mrs Cummings.'

Still a mite perturbed, Rachel smiled briefly at him. 'Take a seat, Graham. I'll see how things are going in the kitchen.' Leaving the room, she quickly crossed the hall and entered the big modern kitchen that was her pride and joy. A far cry from the little scullery in the house she had been reared in on the Shankill Road. Stretching the length of the house, it had the latest in modern equipment.

At times like these, to leave herself free when entertaining someone new, she called on the assistance of two sisters who ran a small catering business. For a nominal fee they could be persuaded to cook a meal in your home for anything up to twelve people. Their cuisine was always mouth-watering and Rachel had no doubts that everything would be just fine. 'How's it going, Evelyn?'

The smaller of the sisters greeted her with a smile. 'Everything's fine, Mrs Cummings. We're ready to serve any time now.'

Rachel drew in a deep breath of appreciation. 'Mm, it smells delicious. Give us another ten minutes, then serve it. Is the dining table set?'

A nod of the head confirmed this. 'Everything's in order, Mrs Cummings. Just leave it to us.'

'Good! Ten minutes then.'

As she crossed the hall again, Susan came down the stairs. 'Well, is he presentable enough for Father?' she whispered.

'Hush!' Her mother gave her an anguished look. 'He might hear you.'

'For goodness sake, Mam, these walls are thick. There's no chance of being overheard. What's he like?'

'Very nice. But . . .' The doubt in her voice caused Susan's brows to rise in query. 'He looks much older than I anticipated.'

'Really?'

'Yes. Come see for yourself.'

Trevor and Graham were deep in conversation, while Alison, looking bored, was leafing through a magazine. Graham rose courteously to his feet when they entered the room.

'Have you met my other daughter, Graham?'

'No, Mrs Cummings, I have not had that pleasure.'

'This is Susan, my eldest daughter.'

'I'm very pleased to meet you, Susan.' A charming smile, exposing even white teeth, accompanied the words, and Susan was surprised to feel the colour rise in her cheeks as his eyes openly admired her. He really was charming, but then, she agreed with her mother, he was much older; old enough to have acquired such charm. Where on earth had Alison met him?

'Likewise, I'm sure.' She returned his greeting with a warm smile.

Graham proved to be a great conversationalist and kept them entertained during the meal. Afterwards they retired to the lounge and Alison became alarmed when her father offered Graham another drink. 'No, Dad. If Graham takes another drink he won't be able to drive.'

'Well, he can get a taxi home and pick his car up tomorrow. Is that all right with you, Graham?'

'I'd like that, if Alison doesn't mind?' With raised brow he awaited Alison's reaction.

'Alison does mind, as a matter of fact! She minds very much.' A baleful glare was bestowed on him. 'You promised to take me to the Orpheus tonight.'

'Orpheus? What's the Orpheus?' Trevor cried in bewilderment.

'It's a ballroom, Dad. It's above the Co-op, in York Street. This will be my first time there. Graham, you promised! You know you did.'

Graham smiled wryly at Trevor. 'I did promise, Mr Cummings, and I'm a man of my word. It was lovely meeting you and Mrs Cummings. The meal was delicious. I really enjoyed it. I hope we will get to know each other a bit better in the future.'

'Feel free to visit us any time you like.'

Alison had shrugged into her coat and, grabbing her handbag, tugged at Graham's arm. 'Oh, come on, Graham, or we won't get in.'

Seeing that Susan had also donned her coat, Graham asked politely, 'Can we give you a lift into town, Susan?'

'Yes, please, Graham.'

On the short journey to town Susan sat in a daze.

Every Saturday night for the past few months she and Jim had frequented the Orpheus. It had come as a shock to her to hear Alison say they intended going there tonight. She always met Jim in the foyer, but now she asked Graham to drop her off at the corner of Donegal Street. When the car stopped Alison twisted round in her seat. 'Where are you going tonight?'

'I'm not sure yet. Thanks for the lift, Graham.'

Before any further embarrassing questions could be directed at her, Susan jumped from the car. What on earth was bringing them to the Orpheus tonight?

She waved the car out of sight on its way to the car park, then set off along York Street.

Jim Brady watched Susan hurry towards him and a wave of tenderness washed over him. She was so beautiful and such a lovely person. He felt guilty wasting her time. They couldn't go on as they were. The longer they continued to meet, the harder it would be to break up and the more hurt Susan would be. The attraction between them was too strong. It was becoming increasingly hard to hold his emotions in check. He wanted her with a desire that put everything else from his mind. If only there was a chance that one day they could wed, he would be the happiest man in the world. But marriage was out of the question and anything less was not good enough for her.

Her eyes lit up when she caught sight of him and a smile of pure joy wreathed her face. She stopped, breathless, in front of him. 'Hi there,' he whispered and his voice throbbed with passion. They gazed at each other for some moments, then he took her by the arm and led her towards the lift. 'Let's get up to the ballroom. I want to hold you close.'

In a daze, she had been following his lead. Now she stopped in her tracks and tugged frantically at his sleeve. 'Jim, Alison and her boyfriend, Graham, are coming here tonight. Can we go somewhere else instead, please?'

He stopped and stood lost in thought for a short while. 'Does it matter if your sister sees us? After all she's bound to guess that you are seeing someone.'

Susan stood undecided and he leant closer. 'Let's stay. I'm just aching to hold you close, more than anything else in the world. Mm?'

Encouraged by these words, she ventured, 'We could go somewhere where we could really be alone.'

He drew back instantly. His passion was too raw to seek solitude somewhere. Afraid of wavering in his resolve, he cried abruptly, 'That's out of the question, and you know it! Come on, let's dance the night away.' And without further ado he took her arm and led her towards the lift from where the strains of 'Misty' could be heard drifting down from the floor above.

Agog with excitement, Alison stood at the entrance of the grand Orpheus ballroom. Used to Sammy Leckie's small dance hall, she was bemused by the size of the Orpheus. And tonight there was an orchestra playing. Imagine dancing to live music instead of records. Her eyes rose to the ceiling, where a huge silver ball slowly rotated, throwing slivers of light on to the swirling bodies below.

A sigh of contentment escaped her lips. She turned to Graham. 'Isn't it marvellous?'

He laughed at her excitement. The band was playing a waltz and the couples on the floor twirled gently to its beat. 'Let's join them.' Without another word he swept her into the swaying mass.

Graham had plenty of practice and was a competent dancer. He twirled her in and out of the other dancers and she closed her eyes and gave herself up to the magic of the music. As the waltz drew to a close, she reluctantly opened them again and was amazed to see her sister and a tall man dancing close by.

Susan hadn't seen her. How could she? She was gazing spellbound at her partner and had eyes for no one else. Not that Alison could blame her! Oh, no. She would be the first to admit that he was a very handsome fellow. Grabbing her sister by the arm as she was about to move off, Alison cried indignantly, 'Susan! Why didn't you say you were coming here?'

Embarrassed, Susan lied. 'I wasn't sure where we would finish up tonight.'

The men shared a perplexed glance and edged their partners to the side of the dance floor. They waited expectantly to be introduced.

The silence lengthened and Alison said, 'Well . . . aren't you going to introduce us?'

Reluctantly, Susan did so.

Shaking Alison and Graham by the hand, Jim – always the gentleman – said cordially, 'Grab a table and I'll fetch some drinks. What would you ladies like?' Fruit juices were ordered and Jim raised an eyebrow at Graham. 'What's your poison, Graham?'

'I'll come to the bar with you. You won't be able to carry them all, and I know from experience that trays are like gold dust in here.'

The bar was crowded and as they waited their turn the two men eyed each other. Graham was wondering how come Alison had no idea that her sister was courting. It was obvious to him that Jim and Susan were very much in love. It was in the air all around them. It was he who spoke first. 'Have you met the girls' parents yet?'

A crooked smile twisted Jim's mouth. 'No, and I don't think I'm likely to.'

'Oh . . .?'

'I'm from the wrong side of the track, you see.'

'But surely, in this day and age, things like that don't matter?' said Graham with genuine surprise.

'My mother's a widow and I've two younger sisters to keep an eye on. My wage is needed every week. Can you see her father welcoming me as a suitable husband? Especially as I'm a Catholic.'

'Hmm, I see what you mean.' After a short pause Graham continued, 'You seem very attracted to each other. I wish Alison would look at me like that.'

Embarrassed, Jim was non-committal. 'It's where it all ends that counts. But there's no future for us.'

'I'm sorry. Forgive me. I should mind my own business.'

'No harm done. Here, grab a couple of these glasses.'

The two girls sat at one of the small tables that dotted the sides of the dance floor. Alison's eyes glowed as she looked around her. 'It's wonderful here. I suppose you come all the time?'

Stretching the truth a bit, Susan confessed, 'Most Saturdays.'

'You're a dark horse, Susan.' Alison's voice was accusing. 'Jim's gorgeous. Why are you making a big a secret of him?'

Susan smiled slightly at her sister's obvious admiration. 'He is gorgeous, isn't he?' she agreed. She had a feeling that her sister would want to stay with them the rest of the evening and she was thinking of ways to put Alison off. She wanted Jim to herself. 'Graham is also very nice. I could see Mam and Dad were impressed with him.'

'I'm sure they'd like Jim, too. Why didn't you invite him to tea?'

'I'm afraid I can't agree with you there. He wouldn't get much of a welcome in our house, I can assure you of that.'

Alison's eyes widened, then closed for a few seconds as comprehension dawned. Her voice was full of pity. 'Of course. How stupid of me. With a name like Jim Brady he has to be a Catholic.'

'Here you are, Susan,' Jim handed her a glass of juice. 'Graham is coming with yours now, Alison. He stopped to talk to someone.'

'I'm here.' With a flourish, a glass of juice was set on the table in front of Alison. 'Cheers.' Graham raised his glass.

A chorus of 'Cheers' was followed by a brief silence as they quenched their thirst.

To Susan's consternation, after a few minutes of desultory conversation Graham asked her to dance with him. With a startled glance at Jim, she reluctantly followed him on to the dance floor.

Alison looked expectantly at Jim and he responded. 'Shall we?'

As they circled the floor Alison gazed up into Jim's face. 'Have you and Susan been seeing each other for a long time?'

'Not very long. Why do you ask?'

'You look very lovey-dovey together.'

A wide grin split his face at the audacity of her remark. 'Do you think so?'

'I do indeed!' An insinuating look accompanied the words.

His deep-blue eyes crinkled at the corners when he smiled and she thought how handsome he was. 'Just what are you suggesting, Alison?'

She shrugged. 'I don't know. But I'd hate to see Susan get hurt.'

'She's a big girl. She knows the score.'

'Are you sure? She believes everything she's told. She's very trusting. Not like me.' Alison tossed her blonde curls. 'I take everything with a pinch of salt.'

He laughed – anyone would think she was the older sister. 'Believe me, she knows the score.'

'Are you planning to marry, then?'

'If you don't mind my saying so, I don't think that's any of your business. Are you going to marry Graham?'

'Who knows? It's early days.'

'Has he asked you to marry him?'

'No.' She laughed aloud. 'But he will,' she added confidently.

They were passing Graham and Susan, who were covering the floor in silence and noting the ease with which Alison was engaging Jim in conversation. Susan remarked, 'Our Alison would feel at home in the company of the Queen. I wish I had her personality.'

Graham grimaced. 'She's not always so forthcoming with me.'

'Really?'

'Yes, really. And there is nothing wrong with your personality. I think you're charming, and it's obvious that Jim is besotted with you.'

His admiration was apparent and Susan coloured slightly under his gaze, receiving the compliment graciously. 'Thank you.'

They smiled at each other and she thought what a nice person he was. Her sister was a lucky girl. Over her shoulder, Graham watched Alison laugh and flirt with Jim and his eyes were bleak. Why couldn't she tease him like that? Did she care about him at all? Surely she must, or why ask him home to meet the family? If only she were more like her sister.

Susan's earlier premonition proved right. After the next dance Alison and Graham sought them out and it was taken for granted that they would share a table. The two men got on like a house on fire and Susan had to admit that she enjoyed the light-hearted banter. Her only fear was that Jim would insist that she go home in Graham's car. These fears were unfounded, however. At the end of the evening Jim politely but firmly turned down Graham's offer of a lift home. He said he was taking Susan for a bite of supper.

'What a good idea,' Alison cried delightedly. 'Why don't we join them, Graham?'

Graham stood silent. He could understand Jim's

dilemma. If he accepted, Jim and Susan would have no opportunity to be alone.

They were standing outside the Orpheus and, to her delight, Jim reached for Susan's hand and tucked it beneath his elbow. 'If you don't mind, Alison, we would like to be alone for a while. Mm?'

'Oh, I see.'

Noting her disappointment, Jim suggested gently, 'Perhaps we could all join up again next Saturday night?'

Afraid that Alison was going to insist on joining them for supper, Graham quickly agreed. 'That's a great idea, Jim. I look forward to meeting you again. Good night. Good night, Susan.' With these words he propelled a protesting Alison along York Street, leaving Jim and Susan alone.

'That puts a stop to our Saturday nights together at the Orpheus,' Susan mused.

'Why? I think it's a good idea that we meet up. I enjoyed their company.'

'So did I,' Susan admitted. 'But I thought you liked being alone with me,' she added peevishly.

They were cutting through Smithfield Market area and he pulled her into the doorway of a pet shop. 'I do. I love being alone with you, so that I can do this.' His hand caressed her breast.

Her eyes lit up and she lifted her face for his kiss. The kiss was long and satisfying and their passions rose.

'You see? This is what happens when we're alone. I can't keep my hands off you.'

'But I want you to touch me,' she cried in bewilderment. 'We were meant for each other, Jim. Surely you can see that? Don't!' He had removed his hand and she tried to pull it back. 'Don't push me away like this, Jim. I love you.'

Reluctantly he widened the space between them even more.

'We can't go on like this, Susan.'

'I know! I know we can't. We could get married quietly, and go somewhere outside Belfast to live.'

'Ah, Susan. Susan.' He shook his head in despair. 'I told you there was no question of us marrying. Remember? It isn't just our religious differences. You know that. I've explained to you that my mam's a widow. I've to provide for her and the girls. You said you wouldn't hold it against me when the inevitable happened and we had to part.'

'Are you saying that you don't want to see me any more?' she cried aghast, fear sending a shiver down her spine.

'No, of course I'm not saying that, but we can never marry.'

'Well, then, whatever you like, Jim. I don't care what people say. I'll live with you.'

Resting his hands on her shoulders, he gazed at her beseechingly. 'Susan, I love you and I will never use you in that way. Now, can we continue to see each other without any strings attached?'

Left without any choice, she nodded glumly, the tears threatening to fall.

'Then let's go get something to eat. I'm starving.'

The idea of eating anything made her feel sick. How could he even think of food? Nevertheless she managed to nibble at a sandwich and drink a few sips of tea while she talked brightly to him. She would tolerate anything just to be with him.

Jim watched the effort she was making and thought how unfair life was. It must soon end; it could only get harder. But not yet, his heart cried. Not just yet. Surely he deserved some time with her? He loved her so much.

To Susan's deep regret, Saturday night at the Orpheus became a regular foursome. Oh, she loved the company, but she missed the intimate moments between dances when Jim sat with his arm around her shoulders whispering sweet nothings in her ear. In spite of sulks from Alison, Graham never again offered them a lift home. There was an unspoken agreement that they part company outside the Orpheus, and this pleased Susan no end. Then, one Saturday night a few weeks later, it was absolutely pouring down when they left the hall after the dance. There had been a slight drizzle when they arrived, but now the rain was literally bouncing off the pavement. They eyed it in silence for some moments.

Graham diffidently offered them a lift. 'I know you would prefer not to, but that rain looks as if it's in for the night.'

Jim drew Susan to one side. 'I think it would be a good idea if you went home with Graham and Alison tonight. I'll get a taxi.'

'No, Jim. I want to stay with you for a while. We haven't had a minute alone all evening. I'll get a taxi home later on.'

'Be reasonable, Susan. Even if we go for a bite of supper, we'll be soaked to the skin by the time we get there. If Graham gives us a lift to the café, Alison will want to join us and it would be churlish to refuse her.

It would become a habit, so it would. Do you want that?'

She could see his point of view and shook her head glumly.

'So please accept Graham's offer of a lift.' Jim tilted her face up to his and kissed her. 'See you on Tuesday night as usual.'

Graham had tactfully led Alison out of earshot to give them more privacy. Now he moved forward as Jim turned towards them, an inquiring look on his face. 'We'd be very grateful if you would give Susan a lift home, Graham. And I'll see you both next Saturday.'

Jim hurried along Royal Avenue and turned up Castle Street hoping to catch the last bus. He was lucky and caught it by the skin of his teeth. Nevertheless, he was already soaked to the skin. But he begrudged paying for a taxi home. He needed to be careful with his money if he was to entertain Susan twice a week. Money was no real problem to her and she didn't understand. He stared at his reflection in the bus window. His hair was plastered to his head and his eyes had a bleak look. Susan's annoyance at his decision to send her home with her sister rankled. After supper every Saturday night he always got a taxi to her street to make sure she got home safely. Then he walked home, but that was out of the question tonight; surely she understood that?

Another problem had cropped up. His youngest sister Louise was due to leave school soon and Sister Vincent, the head nun at St Vincent's School, had sent for his mother and asked her to consider sending

Louise to St Dominic's College for further education. His mother had been against the idea, saying that they couldn't add to the burden Jim already carried, but with his other sister May already at St Dominic's, how could he deny Louise her chance? It was the penalty of having two clever sisters. But with all these commitments, when would he ever be in a position to get married?

It felt as if he carried the worries of the world on his shoulders. He felt like a man who had been married for years. Susan thought that religion was the only stumbling block to their marrying; if only she were right. Why, if that was the case, he would defy the Church and her father, and marry her no matter what the cost.

It was a month later when the bottom fell out of Susan's world. The Saturday night started off as usual. Susan arrived with Alison and Graham, and Jim was waiting in the foyer for them. Greetings were exchanged and they made their way to the ballroom. Soon, however, alert to every nuance where Jim was concerned, Susan became aware that something was wrong. As they circled the floor he held her with a desperation that was very apparent to her.

'What's up, Jim? What's bothering you? Do you feel ill?'

He shook his head in denial. 'I'm perfectly all right.' After all, a breaking heart was not considered an illness.

'Jim, come off it! I know something's wrong.'

His lips trailed her face and a sigh escaped his lips. 'We will talk about it later.'

He would say no more and she had to curb her

impatience and wait. The other two seemed unaware of anything out of the ordinary and the evening passed slowly.

As usual, they said good night to Alison and Graham outside on the pavement. It was a cold night and, arms entwined, they hurried to their special café, where they always sat at the table in the corner and talked and talked. Tonight Jim was silent, locked in his own deep thoughts. Her patience, which had been sorely tried all evening, suddenly snapped.

'All right, Jim, I can't stand the big silence any longer. Let's hear all about it.'

'First things first. What would you like to eat?'

'I'm not hungry, thank you.'

These words brought a reluctant smile to his drawn face. 'You're always hungry.'

'Not tonight, I'm not. Food would choke me.' The waitress had approached their table and Susan gave her order. 'Just coffee for me, thank you.'

'Make that two coffees, please,' Jim seconded her.

He reached across and clasped her hands in his. 'Susan, you know I love you, don't you?'

Sensing bad news, her heart started racing and her nails bit into his hands. 'Yes. What is it, Jim, what's the problem? Is your mother ill? Can you not see me for a while?'

'Not for a while,' he said slowly. 'In fact, I think it's time to call it a day.'

She swallowed deep in her throat, hurt beyond measure. 'What do you mean, call it a day?'

'You know what I mean, Susan. It's not fair to you, to go on as we are.'

'I'm not complaining.' Her lips twisted in a wry smile. 'Well, not often anyhow.'

'You're a young, attractive woman, Susan, and I can't waste any more of your life.'

'What are you suggesting, Jim?'

'I think it's time we parted.'

The waitress arrived with the coffee and Jim released her hands. 'Thank you.'

Susan felt bereft without his touch. This is how she would feel if she never saw him again. 'Just tell me this, Jim. Have you met someone else?' she whispered fiercely.

'Don't be daft! I could never look at another girl while I have you.'

'Well, then, I can't see why we can't keep on meeting. We're certainly not doing anything wrong. Your priests could certainly find no fault in our relationship.'

His lips tightened and an angry colour crept up his face. 'And how long do you think I can stand this? Think, Susan. Do I have to spell it out for you? I'm a man! I can't bear to be with you and not have the right to show my feelings.'

She leant eagerly across the table and whispered urgently. 'But we can show our feelings. I feel the same. You know I do. We will just have to be careful, Jim.'

Her heart sank. He was shaking his head before she had finished speaking. 'I've too many commitments. As you know, our Louise is starting at St Dominic's College. I've already spent the few savings I had tucked away for a rainy day. She needed uniforms, books and other bits and pieces. I've actually had to go into debt. Then there will be extra bus fares. If we had stayed in Spinner Street instead of moving up the Falls, we wouldn't have had a mortgage and the girls could have walked to college. But we did move! It seemed a good idea at the time, but that was before I met you. As things stand, I can't see any hope for us at all.'

'I'll wait, Jim. I'll wait as long as necessary. I didn't realize that you were so worried about money. Why, that's no problem. I can pay for our outings.'

'Do you think I'd let you do that? No. I've made up my mind about this. Lord knows it wasn't an easy decision, but we can't keep on seeing each other.'

Their coffee grew cold as they argued, but he was adamant. In the taxi on the way home, Susan was all over him. She would make him realise just how wonderful life could be, whether or not they were married.

In the shadowy corner shielded by tall hedges, where they usually said good night, she went wild, full of passion and offering her all. To her delight, instead of pushing her gently away, as he normally did when she got worked up, he lost control. Gripping her tightly, he pounded his body against hers, his mouth savagely devouring hers. Feverishly, she clung to him, egging him on. Her heart was singing. At last he was going to be hers. She was wise enough to know that once Jim took her, in his eyes they'd be as good as married. It wasn't the way she would have planned it, but what did it matter if it was here on the corner, so long as it meant he was committed to her?

Suddenly she found herself flung back against the hedge as he turned his back on her. 'Jim?'

For some moments he stood, shoulders heaving, fighting for control. Then he swung round and lashed out at her. 'Stop tempting me, Susan. Can't you see any further than your nose? You're being very unfair.'

'I only want to show you how much I love you,' she whispered. Her arms reached out appealingly to him. 'Come on, Jim. We won't be hurting anyone.'

He shook his head sadly and moved away. 'I'm sorry, Susan. More sorry than I could ever say.'

Without a backward glance he left her. She stood there, petrified, watching him out of sight, unable to believe it was all over.

For some time she remained where she was, trying to come to terms with his rejection. Surely if he had any feelings at all for her he would not have turned down her offer in such a crude way. She felt like a prostitute who had not come up to expectations. Shame sent a hot flush washing over her body as she relived her wanton actions. It abated, leaving her icy cold and shaking all over. There was a sick feeling in the pit of her stomach. Tears rolled down her face and she brushed them angrily away. She would show him, so she would. He'd never get another chance to reject her.

Nerves ragged, she made her way up the street and entered the driveway to her home, all the while muttering angrily to herself. Dismay brought her tirade to a halt as she saw Graham leave the house and head for his car. She turned and hurried down the drive again, hoping to elude him, but he caught sight of her and started towards her. 'Susan . . . Hey, there.'

Forced to retrace her steps, she was glad of the shadows; hoped he wouldn't look too closely.

Peering anxiously at her, he asked, 'Susan, is anything the matter?'

An involuntary shiver passed through her body. He put an arm round her shoulders in concern. 'Come on, let's get you into the house where it's warm.'

'No. No! I can't go in just yet. I can't face anybody at the moment.'

He was in a quandary. He couldn't leave her out here in this state, but what else could he do?

His eye lit on his car and, taking her by the arm, he said, 'Let's sit in the car until you feel better. It will be a lot warmer there.'

I'll never feel better again, she thought bitterly, but allowed herself to be helped into the back seat of his car.

He clasped her cold hand between his and tried to rub some warmth into it. 'You're frozen, Susan. Tell me what's wrong. Have you and Jim quarrelled?'

Suddenly his kindness made it all too much to bear and harsh sobs tore from her throat.

Aghast, Graham gathered her close and murmured words of comfort in her ear. 'It'll be all right. Why, Alison and I also had a tiff tonight. All couples disagree sometime or other. It's human nature.'

Her mouth yawned wide in protest. 'Uh-huh. It's worse than that. He doesn't want to see me again.'

'Don't be silly! He loves you.'

Pressing her forehead against his chest, she burrowed wildly against it, wailing away. 'He doesn't. He doesn't. You don't understand! I made such a fool of myself. I'm so ashamed. I offered myself to him and he pushed me away in disgust.' She drew back and gazed up at him, to see his reaction to her words. 'Would you turn Alison down, if she wanted to . . . to . . . you know what I mean.'

In the dim light he smiled wryly. Turn Alison down? Chance would be a fine thing. She kept him firmly at arm's length. Alison took all she could get and gave nothing in return. He was having second thoughts where she was concerned. Meanwhile he couldn't believe that any full-blooded man would turn a girl like Susan down. Over the weeks he had found himself very attracted to her. She wasn't as pretty as her sister, but she had more between the ears. He had been amazed at how much he looked forward to his dance with her every week. Now here she was, in his arms, and every nerve in his body was aware of her.

'I bet he wasn't disgusted,' he said gently. 'You've misunderstood, so you have. Why, it's obvious Jim loves you.'

His fingers entwined in her hair and he gently drew her head back so that he could see her face. 'No man in his right senses would turn you down, Susan. No man. You're lovely.'

Her eyes widened into great dark pools of mystery and her lips trembled at his words of admiration. He warned himself to be careful; she trusted him and didn't realize how tempting she was being.

'Let's get you inside. Your parents have retired and I'm sure Alison will be in bed by now. Come on, I'll make you a nice cup of tea before I go.' He put her gently from him and turned to leave the car. She was so vulnerable; he had to get away from the temptation, before his body betrayed his desire for her.

Relieved to hear that her parents were in bed and she wouldn't have to face them, Susan relaxed. 'Give me another couple of minutes, Graham. If Alison is still awake, she'll ask all kinds of questions. She won't give up until she hears the truth, and I couldn't bear that.'

He left a space between them and turned in his seat to watch her.

Her eyes searched his face, seeing the sadness there. Momentarily distracted from her own misery, she asked gently, 'Why did you and Alison quarrel tonight, Graham?'

'Oh, the usual. Nothing important. To be truthful, we've quarrelled quite a lot lately.'

A cold hand reached out to cover his. 'I'm so sorry to hear that. You're a very nice person.'

He covered her hand with his. 'You're still freezing.' She moved closer and his arm circled her waist as she snuggled against the warmth of his body and gazed up at him. Her lips were so close. Too close for comfort. Should he risk a kiss? No, it would be too dangerous!

He could never figure out who made the first move, but her lips were soft as velvet and moved beneath his with a hunger that matched his own. Passion mounted as his hands caressed her body; soothing the hurt and pain of rejection away, all thoughts of Jim and Alison were forgotten.

In a daze, Susan groped for the handle of the car door and stumbled out on to the drive. She gaped in confusion at Graham as he followed her. What had she done?

'Susan, I'm sorry. I got carried away. Can you forgive me?'

She tore her eyes away from the anguish in his. 'Just go home, Graham. Please go.'

'No!' He couldn't just leave like this, as if nothing had

happened. He had to make her understand that he really cared for her; had meant no disrespect. The fact that she had been a virgin floored him. 'No. We must talk.' He stepped towards her. 'Let's go inside.'

'No. Go home! Do you hear me? I don't want to talk to you.'

Hearing the hysteria rising in her voice, he hesitated. Then he opened the car door and climbed inside. 'All right, I'll go. But we must talk about this, Susan. It can't be ignored.'

She turned and climbed the steps to the house, fumbling in her handbag for the key as she went. Glad that the house was silent, she quickly climbed the stairs and entered the bathroom. For some time she sat on the edge of the bath reliving the events of the evening. How could she have done those terrible things? Flinging herself at one man and then eagerly succumbing to another man's advances. After Jim's rejection, Graham's lovemaking had been balm to her hurt feelings. And she had enjoyed it! Every single moment of it. Even the sharp pain had only enhanced the pleasure. She hadn't expected to enjoy intercourse, especially in the back of a car of all places, but she had and now she felt sated.

Stripping, she entered the shower cubicle and ran the water as hot as she could bear it. Her body still glowed with the aftermath of passion and she allowed herself to revel in it. It was wrong, her mind cried. You are the lowest of the low, encouraging the man who may be your sister's future husband to make love to you.

Why not? her heart cried. No one need ever know. Graham certainly wouldn't broadcast the fact that he had seduced his girlfriend's sister. And I might never know anything like it again. Tears poured down her cheeks; why couldn't it have been Jim? Jim . . . Jim, how can I live without you? But no, it had to be her potential brother-in-law. She wished she had never been born.

Chapter Two

The train shunted to a halt and Susan rose wearily to her feet. She had been travelling since early morning and every bone in her body ached with fatigue. With each passing hour she had become more depressed. Rushing off to visit her Aunt Edith had seemed the answer to her problems – a chance to sort out her affairs – but what if she sent her packing? What would she do then? She would be stranded in a strange town with little money and nowhere to go. Not that her aunt would just show her the door! No, she wasn't like that. However, she might try to persuade her to return home, and that Susan couldn't do.

Early that morning she had left Belfast in a positive frame of mind, determined to put the past behind her and make a new life for herself over in England, but as the day progressed doubts had set in. Without Aunt Edith's help she would have to return home and face the music. Her heart quailed at the thought of the reception her news would evoke in her parents. Their wrath would know no bounds! Her father would never again be able to hold his head high, would never be able to preach what his daughter was obviously not practising.

Though why he should be held to account for her failing, she would never understand. She supposed it was all in the mind. As for her mother, although kind and gentle, Rachel was such a proud woman, and her daughter's news would absolutely devastate her.

The journey over on the ferry from Larne to Stranraer had been stormy and Susan had felt quite ill, bringing up all she had eaten that day but feeling no better for it. Terrified that she had perhaps put the baby at risk and was about to lose it there and then, she had sent prayers heavenwards. To her great relief they had arrived in Stranraer without further mishap. Once on *terra firma* her heaving tummy had settled and after a short wait she had boarded the train to Carlisle in a better frame of mind. On the journey down through Scotland the still-breathtaking autumn scenery of fiery red and orange hues – especially when mirrored on lochs, doubling their beauty – had absorbed her full attention, lulling her into a sense of calm. Surely in such a wonderful world it was wrong to despair? Life must be worth living, no matter what the hardships might be.

At Carlisle she had changed trains and soon found herself in Newcastle. Here, she knew from past experience, there would be a long wait for the connection to Darlington. She checked and found that her memory had served her right: there was indeed a long time to wait before her next train was due. She did some window shopping, but eventually the sharp wind sent her in search of warmth. Entering the cosy atmosphere of a small café, she ordered some sandwiches and a pot of tea to pass the time. To her surprise she discovered she was quite ravenous and devoured the sandwiches, which were unexpectedly tasty.

Now, at last, she had reached Darlington, her destination. Soon she would know her fate. Her Uncle Billy was meeting her at the station. From there they would go to Albert Hill, known as 'Little Ireland' because so many Irish people had settled there over the years. It was five years since Susan had last been over on holiday. Then she had been a carefree young girl; now here she was, back again, a woman scorned. A woman scorned was indeed a terrible thing. It made one want to lash out at anything and everything. Look what she herself had done when Jim Brady had refused her wanton offer. Shame washed over her as she recalled his words. Gentle, kind words, but rejection nevertheless. Well, in her misery she had encouraged another man and certainly made a mess of things. Now she must pay the price.

She had been a gangly teenager the last time she was in Darlington. Although she had grown little, she had filled out and knew that she looked quite different. Would Billy Devine recognise her now? Straightening her shoulders, she grabbed her suitcase and left the train to stand on the platform amongst the bustling crowd. She had enjoyed her last stay in Darlington and it was every bit as busy as she remembered it. Even at this late hour there was a lot of activity. Anxiously she scanned the faces of those obviously waiting for their family or friends. She saw Billy at once; he stood head and shoulders above the crowd. His eyes examined her face and passed on. Smiling slightly, she gripped her case with both hands and approached the big man. Placing her case to one side, she tentatively touched his arm. He frowned down at her and then his face lit up and he cried, 'In the name of God, Susan, but haven't you grown up. You were this height . . .' a large hand gestured a ridiculous height, 'the last time I saw you!'

Some of the tension left her body as she laughed aloud at the very idea that she had been so small just five years ago. 'I was a bit bigger than that, Uncle Billy. I really haven't grown all that much. I've just filled out,' she laughed gaily.

He reached for her hands and pulled her into a bear hug. 'You look wonderful, love. Let's get a taxi and get you home. Edith is so excited. She can't wait to see you.'

Susan hesitated, not wanting to put him to the expense of a taxi, and said haltingly, 'Can we not walk, Uncle Billy? If I remember correctly it's not very far.'

'Not in a taxi, it's not, and I'm certainly not trailing you through the streets in this freezing weather. Besides, I can afford it, so hold your tongue. Is this your suitcase? Well, then, let's get a move on.'

He was right. In the taxi it was just a short journey from the station through the town to Albert Hill. Her Aunt Edith had the door open and was on the narrow footpath before the cab stopped.

Gripping her by the hands, she gazed into her niece's pale face. 'You look tired, love. But then, sure you've been on the go all day.' Pulling her close, she cried, 'Oh, it's good to see you again. But what am I thinking of, keeping you standing out here in the street? Come on inside where it's nice and warm.'

The house seemed smaller than Susan remembered it. Only the knowledge that her cousin Jack, their only son, had gone to work in London had encouraged her to seek asylum with them. Would she be too much of a burden?

'Take off your coat and hang it behind the door, Susan. Then sit yourself by the fire while I lift the dinner. I've a nice casserole simmering away here. Billy, put that suitcase upstairs and entertain her until I'm ready.'

Billy quickly did as he was bid and, descending the stairs again, took the armchair facing her. He smiled fondly as his wife's excited voice shouted questions from the kitchen. 'She's been like a cat on a hot griddle all week preparing for your arrival,' he confided.

He eyed his niece keenly. She looked worried. He had a feeling this was to be no short visit and it bothered him. Had she fallen out with her da? If they had plenty of room, it wouldn't matter in the slightest how long she stayed. Edith would revel in her company. However, although there were three bedrooms in the house, the smallest was used for storing all those out-of-date bits and pieces too precious to throw out, and the other room was Jack's. If things didn't work out for Jack in London, what then? His son must have a room to return to.

Pushing his worries to one side, for after all he could be wrong, he asked, 'How's your mam and dad, love?'

'Well. Very well.'

A smile cracked Billy's long, solemn face, sending it into a wreath of wrinkles. 'Is your dad still holding up a pillar of the church, then?'

She smiled in return, her heart warming to this big man. Her father never could understand what had possessed his good-looking sister-in-law to run off with

Billy Devine. A married man who had given up a good job with a good pension attached to it, to run off with Edith. He had also left behind a very embittered wife. Edith had been pretty enough to turn any man's head, but what had she seen in him? Ugly as sin and as common as muck, her father had often said of Billy whenever his name cropped up in conversation, which it did often enough over the years. The fact that he was a Catholic hadn't helped matters much.

'And what about Alison? Is she still as lovely as ever?'

'She is indeed. She's courting, you know?' At his shake of the head Susan laughed and said, 'How could you know? But yes, she is. I expect an engagement will soon be announced.' It saddened her to think of Alison marrying Graham. She was so offhand with him. Treated him like dirt. He deserved better. She smiled inwardly. Imagine her defending the very man who was responsible for her present predicament. Wonders would never cease.

Nevertheless, Alison would soon be walking down the aisle on the arm of her proud father. And Trevor would be very proud; anything his youngest daughter did was all right by him. She was the apple of his eye and apparently never put a foot wrong. In his opinion, Graham was a great catch. Would she herself ever walk down the aisle? She doubted it. She doubted it very much. What man in his right mind would settle for second-hand goods?

Edith's voice reached them from the kitchen. 'You can move over to the table now. The dinner is ready.'

They sat at the pine table and Susan sniffed in appreciation as Edith removed the lid from the steaming casserole. 'That smells delicious, Aunt Edith.'

Smiling her thanks at the compliment, her aunt informed her, 'It's lamb, well, I suppose I should say mutton, but the best taste for a casserole comes from mutton, and the vegetables are from the market. Did I hear you right, there? Is Alison about to become engaged?'

'She is indeed. In a few weeks' time – at Christmas, I imagine – she will get engaged to Graham Robson.'

Dishing ladles full of the thick casserole into the bowls that were sitting ready, Edith handed Susan one and eyed her with raised brow. 'She's a bit young, isn't she? The vegetables are in that dish and the potatoes are in the small one.'

'Thank you, everything looks delicious. Alison isn't all that young. She was nineteen in May.'

'Still, that's not very old. And what does my dear sister Rachel think of all this?'

'Actually, she's quite pleased. Graham is a staunch Protestant and manages a big car showroom in the city centre for his father. He's an only child and the business will be his one day. He's also quite handsome. He's a bit older than Alison, but I suppose that's all to the good, as she is a bit of a scatterbrain. Anyway, the parents are thrilled to bits.'

'Huh! And what about you? Any sign of you tying the knot?' Edith watched in amazement as bright colour swamped her niece's face.

'Me, get married? Never! Who would have me?' 'Now' hovered on her lips, but she bit it back.

Edith frowned. 'A bonny girl like you? Why, many a man would consider himself lucky to get you.'

'You're very kind, Aunt Edith, but I don't think so.'

'You're talking nonsense! And you know it.'

Determined to put an end to this embarrassing conversation, Susan quickly piled turnip, carrot and potato on her plate and tucked into the thick casserole. 'Mm . . . this is delicious.' If only she were getting married, she lamented inwardly. Then her problems would be non-existent and she certainly wouldn't be sitting here in Darlington. How could she have been so foolish? Just because Jim Brady had scorned her advances, she had thrown caution to the winds, and look where it had got her.

There was jam roly-poly and custard for dessert and then Edith rose to her feet and started to clear the table. 'You sit over by the fire, love, and I'll make you a nice wee cup of tea.'

Pushing back her chair, Susan objected. 'Oh, no. I'll clear up. You sit down, Aunt Edith.'

'Do as you're told. Tomorrow you can do your share of the work.' She turned to her husband. 'Billy, away down to the club for an hour or so. Susan and I will be having a good old natter. You'd probably be bored to tears listening to us women.'

Glad for the excuse to get out for a pint, Billy grabbed his coat from the rail and, giving Susan a big wink, left the house.

Slowly Susan sank into the armchair, hands clenched tightly between her knees to stop them trembling, and gazed into the fire. Now for the reckoning. Her aunt was bound to ask her reason for visiting them, out of the blue like this, so near Christmas. How much should she tell her? Not everything, that was for sure. She was too ashamed to admit the whole truth. But she would have to tell Aunt Edith about the baby. What would she think of her niece's fall from grace? Would she be disgusted and send her packing? Or would she let her stay here until after the birth? Dear God, please let her be understanding, Susan prayed inwardly.

She sat rehearsing her words, discarding this explanation in favour of that one. To her great relief her aunt thrust a cup of tea into her hand, patted her consolingly on the shoulder and took the initiative. 'Don't look so worried. You're in trouble, aren't you?'

Tears brimmed over and she dashed them away with the back of her free hand. 'Yes, how did you guess? And I'm so ashamed. Oh, Aunt Edith, sure you won't sent me home?'

Taking the armchair facing her, Edith pulled it closer so that their knees were almost touching. Gazing earnestly into her niece's face, she said, 'Tell me all about it, love.'

Susan shrugged resignedly. 'There's not much to tell. I was foolish and now I must pay the penalty.'

'What about the man? Is he not willing to marry you?'

'He doesn't know!' Her voice rose shrilly. 'And anyhow, he can't marry me.'

'Is he already married?'

'No. But he would never marry me. It was just a one-off. We were both feeling low and, well, it just happened. He'd had a tiff with his girlfriend and I'd had cross words with a friend and was feeling very down. I should have known better, Aunt Edith. I liked him, but it wasn't as if I really fancied him. Later he was so ashamed. It was painful when I had to face him again. I just wanted to curl up and die. When I realised I was pregnant, I couldn't tell him. Can't you see? He wouldn't have wanted to know. It would have put him on the spot. Besides, I'm in love with someone else, and so is he. That would be no basis for a happy marriage. I was so stupid! I never thought that there might be consequences and I suppose neither did he. As I said, it all happened on the spur of the moment.'

Edith was incensed at the idea that a child had been conceived because they had both been feeling low. What was the world coming to? She wanted to chastise her niece, give her a good shaking; but, controlling her temper, she said, 'But . . . if he's free, he has a right to know. Surely you can see that, Susan? It's his child as well as yours. He might want to give it his name.'

To Edith's distress her niece became even more distraught, great sobs rasping from her throat and tears rolling down her cheeks. Going to her, Edith gathered her close.

Susan clung to her. 'He must never know. Why do you think I ran away?'

'There now. There now. You'll make yourself ill if you go on like this. Did your mother put you out?'

Stifling her sobs, Susan cried, 'She doesn't know. Oh, Aunt Edith, she mustn't ever find out. Promise you won't tell her.'

Pushing her niece back so that she could examine her face, Edith reasoned, 'Now Susan, she will have to know sometime. Surely you can see that? And the sooner, the better.'

'No! Please let me stay here until after the birth. Please, Aunt Edith. I've always been careful where money is concerned and I've a fair bit saved. Perhaps I'll be able to get a part-time job. Once the baby is born I'll work something out.'

Hearing hysteria rising in Susan's voice, Edith reluctantly assured her. 'Of course you can stay, love, if you really want to. But we will have to go into this more thoroughly and do what's best for all concerned. It's only natural that you're not thinking straight at the moment. Look, drink up your tea and then I'll show you to your room. You try and get a good night's sleep. We'll discuss this tomorrow.'

On his return from the club, Billy saw that his wife was perturbed. A glance around the room and into the kitchen showed him that Susan must have retired for the night. 'Has she gone to bed then?' he whispered.

'Yes, she was absolutely exhausted.'

His eyes narrowed at her expression. 'Why so worried, love?'

Rising to her feet, Edith faced him. She was aware that he was hoping their son would return from London any day, and that Billy would want his room left vacant for him. 'Billy, she's pregnant,' she said softly.

His face closed and he looked stern. 'Now, Edith, that's not our problem,' he warned. 'So don't be getting involved.'

'I know that, but can't we put her up for a while? I'll soon talk some sense into her, make her realise that her place is at home.'

'Did that bitch Rachel put her out?'

'No. Actually, Rachel doesn't know about the baby.'

'What? You'd think she'd be the first to know. Look,

much as I like Susan, she can't stay indefinitely. Jack might want to come home at any time.'

'You know that's not likely.'

'Still, he might!' Billy said stubbornly. 'We must keep his room ready for him.'

She shook her head sadly in disagreement, but went on, 'We'll work something out, Billy. Let's play it by ear. Eh, love?'

With a sigh he reached for her and gathered her close. How could he deny her? He would never be able to comprehend just what she saw in an ugly brute like him. Sinking his face in her soft, sweet-smelling hair, he muttered, 'Whatever you say, love. Whatever you say.'

After a restless night Susan awoke feeling listless. Her Aunt Edith had sounded as if she intended persuading her to return home. But how could she go home? How could she face her family and friends? And what about *him*? He was like part of the family now and, if she returned, he would be sure to guess the truth. She was so ashamed of herself; couldn't believe that she had been so foolish. If only she could wake up and discover it was all a bad dream, how different life would be for her. To think that because of a rejection from Jim Brady and a tiff with Alison, a child had been conceived. If she returned home what a predicament she would be in. Graham obviously loved Alison. How would he react? It would be enough to give him a heart attack. No, she couldn't go back! It would upset too many apple carts.

Slipping from beneath the blankets and thick patchwork quilt, she crossed to the long, narrow window, shivering when her feet left the small bedside mat and hit the icy-cold oil-cloth. Dawn was breaking and she gazed out over the back yards at the frost-covered rooftops with tears in her eyes. Back home she would be standing on warm carpet, gazing out over fields and hedgerows. Well, she had made her decision and she would just have to grin and bear it. That is, if her aunt allowed her to stay.

A glance at the watch her father had bought her for her twenty-first birthday six months ago brought more tears to her eyes. They had thrown a wonderful party for her. Life had been good then. She'd had a good job in Kennedy Construction, where she was personal secretary to the MD, and a beautiful house to call home. When she had met Jim everything had changed. Her love for him had blinded her to everything else. So what if he wasn't prepared to marry her. It wasn't the end of the world. She'd had nice friends and a good social life. How could she have been so blind? In the dim light the small luminous face of the gold watch showed her it was only five o'clock. Thankfully she tiptoed across the icy floorcovering and crept back under the bedclothes, but not to sleep; too many regrets plagued her.

At six o'clock sounds downstairs alerted her that her aunt and uncle had made an early start to their day. Dragging on her dressing gown, she hurriedly descended the stairs.

Billy was on his knees by the hearth of the small kitchenette grate, raking out the cold remains of yesterday's fire. On the hearth rolled-up papers, sticks and a bucket of coal were ready for today's heating. Quietly she approached him. 'Let me do that, Uncle Billy.'

Startled, he glanced over his shoulder at her in surprise, but before he could speak her aunt came in from the kitchen.

'In the name of goodness, Susan, what are you doing up at this hour? Away back to bed and I'll bring you up a cup of tea when the kettle has boiled.'

'You'll do nothing of the kind! I didn't come over here to be waited on hand and foot. Give me something to do, please.'

'I forgot to tell you last night. We have leased a stall in the market. We sell fruit and veg. Billy goes to the wholesalers early every day for fresh produce. However, there is no need for you to be up. I help him on the stall, but I don't leave the house until nine o'clock. So away back to your warm bed.'

'Please, Aunt Edith. Please let me do something to help out.'

'Susan, there is no need for you to rise at this unearthly hour,' Edith insisted. 'Go on, away back to your bed.' Seeing that her niece was about to argue, she relented, 'Okay, okay. Keep an eye on the porridge, if you must do something. Billy always complains that I make it too thick, so keep stirring it. Anyway, I want to talk to you before I go to work.'

Billy was long gone; the breakfast dishes were cleared away and the hearth was brushed and washed. Pouring another two cups of tea, Edith motioned Susan to take a seat by the blazing fire. Sitting facing her, Edith looked long and earnestly at her before speaking.

'Susan, I don't know what to do for the best. Our Rachel married well and, remember, I know the home you come from. I'm sure you were never short of anything. It will be entirely different over here, you know.'

'I know that, but I'll be forever grateful if you let me stay.'

'Let's get this all sorted out first. Why all the secrecy? You won't be the first girl to have a child out of wedlock. It would be a nine-day wonder, and then your parents would rally round. I admit our Rachel is proud and stiff-necked, but she wouldn't let you down.'

'Aunt Edith, you know what me mam is like. She'd die of shame. She wouldn't be able to hold her head up in public again. I couldn't do that to her. I just couldn't! And then there's Alison. The scandal would take all the joy out of her wedding preparations. It wouldn't be fair on them if I stayed at home.'

Struck by a sudden thought, Edith said, 'They do know where you are, don't they?'

'Yes, I left a note.'

'A note?' Edith's voice was shrill. 'You didn't speak to them? Won't they think that a bit strange?'

'No, Dad and I had an argument. You know how it has always been between him and me. I can't do right for doing wrong. And, lately, he can't look at me without finding fault. I admit I've been a bit of a handful this past year. You know – rebelling against everything. Anyway, I threatened to leave home. He told me to go and be damned, so I took him at his word and left.' She gave a wry grimace. 'No, they won't be surprised.'

Dismayed at the animosity against her father that her niece couldn't hide, Edith said, 'All families have these falling outs. He probably regrets it now.'

'Huh!' Susan shook her head in disgust. As if!

Realising that she was making no headway, Edith changed tack. 'What about Christmas? It's not far off. They'll expect you home then!'

'I'll make some excuse. Say you need me here.'

'Your dad won't stand for that. His daughter away from home at Christmas? He'll come looking for you, you mark my words, girl.'

'Aunt Edith, please believe me, he won't care enough. He never has.'

'You're wrong! I'm not over-fond of Trevor Cummings myself, but I know he will be worried and hurt if you don't go home for Christmas.' Her frown deepened. 'When is the baby due?'

'June.'

'June? That's seven months away. Are you sure you're pregnant? You're not just late? I mean, you've just turned twenty-one. Your blood changes every seven years. Your period could come yet, Susan.' It was a forlorn hope, but Edith eyed her niece optimistically.

Her hopes were dashed. A harsh laugh escaped Susan's lips. 'Oh, I'm sure all right! I wish I weren't, but there is no doubt about it.'

'When do you think the wedding will be?'

'Alison confided in me that she would like a June wedding.'

'Surely she'll want you to be bridesmaid?'

'I know she does. But, even if I'm at home, I can't be a bridesmaid. How can I? I can't be fitted for a dress with a big belly. Now can I?'

'But if you're at home I'm sure Alison will give you a chance to get over the birth and settle for a later date, say in August. Eh?'

Susan stretched out her hands in despair. 'Can't you see? That's why I'm here. I don't want to upset everybody's plans. That's why I left home. Please let me stay here. Please,' she pleaded.

'How will you cover this all up, eh? Not going home at Christmas will be bad enough, but to miss the wedding as well . . .?' Edith threw her arms wide, a horrified look on her face at the very idea of it. 'Susan, it just can't be done,' she gasped. 'And after the birth, what then? Are you putting the baby up for adoption? Is that how you hope no one will ever know?'

'No, I'm not. I intend keeping this baby. To be truthful, I haven't planned any further than the birth. Look, let me stay until Christmas, then we can decide what to do. Just give me a chance to sort things out in my own way. Please, Aunt Edith.'

'What if our Jack wants to come home? What then? That's his room you're in. What if he wants to come home for the Christmas break? Which we sincerely hope he does. What then?'

'Well, surely there must be some convent or home over here that will take me in.' At the very idea of a home for unmarried mothers Susan was unable to control her emotions, and tears gushed from her eyes. 'I wish I hadn't been so foolish! Oh, how I wish I could die.'

Going to her, Edith gathered her close and rocked her gently in her arms. 'Hush, now, there will be none of that kind of talk in this house. We'll work something out,' she murmured, but her eyes were bleak. Her sister would never forgive her when she found out – as she was sure to . . . eventually.

* * *

It was with trepidation that Edith joined Billy at the market stall. Although they rarely saw eye-to-eye, Billy thought the sun shone out of his son's backside. He would strongly object to Jack's room being occupied at Christmas.

It was Monday and market day in Darlington. Every Monday and Saturday stalls were erected in the square adjacent to the indoor market and – hail, rain or snow – a constant stream of people travelled from all the small towns and villages around in search of bargains. It also meant extra revenue for the indoor market. As was usual on such days, a steady queue of customers kept conversation between husband and wife more or less on a business level. It was lunchtime, when the crowd thinned out looking for some place to eat, before Billy got a chance to question her.

Unwrapping the sandwiches bought from a neighbouring stall, he asked Edith before biting into one, 'Well? How long does she want to stay?'

'Until Christmas.' Billy swallowed quickly and opened his mouth to protest, but she forestalled him. 'If we hear from Jack and he wants to come home, she has promised to move out.'

'And just where will she go, Edith?' he cried in disbelief. 'Eh? In her condition?'

'I don't know, Billy. She's adamant that she won't go home. Perhaps we could make enough space in the spare room for a single bed. It would only be for a few nights. Failing that, I'll get someone to put her up. In the meantime, can't we play it by ear, love? The chances of Jack coming home are slight. To tell you the truth, I'll be glad of her company. It will take my mind off him.'

He gazed into big, brown eyes filled with entreaty and once again was lost. In his heart he was aware that the chances of Jack coming back to Darlington were indeed slim. He wouldn't come without *her*, and surely she wouldn't have the gumption to show her face around here for some time to come. But what if she tired of Jack? She had, after all, dumped one man to run off with him. What then? To Edith's relief, he sighed and agreed. 'All right, love, if that's the way you want it, we'll play it by ear.'

Trevor Cummings looked up inquiringly from his plate of bacon and eggs when his wife entered the room sorting through the morning mail. He would never admit it, but he was sorry he had been so hard on Susan lately. But in the circumstances, who could blame him?

Meeting his eyes, Rachel shook her head. 'Nothing from Susan.'

From her place at the table Alison said plaintively, 'Mam, she has only been away a week. Give her a chance.'

'She doesn't deserve a chance,' her father said gruffly. 'What did I do that was so wrong, to justify her running off like that? We've had these rows before and she stayed put. What was so different this time? Eh? Tell me that. Your sister Edith has a lot to answer for, Rachel, taking her in like that. She should have sent her straight home.'

'Perhaps she got fed up listening to you, Dad.' Alison ventured to speak out on her sister's behalf. 'You did go on and on at her.'

Tentatively his wife intervened. She knew why Trevor had always been hard on Susan. 'Trevor, I agree with

Alison. You did come down rather hard on Susan lately. And for what? Voicing her opinion? Staying out late? Good heavens, she's a grown woman.'

Trevor's fist descended hard on the table, making his wife and daughter jerk in surprise. 'She should have known better than to answer me back,' he bellowed. 'Good Lord, you can't expect me to tolerate insolence from my own daughter. Can you?'

With a sigh, Rachel carefully mopped up the tea she had spilt. 'Now she's twenty-one we have no control over her. Remember that!' she warned. 'You could have been a bit more diplomatic. When she comes back you will have to bite your tongue now and again to keep the peace.'

'Huh! Chance would be a fine thing.'

'Now, you know you don't mean that. You want her to come home as much as I do.' She glanced quickly at her husband's dour face and said tentatively, 'Perhaps I should go over and try to talk some sense into her?'

'You'll do nothing of the kind! Let her make the first move.'

Clenching her teeth in frustration, Rachel cried, 'I do wish Edith was on the phone. Then I could at least talk to Susan, make sure she's all right.'

'What about me going over?' Alison offered brightly. She had an uneasy feeling that there was more to Susan's escapade than met the eye. There was something fishy going on. She had tried to find out what had happened between Jim Brady and her sister, but Susan had remained tight-lipped, insisting that their parting had been mutual, with no animosity on either side. Why, then, had she been so miserable?

'No, thank you. You'll stay where you are.' Rachel was aghast. 'What would Graham say if you were to go?'

'He would probably come with me. A wee holiday break.' Alison's eyes danced with mischievous glee at the very idea of it.

Her father fixed a stern eye on her. 'Don't even joke about going off alone with Graham until you're married.'

Alison turned aside to hide the smug look on her face. Parents could be so blind. She had no intention of making any mistakes. So far she had managed to keep Graham at bay. If he became too frisky, she would make sure that precautions were taken. Not that she thought he would. He had been quite cool lately and, come to think of it, marriage had not been mentioned between them for a long time. Could he be having second thoughts about marrying her?

It was a Wednesday evening that Susan rang her mother, confident that she would find her alone. She knew her father would be playing bowls. He was in the Churches' League and, when not playing in tournaments, he practised in the church hall every Wednesday night. Wednesday was also the night Alison went to Sammy Leckie's to learn advanced ballroom dancing. Susan was hoping for a private chat with her mother – a chance to assure her that she was all right, without her father giving off in the background. The continuous peal of the phone resounded for some moments. Susan pictured her mother setting her perpetual knitting carefully to one side, before leaving the lounge and crossing the hall to answer it. It saddened her to think that in the normal course of events her mother should be knitting for her first grandchild.

'Hello, Rachel Commings speaking.'

'Hello, Mam.'

Rachel didn't receive many evening calls and she had expected it to be someone leaving bowling fixtures for her husband. Her delight was therefore all the more obvious when she heard her daughter's voice. 'Susan! Thank God to hear your voice. Are you well?'

'Yes, Mam. I'm fine.'

'What on earth possessed you to run off like that?'

'Now, Mam, you were there. You heard me dad. He treats me like a five-year-old.'

'It's only because he worries about you. He's afraid of you falling in with the wrong company.'

The wrong company? If they only knew, she thought resentfully. In their eyes Jim Brady would be the wrong company, but she couldn't persuade him to lay a finger on her. Yet the *other* one had taken advantage of her vulnerability and seduced her. Thoughts of Graham suddenly crowded her mind, making her recall the warmth and excitement of their union. A feeling of desolation swamped her. It was her own fault; she should have known better.

'Susan? Are you still there, Susan?'

She stifled the tears that threatened. 'Yes, yes, Mam. I'm here.'

'Are you crying, love?'

'No. I've got a cold. You know, watery eyes and runny nose?'

'Do take care of yourself, love. You know . . . your father regrets speaking to you like that. We would be so pleased if you would come home.'

'I find that hard to believe, Mam. He's never really

shown concern for me. Alison is apparently giving him the ideal son-in-law, so I don't count at all. Ha-ha, that's all that matters. He couldn't care less about me.'

'Ah, Susan, you've always been so defiant. You get your dad's back up. He's terribly disappointed that you took the huff and ran off like that. Of course he cares and wants you to come home.'

'Mam . . . he isn't taking his spite out on you, is he?'

A silence met these words. Then Rachel cried, 'What on earth do you mean, Susan? Of course he isn't!' She was alarmed at how perceptive her daughter was.

Susan remembered the times her father's spiteful remarks had reduced her mother to tears; remembered the muffled weeping coming from her parents' bedroom, and did not believe her. 'I'm sorry, Mam, if I'm bringing you grief. Don't let him browbeat you.'

'You've got it all wrong, Susan.'

'Have I, Mam?' Wanting to change the subject, Susan asked, 'What about Alison? Is she engaged yet?'

'Not yet. I imagine a ring will be bought at Christmas.'

'You know, I envy her. She's two years younger than me, yet she can do whatever she likes! So long as she is with "Graham" she gets away with murder. Dad doesn't demand that Graham has her home by eleven every night. No, those two can do no wrong. Graham would never do anything ungentlemanly. Huh!'

Unable to understand her daughter's bitterness against Graham, Rachel said soothingly, 'Well, he is older than Alison. We trust him to respect her.'

'But you don't trust me?' Susan felt a hypocrite. Here she was, about to become an unmarried mother, and she was giving off about her parents' lack of trust. Why, they would probably disown her if they found out.

'We do trust you. We were just worried when you refused to bring your friend home. I think your dad was under the impression that you were dating a Catholic?' She waited hopefully for her daughter either to deny or confirm the accusation. Her words hung in the air for a few seconds, then sadly she continued, 'I've been wondering about your work, Susan. Did you ask for time off? Surely you didn't hand in your notice? Not knowing what you told them, I was afraid to phone the office. Is your position still open for you?'

Susan laughed; her mother never did wait for an answer. 'One question at a time, Mam. Yes, Mam, my job is safe. I've managed to get time off. One of the other secretaries will take over until I come back.' Susan wasn't really telling lies. Her boss was a very understanding person and would bring in a temp if required to keep her position open. Knowing it would go no further, Susan had confided in him and she had until after the birth to decide what she wanted to do. However, since she didn't know how long she would be away, she couldn't expect her job to be kept open indefinitely. But there was no need for her mother to know this.

Rachel's relief was obvious. 'Thank goodness for that. Well, you've made your point, so come home at once. I worry about you over in that small, cold house at this time of year.'

'Mam, anyone listening to you wouldn't believe you had been reared in a small kitchen house on the Shankill Road, with no hot water and an outside toilet,' Susan teased. She knew her mother didn't like to be reminded of her roots.

'That may well be! But *you* have known only the best. Will you come home?'

'I'm enjoying my bit of freedom, Mam, so I'll stay on here for a while. And the house isn't cold, it's like a wee palace. Edith and Billy have it lovely and comfortable. Don't worry about me.'

'I can't help worrying. I don't want you led astray.'

Susan sighed inwardly. 'Mam, believe me I have less chance of going astray over here than I had back home. Aunt Edith keeps a close eye on me. You can rest assured, I'm not in any danger of being led astray.'

'How is Edith?'

'She's wonderful, Mam. They are both so kind to me. They have a stall in the market now and sell fruit and veg. It's proving very profitable. I help out sometimes. I enjoy meeting the Darlington people. It reminds me of the market back home.' The pips sounded. 'Mam, I've run out of money. I'll phone you again soon. Give Dad and Alison my love.'

'Susan! Susan,' Rachel cried in distress, but the phone was dead.

The wind had strengthened while she was on the phone and icy gusts whipped at Susan's clothes, moulding them into the contours of her body as she left the phone booth, almost lifting her off her feet with its ferocity. She had eased the woollen beret up off her ears whilst phoning and, as the wind set her ears tingling, she made to pull it back down over her unruly curls, but was too late. The wind wrested it from beneath her hand and tossed it like a feather along the street. With a cry of dismay she raced after it and for some moments struggled against the wind in an effort to retrieve it. However, it eluded her efforts and an extra-strong gust lifted it far beyond her reach. She slowed down in frustration. There was no way she could catch up with it in this gale-force wind.

A figure suddenly sped past her, long legs quickly covering the ground. She watched as he effortlessly retrieved the beret and turned back towards her. As he drew near, to her surprise she recognised him. He and her cousin Jack were close friends. She had often trooped about with them on her last visit all those years ago. Would Donald Murphy recognise her again? With a flourish, he handed her the beret.

'Thank you. Thank you very much.'

At the sound of her Irish brogue he leant closer and dark-blue eyes scanned her face. 'Don't I know you?' One fist hit the palm of the other hand as recognition dawned. 'Ah, yes, you're Billy Devine's niece. I heard you were over here. We met some years ago, but I don't suppose you'll remember.'

'I remember perfectly,' she retorted, pulling the beret down over her ears and tucking her hair in under it. 'I'm not senile, you know,' she teased.

'I didn't mean to imply you were,' he replied stiffly.

She gaped at him in amazement. 'Touchy, aren't you? I didn't mean any offence.'

'No offence taken.' He swung away and then back again. 'I'll walk home with you.'

'There's no need.'

A slight smile curved his thin, sensitive lips. 'I'm going in that direction.'

They walked along in silence, the wind making

conversation difficult. He had grown quite a few inches and filled out since Susan last saw him. She was very aware of the bulk of him as they battled against the wind. He had certainly grown into a very presentable young man. She wondered if he was married. Stealing a glance at his brooding, dour looks, she declined to ask. In her opinion Heathcliff, her hero in *Wuthering Heights*, wouldn't hold a candle to Donald's sullen expression. Hark at her! Imagine thinking along those lines. Would she never learn?

To break the effect he was having on her, she shouted above the wind, 'This is some wind, isn't it? Is it usually this strong?'

'Yes, it is strong,' he agreed. 'Usually we're sheltered here in Darlington. It lies in a valley and we miss the worst of the snow and gales, thank God. Take Barnard Castle, for instance, it's just a few miles away and is not so lucky. It can be cut off for days at a time by snow and we would see nothing here in Darlington. To be truthful, I think we're in for some snow here, at the moment. It's certainly cold enough. However, when it does fall it doesn't lie long. How long are you over for?'

'I haven't made up my mind yet. I just came over for a short holiday.'

At the corner of the street she prepared to say good night, but to her surprise he continued walking around the corner and down the street.

Bemused, she followed him. 'There really is no need for you to come any further, Donald. I'll be quite safe,' she chided.

'Oh, but there is,' he assured her. When they arrived at her door she turned to him. 'Will you come in for a cup of tea? I'm sure Aunt Edith will be pleased to see you.'

'No, I'd better not. It's getting late. I've something to attend to and then I'd better get on home. Good night.'

'Good night, Donald. Thanks for walking me home.'

He lifted his hand in farewell and she watched in amazement as he took a bunch of keys from his pocket and, approaching the house next door, inserted one in the lock. It turned easily and he give her a big wink before disappearing inside.

As Susan entered the house, her aunt rose from her seat by the fire and came into the hall to meet her. 'You look frozen. I'll make us a cup of tea. Did you get through to your mam all right?'

'Yes. She was relieved to hear from me. She asked after you and Billy.'

'Is everything all right at home?'

'Mmm . . .' Hanging her coat on a hook in the hall, she said, 'Donald Murphy walked up from the phone box with me. I didn't realise he lived next door. I thought that house was empty.'

'It is . . . well, not quite empty. When his aunt died he somehow or other managed to get his name put in the rent book. When it became common knowledge there was a bit of an uproar at the time, as half of the street wanted it for someone or other. However, whether or not hands were greased – and they probably were – we will never know. But the landlord stood firm and his word was law. As far as he was concerned, Donald's name was in the rent book and that was the end of it.'

Edith fell silent as if undecided. Then she continued, 'Donald was engaged to a girl at that time and they intended starting married life there, but it wasn't to be. He doesn't live there himself, but comes up and stays a few days every month to keep it aired. I sometimes wonder if he expects her to come back to him.'

'What happened? Did they not get married then?'

'No. Apparently she fell in love with someone else.'

'So that's why he's so different. I can sympathise with him. He must have been very unhappy. If I recall correctly, he used to be such a happy-go-lucky sort of lad, and now he seems quite surly. I asked him to come in for a cup of tea, but he was in too much of a hurry to get back home.'

Edith sighed and her eyes took on an empty look. 'I suppose I may as well tell you the rest of it. He isn't very friendly towards us Devines.'

'Oh, why's that? Didn't he and Jack used to be best mates?'

'They were. That's why he avoids us when he can. You see, it was our Jack she ran off with.'

'Oh, no. How awful for him. He must have felt betrayed.'

'Don't put all the blame on Jack!' Edith tersely defended her son. 'These things happen. It nearly broke Billy's heart. This community is so close-knit, you wouldn't believe it! They all rallied round Donald, because he was the injured party and his family were here long before Billy and me. In fact, Donald was born over here. They said some awful things about Jack. Billy also turned on him. Railed at him about doing the dirty on a mate. That's why I don't think Jack will ever come back. I could tell he was hurt at his father's attitude. I suppose, knowing our own history

– how Billy fell in love with me and left his wife – Jack must have thought his father a right hypocrite. But there were extenuating circumstances. You see, Donna, Billy's wife, didn't love him, or I would never have agreed to come away with him.' Tears welled up and ran down her cheeks.

Reaching across, Susan gripped her aunt's hands tightly. 'Oh, Aunt Edith, don't upset yourself. I'm so sorry for you both. What an awful thing to happen. What was this girl like? Did you like her? If things had been different, would you have welcomed her as a daughter-in-law?'

'How can I say? I never really got to know her.' Edith's voice was sad. 'Her name was Margaret McGivern. I say was, because for all I know she might be Mrs Devine now. She was attractive all right. Not what you would call a raving beauty like, but attractive, with pale-blonde hair and great dark eyes. She came from the other end of town, Saltersgate. She and Donald were to be married at Christmas and Jack was to be best man. The three of them ran about together everywhere; to the dances and the picture houses and the clubs. They were inseparable. However, she was only in this house one time. If she and Jack were carrying on behind Donald's back, we weren't aware of it. I would never have tolerated it under my roof and neither would Billy.'

She fell silent and Susan waited patiently, convinced that more was to come. She was right, for after some moments of contemplation her aunt continued tearfully. 'The night she told Donald she was in love with Jack, Donald went berserk and came looking for him. They had one hell of a brawl out there in the street. It was awful. They beat each other from one end of the street to the other. No one else was allowed to interfere. Billy tried to separate them, but the men crowded round him and warned him to let them be. They near murdered each other. Margaret was hysterical, so I brought her inside. Somebody phoned the police and an ambulance, and both Jack and Donald ended up in casualty in the Memorial Hospital, under police guard. When they had taken statements and knew the full story, the police wanted Jack to press charges, on account of it being Donald who started the fight, but he declined. The next morning he and Margaret left for London. It was heart-breaking, so it was, watching them drive off for the station in a taxi. Jack's ribs were bandaged and his face was a right mess. He was obviously in great pain.' She paused, lost in unhappy memories. Her voice was bitter when she continued. 'Donald vented his spleen on us. You'd think it was our fault, the way he treats us. He never gave us the benefit of the doubt. It's awful annoying. He just can't be civil towards us. But we honestly hadn't a clue what was going on. As I say, she was only in this house that one time.'

Susan sat, head bent, as the implications of what she had just heard penetrated her brain. It seemed to her that, in the circumstances, Jack would be unlikely to come back to Darlington. Not to live anyhow. Not in this house, with Donald renting the house next door. She recalled the old adage 'Every cloud has a silver lining'. Did that mean there was hope for her? Would she be able to settle here and keep her shame a secret from those in Belfast? Oh, if only . . .

'What about her parents?' she asked tentatively. 'Will

they not be able to persuade her to return. Won't she miss her family?'

'Margaret's parents died young and she was reared by her grannie. She died about a year ago. There's nothing to bring Margaret back here. Nothing at all. Oh, God, why couldn't she have married Donald Murphy and left our Jack alone? She has ruined all our lives. You hear such bad reports about life in London. For all we know, they might be living on the streets,' wailed Edith.

'Have they any money?'

Edith nodded sadly. 'The money we had saved for a van – Billy insisted that Jack take it. He accepted it on the understanding that he would pay it back when he was able. And I know he will, but it wasn't all that much, it won't last for ever.'

'So long as they have some money, they'll find some kind of accommodation, and if they really love each other, they'll be happy no matter where they are. Jack has a trade, hasn't he?'

'He was a fitter in Cleveland Bridge, but will he be able to get that kind of work in London? I doubt it.'

'A fitter can do all different kinds of jobs, Aunt Edith. There's plenty of work in London. He will get into a factory or a garage. Have you not heard from him at all?'

'Huh! One miserable letter to let us know they had arrived safe and well. One miserable letter. Not a word of regret or sorrow for all the trouble he'd caused.'

'He's been too ashamed, so he has. I know how he feels. It's shame that keeps you from getting in touch. But he'll write again, Aunt Edith, when he has some good news to tell you. Just you wait and see.'

Edith wiped her eyes and said, 'I hope you're right. It's great to be able to talk about him. Billy won't let me mention his name in this house. He doesn't like me worrying about them. But I can't help worrying. It's what mothers do best.'

Rachel slowly replaced the receiver in its cradle, a worried frown on her brow. To her, Susan had sounded homesick, so why didn't she come home? As she crossed the hall to the lounge the headlights of a car flashed across the windows as it turned into the drive. She changed course and went to open the door for Alison and her friend, surprised that they had come home by taxi. It was a terrible extravagance. Young people these days were hopeless where money was concerned. You would think it grew on trees.

It was starting to rain. Rachel drew back the net curtain and peered through the window at the side of the door. Great spots splattered the car and she saw that it wasn't a taxi but a comparatively new saloon car that stood outside in the driveway. Through the gloom she was amazed to see her daughter lean forward and kiss her companion, a young man, on the lips. A slow, sensuous kiss. He made to gather her close, but she laughingly broke away from him and, leaving the car, dashed up the steps and turned to wave him off.

Rachel opened the door and Alison laughed. 'That was good timing, Mam.' She shook the loose raindrops from her short blonde curls and eyed her mother keenly. 'Are you all right, Mam? You look a bit pale.'

'Who was that?'

'Just a boy I dance with in Leckie's.'

'You kissed him!' Rachel accused her.

'Just a peck, Mam.'

'It looked more than a peck to me. I thought you were going to eat him. Alison, remember you're practically engaged to Graham.'

'Oh, for goodness sake. What he doesn't know won't harm him.'

'That's the wrong attitude to take when you're contemplating marriage to someone, Alison. I'm surprised at you.'

'Mam, things are different now from what they were in your day.'

'Huh! Not all that different. You had better be careful, girl, or you will lose Graham.'

'I couldn't care less, Mam. There are plenty more fish in the sea. It's Graham who's pressing for an engagement, not me. I'm willing to wait.'

Rachel looked at her beautiful, wilful daughter and could understand why Graham was in such a hurry. He was afraid of losing her.

'Why are you looking at me like that?'

'Hmm. I want to remember what a fool looks like when Graham says "Let's call it a day."'

Alison pulled a wry face and headed for the stairs. 'See if I care.' And she didn't! Life had suddenly become more exciting now that she was learning advanced ballroom dancing. Once she could go to the big ballrooms, the world would be her oyster. The young men were queuing up to dance with her as it was. But they were too young. She preferred the older, more sophisticated man. That was why she had started going out with Graham in the first place. He had prospects and money, but now he bored her. To be truthful, he didn't seem interested in her any more either.

Her mother's voice halted her. 'Susan has just this minute been on the phone.'

She turned, her voice full of regret. 'Oh? I wish I'd been here. How is she?'

'She seems well enough, but I thought she sounded a bit homesick. Probably wishful thinking on my part. She certainly has no intention of coming home just yet.'

'I don't blame her. She's probably having a whale of a time over there. I wish I had her nerve. Imagine taking off like that! I wish something exciting would happen to me.'

'Is getting engaged not exciting enough for you?'

'Catch yourself on, Mam! What difference will it make?'

'You will have an exciting time planning your wedding and looking for a house.'

'Balderdash! It will be years before we marry. Meanwhile, I intend to enjoy myself. Good night, Mam.'

'Good night, Alison.' Rachel watched her climb the stairs, a frown creasing her brow. 'Sweet dreams,' she whispered, 'And I sincerely hope they are of Graham.' Was their youngest daughter as innocent as they would like to believe? It was bad enough Susan proving difficult. Please God, let Alison behave, or life with Trevor would be unbearable.

Susan made her aunt a cup of tea and insisted on adding some of the precious whiskey set to one side for medicinal purposes.

'Oh, you really shouldn't, Susan. That's for emergencies.'

'This is an emergency. You need a good night's sleep, Aunt Edith. After all this reminiscing you won't be able to settle without a little help. Here, drink up.'

Edith sipped at the hot liquid and felt the warmth spread throughout her body, easing the tension from her limbs. 'You really are a blessing in disguise, Susan. I'm glad you came over. Although I wish for your sake the circumstances were different. Did your mother not demand that you go home?'

Susan grimaced. 'She did indeed, but I put her off.'

'I worry about you, Susan.'

'Don't, Aunt Edith. The last thing I want is to be a burden on you.'

'Never that, love. You'll never be a burden. I'm so glad you're here.'

They sat in silence sipping their tea and pursuing their own thoughts. The heat of the fire and the effect of the whiskey took their toll, and soon Edith rose to her feet, her eyes heavy with sleep.

'I think I'd better go to bed before I fall asleep here. I'll see you in the morning, Susan. And thanks for everything. If you're going to bed, love, don't bar the door. Remember Billy isn't home yet. It would never do to lock him out.'

Susan also retired early. She had a lot to think about. If she could just manage to stay here in Darlington until the baby was a few months old, she could claim that it was conceived over here. That way no one would ever guess who the father was. She was glad she had met Donald Murphy tonight. The subsequent conversation with her aunt had made her future look brighter. She hoped that Jack did well down in London and had no desire to return to Darlington. If he should happen to return for the Christmas break, then she would persuade Donald to rent the house next door to her.

Feeling more secure about her future, she fetched a writing pad and pen and, sitting propped up in bed, commenced to write to her friend Ruth Vernon. It was about time she let her best friend know her whereabouts. But she would not mention her reason for coming to England, oh no! If she could help it, no one would ever know the truth. Still, it would be nice to hear from Ruth and be kept up to date on what was happening back home. She bit on the end of her pen for some moments, sorting out in her mind what she wanted to say. Then, happily, she put pen to paper and soon had covered several pages, without giving any secrets away.

Chapter Three

A few days after posting the letter Susan received a reply from Ruth.

Dear Susan,

How mean of you to leave without letting me know. I always thought of you as my dearest friend. I couldn't believe my ears when I phoned and Alison told me you'd gone over to England. I was devastated! However, I do understand and accept your apologies. I know you were in the doldrums since you split up with Jim Brady. You shouldn't have let him get to you like that! There's no man worth all that emotion. By the way, he has also disappeared from the scene. He isn't, by any chance, over there with you? Eh? Only joking. Life over here is dull at the moment. I sure as hell miss you and I'm looking forward to seeing you at Christmas. Darlington sounds like good fun, but don't you go getting too fond of it. Your place is back here in Belfast, with or without Jim Brady. At the moment I'm seeing Dougie Smith, remember him? He's all right, I suppose, but the earth doesn't move when he kisses me. Is that important? Did it move when Jim kissed you? Do people just drift into marriage, Susan? Oh, how I wish you were here, so that I could discuss all my problems with you, face-to-face.

Goodbye for now, please write soon.
Your true friend
Ruth

Susan read the letter over and over and the tears rolled down her cheeks. There was no way she could have told Ruth she was leaving Belfast. Ruth would have wheedled the truth out of her, and no one – but no one at all – must know that the baby was conceived back home. How she wished that she was footloose and fancy-free like Ruth. She missed her friend dearly. Wait until Ruth heard she was not coming home for Christmas. She smiled grimly at the idea. The air would surely be blue. She would wait until nearer Christmas before answering this letter and send Ruth a small present. She folded the letter carefully and placed it under her pillow. It brought her best friend and the past close to her, and she had a restless night thinking of what might have been.

Edith was quick to notice Susan's pallor the next morning. 'Do you feel ill, love?' she inquired anxiously. 'I suppose it's time you saw a doctor. Shall I try and get you an appointment with Dr Allen today?'

'No. Time enough for that after Christmas, Aunt Edith. I feel fine, so I do.'

'Well, you sure as hell don't look it! You don't want to risk losing the baby, so you don't.'

Susan turned away to hide her expression. Didn't she just? If only she could miscarry, it would be relief beyond belief. She would do nothing to harm this baby, which at the moment she just knew was there. A couple of mornings of queasiness and a missed period had alerted her, and the pregnancy kit she bought had proved positive. But other than that it wasn't real to her as yet. If the baby was to voluntarily leave her body, she would look on it as an act of God.

However, she felt so well in herself that it was unlikely to happen. She explained to her aunt, 'That letter I received yesterday was from my best friend. It made me a bit homesick, that's all. But I'll get over it. Come on, we'd better get a move on or we'll be late for work.'

Still worried, Edith hesitated. 'Look, you go back to bed. I'll tell Vera you're feeling poorly. She'll understand.'

Shooing her gently towards the door, Susan assured her, 'You'll do no such thing. I'll be fine.'

At her newly acquired job, in the stall next to her aunt's in the market, Ruth's letter played on Susan's mind throughout the day. Ruth had said that Jim was also missing. But then Susan hadn't set eyes on him since he had rejected her advances and walked away, without even so much as a backward glance, so what was new? Was he involved with someone else? No matter! Even if he still cared for her, he wouldn't have anything to do with her now. As far as he was concerned, she had certainly burnt her bridges good and proper. She must look to the future.

A blanket of snow covered the ground as far as the eye could see, turning the town into a winter wonderland. In a happier frame of mind than she had been for some days, Susan picked her way carefully along the slippery footpath, along Albert Hill and on to North Road, stopping cautiously to look in the shop windows. There was nothing of particular interest to her in these shops and, after a lot of near tumbles, she arrived breathless on Northgate. Here the big-name stores were prominent and her attention heightened. The pavements seemed safer and she stepped out more confidently. She stopped at the windows of Marks & Spencer to admire their wares, before moving along to British Home Stores, which was vying with M&S in its endeavours to outdo their Christmas displays. She was looking for suitable presents to send home. Already some goods were marked down in price and she saw a couple of bargains that would come in handy, particularly a pink sweater that she knew would suit Ruth. During the week she would hunt down these bargains when her employer granted her the few promised hours off work. She bypassed John Collier and Alexandre, not being interested in the latest fashions for the male sex. There was no special man in her life to buy for, and the others would receive aftershave.

A glance down Crown Street showed there was nothing of interest to her there. At the General Post Office she crossed the road and backtracked a bit to view the fashions in the windows of Doggarts' store. She gulped at the price tags, which at the moment were well beyond her pocket. Still, it was a store that seemed to stock just about everything and she had heard good reports about the quality of their goods. She silently resolved to have a look inside when she had some spare time.

Reaching the junction of Northgate and Bondgate, Susan hovered close to the Midland Bank on the corner of Prospect Place, to shelter against the flurry of snow blowing down Bondgate. The heart of the town stretched before her, dominated by the market clock tower, and she paused to admire the view slumbering in a virgin-white mantle. Any other day and this vast white mass of snow would already be broken and slushy, but it was early Sunday morning and so far hardly a footprint marred the scene. Glancing behind her, she saw how her own isolated footprints were already obliterated beneath the fresh fall of powdery snow. It was as if she was in a world of her own. Even the sky was a thick white cover capping all this beauty. The snow muffled all sounds and a peaceful hush seemed to embrace the scene. A calmness settled in her soul at such tranquillity.

When she awoke early that morning and saw the thick layer of snow on the rooftops she decided that the time had come to do the window shopping she had been promising herself. The stall next to her aunt's in the market sold greeting cards and wrapping paper. The owner had bought in toys and novelties for the festive season and had been looking for someone to help out with the Christmas rush. Her aunt had put in a word for Susan and an interview was set up. To her great delight, the owner, Vera Crabtree, and she had hit it off right away and the job was hers.

The idea of earning some money and being able to pay her way without breaking in on her savings had come as a great relief. Also, she had not much time to brood and found that she was settling in nicely. It did, however, mean that her days were taken up – even Saturdays – and she had no time to do her Christmas shopping. Only two weeks to Christmas and she still hadn't bought all her presents.

She loved the snow and now, as she gazed at the scene before her, she realised how much at home she felt here. Darlington was an old Quaker town and the architecture of the buildings appealed to her eye. The Pearl Assurance building on the corner of High Row and Bondgate, in particular, was very imposing, especially this morning when snow covered its ornate domed roof and high chimneys, which towered above the roofs of the smaller buildings. Close by, Dressers, the stationer, also looked very attractive with its colourful name sign and posters calling attention to its wares. Jackson's Dry Cleaners and Dunns separated it from two more imposing structures housing the Yorkshire Penny Bank and Barclays Bank.

Standing majestically on an island at the junction, the statue of Joseph Pease stood in all its glory as he silently surveyed the town he had helped to fashion back in the 1800s. She had been reading a lot about this man in a book that her aunt had lent her. To all intents and purposes he had been a spectacular figure, becoming the largest coal merchant in the North-East and generously donating the land for South Park to be laid out for the pleasure and recreation of the people of Darlington. He became the first Quaker MP, entering the House of Commons in 1833 – a pursuit that he had carried on, in spite of opposition from his father and the Society of Friends, of which he was a dedicated member.

The statue itself was weather-beaten and today had a white hat of snow, becoming higher by the minute. This served to make Pease look very formidable. Becoming aware that her toes were beginning to go numb in her thin-soled patent boots, Susan stamped her feet and headed for the Saxone shoe shop on the far side of the road next to the King's Head Hotel. She was reluctant to trespass on the virgin-white carpet, but consoled herself with the knowledge that the falling snow would soon fill in the gaps. It would be trampled anyhow, by church-goers and the like, she reminded herself.

Having caught a glimpse of a pair of fur-lined boots in the window of the shoe shop on her way home from work, she now wanted a closer look. If they had thick soles and weren't too expensive she intended treating herself. At first she thought they had gone, but sighed with relief when she saw they had merely been moved to a higher place on the display shelves. To her great joy she discovered they had also acquired a 'Sale' tag and were a bargain. Tomorrow she would nip out and, if they had her size, she would buy them during her brief lunch break, before they were snapped up.

Pleased with herself, she crossed the main road and carefully climbed the few steps to High Row, pausing on the way for a closer look at Joseph Pease and reading the four bronze plaques around the plinth at the base of the monument. These illustrated important episodes in the great man's illustrious career: politics, education and involvement in the railways. On High Row itself, the shops were also trying to outdo each other in their Christmas displays. Suddenly struck by thoughts of home, Susan was overwhelmed by the memory of the decorations that would be lighting up Belfast city centre. The usual giant Christmas tree outside the city hall would be decorated and ablaze with hundreds of colourful lights, and Royal Avenue would be a sight to behold. Every year she and Alison went down town just to see the wonder of the lights being switched on. She supposed Graham had accompanied her sister this year. Discovering tears trickling down her cheeks, she brushed them away with a swipe of her hand. It was senseless moping over the past. If she could arrange it, this would be her home from now on.

Her mother had been astounded when Susan had told her she would not be home for Christmas. Angrily brushing aside her excuses, Rachel had demanded to know how she could put Edith before her own family, especially at this time of year. Susan was ashamed to use her cousin Jack's absence from home and her aunt's unhappiness as an excuse to stay here. God forgive her, she was building a web of lies and deceit that might one day strangle her.

Determinedly pushing all worries to the back of her mind, she paused at the bottom of Post House Wynd and glanced across to survey her place of employment, the indoor market. Dwarfed at one end by the magnificent town clock, which had also been donated by that generous man, Joseph Pease, the market stretched the length of West Row and was embraced at the other end by the town hall on Horsemarket. All looked splendid in their Christmas finery. Continuing on along High Row, she paused between shops to peer up into Buckton's Yard, Clark's Yard and the Mechanic Institute Yard. All these intriguing, quaint little entries contained a conglomeration of small shops, which she had as yet to explore. It would be something to do after Christmas when she had more time to herself. Who knew what treasures of the past she would find there? This must be how children felt as they anticipated Christmas, she thought, and promised herself that one day in the not too distant future she would explore all these intriguing yards.

She was gazing into Binns' store window when a voice close at hand startled her.

'What has you out so early? Could you not sleep?' Donald Murphy teased. 'Perhaps a guilty conscience?'

Startled, she spun round and gazed up into his dark, brooding face, lightened slightly by the hint of a smile. A fine dusting of snow covered his thick, dark hair and clung to the edge of long eyelashes. 'You frightened the life out of me, Donald Murphy! Creeping up on me like that.'

'Sorry. I didn't mean to alarm you. It's the snow muffling my footsteps. Normally you would hear me a mile off. And you haven't answered my question,' he insisted. He had been admiring the figure in the bright-red coat and knee-length white patent boots and was surprised to discover it was Susan. Why, she was lovely! How come he hadn't noticed earlier? Margaret McGivern must have dulled all his senses towards women. How he missed Margaret! He must have neglected her, for her to turn to Jack Devine like that. He wished he could turn back the clock, but it was too late now. However, this girl exuded sensuality. How come he hadn't noticed before? The white fur snood that Susan wore showed off to perfection her pink-and-white porcelain complexion, which glowed with health. Big, smoky-grey eyes, fringed with long, thick lashes, gazed at him from under exquisitely curved black brows, and her soft, sensuous lips were pink and enticing.

Aware of his admiring scrutiny, Susan blushed. What was he playing at? she thought angrily. Anyone would think he was seeing her for the first time! A pink tide of colour rose from neck to hairline, making him aware that he was staring. He apologised at once. 'Sorry for gawking, but I suppose you already know how pretty you are. Mm?' A light laugh accompanied the words and her embarrassment deepened. Taking pity on her, he let her off the hook by returning to his former question. 'Well . . . what are you doing out so early on this marvellous Sunday morning?'

Still acutely embarrassed by his admiration, she retorted, 'I could ask you the same question. What brings *you* out so early on a Sunday morning?'

'I'm on my way to Mass in St Augustine's.'

'Oh, sorry, I never thought of that. Well, I'm ashamed to admit that I'm not as clean-living as you. I'm just window shopping. I don't get a chance during the week.' She tilted her head and gazed up at him. 'I'm working now, in case you don't know.'

'Really?'

'Yes, Vera Crabtree – you know, she has the stall next to Aunt Edith's in the market – has taken me on to help during the Christmas rush. That's why I'm window shopping. This way I'll know just where to go when I do get a few free minutes.'

'I know Vera. She's a very nice woman.'

'I couldn't agree more. She's so easy to get on with.'

When Susan moved off, Donald fell into step beside her and, after a short silence, asked diffidently, 'Is Jack coming home for Christmas?'

'Not that I know of. Aunt Edith got a letter from him on Wednesday and he told her that Margaret's pregnant.' She watched him from under lowered lashes and felt heart-sore when she saw the raw misery etched on his face. It was obvious he still loved the girl. She could certainly appreciate how he felt. To lose the one you love and then hear she was expecting your best friend's child must be a traumatic feeling. It made everything so final.

He sighed. 'I suppose it's only to be expected. Are they married?'

'I honestly don't know very much about them. It pains Billy to hear Edith talking about Jack, so I just mind my own business. I don't want to upset them by asking embarrassing questions.' She and Donald had met a few times and indulged in casual conversation since her arrival here, but so far she had not ventured to mention Jack and Margaret. Now she said hesitantly, 'I'm so sorry about what happened, Donald. You and Jack were such good friends. It must have been an awful experience for you.'

He shrugged. 'Ah, it was! But it's all water under the bridge now.'

'Aunt Edith and Uncle Billy are heartbroken, you know. They not only lost a son, but a very good friend. Do you not think you should bury the hatchet?'

'That's easier said than done. They must have known. Everybody else did.' His face tightened and his voice thickened. 'They must all have had a good laugh up their sleeves at my expense.'

'I'm sure no one was laughing at you,' she said softly.

'Edith could have dropped me a hint, and perhaps things would have turned out differently. But then, it was their Jack who was the culprit. In their eyes he can do no wrong.'

'They honestly didn't know. It came as a terrible shock to them. Edith told me that Billy said some terrible things to Jack, and now he fears he will never see him again. They're hoping desperately that he will come home for at least a few days at Christmas. I feel guilty as hell, because I know how much they want him to come but I hope he doesn't.'

'Why's that?'

She laughed. 'Oh, all self-interest, I'm afraid. I'm occupying his room at the moment. I don't know where I'll end up if he comes home.'

'You don't intend going home to Ireland for Christmas, then?'

'No.'

Her tone and attitude should have warned him off, but he persisted. 'I hear you're married. What about your husband? Will he not expect you home?'

Her lips tightened. She had not wanted to pretend she was married, but Edith had produced a wedding ring that had belonged to Billy's mother and suggested that Susan wear it, saying there was no need for people to know her business. Thinking that perhaps, when she started to show, her condition might prove embarrassing to Edith and Billy and not wanting to bite the hand that fed her, Susan had agreed to wear the ring. However, the deceit bothered her.

'No!' Her voice was curt, her face closed. 'He won't be expecting me! And, if you don't mind, I don't want to talk about it.'

Donald longed to question her further; to find out how one so young and beautiful could already be separated from her husband. The man must be a fool. But in view of her attitude he decided to hold his tongue; at least for the time being! They had reached the corner where High Row meets Blackwellgate.

'Sorry. I didn't mean to be nosy back there. Look, I'd better not dally. I don't want to be late for Mass.'

Looking around her, the only spire that Susan could see was the one to the right of the three big coolers of the power station that dominated the skyline. This spire she knew belonged to St Cuthbert's Church, rising as it did beyond the roof of the market. 'Where is this St Augustine's Church, then?'

Donald smiled at her bewilderment and pointed ahead. 'Just up there on the right.' Impulsively he added, 'Come with me and see for yourself. It's a beautiful old church. Well worth a visit.'

She laughed aloud. 'I'm not a Catholic.'

'Oh . . . I thought you were. I saw you at St William's last Sunday with Edith and Billy.'

'Nevertheless, I'm not Catholic.'

'Come on, coax yourself. You'll love it.'

Still she hesitated. 'Tell you what. I'll come with you and pray that you will in the near future make your peace with Aunt Edith and Uncle Billy. What's the chances of that happening?'

For the first time since her meeting with him outside the phone box, she saw a real smile light up his face, dispelling the dour look and making it rugged and quite handsome. 'I think the chances are very good.'

'You're on then.'

Happily she walked beside him, unable to hide the smug look on her face. Edith and Billy would be very pleased. She was so lost in thought that it came as a surprise when Donald suddenly stopped at a wrought-iron gate. It divided a row of houses and a great big detached house on the corner of Larchfield Street.

He laughed as she glanced around in obvious surprise. 'We're nearly there.'

He ushered her through the gate and she could see by the trampled snow that others had been here before them. At the end of the narrow entry she saw St Augustine's Church for the first time. She was mesmerised at how a church so near the main thoroughfare could be completely hidden from view. When they left the short entry, on their right beyond a snow-covered lawn a sprawling building was obviously the parochial house. Donald soon confirmed her suspicions and said that the building now on their left was the junior school, the main entrance to it being in Larchfield Street.

The church itself was very old. They entered the porch and she watched as he dipped his fingers into the font of holy water and crossed himself. Nodding to stairs to the left of the door, she asked where they went and was informed that they led to a balcony along the back of the church, where the organ was and the choir gathered to sing the hymns. Donald pushed open the heavy inner door and ushered her through.

She paused inside and gazed around her in wonder. 'It's lovely,' she whispered and without any prompting from him made her way up the church, admiring the beautiful stained-glass windows on either side, as she went. She sat in a pew near the front and took in the intricate detail of the three altars. It must have taken years to perfect.

They were early, but soon the church filled up and the altar boys, followed by the priest, came through a door to the right of the altar and Mass began.

Susan found herself kneeling when Donald knelt and, as there was no choir at this early Mass, singing the hymns from the hymn book. As she participated in the solemn service, peace settled on her heart and she felt that things would surely work out for her.

The service proved all too short and soon they were on their way back through the town. The return journey showed how the beauty of the snow had already been impaired as people went about their business this lovely winter's morning. At the corner of Skinnergate Susan indicated that she was going in that direction to continue her window shopping.

Catching sight of the Pali sign up on the left-hand side of Grange Road, he was struck by a thought. Dare he? Would she go on a date with him? She could only say no.

To Susan's surprise, with a nod of the head across the road, he asked tentatively, 'I wonder . . . would you like to come to a dance with me at the Pali next Saturday night?'

She had heard of the Pali. It was a very popular dance hall. Her heart missed a beat. Go to a dance? How she wished she could. 'I'm sorry . . .'

'Look,' he interrupted hastily. 'I know you're married, and you know I don't want to get involved, otherwise I wouldn't dare ask. We understand each other. Can't we be mates? Enjoy a night out together?'

She pondered for a moment. He didn't know, of course, but it was the thought of her condition that was causing her to hesitate. She came to a decision. She wasn't showing yet, so why not? God knows when she would ever get the chance to go to a dance again. She could wear a loose top; hide her slight bump. Before she could change her mind she said, 'I'd love to.'

Again a smile transformed his face. 'Great! I'll pick

you up at seven-thirty then. It will give me a chance to bury the hatchet with Edith and Billy.'

He was gone before she could express her delight.

The news that Susan would not be home for Christmas enraged Trevor Cummings. He glared at his wife as she read extracts from the letter in her hand. 'Just who the hell does she think she is? What must that big galoot Billy Devine think of us, that our daughter prefers their company to ours at this important time? You write and tell her that if she doesn't come home now, she won't be welcome here ever again.'

'You don't mean that, Trevor.'

'Oh, but I do, Rachel. I mean every word I say, so you be sure to tell her that.'

'Dad, she might have a very good reason for staying in Darlington. Perhaps she has fallen in love with someone.' Alison was trying to keep the peace, but her father rounded on her in anger.

'If that's the case, she can stay over there! She won't be welcome here any more, the way she's carrying on.'

A worried look passed between mother and daughter. Rachel's chin rose in the air and she cried defiantly, 'Then I'm afraid you will have to tell her so yourself for a change. As far as I'm concerned, this is her home and she will always be welcome here.' With a pronounced flounce she left the room, to hide the tears that threatened.

'Dad! How can you be so hard?' Alison exclaimed. 'Susan's your eldest daughter. It could have been much worse, you know. If she had remained here she might have married a Catholic.'

Once more Trevor rounded on her in fury. 'So she was seeing a Taig. Was she?'

'I didn't say that.' Alison was dismayed at her slip of the tongue. 'I know she dated one for a time, but obviously it wasn't serious or she would never have gone over to England.'

Still glaring at her, Trevor asked in a soft voice that was more insinuating than a roar, 'Is there more to this than meets the eye? Eh, Alison? Are you keeping something from me? Did Susan go over to England because she has something to hide?'

Alison gaped blankly back at him. What was he getting at? Then, like a bolt from the blue, comprehension dawned and she gasped, 'How can you think a thing like that? If that were true she would have stayed here and got married.'

All the fire left Trevor and he slumped in his chair. He knew only too well how some men used young girls and then discarded them. 'Only if he was *willing* to marry her,' he said sadly. 'Only if he wanted her.' He reached a hand towards his daughter. 'Come here, love.' Hesitantly she approached him. Gripping her hand between his, he whispered, 'Ah, Alison, at least you are fulfilling my hopes. No one could ask for a better son-in-law than Graham.'

Alison looked at him in misery. She didn't want to fulfil his hopes. She wanted a life of her own. Tugging her hand from his, she turned on her heel and hurried from the room. Trevor gazed after her in amazement. What had he done now? Bloody women! He'd never understand them as long as he lived.

* * *

Graham listened in dismay as Alison ranted on about her sister's decision to remain in Darlington over the festive season. He had not had a chance to make his peace with Susan concerning his licentious behaviour. Each time he had been in the Cummings' home she had managed to elude him. Only once had he actually come face-to-face with her. A few days after the episode in the car he had arrived back from town with Alison, and Susan had been in the act of leaving the house. He had managed to block the doorway, forcing her to stop. Glad that Alison had continued on into the kitchen with her purchases, he had whispered urgently, 'Susan, can you ever forgive me?'

'Hush!' She looked furtively around to make sure they were alone. The shame that clouded his hazel eyes made her cringe. To think she had brought him to this. It was awful that she was the cause of his despair. 'Forget it! I have,' she hissed curtly.

Alison's voice hailed him from the kitchen. 'Will you kindly bring the rest of those groceries in here, Graham.'

'Coming, Alison.' Still he blocked Susan's path, whispering fiercely, 'We must talk. Let me at least give you a lift into town, please?'

Angrily she shouldered past him. 'No, thank you. I'll get the bus.'

He gazed after her in dismay. Remembering her hissed remark '*Forget it! I have*', he squirmed inside. Had she really been able to forget what happened? He had found it the most wonderful experience, and she had participated with enthusiasm. He had never known such heights of passion until that night with Susan. Or was that because it was sweet, forbidden fruit? Was that why it had seemed so wonderful? He must try and get her to speak to him; discover if it really was all over between her and Jim Brady. If so, he would make a point of gradually breaking free of Alison and would pursue Susan. He was convinced that it was her he now loved, and given the chance he would do all in his power to win her. Had she really felt nothing that night?

To his great distress, in the following weeks Susan had continued to avoid him and, as things stood between him and Alison, his hands were tied. It came as a shock to hear that she had run off to stay with an aunt in Darlington. Was Jim Brady pestering her? Was she still besotted with him? Had she run away to avoid bumping into him? Graham determined that when Susan came home at Christmas he would have it out with her. Now Alison was saying that her sister was not coming home.

'Mam is so disappointed, and as for Dad, he's incensed. I don't know how she can do this to us.'

'What reason does she give?'

'Huh! She says Aunt Edith needs her, because my cousin Jack is away living in London. Do you know what I think, Graham? I think she has met some man over there. That's what I think! Why else would she stay away at Christmas?'

Graham's heart sank. 'If that's the case, why not say so? It's nothing to be ashamed of,' he reasoned. 'Does she say when she will be home?'

Alison shook her head glumly. 'One good thing! Aunt Edith is moving house in the New Year, and Susan says they'll be getting a phone installed. At least we'll be able to talk to her when we feel like it. Not wait until she deigns to go to a phone box.' Then she would find out whether or not what her father had hinted at bore any truth. She found it hard to believe that her sister could be so foolish, but she and Jim Brady had been very close. Susan had been besotted with him! Like putty in his hands. There was no denying that.

She mustn't mention these doubts to Graham. It wasn't fair to condemn her sister without proof. She moved closer to him and raised her face in invitation. It was beginning to annoy her that lately she had to make the first move every time they were alone. She recalled how keen he had been at the beginning. Kissing her at every opportunity. Trying to excite her with his body. Positively annoying it had been. Now they may as well be brother and sister, for all the attention he paid her. But then, hadn't she told him that they must wait? To be truthful, she was surprised that he had taken her rejection so much to heart. Also, there had been no pressure to get engaged lately. Had he changed his mind? Surely not! Everyone envied her, and kept asking when the big day was. Pressing closer, her eyes questioned him.

Reluctantly Graham embraced her. He was finding it more and more difficult to put on a show. He couldn't believe that he no longer desired Alison. At the beginning he'd had difficulty keeping his hands off her; in fact, just the sight of her small, firm breasts in the tight sweaters she wore had been enough to excite him. Now all his thoughts were of Susan. Memories of her fiery passion constantly plagued him. How he longed to see her again. He didn't for one moment think that Alison would be exactly heartbroken if he decided to call it a day. She cared little for him. He realised that he shouldn't let it drift on like this, but how could he keep tabs on Susan otherwise? Still, he was being unfair to Alison. It was time he broke off their relationship. Huh! If you could call it that!

To his dismay, Alison pressed closer still. The pressure of her body against his was obviously a come-on and shock gripped him at the idea. Surely he was mistaken? Alison had never before acted as if she desired him.

'Graham,' she whispered tenderly. 'I've been very unfair to you, darling, holding you at arm's length all this time.'

'Perhaps it's all for the best, Alison,' he said gently. 'To tell you the truth, I'm beginning to think that we aren't really suited to each other.'

Shock coursed through her body, but she smothered it. 'What do you mean?' she asked in bewilderment. It was unthinkable that Graham should let her down. She would be a laughing stock.

'Well, it's obvious that you don't seriously care for me . . .'

'What on earth gives you that idea?'

'Huh! The way you treat me.'

She pressed urgently against him. 'Oh, but I do. Indeed I do care. That's what I'm trying to tell you. I know now that I was wrong to keep you at arm's length. I care deeply for you.' Her mouth was urgent beneath his, her hands frantically caressing his body. Everybody was expecting an engagement at Christmas, and she had no intention of disappointing them. Dismayed at her actions, Graham tried to arrest the unexpected flow of passion. Somehow, it didn't ring true. To his great relief, he heard the doorbell sound and someone cross the hall to answer it.

Talk about being saved by the bell. Thankfully he drew away from her. 'Somebody might come in and catch us.'

Her head tossed in the air and she glared at him. 'I hope you haven't been leading me up the garden path, Graham Robson. I think this weekend would be the right time to choose the ring, don't you?' she taunted daringly. What if he really wanted them to cool it? How could she face everyone? Her parents would put all the blame on her.

She watched anxiously as she put this ultimatum to him. Graham dithered. He knew he should take this opportunity to persuade her that they weren't meant for each other, and that it wouldn't work out between them, but he was too cowardly. He found himself nodding in agreement. After all, he reassured himself, engagements could always be broken.

It was Billy Devine who answered Donald's knock on the door on Saturday evening. Thrusting out his hand, he gripped Donald's and drew him into the house.

'It's good to see you, son.'

'You too, Billy. I've been a fool, so I have.'

There were tears in Edith's eyes when she hugged him close. 'You know, son, we really didn't have a clue what was going on.'

'I realise that now, Edith, and I'm sorry if I caused you a lot of grief. You had enough on your plate at the time.'

'You're here now, Donald, and that's all that matters. Sit down, son. Susan will be down in a minute.'

Hesitantly Donald said, 'Edith, I've been thinking . . . Perhaps the Pali isn't exactly the right place to take a girl like Susan. She strikes me as upper-class. Should I suggest somewhere else?'

Before Edith could answer him, Susan entered the room. He rose to his feet at once, his gaze admiring.

'You look wonderful,' he said softly.

A blush covered her face at the compliment. 'Thank you, kind sir,' she replied.

They left in a flurry of goodbyes, with Donald – at Edith's pleas to visit them more often – assuring her, with an admiring look at Susan, that he certainly would. After they'd gone Edith turned to Billy, her face puckered with worry.

'Billy, you don't think . . .?'

He put a finger gently to her lips. 'I'm not going to think anything, and neither are you, my love. They are adults after all, and they are both free.'

'She's pregnant, Billy! Do you think she's told Donald about the baby?'

'As I have already said, it's none of our business, Edith. At the moment all I can think of is the fact that for the first time in weeks we have the house to ourselves.' He was urging her towards the stairs; his mouth stifled her objections.

Pushing him away, she cried, 'All right! All right, there's no need to smother me.' And, with a girlish giggle, she preceded him up the stairs.

'I heard what you said to Edith about the Pali. Do you think I'm some kind of a snob, Donald? Is that how I come across to you?'

'No, not really, but the Pali is frequented by the soldiers from Catterick Garrison and can get a bit rough at times. It gets a bit of a name, but no one will bother you as long as I'm with you.'

'It sounds like the Plaza back home. That's where all the servicemen who come into Belfast go. I was only there the once with my best friend. I thought it was brilliant, all those men queuing up to dance with us. We had a great time.'

The Pali wasn't as spectacular as the Plaza. There was the same dim lighting, the big silver ball revolving in the centre of the ceiling, throwing fingers of light on to the white shirts and coloured dresses of the dancers; and the hushed, excited chatter against the throbbing music. There the likeness ended. The Plaza had bars where wine and beer was sold. Susan could see no bars here. After a visit to the cloakroom to leave her coat and change from her boots to her dance shoes, she returned to Donald.

Her eyes were glowing with excitement and he laughed as he led her on to the dance floor. 'I can see you're impressed.'

She nodded. Her happiness was apparent. 'It's a bit like the Plaza back home,' she repeated. 'I feel very daring being here.'

'Where did you usually dance?

'The Orpheus and Club Orchid.'

'With your husband?'

Her happiness faded. 'No.'

Annoyed at himself for putting a damper on her feelings, Donald cried, 'Look, forget I said that. I didn't mean to spoil things. Let's just enjoy ourselves.' With practised steps he swung her in and out of the dancers to the strains of a quickstep. They finished at the bottom of the hall as the music came to a halt and, seeing two empty chairs, he steered her over to them.

'That was wonderful, thank you. I can't believe my luck!' she sighed.

'What do you mean?'

'You being able to dance so well.'

He threw back his head and laughed aloud. 'Oh, so you thought I'd have two left feet, did you?'

'No! No, I'm only admitting I'm not much of a dancer and I need a good partner to lead me around the floor.'

'Aren't you being a bit modest? I bet you could dance with anybody in this hall,' he teased.

She just grinned happily at him and again he was struck by how lovely she looked. The first chance he got he would take Edith aside and find out what had gone wrong with her marriage.

The music started up again and he eyed her. 'Fancy a slow foxtrot?'

'My favourite dance,' she said as she slipped into his arms and was drawn close.

As he nodded to friends and acquaintances, Donald was aware of the envious glances cast in his direction and for the first time felt free of the hurt invoked by Margaret's betrayal. Susan was indeed a partner to be proud of. Her soft brown hair glowed with copper highlights and her eyes were dark, mysterious pools. Although they knew she was with a partner, even the soldiers were cheeky enough to give her the eye. Very much aware of their interest, he unconsciously drew her closer still. Her head rose in the air and she gazed reproachfully up at him. Immediately, he loosened his hold. He mustn't give her the wrong impression. After all, it wasn't as if he was actually making a play for her. He still loved Margaret McGivern. No one else could ever take her place.

'Sorry, I got carried away. You're very lovely, you know.'

She blushed and stiffened in his arms and he regretted his actions. 'Don't look like that. I promise to behave myself.'

She remained stiff and unyielding for the remainder of the dance. When it ended he led her to the long table where soft drinks were sold. 'What would you like to drink?'

'Orange, please.'

The chairs were all occupied, so they stood to one side and sipped their drinks. Seeing a worried frown pucker her smooth brow, he leant towards her. 'Look, Susan, please don't be worrying. I didn't mean any harm. We can go home any time you like.'

'It's all right, Donald,' she sighed. 'It's just that I can't afford any more complications in my life. As things stand, I've enough to worry about.'

'I realise that, Susan, and I don't want to add to your troubles. I promise to be on my best behaviour from now on. I'll be the best mate you ever had.'

She still looked unconvinced, but nodded her head. If only she could believe him. It would be lovely to have someone she could go out with, with no strings attached; someone to depend on. But in her heart she thought it would be better if she didn't see him again. This must be their first and last date. It was too dangerous! Something about him reminded her too much of

Jim Brady and she wanted him to hold her close; she longed to close her eyes and pretend she was with Jim. She was lost for companionship, but Donald, like herself, was on the rebound. It could cause all kinds of problems.

In spite of the uneasy start, the night was a great success. They danced every dance and Susan felt happier than she had been for a long time. They walked home in the crisp, frosty air and she did not demur when he took her hand and tucked it beneath his elbow.

'I really enjoyed myself tonight, Susan.'

His voice was like a caress and she sighed. Was he going to start all that again? Her hand wriggled to get free, but he tightened his grip on it. 'I promise I won't overstep the mark again. I realise you're not free, but then in my heart, neither am I. I still love Margaret and I'll never change. Nevertheless I value your friendship. Please say you will come out with me again?'

'It wouldn't be fair, Donald. You know nothing about me. There might be talk.'

'Why would there be any talk? We're doing nothing wrong. I honestly don't see why we can't be friends,' he cried in bewilderment. 'It won't cost you anything. At least say you will come to the dance with me on Boxing Night. Please?'

It was on the tip of her tongue to tell him she was pregnant, but then he might not want to be her friend. He would know soon enough. 'All right. But, Donald, please don't expect anything from me. I admit that I don't know many people over here and I'm very lonely at times. I do need a friend, but I'm in love with someone else, and friendship is all there can ever be between us.'

His mind went blank, then rushed into overdrive. She was in love with another man? So that must be why her marriage was on the rocks. He wouldn't have believed it of her. Where was this other man now? Had the break-up of her marriage been in vain? Surprised and saddened at her situation, he was silent until they reached her door.

Susan made no effort to break the silence; just gently removed her hand from his now-loose clasp. Nor did she invite him in when they arrived home. 'If you still want me to come to the Pali with you on Boxing Night, just let me know. I'll understand if you don't. Good night, Donald.'

She unlocked the door and was through it before he could gather his wits about him. He stood dumbfounded, staring at the door. What was he thinking of? He had acted like an idiot. Of course he still wanted her to go to the dance with him on Boxing Night. He would call in during the week and make sure she understood that. More at ease in his mind now, he headed home. After all it was no concern of his if she loved in vain. Wasn't he in the same boat? It was a friend he wanted – a dance partner – and he couldn't think of anyone he would rather have.

To Susan's dismay, her aunt and uncle were still downstairs and sitting by the fire sipping cups of tea. 'I thought you'd bring Donald in for a cuppa. It would have given us a chance to talk,' Edith said.

'I thought you would be in bed and I didn't want to disturb you,' she lied convincingly.

'Never be afraid to bring him in, love. Even if we have retired, you won't annoy us. Did you enjoy the Pali?'

'It was great, Aunt Edith. I don't know if you were ever in the Plaza back home? It reminded me of there. Donald's an excellent dancer. I really enjoyed myself.'

'Pour yourself a cup of tea and sit down, love. You look frozen.'

With a resigned look, Susan did as she was bid and joined them by the fireside.

'We got some good news tonight.' Edith sounded nervous and Susan moved restlessly on her chair. 'You know Mrs Duggen down the street?'

'Yes. The woman who lives in the corner house?'

'That's right. Well she came for me earlier on. Our Jack had phoned her and asked her to fetch me. And . . . what do you think? He's coming home for Christmas after all.'

Slowly Susan set her cup shakily on the table, grateful that the tea didn't slop over the edge. She forced a smile to her face. 'Oh, I am pleased for you. You must be delighted.'

'We are. We're over the moon. But now, love, I don't want you to be worrying. We'll sort out somewhere for you to stay. They will only be here a few days. They said they'd come on Friday, stay over Christmas Eve, Christmas Day and Boxing Day, and leave on Tuesday. I'm so happy I could cry.' Without more ado she proceeded to do so.

Edith's tears blinded her to Susan's reaction, but Billy could see that, although his niece tried to show pleasure, it didn't ring true. He realised that she was worried and said, haltingly, 'Susan, we will make room for a bed in the spare room for you, if that's all right? It will only be for a couple of nights, after all.'

'That would be great, Uncle Billy, but won't I be in the way?'

'Don't be silly. You're family. Everything will be fine, so it will.'

Tears ran down Susan's cheeks as she lay in bed that night staring at the ceiling. She was glad she had managed to put on a good show in front of her aunt and uncle. She was also glad she had sent all her presents off to Ireland during the week. Although Jack wasn't coming until next Friday, her aunt would want to get this room ready for him and Margaret, and she would have to find somewhere to live right away. She didn't agree with her uncle. The spare room was out of the question. Oh, she didn't mind being in cramped quarters for a while, but it wouldn't work out. She would feel that she was intruding on their privacy. Jack would want to patch things up with his parents and he couldn't talk freely if she was there. Her aunt had agreed with her that the junk room, as she called it, was unsuitable, saying that she would see that Susan found somewhere comfortable to stay. God knows where she would end up while her cousin and Margaret were here. After the way she had treated Donald's overture to friendship, she could hardly now ask him to rent the house next door to her.

Her thoughts turned to Vera Crabtree, as she tried to remember if any of her family were still living at home. She must ask Aunt Edith. Poor Donald. His face appeared before her mind. He would be devastated, seeing the woman he loved pregnant by another man. And . . . what if her cousin decided to stay in Darlington? What would happen to her then? God alone knew the answer to that.

Chapter Four

While Susan was tripping the light fantastic around the dance floor in Donald Murphy's arms at the Pali, Alison was doing likewise at the Orpheus.

The dance was almost over when, to her surprise, she saw Jim Brady approaching their table. 'Look who's here, Graham,' she muttered.

Graham rose to his feet at once, hand extended in welcome. 'Why hello, Jim. It's good to see you.'

'You too, Graham. I've just arrived. Hello, Alison. I trust you are well?' His eyes roamed over the table noting that there were only two glasses. 'Is Susan not here tonight?'

'No!' Alison's voice was abrupt. She volunteered no further information.

Embarrassed, Graham said, 'We haven't seen you in a while, Jim. Where have you been hiding yourself?'

'I've been busy, Graham.' He smiled slightly. He wasn't going to admit that he'd been broke lately. Couldn't afford to go out. That was nobody's business but his own. Besides, these people wouldn't know the meaning of the word skint.

The music started up and he said, 'Graham, is it all right if I dance with Alison?'

'Be my guest.'

'Huh! Have I no say in the matter?' Alison cried, greatly affronted.

Both men grinned at her chagrin. 'Please may I have this dance, Alison?' Jim extended a hand and smiled disarmingly, sure of her reply.

God, but I'd love to turn him down, she thought angrily; wipe that smirk off his face. But she wanted to question him about her sister, so needs must. With a great show of petulance, she allowed him to lead her on to the dance floor.

Waiting until they were out of earshot of Graham, she looked up at him and demanded, 'What did you do to my sister that sent her scurrying over to England in such a hurry, eh?'

'Susan's in England?'

She could see that he was flabbergasted, but taunted, 'As if you didn't know!'

'On my honour, I didn't. I came here tonight looking for her. I've missed her terribly. I couldn't stay away any longer.'

'Well, I'm afraid you've left it too late. You've no chance of seeing her. She took off weeks ago and is now staying with Aunt Edith in Darlington. She's got herself a job and all. What do you think of that?'

Jim was dumbfounded; didn't know what to think. Perhaps it was as well. Now he wouldn't be able to ask her forgiveness and beg her to be friends again. After all, he could still not offer her marriage.

'Tell me something, Jim. Has she run away to hide something from us?'

She watched him closely. His brow furrowed and he

looked bewildered. 'I don't understand. Hide what?'

'Come off it. You know damned well what I'm getting at. Is she pregnant? Is that why you dropped her?'

His jaw dropped and his face stretched with horror. Then, grabbing her by the upper arm, he hustled her off the dance floor and into a corner. 'Explain yourself, miss,' he said tersely.

Flustered, she cried, 'My dad is convinced she ran away because she's . . .' The words refused to come. 'In the club.' She shrugged. 'You know what I mean?'

'Well, let me tell you something, Alison Cummings. If Susan is pregnant, it's not my doing.'

'Huh! You would say that anyway, wouldn't you?'

The urge to strike her accusing face was so strong that Jim turned on his heel and walked away. Her dad, with his filthy mind, was absolutely wrong. There was no way Susan could possibly be expecting a baby. He hadn't laid a finger on her and, as far as he knew, there had been no one else in the picture at the time. He lifted a hand briefly in farewell in Graham's direction and headed for the door. Tomorrow night he would go to the Club Orchid and find out what Ruth Vernon had to say. Susan and she had been as thick as thieves. If anyone knew anything about Susan, it would be Ruth. He would clear Susan's name once and for all.

Ruth Vernon was surprised when Jim, for the first time ever, asked her to dance with him the following night in the Club Orchid. 'This is a surprise,' she exclaimed. 'Where've you been?'

'Oh, here and there. Look, I've a favour to ask you. Could we sit this one out and talk?'

'I'm with Dougie Smith. If we sit out together, he won't like it. He'll wonder what I'm up to.'

Jim's disappointment was so acute that she asked, 'Is this about Susan?' He nodded eagerly and she pondered for a moment. 'Go down to the bar and get yourself a drink and buy me a Coca-Cola. I'll explain to Dougie what's happening and I'll meet you over there,' she nodded towards the door, 'in ten minutes. Okay?'

'Thanks, Ruth. I won't forget this.'

Ten minutes later they sat outside the ballroom, on the stairs that led to the ladies' cloakroom. Ruth touched her glass to his. 'Cheers.' She added warningly, 'If I'm very long, Dougie says he'll come looking for me.'

'This won't take long. Tell me, did you know that Susan was living over in England?'

Ruth nodded, but explained, 'Mind you, she went off without saying a word to me, or anyone else for that matter. Just took off out of the blue. I only found out when I phoned her house and Alison told me.'

'But why go to England? She must have hinted at something.'

Ruth's shoulders lifted in a shrug. 'I honestly don't know. I do know that she was terribly cut up about you, but I thought she was coming to terms with it.' She paused and reflected. 'To be truthful, I got an awful shock when I heard the news. Alison wouldn't even give me her address, but eventually I received a letter from Susan and she apologised for not telling me she was leaving.'

'And she didn't say why she went away?'

'No, not a word.' Ruth gave him a glare from her big,

brown eyes. 'But I think that's obvious, don't you? She was running away from you, so she was.'

Relieved to hear this, Jim said tentatively. 'Her father thinks she was hiding her pregnancy.'

'Mr Cummings thinks that?' Ruth gasped, her head swinging from side to side in denial. 'He's got it all wrong. She would have confided in me. She'd have needed someone to talk to.'

'Alison thinks that if her sister is pregnant, I'm the one to blame.'

'Well, that's understandable! You're the only one Susan was seeing. She was nuts about you.'

'She didn't see anyone else after we split up?'

'No, she was too heartbroken.'

'Then she's not pregnant. I never laid a finger on her. And that's God's honest truth.'

'I'm glad to hear that, Jim. It would have caused a lot of problems.'

'Will she be home at Christmas then?'

A sad shake of the head. 'I'm afraid not. I received a present from her yesterday morning and a letter. She says she won't be home.'

'Did she say why?'

'Some cock-and-bull story about not wanting to leave her aunt.'

'Ruth, can I please have her phone number?'

'Unfortunately her aunt isn't on the phone.'

'Her address, then?'

'Jim, I would have to ask her permission first. Give me your address and, if she says all right, I'll post it on to you. That's the best I can do. After all, she must have left to get away from you. What other reason would she have? And who knows, maybe she's met someone else.'

Jim searched his pockets and found an old receipt. Quickly he jotted down his address on the back of it. Ruth's remark that Susan might have met someone else dismayed him. 'Let me know as soon as you can, won't you, Ruth?'

'Sure. I'd better go now, Jim. See you around.'

Graham watched dumbfounded as Jim left Alison standing in a corner and, with a wave of farewell in his direction, left the room. He hurried to meet her. 'What was all that about?'

'Nothing.'

'Come off it, Alison. It's obvious something's wrong. Surely he didn't chance his arm?'

'Don't be silly!' She was silently debating whether or not she should tell Graham about her father's accusation against Susan. If Jim was telling the truth, and somehow she believed he was, it would be foolish to besmirch her sister's good name by repeating her father's insinuations. She decided against telling him.

'He wanted Aunt Edith's address and, when I refused to give it to him, he stormed off,' she lied, then asked tentatively, 'Did I do the right thing?'

Quickly Graham agreed with her. 'You sure did! She's better off without him. Still, you must try and persuade her to come home for Christmas. It's unthinkable that she should stay over there.'

'She phones me mam every Wednesday night, so I'll stay in this week and have a word with her. But, mind you, I don't think it will do any good.'

'It's worth a try. She should be with her family at this time of year.'

'You're right! I'll do my best to persuade her.'

Donald strode along North Road trying to get his mind around the enigmatic puzzle of Susan Cummings. What age would she be? Twenty? Twenty-one? Certainly no more than twenty-two. And she had a failed marriage behind her. She had confessed to being in love with another man. Where was this other man? Had she left her husband, only to find out this man didn't love her in return? Or had he a wife he refused to leave? Was that why she had come over to Darlington? He really must make an effort to get Edith on her own and find out just what the situation was. Suddenly he realised he had no need to do that. He had no designs on Susan. They would just be good mates, and mates took each other on trust. He would make sure he was around when she needed him. If she wanted to confide in him about her past, she would tell him in her own good time. That would be a bonus; a sign of her trust. Meanwhile he must not pry into her private affairs. After all, he was in the same boat as Susan with a failed romance behind him. They needed each other, and he had certainly been no comfort to her tonight. What must she be thinking of his silent condemnation? That's what it had amounted to, condemnation. He was thoroughly ashamed of his attitude. At the first opportunity he would seek her out and put matters right.

The chance of earning some extra money for Christmas had encouraged Donald to work every night. It was

Friday, the day before Christmas Eve, when they had stopped for the holiday break, before he was in a position to call and ask Susan if she would still accompany him to the dance on Boxing Night. Who knows, perhaps if he played his cards right, she might even agree to go out to the pub with him tonight for a drink?

He sang lustily as he showered, causing his mother to eye him suspiciously when at last he put in an appearance. She had sorrowfully watched him nurse a broken heart and was fearful of him making another mistake on the rebound.

'What has you so happy?'

'Mam, I'm going to ask a very beautiful girl to come out with me for a drink and I'll be the happiest man in the world if she says yes.'

A worried frown gathered on Mary Murphy's brow. 'Now you be careful, son,' she warned. 'You know what happened the last time.'

'That's all in the past, Mam. This girl and I are just good friends. No strings attached. So you have nothing to worry about.'

'Do I know her?'

'No, but you'll have heard of her. She's Edith Devine's niece.'

'Jack's cousin?'

He nodded. 'You'll like her, Mam. There's no nonsense about her.'

'Will you never learn? Has that family not caused you enough heartache?'

'Mam, I've explained. We're just good friends.' He gave her a hug and an affectionate kiss on the cheek.

'Stop worrying about me and don't wait up, I might be late.'

'Donald, no matter what you might think, there's no such thing as platonic friendship between a man and a woman. Do you hear me? You take care!'

'I will, Mam, I will.'

His assurances rang in Mary's ears long after he had gone. She sent a prayer heavenwards. 'Please, dear God, don't let him be hurt again.'

It was almost nine o'clock when Donald eventually arrived at Edith's house. He stepped into the hall and raised his hand to knock on the kitchen door, but hesitated as animated voices reached his ears. They seemed to have company. One well-remembered voice stood out from the rest, causing a fist to close around his heart. 'That was a lovely meal, Mrs Devine. It's great to be home. Thank you for having us.'

'You're welcome, Margaret. I only wish you were home for good.'

Jack's voice came next, sounding worried. 'Mam, do you think Susan will be all right in that wee spare room?'

'Your dad got a mate to store all the rubbish he won't part with, and that single bed up there is very comfortable, so it is. I wanted her to go into a guest house, but she said she was all right. She's been sleeping there since Monday.'

Careful not to make any noise, Donald backed out on to the pavement and hurried down the street. He felt gutted. The old feelings of betrayal had returned to torment him. Why did they have to come back now, just when he was getting over her? But then, there was no need for him to see Margaret. He would make himself scarce until they left.

At the corner of the street he almost bumped into Susan. Seeing his distress, she gripped his arm in concern. 'You saw them, then?'

'No. I heard their voices.' A bitter laugh accompanied these words. 'That was enough to send me scampering away.'

'I'm sorry, Donald. I wish I could have prepared you, but I didn't know where you lived and I didn't want to ask Aunt Edith. It would have taken the joy out of their coming, if you know what I mean? She's sure to be worrying about the effect it will have on you. I hoped you'd come and see me before they arrived.'

'I've been working every night. It's you I was coming to see, but when I heard their voices I just couldn't go in.'

'They arrived this afternoon. I offered to stay behind and get the stall ready for tomorrow's last-minute rush. I wanted to give them some time alone. Get the awkwardness out of the way. I dread it, so I do. I'm going to be in the way, I know I am, but I couldn't find anywhere to rent and I've nowhere else to go.'

He nodded. 'I heard them talking about you. They were wondering if you would be comfortable in the spare room. I wish I could be of some help.'

She took the bull by the horns and cried, 'You can!'

'Can I?' he said in bewilderment. 'How?'

'You can rent me the house next door.'

He gazed at her blankly for some moments. Then the penny dropped. 'Of course you can stay there! How come I never thought of that?'

Relief made her voice shake. 'Oh, Donald, you don't know what this means to me.' She looked at him anxiously. 'Will you come back with me now? You could help me move my stuff in.'

He backed off a little. 'I don't think that would be a good idea, Susan. Look, here are the keys. I'm sure Billy and Jack will give you a hand with your stuff.'

She moved close and stared earnestly into his eyes. 'Does this mean I won't see you while they're here? I'm depending on your company, Donald.'

'Of course you'll see me. We can meet away from the house.'

'Donald, you will have to face them sooner or later. Please come back with me now and get it over with. I haven't much stuff. It'll only take a few minutes to move me into your house, and afterwards we can go out for a drink if you like? Mm, how about it?'

'I'm sorry, Susan, but I just can't face them.' With these words Donald turned abruptly on his heel and was off.

Susan pocketed the keys with a sigh. She could understand his reluctance to face the enemy, but she wished he'd been a bit stronger. It would be better in the long run.

She had almost reached the house when he again fell into step beside her. 'You're right, of course, Susan,' he said with a rueful smile. 'I may as well face the music and get it over with. You will help me all you can, won't you?'

A delighted smile brightened her face. 'Of course I will, Donald. But remember, I've yet to meet Margaret.' She stepped into the hall. 'Are you ready?' she whispered. He nodded and she pushed open the door.

Jack rose to his feet at once and came towards her, a welcoming smile on his face. The smile faltered when Donald followed her into the room.

It was Billy who broke the awkward silence. 'Come in, Donald, and pull up a chair. Would you like a beer?'

Relieved that there was no sign of Margaret, Donald replied, 'No thanks, Billy. Hello there, Jack. How's things with you?'

'Hello, Donald.'

Before tension could set in Susan quickly intervened. 'Donald has suggested I move into his house next door while Jack is here. He's come to help me move my stuff in.'

'That's a wonderful idea – you'll be more comfortable there than in the spare room. In the circumstances, it's very kind of you to offer, Donald.'

In the kitchen Edith and Margaret stood silently throughout this discourse. At last Edith whispered, 'Do you want to face him now or later?'

'It's best to get it over with.' Slowly Margaret dried her hands and headed for the door.

Donald felt his heart contract at the sight of her. Pregnancy obviously agreed with her. Light-coloured hair framed her head like a golden halo, her white skin gleamed like thick buttermilk and her sensual lips needed no make-up to enhance them. She positively bloomed. How come he hadn't noticed the way the wind was blowing and had allowed Jack to walk off with her?

'Hello, Donald, how are you?'

'I'm very well, Margaret.' He was glad that his voice sounded strong and confident. 'Susan here is going to stay next door for a few days. I've come to help her move in her bits and pieces.'

Jack hastened to introduce the two girls. 'Margaret, you've never met my cousin. Susan, this is my wife.'

'I'm very pleased to meet you,' Susan said formally. She could understand both men lusting after this girl. She had that spark that would always turn men's heads. 'I've heard all about you.'

'I'll bet you have.'

Taken unawares by the bitter note in the other girl's voice, Susan turned abruptly to Donald. 'Is there any bedding next door?'

'Plenty of blankets, but you'll need some sheets and pillowcases.'

Glad to escape the tension that was building up, Edith headed for the stairs. 'That's no problem. I'll fetch some.'

Remembering her promise to help Donald over this awkward situation, Susan said, 'Donald, if you come up I'll show you what I want moved.' And she followed her aunt upstairs.

Tentatively Jack offered, 'Can I be of any assistance?'

'No, no, you're all right. We'll manage.'

When Donald had followed the women, Jack went to his wife and took her in his arms. 'Don't you distress yourself,' he warned. 'Think of the baby.'

Fighting back tears, Margaret released herself from his embrace. 'I'll finish the washing up.'

'I'll help you.'

Left alone, Billy sank down on to the settee and buried his head in his hands. He was delighted to have his son home, but felt uncomfortable in the presence of Margaret. No matter how often he told himself it took two, he could find no fault in Jack. He was convinced that his son would not have seduced her behind his friend's back if he hadn't had plenty of encouragement from her. He placed all the blame firmly at Margaret's door. Donald was a good man, and she shouldn't have two-timed him. She should have been honest with both men. However, for Jack's sake he would do all in his power to make her welcome.

With a deep sigh, he rose to his feet and climbed the stairs to give Donald a helping hand.

Upstairs, Edith looked around the small room she had done her best to make comfortable. 'I got the impression that you were all right here, Susan,' she said accusingly. 'You should have said, and I would have found somewhere else for you to stay.'

'Oh, Aunt Edith, please don't be annoyed,' Susan cried in alarm. 'It is comfortable. Honestly! But can't you see? I'd be in the way. You need time alone with your daughter-in-law to get to know her. This way, we won't be falling over each other. You will have more time with your own family and won't be worrying about me.'

Edith remained tight-lipped and, going over to her, Susan whispered, 'Please understand. I wouldn't offend you for the world.'

Her aunt's expression relaxed. 'Promise me you'll come in for all your meals.'

'All except breakfast. I can manage to make that myself,' Susan teased. 'I will also be able to have a lie-in, if I feel like it.'

Edith frowned in Donald's direction. 'I know it's none of my business, but will he be staying there with you?'

'You can rest assured, I won't, Edith. I'll not sully your niece's good name.'

'Well then, let's move her stuff in next door.'

An hour later they smiled at each other across the pub table. 'That wasn't too bad, now was it, Donald?'

'No. As you said, it's better to get it over with. But . . . I'll tell you something. I'm glad she wasn't there when we went in to say farewell. I was all tied up in knots.' Susan remained silent and he eyed her covertly. 'What did you think of her?'

'She's very pretty.'

'Did you like her?'

'Ah, come off it, Donald! How can I tell? I only exchanged a couple of words with her.'

'I fell for her the first time I saw her.'

'Well, I'm not you. Whether or not she and I become friends remains to be seen.'

Last orders were called, and Donald appraised her. 'Do you fancy another one?'

'No, thank you. I've an early start in the morning.'

'Fine. I want to go back with you and make sure that fire I lit is okay.'

'There's no need for you to come back, Donald. I'm sure the fire will be fine.'

'I'm coming back.' His tone brooked no argument and she silently followed him from the pub.

The house was much warmer than it had been earlier on. 'It's lovely and cosy. Thank you, Donald.' Edith had insisted that Susan bring tea, sugar and milk in with her and now she said, 'I'll make a cup of tea and then we'll discuss the rent.'

'Get away with you! I don't want any money from you.'

'All the same, I'll feel better if I pay my way.'

'How about you making me a meal on Boxing Night before we go to the dance?'

'So you still want me to go with you?'

'Of course I do, Susan. I know how it must have looked to you last week. As if I was sitting in judgement. I didn't mean to. I promise to mind my own business in future. Can you forgive me? I need a friend more than ever now, especially if they decide to remain in Darlington.'

'Do you think there's any chance of that happening?' Susan asked in dismay.

'To be truthful, I can't see Jack staying in London. It's not his scene. I think they'll be back in the not-too-distant future. Margaret will want the baby born here.'

Handing him a cup of tea, Susan sat down on an armchair at the side of the fire. Donald took the only other chair in the room, facing her, and waved a hand vaguely around. 'As you can see, there's not much furniture. When my aunt died I got rid of most of her old stuff. I knew Margaret wouldn't want an old woman's bits and pieces. Mind you, I had plans. I would have worked my fingers to the bone to make it nice for her.'

'It could be made very comfortable indeed,' Susan agreed.

To her dismay, his head sank on to his chest and she knew he was fighting back tears. 'How am I going to get through this, Susan? I thought I was getting over her. Now look at me! A right bundle of nerves.'

Going to him, she put an arm across his shoulders

in sympathy. 'You'll get over her. Just wait and see. I'll help you all I can.'

Turning, he put his arms around her waist and sank his head on to her breast. 'I'm glad you're here, Susan.'

Gently she edged away from him. It would be so easy to become involved. She was also at a low ebb at the moment, but it wasn't a lover she needed – it was a friend. 'We'll help each other, Donald. Now it's time you were leaving, or Aunt Edith will be getting worried. She's probably taken up sentry duty behind the blinds,' she laughed.

Reluctantly he rose to his feet and reached for his coat. At the door she gave in to the temptation to give him a hug of comfort. Too late, she saw Jack unloading the car he had arrived in. He nodded in their direction and his eyes were full of speculation. Ah well, it would give him and Margaret something to talk about, she lamented.

At work the following morning Edith gave Susan a handful of mail. She smiled as she opened it. There were last-minute cards from her family and friends who had expected her home at Christmas. Ruth's contained a short letter explaining about her meeting with Jim Brady at the Club Orchid. The market doors were opening to the public and Susan put all her mail carefully under the counter to be enjoyed later, but Ruth's note played on her mind as she attended to her customers.

What could Jim possibly want to write to her about? It would be a waste of time corresponding with him. They could never meet again. He wouldn't want her now, in any case, if the truth ever came out.

Jack and Margaret stopped by the stall while doing some last-minute shopping and were greeted excitedly by Vera. 'Oh, it's lovely to see you again, Jack. Mind you, you were a naughty boy.' Releasing him from her bear hug, she turned to Margaret. 'You too, young lady. You know you broke poor Donald Murphy's heart when you ran away with this scallywag.'

Jack gave Susan a sly look. 'I wouldn't worry too much about Donald if I were you, Vera. He's already found consolation.' He drew Margaret towards him. 'You haven't been introduced to my wife, have you?'

'No, I haven't had that pleasure. And a bonny girl she is. I wish you all the very best, love.'

'Thank you. You're very kind.'

'Where's Mam?'

'She's just nipped out to get something for her lunch,' Vera informed him. 'And your dad has run out of tomatoes, so he's away to get some more. Here's your mother now.'

'Jack, Margaret! What are you doing here?'

'Just dropped in to say hello to Vera. We've been doing some shopping. Now we're off for something to eat.'

'I say. Excuse me,' Vera interrupted. 'Would you take Susan with you, please? She must be starving. She's been working like a trooper all morning.'

'Oh no, I couldn't,' protested Susan. 'We're too busy.'

'This is our slack time. I'm ordering you to take a break,' Vera insisted.

Susan threw an imploring look at her aunt, but no help was forthcoming from that quarter. Reluctantly she slipped her arms into her coat, which Vera held ready for her. 'I hope you don't mind, Jack? I don't want to impose.'

'Not in the slightest. We'll be delighted to have you join us, won't we, Margaret?' But his wife had already moved away from the stall and her reply was muffled.

They had lunch in a small café in the Market Square. Conversation consisted mostly of Margaret trying to find out all about Susan's background and her relationship with Donald. Susan answered as best she could without giving away any secrets, but her patience was sorely tried and it took all her willpower not to tell this inquisitive girl to mind her own business.

When Jack left them for a short time, she made a point of turning the tables on Margaret. Pretending sympathy, she quizzed the girl on her own relationship with Donald.

'It must have been very upsetting for you to have had to choose between Jack and Donald?'

'Yes. It was. I was in an awful pickle at the time. Donald was so upset. I suppose you heard all about the big fight between them?'

'I did. But you can't blame him for being angry. After all, weren't you engaged to him? It must have come as an awful shock to discover that you were two-timing him.'

'It wasn't like that! It wasn't like that, at all. He shouldn't have taken me so much for granted. Had he paid more attention, we'd be getting married on Boxing Day.'

Susan was taken aback. 'I didn't realise a date had been set.'

'Huh! Donald will only tell you what he wants you to know. Are you in love with him?'

'I beg your pardon?'

'I suppose you are. He's hard to resist when he turns on the charm.'

Susan leant across the table. 'It sounds to me as if you're still in love with him?'

A dark flush covered Margaret's face. 'What gives you that idea?'

Susan remained silent, and just sat scrutinising the girl's embarrassed face. Jack, coming back to the table, put an end to the conversation, but Susan was convinced that this girl did indeed still carry a torch for Donald. So how come she had married Jack?

Quickly Susan finished her meal and rose to her feet. 'That was lovely. I enjoyed it. Thank you both for treating me, but you do realise I must hurry back, don't you?'

Her cousin waved her off. 'Away you go, Susan. We know you're busy. See you at dinner tonight.'

Smiling brightly, Susan hurried off. She had plenty to think about. If Donald found out that Margaret was still in love with him, it could cause all sorts of problems. What would he do? Would he try to win her back, or would he see her for the fickle person she was?

Jack and Margaret decided to go to midnight Mass with his parents on Christmas Eve and, wishing them a happy Christmas and promising to come in early the next morning, Susan retired to the house next door. Making herself a cup of tea, she carried it upstairs and, once snug in bed, settled down to read her mail.

In her letter Ruth didn't give any reason why Jim Brady suddenly wanted to contact her. But then, she probably didn't know his reason. Jim was the type of person to confide only in close friends. Should she write to him? No. There would be no point. It would just prolong the agony. They certainly had no future together. To take her mind off Jim, she recalled the conversation she'd had with Margaret. Was Jack aware of the risk he was taking in coming home? It was obvious that he loved his wife very much.

A loud knock on the door brought her slowly from her bed. Pulling the curtains slightly away from the window, she peered down into the darkness. It was Donald. What did he want at this time of night?

When she opened the door she could see that he was the worse for drink.

'Can I come in for a while, Susan?'

'It's very late, Donald. We don't want to start any gossip, do we?' she warned.

'I'll not stay long. I was on my way to midnight Mass when I realised that I was in no fit state to go.'

'Ten minutes! No longer, mind. Sit down and I'll make you a strong cup of coffee. It will help sober you up.'

He removed his coat and shivered slightly. 'It's cold in here. Did you not light the fire?'

'There was no need. I've been next door all evening. I was nice and warm in bed when you came.'

'I'm sorry, Susan. I shouldn't have come here, but I needed someone to talk to.'

'What about? As if I didn't know!' Susan said drily as she spooned instant coffee into the cup.

'I can't help myself. I can't stop thinking about her.'

The kettle boiled and she handed him the steaming mug of coffee. Sitting on the armchair, she pulled her legs up underneath her and wrapped her candlewick dressing gown tightly around her to capture some warmth. 'Remember, she's married now, Donald. And the Catholic Church forbids divorce, so don't start something you can't finish.'

'I know all that. And if she wouldn't have me before, why should she want me now, eh?' He looked blankly at her empty hands. 'Are you not having one?'

'I've just finished a cup upstairs. I don't really know much about what happened between you and Margaret. Why did she turn to Jack in the first place?'

He shook his head in despair. 'I honestly don't know! I thought we were so well suited. And . . . I respected her, mind! Never made a wrong move. Never once touched her up, if you know what I mean.'

Thinking of how she had longed for Jim Brady to touch her, Susan said, 'Perhaps she wanted you to touch her, show how much you cared?'

He looked scandalised. 'There was no need for that! She knew I loved her.'

Susan shrugged. 'Well then, why did she turn to Jack?'

'I wish I knew.' Putting his cup on the hearth, he moved over and knelt in front of her chair. Placing his hands on her thighs, he looked beseechingly at her. 'I want to ask you a favour, Susan.'

She could feel the heat of his hands through the towelling material and was filled with a longing for close bodily contact. Not sex, just contact with a strong male body. Pushing his hands away, she cried, 'Well? What do you want to ask me?'

He looked at the hands she had pushed away and was at a loss as to what to do with them. Steepling them as if in prayer, he said, 'While Margaret is here could we pretend we have something going between us?'

His nearness was unsettling her and, unfurling her legs, she sprang from the chair and moved restlessly about the room. 'That's impossible. For a start, no one would believe it.'

He moved to stand in front of her, his head bent so he could look into her eyes. 'I wouldn't take advantage. Just subtly give out the idea that we're seeing each other. Please? It won't cost you anything.'

'I can't do it. It wouldn't work.'

He put his hands on her shoulders. 'Why not? Who knows, we might even learn to care for each other.'

She gazed up at him, little knowing how vulnerable and appealing she looked. His mouth hovered over hers, but before he could claim her lips, she found the courage to push him away. 'It's time you were going. They'll be coming home from Mass soon and I don't want Aunt Edith to see you leave and get any wrong ideas.' She lifted his coat from where he had hung it on the floor and, thrusting it at him, pushed him none too gently towards the door. 'Remember, Aunt Edith has invited you to join us tomorrow night. Are you up to it, or shall I make excuses for you?'

He shrugged into his coat. 'I'll be there. Thanks for the coffee.'

'Happy Christmas. See you tomorrow.'

She closed the door on him and leant against it, trembling like a leaf in a storm. It had been too close for comfort. He must never realise just how close, otherwise he'd never be away from her doorstep. Tense and irritable now, she climbed the stairs, but her Christmas mail failed to hold her attention. She was remembering the great longing and need he had aroused in her. Was she forever to be unfulfilled?

There were a lot of people about so late at night. At first Donald was bewildered, then he remembered midnight Mass. These people must be returning from there. He recognised Jack's voice approaching and drew into the shadows, away from the street lights, not wanting to speak to him. Billy, Edith and Jack all passed by, but there was no sign of Margaret. Perhaps she had felt unwell and come home earlier.

He was about to turn the corner of the street when her laughter rang out. She was talking to two girls whom he recognised as old school mates. He was about to pass on when, bidding them all good night, she caught at his sleeve, bringing him to a halt.

'Hello, Donald. Walk me back up to the house, please. I want a word with you. Good night, girls, see you around.'

In spite of the speculative glance from the girls – well, they would have heard about her treatment of him – and surprised that she wanted to speak to him, Donald suited his step to hers and they dandered back up the street.

'I hope you didn't mind me stopping you like that, but I couldn't get away from them.'

So she didn't really want to talk to him; he was the lesser of two evils. Disappointment stabbed like a knife in his chest. She proved him wrong by stopping well before they reached Edith's door and drawing into the shadows. He followed her, trying to hide his bewilderment.

'Donald, I'm glad of this opportunity to apologise for all the hurt I've caused you.'

'Don't worry about it, Margaret. It's all in the past. The best man won.'

'Did he, Donald? I'm not so sure about that.'

Her voice was soft and caressing and he wasn't sure he'd heard her correctly. While he was still in a daze she moved close and raised her face to his. 'Happy Christmas, Donald.'

Her lips were inviting and, without thought, he drew her closer still and claimed them. The kiss went on and on as they swayed together and their passion flared. Before it could get out of control, she came up, panting for breath. 'Not here. Not now. Jack will come looking for me. Do you still think the best man won, eh, Donald? See you tomorrow night.' With a light laugh she left him standing there, gasping, his mind racing. What on earth was she playing at? Perhaps he would find out tomorrow night. His thoughts were in turmoil, but his step and heart were a good deal lighter as he headed home.

Christmas dinner was a leisurely affair stretching over a couple of hours. The starter, chilled melon and prawns, made the day before and kept refrigerated, was doused in crème de menthe and was mouth-watering. Billy was not a lover of turkey, so a large goose had been chosen to grace the table. Sizzling and crackling, it was perfectly complemented by dishes of fresh vegetables and creamed, roasted and delicious boiled small potatoes. Last but not least, a rich plum pudding tempted them to find room for it.

Praise for Edith was profound and she could barely conceal her pleasure. When everybody had eaten to bursting point, the table was cleared and they all lolled on the sofa and chairs, striving to keep their eyes open. Giving his head a good shake to dispel his sleepiness, Billy rose to his feet and announced, 'You girls are welcome to retire for an hour or two. Remember, we are entertaining tonight. I'll wash the dishes and clear up the kitchen.'

'I'll give you a hand, Dad,' Jack volunteered.

'Well, now . . . if you're sure you're up to it, I'll be glad to take you up on your offer, Billy.' Without more ado Edith headed for the door.

'I feel sated. If I don't lie down for a while I'll not be fit to see anyone this evening.' With a wag of her hand Margaret followed her.

Billy eyed Susan. 'What about you, love? Won't you go up to the spare room for an hour or so?'

'I'd prefer to go out for a stroll and get some fresh air, if you don't mind. I'll walk down to the phone box. I promised the family I'd ring today, but I hate leaving you two to do all the hard work.'

'Don't worry your head about us, Susan. You'll probably get roped into helping prepare the buffet for later on. Away and phone your folk. Give them my best regards.'

'Thanks. I'll do that. See you later.'

The wine had flowed freely during the meal and Susan felt quite tipsy as she made her way down the street, anticipating the conversation she would have with her parents. Would her father consent to talk to her? Perhaps, if he was cornered by her mother and sister, he would feel obliged to.

She dialled the number, smiling as she waited for someone to pick it up at the other end. A great sadness enveloped her as she listened to the phone ring on and on and on. A glance at her watch showed her it was four o'clock. She pictured the scene back home. It would be somewhat similar to the one she had just left. Her dad would be out for the count on the chair by the fire. Her mother would have gone to have a lie down, sure that she would hear the phone if it rang. But what about Alison? Probably she had gone over to see Graham's parents.

Tears blinded her as she hung up the receiver and left the phone booth. This was the loneliest she had felt since leaving home. Until now she had been too busy and had managed to keep her fears and worries at bay. Now she was swamped with unhappiness. Before she realised it, she was walking along North Road. On the opposite side, Northgate Park seemed like a good place to pull herself together.

It was bitterly cold and the trees lifted frost-coated branches towards the slate-grey sky. The grass crunched under her feet and an icy wind tugged at her clothes. The park was empty except for a couple of parents obviously there under pressure while their children tried out their new bikes and roller skates. A few men were walking their dogs. She was glad there was no familiar faces about; no need to put on a brave front. Snuggling deeper into the collar of her coat to keep out the chill, she walked quickly along the path until no one else was in sight. With no one to notice, she let the tears rain freely down her face. What had she to look forward to? A very lonely life, by the look of it. Would things be any better if she had stayed at home in her own familiar – if perhaps unfriendly – surroundings? Would her parents have forgiven her by now?

Graham would most likely have realised the child was his! Would he have cared enough to give up the woman he loved to marry her? No, why should he? She had been more than willing. The child was her responsibility alone. Besides, the scandal would have been too great. Her parents would never have recovered from it. She had done the right thing, she thought. Her place was here, now. Wiping her face dry on the back of her gloves, she turned for home. At least the tears had released all the pent-up emotions she had been harbouring, and she felt better for it.

Her thoughts returned to Graham. Had he and Alison become engaged today? And what about Jim Brady? Should she write to him? She left the park and was crossing the road, deep in thought, when a voice hailed her. It was Donald Murphy. Realising there must still be some signs of her recent breakdown, she waved, silently willing him to go on. He appeared not to get the message and waited for her to reach him and his companion.

He eyed her closely, noted the sign of tears but held his tongue. Turning to the woman by his side, he said, 'Mam, this is Susan Cummings. I've mentioned her to you. Susan, this is my mother.'

The women silently greeted each other with a nod.

'I'm taking Mam to her sister's. She's spending the next two days there. Are you stretching your legs, Susan?'

'Yes. I tried to phone home, but apparently no one

was there, so I took a walk in the park to try and burn off some of the Christmas dinner calories before trying the phone again. If you'll excuse me, I'll give it another go. Nice meeting you, Mrs Murphy.'

Without waiting for an answer Susan walked away. She had been very aware of Mrs Murphy's disapproval and it annoyed her. Why was this woman finding fault in her? She didn't even know her.

This time the phone was answered on the third ring and an apologetic Alison made excuses for missing her earlier. Glad to hear her sister's voice, Susan brushed these to one side. The next forty-five minutes were spent talking to each member of the family. Even her father contrived to sound sincere as he wished her a happy Christmas. Then Graham came on the line. 'Hello, Susan. How are you? I hope you're enjoying yourself over there.'

The misery of earlier on had evaporated as she spoke to her family and she answered him truthfully enough. 'Yes, Graham, I'm enjoying myself. Alison has been describing her ring to me. It sounds lovely. Congratulations.'

He lowered his voice. 'Susan, have you forgiven me?'

Ignoring his question, she said, 'Graham, I wish you and Alison the best of everything.'

'When are you coming home? Everybody asks after you. Even Jim Brady went out of his way to inquire about you. Come home soon, Susan. We all miss you.'

'I'll phone again in the New Year, Graham. Happy Christmas.' Slowly replacing the receiver, she pondered his words. It was probably her imagination, but she'd thought he sounded as if *he* really missed her. That was nonsense of course! Hadn't he become engaged to her sister? And . . . Jim had been asking about her. Why? What could possibly have happened to make him inquire about her, after the way he had treated her?

Donald was waiting a short distance from the phone box. 'I thought I'd catch you. You look much happier now. Why the tears earlier on?'

'Oh, you know how it is. There was no answer when I rang home and I felt a bit homesick. You know what it's like at Christmas when you're away from home.'

'And now?'

'Now I feel much better.'

'Did you enjoy your Christmas dinner?'

'It was delicious. To be truthful, I was surprised when I heard we were having goose. Back home we always have turkey at Christmas and I didn't fancy the idea of goose. But it was mouth-watering. Aunt Edith made an orange sauce to complement it and I thought it was very tasty indeed.'

He smiled down at her. 'Edith would be pleased to hear so much praise of her cooking. Do you want to go for a walk?'

'No. I'm helping to prepare the buffet for tonight. I'll see you then.'

'I'll walk to the corner with you.'

She stopped at the top of the street. 'No need for you to come any further.' She paused. 'Tell me, Donald, why does your mother dislike me so much?'

His face coloured. 'She thinks anyone connected with the Devines is bad news as far as I'm concerned. I explained that we were just good friends, but she said there was no such thing as platonic friendship between a man and a woman.'

Susan grinned at his embarrassment. He sounded like a young lad. 'Then we'll just have to prove her wrong, won't we? See you later on.'

Chapter Five

Alison heard the phone ringing as the car drew to a halt in the driveway and, scrambling from it, she raced up the steps and into the hall. It stopped just as she reached it. Graham locked up the car and slowly followed her inside.

She swung round to face him with a grimace. 'That was probably Susan.'

'I imagine it was. I told you we should have waited until after she phoned.'

He was tight-lipped with anger and she gazed at him in amazement. 'It's no big deal. She'll ring back later. After all, she can't expect us to stay in all day waiting for her to ring. She should have given us a definite time.'

'Perhaps she can't make definite arrangements,' Graham said defensively on Susan's behalf. He was trying to keep a rein on his temper. He was so disappointed to have missed her, and all because Alison wanted to show off her ring to a friend. And he might not be here when she rang again, might not get a chance to speak to her. 'Remember, she has to get to a phone box and she might not be able to get away when she feels like it.'

'Well, that's just too bad then! After all, it was her choice to stay in Darlington. We certainly did our best to persuade her to come home.' Aware that Graham was still displeased and unable to fathom the reason why, but not wanting to spoil Christmas Day, she asked coaxingly, 'Would you like a drink?'

'Would I not!' he answered grumpily. 'But you know fine well we're going to Mother's for tea, and I'll be driving.'

'We can always get a taxi.'

'They'll be like gold dust today. But . . .' She waited patiently as he pondered. 'Dad doesn't usually drink during the day. Even Christmas Day. I'll phone and find out if he will be able to pick us up here. However, you'll have to stay the night at our house.' He held her eye, knowing she would not like this idea. Alison and his mother did not really hit it off.

'That's all right,' she agreed, all the while consoling herself that it wouldn't be too bad, for there would be other people there.

Mr Robson himself answered the phone. He said there would be no problem and he would pick them up about seven. They sat on the settee and, mollified, Graham raised the glass of beer she had poured for him. 'Happy Christmas.' He comforted himself with the thought that Susan would surely ring again before they left.

'Happy Christmas, and here's to our future together.'

The fact that Graham only half-heartedly returned this salute wasn't wasted on Alison. She couldn't understand him. She turned her left hand this way and that, examining the solitaire diamond ring on the third finger. It was beautiful and had cost a pretty penny. Surely he must care for her, else why go to the extent of getting engaged? She glanced across at her father, spreadeagled asleep on the armchair. He had certainly been as pleased as Punch, plying Graham with drinks and insisting that he stay over the night before. Already he was planning a New Year party in their honour. Her mother had been more subdued; her congratulations no less sincere than her husband's, but looking as if she had reservations. But then, didn't her mother think her the flighty type?

'I've been thinking, Alison . . .'

With a start she brought her attention back to Graham. He paused so long that she prompted, 'Well?'

'Why don't we go over and see for ourselves how Susan is?' At the look of amazement that she turned on him, he added hastily, 'It would be an excuse for a wee holiday.'

Still looking surprised she cried, 'Don't be daft! Me dad would never hear tell of it. You and me go away together?' Her eyes became suspicious. 'Anyway, how come you're so worried about our Susan?'

'Surely it's only natural? After all she'll soon be my sister-in-law. And I'm really being selfish. A winter break would do both of us the world of good and we would be killing two birds with one stone.'

Still she looked unsure what he was going on about. 'Well, anyhow . . . Dad would never hear tell of it.'

As if aware that they were talking about him, Trevor awoke with a grunt and a snort. He stretched his limbs and peered at them, bleary-eyed. 'Did someone speak to me?'

'No, Dad. But your name was mentioned,' Alison admitted.

Deciding to grab the bull by the horns, Graham said, 'Mr Cummings, I was wondering if Alison and I should visit Susan early in the New Year, just to make sure she's all right?'

'If you mean before you're married, the answer's no. At least, not with Alison, you won't! Once you're married you can do as you please, but to be truthful, I don't really think Susan merits your concern. She has shown very little for us.' Rising with difficulty from the deep chair, Trevor left the room, disapproval showing in every line of his body.

Alison shrugged her shoulders and sighed. 'I told you so.'

Graham grimaced. 'Pity. A wee break would be very nice. Perhaps if we worked on his compassion?'

'My father doesn't know the meaning of the word. At least not where our Susan's concerned.'

'Oh, you never know. We'll keep plugging away at him.'

Alison turned away to hide her expression. She couldn't understand why Graham was being so persistent. Suddenly her demeanour brightened as a possible explanation developed. She was holding him at arm's length. Perhaps he was being devious. What if he really wanted to get her completely alone and was using a visit to Susan as an excuse to do so?

It was late, after nine o'clock, before friends and neighbours started to drift into Edith's home. This was usual, Susan was told. The effects of the Christmas meal were allowed to settle before any more food could even be considered. Soon the house was full to capacity, and still they came. It was ten o'clock before Donald eventually arrived.

Susan was chatting to Margaret when she sensed, rather than saw, her tense up. Following the direction of her look, she saw that Donald had entered the room. Seeking Edith out, he gave her a bottle of whiskey. Relieved of this duty, he scanned the room. Margaret was obviously waiting for his glance and their eyes locked.

Embarrassed at witnessing such naked longing in the girl's eyes, Susan swung her gaze to Donald. He had yet to notice her, but she could see he was taken aback by Margaret's reaction as well. Then he became aware of Susan and a grin split his face. Slowly he gently shouldered his way towards them, stopping to greet this one and that on the way. Margaret still stood galvanized to the spot and Susan looked frantically about for her cousin, afraid he might be witnessing this dramatic scene.

Fortunately, he was nowhere to be seen. Nudging Margaret with her elbow, she whispered furiously, 'Get a grip on yourself, Margaret. Do you want another brawl to start?'

Margaret blinked and gave her head a slight shake as if to free it from the hypnotic trance. Just in time! Jack was suddenly there at her side. 'Are you feeling all right, love? You look a bit pale.'

A blank gaze met these words and then Margaret seemed to become aware of her situation. She made her excuses in a whisper. 'It's a bit warm in here, Jack. Could we go outside for a few minutes for a breath of fresh air?'

'Yes, of course. I'll fetch our coats and we can go for a short walk. The air will do you good.'

He made his way out to the hall, passing Donald without a glance.

Arriving at their side, Donald avoided Margaret's intense gaze. 'Hello, girls, that's a smashing spread you have ready. I'm looking forward to it. Meanwhile, can I get you a drink?'

'The heat's too much for me at the moment, Donald. Jack and I are going for a walk. Perhaps you would like to join us?'

'Thanks all the same, Margaret, but I've just arrived. I warn you, wrap up well, it's freezing out there.'

'Here, love.' Tenderly Jack wrapped a thick woollen scarf around his wife's neck and helped her into her coat. 'Let's go. See you two later.'

Not once did he meet Donald's eyes. This led Susan to believe that he had indeed been aware of his wife's interest in her old flame. Dismayed, Susan sipped at her drink. Poor Jack. He must know how the wind was blowing. She eyed Donald covertly.

He was well aware of her sly glance and challenged her. 'What are you looking at me like that for?'

'I saw the way you two looked at each other just now, and it worried me,' she confessed.

'Just what did you see, eh? I was as taken aback as you.'

'She's still in love with you, Donald.'

'You're imagining things. She married the one she wanted.' The urgent kiss of the night before that had plagued him came to the fore again. The sheer intensity of it had excited him all day. Hadn't Margaret implied that Jack wasn't the right man for her after all? If that were the case, what did she intend doing about it?

Susan was eyeing him intently. The strains of a waltz came from the next room and he asked abruptly, 'Would you like to dance?'

'Donald, they're packed in there like sardines in a tin. There won't be room to move, let alone dance. Let's save our energy for the Pali tomorrow night, eh?'

'You're right. Let's try and find somewhere to sit.'

They made their way from the room and eventually sat crushed together on the lower stairs. She smiled at him. 'How long will the party go on?'

'There will still be some diehards here in the morning.'

'You're joking!'

'I'm not.'

'Thank God I can slip next door when I've had enough of it.'

'I wish I could come with you,' he said wistfully.

'You can always curl up in one of the chairs,' she offered. 'But I wouldn't recommend it.'

'You didn't think I was suggesting anything else now, did you?' he teased.

'I just don't want there to be any misunderstanding between us.'

'You know, I might just take you up on that offer.'

She shrugged. 'Feel free. After all, it's your house.'

They sat in silence for some moments, but at last, unable to curb her curiosity, she asked, 'If Margaret finds she still . . .' Her tongue faltered. She could not believe that 'love' was the right word to use here. '. . . fancies you, will you be pleased?'

He shrugged. 'I don't think "pleased" is the right word. Flattered, perhaps. But what difference would it make now? She married Jack.'

'Maybe she's discovered she made the wrong choice. What then?'

He smiled ruefully. 'You know, that's what *she* said last night.'

Susan's mouth fell open. Gently he put a finger under her chin and closed it. 'You may well look surprised. You could have knocked me over with a feather when she said it.'

'You said . . . last night? How come?'

'When I left you they were all coming up the street from midnight Mass. I managed to avoid them, as I thought, but when I rounded the corner, there she was talking to some friends. I walked back up with her.'

'Alone?'

'Yes, alone. Her friends were going in the opposite direction, so of course we were alone. She asked me to walk up to the house with her.'

'And she told you she had made a mistake?'

'Yes, she wished me a happy Christmas and . . . well, we shared a Christmas kiss.'

Susan could imagine how it had been and was disgusted at these revelations. 'I suppose you pushed her away and sent her home to her husband?' she cried scornfully.

Remembering his response to the kiss and the anticipation that had hovered just below the surface all day, he felt ashamed. He lashed out at her rebuke. 'It's none of your business. I'm not allowed to probe into your past, so why should I let you interfere in mine?'

She was on her feet instantly, hissing into his face, 'Because this isn't *past!* This is *present*. And in case you've forgotten, she's my cousin's wife and I'm very fond of Jack!'

She swung away, glad the hall was now empty, as people had drifted into the kitchen to help themselves at the buffet table. He grabbed her arm and pulled her back. 'Is it just because of Jack you're so annoyed?'

Her brows gathered together in a frown. 'What do you mean?' Then comprehension dawned. 'Huh! You don't imagine for one minute I'm interested in you, do you? Hah! Chance would be a fine thing. Where women are concerned, you don't seem to be able to tell your arse from your elbow.'

He relaxed his hold on her and she was off in a flash. He winced at the sound of his front door slamming shut. Susan must be really fond of her cousin to be so upset. He remained deep in thought until the door opened again. He looked up, all smiles, thinking Susan had returned, if only to sample the buffet.

It was Jack and Margaret. Quickly she slipped off her coat and, handing it to her husband, sank down on the stairs beside Donald. 'You were right! It is freezing out there, but I enjoyed our walk. How about you fetching some grub now, Jack?'

Reluctantly Jack hung their coats on the hall stand. 'Would you not come and pick your own? There's such a variety in there, I'll not know what to get you.'

'Oh . . . just get me anything! I'm easily pleased, as you well know.'

'Is there anything in particular you'd like?' he persisted.

'A couple of slices of meat and something savoury will do lovely, thank you.'

Donald saw the worried speculation in Jack's eyes and felt sorry for him. 'Will you mind my place, Margaret, while I get something to eat as well? All this talk of food is making my tummy rumble.'

She rose to her feet at once. 'If you two think I'm sitting out here on my own, you can think again. I'm coming with you.'

They queued at the table and filled their plates. Donald made his way back to the stairs and was delighted to see they were still empty. Margaret was on his heels and sank down beside him.

'Where's Jack?'

'He was following behind us. He'll probably be out in a minute or two.'

Donald felt uncomfortable. Susan's words, 'I suppose you pushed her away and sent her home to her husband?' echoed in his ears. He shouldn't be sitting here in the hall, alone, with Margaret. But what excuse could he fabricate if he left her? And, come to think of it, why should he worry about Jack's feelings? Jack certainly hadn't worried about him when he was seducing Margaret.

Aware that she was looking at him, he avoided her eye. He was also very conscious of the pressure of her thigh against his on the narrow staircase. He stirred restlessly and she increased the pressure. 'Stop it, Margaret!' he said tersely. 'You're a married woman now,' he chastised her. 'Why couldn't you have been like this before?'

She gaped at him in disbelief. 'I tried. God knows, I tried. But you were such a goody-goody. You refused to be tempted. Why do you think I used Jack to try to make you jealous?'

He couldn't believe what he was hearing. 'I was showing you respect,' he muttered, glancing around to see if they could be overheard, aware this wasn't the place for an argument! What if Jack put in an appearance? The nervous state Jack was in at the moment, there could very well be another fisticuffs and he was having none of that. He rose to his feet. 'Look we can't sit here like this. What if Jack comes back? He might get the wrong idea.'

'I don't care. It's better to get it all out in the open.'

He gazed down at her in panic, in his agitation knocking over his can of beer. 'Now look what you've made me do. And listen, Margaret, as far as I'm concerned, there's nothing to get out in the open! After all, you married Jack! You're expecting his child.'

Flushed with temper, he left her and went to fetch something to mop up the spilt beer. When he returned, to his great relief she had gone.

When it became obvious that Susan wasn't going to return, he sought out Edith and explained, 'Susan went next door with a headache earlier on. I want to bring her in a plate of food, but I've no idea what she likes.'

'Oh dear, I'm sure she'll be starving. Look, I'll fill a plate and you fetch a couple of cans to bring with you.'

'Thanks, Edith.'

For some moments he thought Susan wasn't going to answer his knock, but at last the door opened a crack and she glared out at him. 'What do you want?'

He gestured to the covered plate and held up the cans. 'Peace offering, I didn't mean to offend you.'

Slowly the gap widened and she stood back to let him pass. 'I must admit I'm feeling peckish,' she said, closing the door and motioning him into the living room. A fire burnt brightly in the grate, affording the only source of illumination to the room. He reached for the light switch, but her voice stayed him. 'Don't put the light on, please.'

Placing the cans on the floor, he pulled the small table close to the chair by the fire and, unwrapping the plate, set it down. Taking her hands, he drew her forward and by the light of the fire examined her face. 'Am I the cause of those tears?' he asked gently.

'Donald Murphy, I wish you'd stop thinking you have any power over my emotions! I was crying because it's Christmas night, and I'm far from home and lonely, and nobody seems to care about me. So there! It had nothing whatsoever to do with you.'

'I'm glad to hear that, Susan.' His hands cupped her face. 'I hope I never cause you pain.' He brushed her lips with his and, before she could complain, assured her, 'Just a Christmas kiss. Now, sit down and eat up.'

He watched her eating, reaching over now and again to help himself to some titbits from the plate. Noting the sad droop of her wide mouth, again he pondered the reason why she had run away from her family and friends. Surely if the man she loved was over in Ireland, that's where she should be?

Finishing the last sausage roll, she licked her fingers and gave a contented sigh. 'I enjoyed that, Donald. Thanks for thinking of me.' She made to rise, but he was on his feet at once and gently pushed her down again. 'Really, Donald,' she demurred. 'I should be next door helping to keep the dishes cleared.'

'Just you sit there. Let Margaret pull her weight for a change.'

'You know,' she mused, 'I really do wish I liked Margaret. After all, she's family now, but somehow or other I can't warm to her.'

'Maybe you just need some time to get to know her?'

A sad shake of the head rejected this idea. 'I don't think so.'

He sat on the floor beside her chair and took her hand. 'Listen, Susan. I don't know what way things will go. Margaret keeps coming on to me, and I'm only human. Could you not pretend we fancy each other and I'll have an excuse to keep her at bay?'

She gently touched his face. 'Poor Donald. It's not fair the way she's treating you.'

'What do you mean poor Donald?' he cried indignantly. 'I should be delighted to know she still cares. After all, Jack seduced her from under my very nose. I can't believe I was so blind! I wouldn't be human if I wasn't pleased the tables are turned. But still, every time I look at Jack I feel ashamed. She's making mugs of us both.'

'I'm glad you can see that.'

'Mind you, it doesn't do my blood pressure any good when she flashes those big eyes at me. Believe you me, if we're ever alone I don't think I'll be able to control myself.'

'Do you really think it will help if we pretend to fancy each other?'

'I do. Then she won't be so ready to flaunt herself about.'

'All right then. I suppose I can pretend for a day or so. Meanwhile, I must go in and give Aunt Edith a hand.'

He helped her to her feet. 'First I'm going to heat the

two water bottles, belonging to my dear departed aunt, that are under the stairs,' he announced. 'You will then have a nice warm bed to come back to.'

'That's very thoughtful of you, Donald. You'll make some lucky girl a good husband one day. While you fill the bottles, I'll go and freshen myself up a bit.'

Margaret was sullen as she helped in the kitchen. Edith worked in silence alongside her. A neighbour was also helping out and conversation had been sporadic. It had now dried up. All the women turned with obvious relief to greet Susan when she arrived.

'Sorry I was away so long, but I had an awful headache.'

'How's your head now, love?'

'It's fine, Aunt Edith. I took a couple of aspirin and then Donald brought me in some food and now I feel great.' Her eyes became distressed when she saw the tired lines on her aunt's face. Her neighbour also looked as if she was on her last legs. How come some had to work so that others enjoyed themselves? 'You two take a break. Margaret and I should be able to manage in here.'

When the door closed on them, Margaret muttered, 'What makes you think I want to be stuck in here? Huh, some holiday break!'

'I didn't think you'd mind. Aunt Edith has been kindness itself to you, and she does look awfully tired,' Susan reprimanded her.

'It's all right for you to talk! You've had a break. I saw Donald go off with a plate of food. Did you enjoy your little tête-à-tête? Or was it more than that? He looks after you well. Better than he ever looked after me.'

Susan was astonished at the jealousy that emanated from this girl. Had she no pride at all? And what about poor Jack? As if he had been evoked, the door opened and Jack's head appeared.

Immediately aware of the tension, he asked tentatively, 'Need any help, girls?'

'You can take over from me. I seem to have been in here for ever. I need a rest,' Margaret whinged.

'Why don't you go on up to bed, love?'

'I'll go soon. I'll listen to the singers for a while. There's some good voices in there.'

Silence reigned for some time after Margaret had left. It was Jack who broke it. 'This isn't working out as I had hoped.'

'Oh . . .' Susan's voice was non-committal. She didn't want to hear his gripes.

'I hate London! I hoped if we came up here for Christmas I might be lucky enough to get a job when the factories open again. I'd still have to go back down for a while and work my notice, and stay long enough to get the bond money on the flat back, but I wouldn't mind. The thought that I was coming back here would make it all worthwhile.'

'Then you won't be going back on Tuesday?'

'To tell you the truth, Susan, I don't know what to do. Margaret doesn't want to go back down south at all, but where would she stay?'

'Don't worry about me, Jack. She can remain in your parents' house. Donald will let me stay next door for as long as I like.'

He gave her a sideways glance. 'Are you and him . . . ye know?'

Remembering her promise to Donald, but mindful of the fact that Jack thought her a married woman, she said vaguely, 'It's in the early stages yet. Who knows what will happen. And remember, we're both on the rebound . . . so we're taking it a day at a time.'

'So you and your husband really are separated?' She nodded. 'And you do like Donald?'

'Very much. He's a fine person.'

'I know he is. We were best mates once. I hoped he'd understand when Margaret and I fell in love.'

'Was that not expecting too much?'

'To tell you the truth, Susan, I don't know how it came about. Margaret was Donald's future wife, and I was just their friend. We went everywhere together. Then all of a sudden I was obsessed with her. I was actually jealous when she danced with Donald. I couldn't think straight. I had to have her, no matter who got hurt in the process.' He was silent for some moments. 'I've been thinking . . . What with my parents being caught up in the business, Margaret would be lonely and bored. Could she possibly stay next door with you? You'd be company for each other.'

Susan had no difficulty whatsoever figuring out how his predicament had come about. Margaret was a very devious person. Her refusal was swift. 'No! I'm sorry, but the answer is no. You'd be better taking Margaret away with you.' The very idea of living under the same roof as Jack's wife repulsed her.

'Don't just dismiss the idea offhand, Susan. At least give it some consideration.'

She opened her mouth to refuse again, but he forestalled her. 'Just think about it. Please?'

* * *

Donald saw Margaret enter the living room and was glad there was no empty space beside him. He kept his eyes averted and hoped that she would take the hint and stay away from him. She wasn't put off. Crossing the room, she sat on the arm of his chair. Quickly he rose to his feet and, with a smile, offered it to her.

'No, stay where you are. I'll be quite comfortable here.'

When he insisted, she sat down and patted the arm of the chair. 'Stay beside me, please. I know hardly any of this crowd.'

Reluctantly he joined her, glad that another singer had been called on to perform and that the strains of 'Danny Boy' rising in the quiet room made conversation difficult. When the applause had died down and another singer was being persuaded to do his piece, Margaret tugged at his sleeve. Donald bent low to hear what she had to say, very aware of the luminous skin, the shining hair. He fought down his rising emotions. What was keeping Susan? She had promised to help him.

'Donald, do you care for me at all?'

'Margaret, there's no use bringing that all up again. It's all over between us.'

'You like Susan, don't you?'

'Yes, I do! Very much.'

'Are you seeing each other?'

He nodded and she sighed.

'Then the baby is yours?'

He was very still as he digested these words. What on earth was she talking about?

'I must say I'm surprised,' she continued. 'You professed

to love me, but you held me at arm's length. Yet you must have jumped into bed with her as soon as she arrived in Darlo. What's she got that I haven't? Was it because of the way I treated you? Were you feeling rejected? Is that why you were so easily tempted? Was I that easy to forget, Donald?'

His endeavour to turn the conversation and question her was frowned upon, as a woman's soprano voice took off, filling the room with sweetness as she sang 'This is my Lovely Day'.

He was glad of the respite. It saved him from putting his big foot in it. His mind was in turmoil. Was Margaret trying to cause mischief, or was Susan really pregnant?

The door opened quietly and he saw Susan slip into the room. His eyes slid over her figure, but she wore a loose sweater that covered her well. But surely he would have noticed before now, if she really was expecting? Hadn't they danced together? Still, she might not be showing yet. He glanced down at the girl by his side. Her bump was small but noticeable; there was no doubt she was expecting a child. He saw Susan whisper to Edith and Billy and guessed that she was saying good night. The song finished and, amidst the applause, Susan used the respite to cross the room. Ignoring Margaret, she leant close and smiled into his eyes. 'I'm going home now, Donald. Want to come in for a nightcap?'

For the life of him he couldn't respond to her teasing invitation. He knew she was doing as he had asked and was pretending that they were on more than friendly terms, but his mind baulked at the idea that she might be expecting a child. Good God, would everyone think it was his?

'I think I'll stay a while longer and listen to the singers,' he eventually managed to answer her.

Shock blocked all expression from her face. She slowly straightened, her eyes raking his face with contempt. She shrugged. 'Suit yourself. Good night, Margaret. Looks like you win. Enjoy yourself.'

He half-rose to follow her, but Margaret had a vice-like hold on his arm and, as someone else was about to sing, he didn't want to cause a fuss. 'I'll see you tomorrow.' His voice followed her, full of apology, but Susan hardened her heart. He had warned her he would be unable to resist Margaret, but he shouldn't have let her make a fool of herself like that.

'Don't bother! I'll be busy.'

'What about the dance tomorrow night?'

She didn't deign to answer him, but Margaret was quick to ask, 'What dance?'

'In the Pali,' he said abruptly.

'I'll get Jack to take me. Why not join us?'

'I think not, Margaret. I'm sure I can persuade Susan to go. Will you excuse me, please?'

He collected his coat and muffler and left quickly. His house was in darkness and he knew better than to try to get Susan to admit him again. She had been angry! And no wonder. Hadn't he asked for her support and then, when it was offered, had refused it? But Margaret had taken him unawares. Was Susan really pregnant? If she was, why hadn't she told him? What would people think when she could no longer hide it? They were bound to think it was his. Well, what about it, he lamented inwardly, so long as those who mattered knew the truth? However, he found that it did matter! It mattered a lot. There had been enough gossip about him lately.

Tomorrow he would find out what she was playing at. After all, they were friends, not lovers. She didn't have to confide in him, he reminded himself for the umpteenth time. But she should have told him! Prepared him. After all, it would only be natural for people to assume he was the father.

Margaret watched him leave the room, a grim smile on her face. She had noted different expressions flit across Donald's face. She had seen the perplexed frown puckering his brow and drew her own conclusions. Susan had obviously not yet told him he was about to become a father. Now why was that? she mused.

It was lunchtime when he first arrived at Susan's door. Receiving no answer to his knock, he braced himself and banged on Edith's door. It was opened immediately by Margaret.

'Is Susan not in?' she asked, a hint of a laugh in her voice. 'Mind you, I thought she was. Come in.'

'It's all right. If she's not here, I'll call back later.'

'She'll probably come here for her lunch. Why not join us?'

Reluctantly he entered the hall and, to his dismay, the house appeared to be empty. 'Where is everyone?' he asked as he hung his coat on the rail.

'Edith and Billy went off to visit somebody and Jack has gone to see a friend about a job.'

His heart skipped a beat. They were alone. He shouldn't be here. 'So you aren't going back to London then?'

'Not if I can help it. For heaven's sake, stop hovering

about there and sit down. I won't bite you.'

Suddenly she gave a pleased cry and patted her stomach. 'Oh, the baby just kicked me. Look.' She moved close to his chair and he could indeed see her stomach moving. 'It's turning over. Feel!'

He cowered back in the chair with a grimace of distaste. She laughed in derision. 'You really are the limit, Donald. Imagine being afraid to touch a little baby.'

'I'm not afraid. It just doesn't seem decent. Besides, it isn't a baby yet.'

'It is, you just can't see it yet. Does Susan's move? How far on is she?'

He had decided not to let her guess he was in the dark regarding Susan's condition. 'I'm afraid you'll have to ask her that.'

She stared intently at him. 'I do believe she hasn't told you about it. Now, I wonder why? Can it be that she's not sure of you?'

She was bending over him, her soft blonde hair brushing his face.

'Eh, Donald? Why is she not sure? Could it be you still care for me, and she knows it?' Her breath fanned his cheek and he waited for the remembered soft feel of her lips against it. Instead she leant closer and her lips and tongue teasingly caressed the corner of his mouth. All the old yearning awakened and he turned his lips to meet hers. It was wonderful to be near her like this. The gentleness of the kiss intensified and he rose and gathered her close.

For some moments they devoured each other and then, dragging his mouth from hers, he cried, 'Margaret, where did I go wrong?'

'You didn't,' she wailed. 'It was my fault. All my fault. I was impatient and tried to hurry things on by making you jealous. Then it all went haywire and ran out of control. I didn't realise Jack was such a passionate man and we got carried away. After that, there was no going back. It was exciting, but it was you I wanted. I thought that perhaps, if I explained everything to you, you'd understand, but then before I had the chance to talk to you, you and Jack had that big fight. And then I had no choice – I had to go off with him.'

'And there I was trying to do things decent, managing to keep my hands off you, and you were letting Jack get his leg over. I don't understand! I wanted you to know I respected you. That's why I hung back,' he cried bitterly.

'I realise that now. But at the time I thought you were being offhand and didn't care enough.'

'Offhand? How could you think that?' Aware that his passion was getting out of control, he tried to put her from him, but she clung on.

'To be truthful, Jack's passion took me unawares. I never dreamt he could be so fiery. He's a wonderful lover, but it's *you* I love, Donald. I can't stop thinking about you. I should never have married Jack.'

Pictures of her and Jack together flashed before his mind and he felt repulsed. How could she have carried on like that with Jack if she loved him? 'It's too late, Margaret. Besides, what if I didn't come up to your expectations as a lover, eh? You'd be throwing away a good marriage for nothing.'

She pressed closer still and he groaned with desire. 'I don't think I'm likely to find you wanting.'

'Behave yourself, Margaret. Someone is sure to come in.'

'Meet me, Donald! Just say where and when and I'll make sure I'm there.'

His mind baulked at what she was asking of him. 'It wouldn't work, Margaret. I couldn't do that to Jack. We were best friends at one time.'

'He didn't consider your feelings when he seduced me, now did he? So why should you consider his? You want me! That's obvious. Come on, no one need ever know.'

'You're expecting a baby,' he cried, horrified.

'Do you think I could ever forget that? But there'll be no harm done, if that's what you're afraid of. It's not a sickness, you know.'

The doorknob rattled and then a loud, angry knock heralded the arrival of Jack. Margaret reluctantly withdrew from the warmth of Donald's embrace. Drawing a deep, steadying breath, she smoothed the hair back from her face and went to let her husband in.

'Why did you lock the door? You knew I wouldn't be long,' Jack said accusingly. He looked closely at his wife. 'Are you feeling all right? You look flushed . . .' For the life of him he couldn't describe just how she looked. His nostrils flared when he entered the living room and saw Donald sitting by the fireside, a newspaper open on his lap.

Jack's eyes darted from one to the other of them suspiciously. He hated the way his jealousy bounded out of control when he saw them together.

Donald rushed into speech. 'I'm waiting for Susan. You haven't by any chance seen her?'

'Yes. I've just walked up the street with her. She's just gone in next door.'

Donald wondered if it was safe to get up. Margaret guessed his predicament and, grabbing his coat from the rail, threw it at him. 'I told you she wouldn't be long.' She turned to her husband, keeping his attention. 'Well, any luck, Jack?'

Glad of the chance to escape, Donald said, 'I'll nip in and see her.'

Still Margaret detained him. 'Oh, before you go . . . Jack, there's a dance on at the Pali tonight. Donald's taking Susan – can we join them?'

'I don't think you're in any condition to go dancing, Margaret.'

'Why not? I won't be the only expectant mother there, you know. Besides, we're married. We've nothing to be ashamed of.'

From Jack's bewildered expression, Donald guessed he was not aware of his cousin's condition. Trying to retrieve the situation, he cried, 'Susan could very well refuse me. After all, she might just want a quiet night at home.'

'Then you can come with us. Can't he, Jack?'

Donald was out of the door before Jack could reply.

He walked the length of the street to give his emotions a chance to cool down. He really shouldn't let Margaret get to him like this. It was reckless the way she kept throwing herself at him, not caring who noticed. He would have to put an end to it once and for all. She was married and pregnant, and had already made a fool of him once before, and he had no intention of letting it happen again. Feeling much calmer, he approached his house and quietly knocked on the door.

Susan scowled at him. 'What do you want?'

'Can I come in for a minute? . . . Please?'

Reluctantly she moved aside and, passing her, he entered the living room.

'You will have to come into the kitchen. I'm making myself some lunch.'

'Margaret said you'd be going next door for your lunch.'

'Huh! After the way you behaved last night?' She tossed her head angrily. 'I wouldn't give her the satisfaction to gloat. She probably thinks I'm running after you. Besides, I can't stand that girl. She's always asking questions. Probing into my affairs. Why should I tell her any of my business?'

His eyes intently on her face, Donald said softly, 'You must have become quite pally at some stage, since you told her about the baby.'

Hot colour flooded her face and then receded, leaving her deathly pale. 'I told her nothing of the sort!' she whispered. 'What exactly did she say?'

'She asked me when *our* baby was due.'

Her hand clutched at her throat. 'Oh my God. What did you say?'

'I was gobsmacked. Didn't know what to say. I told her she would have to ask you about that. She could see I was flabbergasted and I think she surmised that you had not told me I was to become a father, so I didn't enlighten her.'

'I'm so sorry, Donald. She must have guessed. Probably because she's pregnant herself, she recognised the signs.

I know Aunt Edith would never have broken my confidence. But for her to accuse you? Why, that's monstrous, so it is. She's just jealous, that's what it is. Jealousy!'

He shrugged. 'It's what everyone else will be thinking once they know.'

'Don't worry, I'll soon make it clear you're not the father.'

Her voice was bitter and, his ego dented, he retorted, 'Thanks a lot! I'm not all that bad, you know.'

'Oh, for heaven's sake don't go seeing slights where there aren't any. You'd make a fine father, but we must keep the record straight.'

'Is your husband the father?'

She turned away. Should she admit there was no husband? No, that would only complicate matters further. Donald would think he was dealing with a nutcase. 'No, he isn't the father.'

His mind ticked over and slowly he voiced his thoughts. 'So the baby is the reason your marriage broke up?' She made no comment, just continued buttering bread. 'You must care very much about this other man, so where is he? Did he let you down?'

She turned and stared intently at him. 'I don't want to talk about this, Donald, so would you like to leave now, or stay to lunch?'

He saw that he was going to be none the wiser and replied, 'I'd like to stay for lunch.'

'Then take off your coat and make yourself useful, like setting the table for instance.'

Against Susan's better judgement she agreed to accompany him to the dance that night. Margaret had persuaded Jack to bring her along and it was no surprise when they joined Susan and Donald. Every dance, the minute the music started up, Donald hustled Susan on to the floor. Finding all this activity too much for her, she chided him, 'Much as I enjoy dancing, I'm afraid this is getting too much for me. I'm getting a bit exhausted.'

'You never complained before.'

'We did have wee breaks before . . . You know, like sitting out a dance for a chat or a drink?'

He looked crestfallen. 'I'm sorry, Susan. I just want to keep as far away from Margaret as possible.'

They were near the table where the drinks were on sale and she steered him towards it. 'I'm gasping for a drink.'

He smiled down at her. 'What would you like?'

'An orange juice, please. Oh, there's two seats. I'll grab them and you hurry, before they discover where we are.'

Their seats were screened from the dancers' view by the couples who were standing on the edge of the floor sipping their drinks. They relaxed, secure in the thought that they had some time to themselves.

'Do you know something, Susan? I'll be glad when Jack goes back to London tomorrow.'

'Even if Margaret stays behind?'

Donald jerked upright, spilling his drink down the front of his shirt. 'You can't mean that!' he cried, feverishly mopping at his shirt with a handkerchief.

'Oh, but I do. He asked me if I would let her stay with me.'

'*What?* Why you? Surely the obvious ones would be his parents?'

'I know, but he thought she might get bored, what with them working all day at the market. And it wouldn't do for Margaret to be bored, now, would it?' she added sarcastically.

'You surely didn't agree?'

'No, I certainly did not, and I made it quite plain to Jack. If she should agree to stay with Aunt Edith, can I remain in your house?'

Eyes bright with laughter fixed on her face and he said teasingly, 'Well . . . I don't know about that. You never paid your rent and I was considering eviction.'

Consternation widened her eyes. 'I forgot all about that. It's because I got such a shock at lunchtime. It went completely out of my head.'

A shadow fell across them. 'So here you are! Hiding away. You two must really be in love.' Margaret stood before them, hands on hips, disapproval apparent in every line of her body.

Reluctantly Donald rose to his feet and motioned her to sit down. 'Where's Jack?'

'He's getting me a drink.' The music was just starting another quickstep. 'How about giving me a dance, Donald? If I didn't know any better, I'd swear you were avoiding me.'

'Here!' A glass of lemonade was thrust into her hand, and Jack glared at her. 'I think you've danced enough for one night. Don't forget your condition. We don't want any accidents, do we?'

Her lips tightened and her nostrils flared in anger. How dare Jack speak to her like that in front of them. 'Susan is dancing just as much, if indeed not more than me. Are you not going to advise her to take it easy?' she retorted.

'What on earth are you talking about, Margaret?' His bewilderment was obvious.

Her smile was malicious. 'Has your dear cousin not confided in you then? She's also expecting a baby.'

Shocked eyes rested on Susan. 'Is this true?'

She rose to her feet. 'I can't see what business it is of yours, Jack, or anybody else's, for that matter. But yes, I am. Now if you'll excuse me, I'm tired and I think I'll go home.' Donald moved to join her, but she stayed him with a raised hand. 'There is no need for you to accompany me, Donald. Stay and enjoy the rest of the dance. I'll be perfectly all right on my own.'

'Oh, but I want to see you home. If I'm lucky I might even get something to eat,' he teased, trying to lighten the atmosphere.

To his relief, she laughed and agreed with a smile. 'You just might at that. Good night, Jack.' An abrupt nod was all she allowed herself in Margaret's direction.

It was a beautiful night; stars twinkled brightly against a dark sky. The air was crisp and their breath was like fine mist hovering on the frosty air as they made their way through the town centre towards North Road.

'Isn't it a lovely night?'

He glanced sideways at her. 'It certainly is, and so are you.'

She laughed aloud. 'Are you trying to boost my morale?'

'I'm trying to figure out what makes you tick. You married one man and are expecting another man's child. Why aren't they here fighting over you? I don't understand.'

'Because until Margaret opened her big mouth, no one but Edith and Billy knew about this baby. It's the best-kept secret. Certainly no one in Ireland knows, and that's the way I want it to stay.'

'Surely the father has a right to know?'

'He isn't free.'

'Ah, I guessed he must be a married man.'

'No, he isn't married. He is, however, engaged. Look, I'm talking too much. Please don't ask me any more questions on this subject. It'll only end in tears.'

'Just one more! Why not tell him? If you love each other, he will probably break off the engagement and marry you.'

'Ah, but you see, that's the snag. He doesn't love me.'

In spite of the fact that she felt far from laughing, the expression on his face brought forth a reluctant chuckle. 'It's all very complicated, Donald, and I'm too ashamed to tell you the truth. So can we just forget my problems and concentrate on yours?'

'I must confess mine are nothing compared with yours.'

'Take my advice and let them stay that way. Forget Margaret! She's nothing but trouble. You'll meet some nice girl one day who is free to return your love. Now let's change the subject. I'm going to keep my side of the bargain and cook you something tasty for supper. What do you think of that?'

'I think that's a very good idea.' He reached for her hand and drew it under his arm, quickening his step at the same time. 'I'm starving. Remember, I missed dinner today.'

She laughed aloud. 'You're not going to let me forget, are you?'

For the remainder of the journey they were locked in their own thoughts. Susan was very aware of his body brushing against hers. Through her own stupid fault she was missing out on so much. She warned herself to be careful. In her vulnerable state she might send out the wrong signals and, since this was to have been Donald's wedding day and he was missing Margaret, anything could happen. Why had she promised to cook him a meal? The rest of the evening could be fraught with danger.

Donald's thoughts were running along similar tracks, only he couldn't see what harm it would do if they comforted each other. Who knows, perhaps if he played his cards right, he might win her around to his way of thinking. He was humming softly, his nerves tingling with anticipation, when they at last arrived at his house.

Inside, he closed the door and drew her into his arms. In the semi-darkness she stood very still, her big, haunted eyes gazing up at him. His head bent and, receiving no resistance, he trailed his lips gently over the contours of her face. Aware that she should be stopping him before it got out of hand, she nevertheless pressed closer, savouring the sweetness of his caresses. Encouraged, he was slowly edging her towards the stairs, all the while seducing her with his mouth and hands.

Suddenly she twisted away from him. 'No, this is wrong!'

'Why? Why is it wrong? We're not trespassing on anyone else's preserves. We're two lonely people who are attracted to each other.'

'I don't want this. I want true love, not just a one-night stand.'

'Who knows where it might lead, eh? I do care for you, Susan. Once your divorce comes through, we might very well care enough about each other to marry.'

She grasped at this excuse. 'That might well be, but until I'm free I don't want to be used by someone who's running away from someone else.'

He stepped back as if stung. 'I wouldn't use you like that,' he protested.

'Oh no? What would you call it?'

'I was trying to comfort you.'

'Thank you very much, but I don't need that kind of comfort. I think you should go now. More than anything else in the world, I need to be respected.'

He looked incredulous. 'You think I don't respect you?'

'How could you, when you think I'm ready to jump into bed with you?'

Without another word he turned on his heel and left the house. She gazed at the door and then kicked it violently again and again. She wished she could kick herself; meanwhile she could only take out her frustration on the door. Struck by a thought, she smiled wryly. He must be starving. And she still hadn't paid her rent.

She was in the kitchen heating the kettle for the water bottles when there was a knock on the door. Convinced it would be Margaret thinking Donald would be here and wanting to invite herself and Jack in for supper, sharp words were hovering on Susan's lips as she wrenched open the door.

Donald stood there looking sheepish. 'I'm sorry.' He shrugged. 'I'm afraid I'll never learn, Susan. I do admit I was hoping to get you into bed, but I honestly didn't mean any disrespect. I really did think we could comfort each other.'

'Okay I understand, and I forgive you.'

She made no effort to invite him in and he grimaced. 'I suppose I've forfeited any chance of some grub?' She hesitated and he pleaded, 'I really am starving, Susan.'

'Oh, come on in then, but you had better behave yourself.'

'You can count on that. I've learnt my lesson.'

The engagement party arranged for New Year's Eve was a great success. Held in the Royal Avenue Hotel, the lavish buffet and constant flow of wine and beer ensured that everyone enjoyed themselves. Rooms were also available at a discount for those who wanted to stay overnight. Alison was flushed with triumph, and Graham had put all thoughts of Susan to one side and had convinced himself he was a very lucky man that such a lovely girl had consented to be his wife.

He eyed his parents chatting to his future in-laws. His father had been won over long ago by Alison's beauty and charming manner, but he knew that his mother still had reservations. She was not over-enthusiastic about the match. Not that it mattered. In her opinion no one would be good enough for him. She had hoped for someone better for her only son. A politician's daughter, for instance. And there had been little chance of that.

In spite of her family's ranting and raving, Susan had resisted all efforts to persuade her to come home for the engagement party. She sent Alison some good-quality towels for her bottom drawer, but Graham still thought it very heartless of her to let her sister down. Even if she couldn't face him, she could have avoided him, as usual. She was very good at doing that, he thought resentfully.

A June wedding was being suggested by his in-laws and he was glad that Alison didn't appear to agree with them, saying she was too young to start having babies. And that would be the next thing on the agenda, if their parents had their own way. Then why had she been so determined to get engaged at Christmas? For the life of him he could not understand how a woman's mind worked.

The atmosphere was wonderful and the crowd laughed and danced the night away. As midnight drew near, Alison and Graham joined those closest to them to see the New Year in. The only blot on the landscape had been Susan's absence. When all the excitement had died down and the New Year greetings were over, Graham drew Alison to one side.

'I know we have two single rooms booked, but can't we share one of them, eh, love?'

He saw dismay register in her eyes before she came up with an excuse. 'But my room is next door to my parents. One way or the other they would be bound to know.'

He gathered her close. 'Did no one ever tell you that where there's a will there's a way?'

'It would be too risky, Graham. I'd die of shame if we were caught. Look at how me dad treats Susan, and we aren't even sure she's pregnant.'

He drew back, brows gathered in a frown. 'Susan pregnant? You never said.'

'Well, we don't *know* that she is. And Jim Brady denies it. But why else run over to Aunt Edith and refuse to come home under any circumstances, if she has nothing to hide?'

Graham was flabbergasted. He felt all at sea, as if he had missed the important part of a film. 'How come you never mentioned any of this to me before?'

'It was me dad who first put the idea into my head. And then when she refused to come home at Christmas and for my engagement party as well . . . You have to admit it does look very suspicious.'

'But why did you not say anything to me?'

'I didn't say to anyone, except Jim Brady – remember that night at the Orpheus? I wanted to find out if he knew anything. But he denied all knowledge of it. Of course he might very well be innocent. If it does happen to be true, she could have met someone over there.'

'You should have told me, Alison.'

'What difference does it make?'

'I'm your future husband and you should tell me these things.'

He turned away and Alison watched him head for the bar, relieved that apparently he had given up the idea of sharing a room tonight. Time enough for all that when they were married, she thought.

At the bar Graham ordered a double Black Bush, and armed with his drink found a quiet corner. Lighting a cigarette, he mulled over the news he had just heard. He recalled that Susan had been a virgin the night he had taken her. Could she possibly be expecting his child? No! It was out of the question. She would have had no reason to hide. All she had to do was tell him.

Alison watched him head for a secluded corner table without so much as a glance in her direction and slowly followed him. He must be very annoyed since he didn't even offer her a drink. Absorbed in thoughts of Susan, Graham had completely forgotten her existence, but to his surprise suddenly Alison was on her knees beside him.

'Graham, have I offended you? I honestly didn't mean to.' She had decided to give in to his wishes and keep him happy. 'As you say, where there's a will there's a way, so shall I come to your room when I'm sure the coast is clear? Most people have already retired, so it shouldn't be too long.'

He looked into her lovely face and discovered that the passion he had felt earlier had completely evaporated. Placing his drink to one side and his cigarette in an ashtray, he cupped her face in his hands. 'It's all right, love. I respect your wishes. Let's wait until we're married.'

'You mean that, Graham?'

He brushed her lips lightly with his. 'Yes, dear. Now off you go to bed. I'll just finish my drink and then I'll be off, too. See you at breakfast in the morning.'

Feeling that she was in the wrong and he was dismissing her like an unruly schoolgirl, she repeated, 'Are you sure?'

'Yes, I'm sure.'

'Well, all right then. I'll see you in the morning.' Still apprehensive, she left him.

He sat for a long time after she had gone, going over and over again in his mind the few encounters he'd had with Susan after that fatal night. She had obviously been embarrassed and avoided him, but then it was an embarrassing situation. But surely she must have known he would stand by her. Still, she would have been considering Alison's feelings as well. If – and he very much doubted it – she was pregnant, it could still be Jim Brady's. There was nothing to prove that she had not been seeing him again. Or, as Alison had pointed out, she might have met someone over in England.

He sat on, imagining what it would be like for Susan to have his child. It would cause a scandal! No doubt about that. Could it possibly be true? Was that why she had taken off like that? Some time passed as he sat lost in thought, until the silence that had descended on the hotel made him aware of the late hour. A glance at his watch showed it was half-past four. He found when he rose to his feet that he felt very unsteady. Making his way to the lift, he pressed the button and was soon in his bedroom. Not bothering to remove his clothes, he threw himself on the bed. His last thought was of Susan. Somehow or other he must see her. But how?

Chapter Six

To his great joy, Jack was promised a job in Cleveland Bridge as soon as he could tie up all the loose ends in London. Margaret adamantly refused to go back down with him and, glad that her beloved son was going to be living close at hand, Edith agreed that she could live with them until he came back.

She was full of apologies to Susan, explaining that she really had no choice in the matter. Susan hastened to assure her that she was happy enough the way things were. She loved this time of day when she and her aunt could talk freely. Margaret never rose early and they were having coffee together, as usual.

'Billy has agreed to start looking at houses,' Edith informed her niece. Then we three can move and leave Jack and Margaret in this house. What do you think of that?'

'Aunt Edith, please don't worry about me. I think I can persuade Donald to let me keep on renting his house. That's a laugh. He won't take any money off me. But you know what I mean – he will let me stay. Once the baby is born, I'll have to think seriously about my future.'

'Susan, I can't help worrying about you. It's time you saw a doctor, you know.'

'Yes, I realise that. Can I join your doctor's surgery?'

'I don't see why not. I'll make an appointment for you to go and see him. I'm sure he will take you on. I'll make it for Wednesday, shall I?'

Vera Crabtree had asked Susan to continue working part-time: Fridays and Saturdays, so Wednesday suited her fine. 'That would be great, Aunt Edith.'

'Would you like me to come with you?'

A definite shake of the head accompanied her answer. 'No, that won't be necessary.' She smiled wryly. 'You've enough running about to do with Margaret, without me adding to your list.'

'Ah now, Susan, you know I wouldn't mind in the slightest.'

'I know you wouldn't, but I'd rather be independent. I'll keep you up to date on all matters, I promise.'

'I wish you and Margaret had hit it off . . .' Her aunt's voice trailed off and she looked appealingly at Susan. Getting no response, she added, 'You would be company for each other, you know, going to the clinic together.'

'Margaret has plenty of friends in Darlington, Aunt Edith. She'll be all right. I'm a bit of a loner. I prefer my own company.' This wasn't really true. She missed her own friends back home and Margaret would be a very poor substitute. She would rather do without than befriend someone like Margaret. 'I'm fine, really I am.'

Edith still looked worried, but Margaret was her daughter-in-law and must come first. Susan had asked her not to reveal that she was already pregnant when she arrived. Aware that Donald would therefore be regarded as the father, Edith had questioned the wisdom of this, but was assured that Donald knew which way the wind blew and was quite happy with the way things stood.

This was true, it kept Margaret off his back.

They looked at lots of houses and at last put in an offer for one on the outskirts of town in Cockerton Village. A semi-detached house, it had three big bedrooms, two reception rooms, a kitchen, bathroom and gardens at front and rear.

Edith was in her glory and, with shining eyes, confided in Susan that she had despaired of ever owning a house, and to her, this one was like a mansion. It required some work on it, but this was reflected in the asking price, and she and Billy would willingly work their fingers to the bone to get it just the way they wanted. They hoped to move in before Easter. Easter Sunday was early this year. It would fall on 6 April and Margaret's baby was also due around that time.

They had expected Margaret to be delighted to have a home of her own, albeit a rented one, but when Billy offered to get Jack's name put in the rent book she just shrugged indifferently, and agreed it would do until Jack arranged something better.

Jack had been spending weekends at home with his wife, finding it harder and harder to leave each Sunday evening. Eventually, at the end of January, he returned for good. It was soon obvious that he did not share his wife's view about living in a rented house. He was over the moon at the idea of getting his parents' comfortable home, saying that it would be long and many a day before they could afford to buy a house. Margaret was far from happy at this idea and an expression used back home came to mind as Susan looked at her dour countenance: 'She had a face like a Lurgan spade.'

Donald invested his savings in a second-hand Austin Mini. A cute little red number. The first time it drew up to the door they all gathered on the pavement to admire and exclaim over it. And not just the family! It was such a close-knit community that the whole street was out giving it the once-over; passing knowing comments on its good points and ignoring its bad.

Had it been a brand-new Aston Martin, Donald could not have been more proud. Every Sunday after Mass he collected Susan and introduced her to all the towns and villages round about. Places like Barnard Castle and Richmond, and Durham and York, where she was enthralled by the quaint cobbled streets in The Shambles and by great York Minster. She was aware that when he arrived each Sunday morning they were watched from behind her Aunt Edith's net curtains, and she could guess who was spying on them.

True to his word, Donald's conduct was beyond reproach. He was a real mate, helping her in every way he could, and she grew to depend on him. When her pregnancy started to show, he confided in her that he didn't care if everyone thought the baby was his, adding sadly that indeed he wished it was.

The car was another thorn in Margaret's side; something else to whine about. Why couldn't Jack buy a car and take her out and about? she lamented the first time they were alone.

'For the simple reason that we are still in debt to my

parents. When we clear that, then – and only then – will I consider going into more debt for a car.'

'But that could take years,' she gasped.

'So be it! There are more important things to consider than a car. Like, for instance, the baby.'

She scowled. 'You know, sometimes I wish . . .' Her voice trailed off.

'What, Margaret? What do you sometimes wish? That you'd never married me?' he said bitterly. 'Well, let me tell you something. Sometimes I wish I was footloose and fancy-free, just like Donald Murphy! He seems to be having a whale of a time gallivanting about in his new car, and maybe, just maybe, you would then look at me with cow's eyes.'

Fear entered her heart. He had never spoken to her like this before. Terrified that he might find her wanting and start to look elsewhere, she said quickly, 'I didn't mean that at all.'

'Didn't you?' With a scornful look he turned on his heel and left the room, glad he had given her something to think about. He was fed up to the teeth with her griping. She hadn't a kind word to say about anyone or anything these days. There was simply no pleasing her.

The house in Cockerton was pronounced habitable in the middle of March, in so far as the bathroom had been refitted and most of the kitchen cupboards replaced. It still needed a lot doing to it, but Edith and Billy couldn't wait to move in and decided to do so right away and refurbish as they went along. Susan was invited to move with them and, although she had vowed to stay where she was until the baby was born, she was glad of the opportunity to get away from the ever-simmering envy of Margaret, who made a habit of popping in to see her whenever she got the chance. The next week was spent carefully packing books and knick-knacks into cartons and tea chests in preparation for the move.

Donald immediately gave notice to the rent man that his house would soon be empty, much to the delight of Jack, who would be glad to see the back of the man who had once been his best friend. Susan, however, was dismayed when she heard, sure that Donald would regret his decision when he met and wanted to marry some girl. He assured her that he was glad not to have to visit the house any more. Nothing else was said, but Susan wondered just what Margaret had been up to, when given the chance, to make Donald so relieved to escape. She tried to pry, but Donald just tapped the side of his nose with a forefinger and would say no more.

It was near Easter when fate created an unexpected opportunity for Graham to visit England. The business was booming and his father was eager to open another car showroom. Something different, a completely new design. Graham, who that very day had been admiring the latest building designs in Newcastle, hastened to get the magazines to show him.

His father examined the pictures presented to him and exclaimed, 'These are in Newcastle, England. Why would we want to go and see them when we have fine architects here in Ireland?'

Seeing his chance to get across the water slipping away, Graham confided, 'Dad, I need a break. Just a few days away on my own.'

George Robson eyed his son closely. 'I've noticed you're not yourself lately, something's bugging you. If you aren't happy about your engagement to Alison, son, break it off now. I realise you won't want to hurt her, but the longer you leave it, the harder it will be.'

'It's not that, Dad. There's something else I need to get sorted out in my mind and I need some space to think.'

'Mind you, you will only be going over to have a look.'

'I know that, Dad. But, you know, it wouldn't be a bad idea branching out. Newcastle, after all, is less than an hour away by plane.'

'You can get that idea out of your head, young man. Your mother hates flying.'

With a cheeky grin Graham said, 'Ah, but then, she wouldn't have to go.'

George returned the grin, glad to see his son looking more relaxed. 'Away and book your flight, before I change my mind.'

'Thanks, Dad. Thanks a million.'

There was nothing wrong with Alison's geography and when she heard his plans, she was quick to point out how close to Darlington he would be.

'You know, I didn't realise that,' he exclaimed. 'Tell you what. If I can find the time, and it's not too far away, I'll go and surprise Susan.'

'I wish I could go with you,' Alison lamented. 'It's not fair.'

Successfully hiding his dismay at her suggestion, Graham said, 'I know. But your dad would never hear tell of you coming along. Besides, I won't be free to entertain you. I'll be busy meeting different people and going out to look at buildings. You'd be bored stiff.'

'Not if you dropped me off at Susan's while you were carrying out your business. I'll have a word with Dad.'

However, Trevor was not so forthcoming, accusing Alison of following in her sister's footsteps. Disappointed, but knowing how much her mother was missing her eldest daughter and not wanting to cause any more friction than was necessary, she agreed to remain at home while Graham was away. Ashamed of the relief he felt, Graham was extra-attentive to her and promised to buy her a nice piece of jewellery while over in England.

Uneasy, but unable to figure out why, she clung to him as he was about to leave for the airport. 'Don't you go falling for one of those English girls,' she warned.

'Don't be silly! I'm going over on business, remember,' he admonished her. 'I won't have any free time to chat up the girls.'

'If you get a chance to see our Susan, try and get her to come home. Tell her how much we all miss her.'

'I will. I'd better go, love. I'll ring tonight. Okay?'

She nodded and lifted her face for his kiss. With a peck on the cheek and a quick hug, he put her from him.

'See you soon.'

She watched him drive off through a blur of tears. If only she had been more forthcoming at the beginning of their relationship there wouldn't be this invisible barrier between them. Now, try though she might, she couldn't get close to him. When had it all gone wrong?

At their engagement party. They had been so close that night; the closest she had ever come to feeling any passion for him, and he must have sensed it, but when he had proposed that they sleep together she had reacted like a Victorian lady. No wonder he seemed to have gone off her. When he came back she would make it up to him. But did she really want to start all that? Surely there should be more to marriage than two people taking vows. There should be passion, excitement, awe. Shouldn't there? Or was it just in books that passion throbbed and they couldn't keep their hands off each other? She certainly had no inclination to fondle Graham's body. Quite the opposite; the idea repulsed her. She had the greatest admiration for him, but he did not appeal to her in that way and sometimes this worried her.

From remarks made by her friends she gathered that most of them felt the same; not sure if they had met the right one, yet afraid to let them go and end up old maids. The first time she had met Jim Brady, that night at the Orpheus, before he and Susan had been aware of her, she had sensed deep emotions between them. It had been like an electric current in the air. She had envied her sister her good fortune. Yet apparently it had ended in heartbreak. What did one do for the best?

The move into the new house went smoothly. Billy's friends in the market rallied round and on Sunday, with a lot of vans and open-backed lorries available for transport, the contents of the old house were soon transferred to the new home. Jack and Margaret had also helped out, as had Donald. The six of them were sitting amidst a jumble of boxes and crates having their first cup of tea on the new premises, when a knock on the door brought Edith proudly to her feet.

'I bet you that will be one of the neighbours to wish us well. Our first visitor. I'll answer it.'

Edith, who had visited the house regularly, painting and polishing, was already on nodding acquaintance with a few of her neighbours, but the man standing on her doorstep was not one of them. They eyed each other for a few seconds. He recognised Edith's resemblance to her sister. 'I'm looking for a Mrs Devine,' he said politely and she immediately recognised the Belfast brogue. 'I went to her old address and was directed here.'

'I'm Edith Devine.'

'I was told your niece, Susan Cummings, would be here with you?'

A frown gathered on Edith's brow. 'Who wants to know?'

'I'm a friend from back home. I'd business in Newcastle and thought I'd take the opportunity to call and see her.'

Jumbled thoughts filled Edith's mind. Was this the child's father? Had he somehow or other heard about her niece's predicament and come to claim her?

Back in the sitting room they sat with strained ears. They heard Edith open the door and the murmur of voices. Then Edith returned, a worried look on her face and a tall man at her heels. 'It's someone to see *you*, Susan. Someone from back home.'

Shock coursed through Susan's body and she went

deathly pale as she gazed in amazement at Graham Robson.

He could see that she was upset and rushed into apologies. 'I'm sorry for not letting you know, Susan, but I had business in Newcastle and thought I'd pay a flying visit.'

Susan swallowed to try to remove the lump that was lodged in her throat and rose slowly to her feet. With hand outstretched and a sickly smile of welcome on her face, she approached Graham. 'It's wonderful to see you.' His eyes swept over her, taking in her obvious pregnancy, and she thought he looked excited. But why? She rushed into introductions. 'Graham, let me introduce you. This is my Aunt Edith.'

Cordially Edith clasped the hand offered to her. 'I realise now who you are,' she exclaimed. 'You're Alison's young man. Welcome to my new home. We just this afternoon moved in, so you will have to forgive the mess.' To Susan's relief she took over the introductions. 'This is my husband Billy and son Jack. That girl is Jack's wife and this is a friend of the family, Donald Murphy.'

Donald could see how dismayed Susan was and, remembering how hard she had worked to keep the knowledge of her pregnancy from those back home, he shook Graham warmly by the hand. 'This is a pleasure. I've been looking forward to meeting Susan's family.' It was up to Susan now whether or not she wanted this man to think they were a couple.

She shot him a grateful look. 'He has indeed been torturing me to take him home to meet you all,' she agreed, with a fond smile in his direction. 'But I wanted to wait until the baby is born.'

Graham looked deep into her eyes. This conversation was ad lib. It didn't ring true. Before he could think of a reply, Edith cried, 'Look, we haven't even offered the man a chair. Sit down, son. Make yourself comfortable. I'll rustle up something to eat.'

'That won't be necessary, thank you. I would just like a word with Susan, if I may?' His gaze was pleading. 'Bring you up to date about things back home. I've hired a car. Perhaps you will come for a drive with me?'

'I'll just tidy myself up a bit. Excuse me, please.' On reluctant feet she climbed the stairs to the bathroom. What on earth had brought him here? How should she handle this?

A silence fell when she left the room. It was Edith who broke it. 'I hear you have just become engaged to my other niece, Alison. Congratulations, son.'

'Thank you.'

'May I second that, son. She's a lovely girl.'

Graham smiled at Billy. 'I'm a lucky man.'

This Alison was a very lucky girl, Margaret thought. Those shoes were hand-made and that suit and Crombie overcoat must have cost the earth. Besides, there was something funny going on here. How come Susan hadn't told her family about the baby? To her, it was obvious that they didn't know! This man had been gobsmacked, and something else . . . An elusive expression had flitted across his face; too swift for her to put a name to it.

When Susan returned she was dressed for outdoors. 'I'm ready, Graham.'

'Graham, I insist you come back here for a bite to eat before you go back to Newcastle.' He opened his mouth to make an excuse, but Edith was adamant. 'I insist. It won't be a feast, but it will fill the gap.'

'I don't want to be any bother.'

'I assure you, it will be no bother at all.'

He nodded. 'Thank you very much. I'd be glad to.'

In the car Graham turned to her. 'Which direction?'

'Turn up West Auckland Road and then straight on,' she said.

Soon they were out in the countryside, with trees and hedges flashing past on either side. It was a typical March evening, cold and blustery. Great dark clouds buffeted each other low in the sky, as if anxious to shed their heavy load. Susan gazed blindly out of the window, waiting for the interrogation she knew was to come. Graham was silent, trying to figure things out in his mind. He didn't want to put his foot in it. Where did this Donald fellow fit into all this?

Ten minutes passed and, unable to bear the silence any longer, Susan turned a reproachful gaze on him. 'Why did you come here, Graham?'

'I told you. I had to come to Newcastle on business, so I thought I'd kill two birds with one stone. Everybody's worried sick about you, you know, and it looks like they were right to be worried.'

'There's no need. I told them I was all right,' she said stubbornly.

His eyes fastened briefly on her stomach. 'You call *that* all right?'

'It's nobody's business but mine! I've settled in over here. If I was to go home, my dad would give me no peace. I'd be the lowest of the low.'

'Don't let Trevor keep you away from your family and friends, Susan. He has already guessed you're pregnant. Believe me, it would be a nine-day wonder.'

She gaped at him in horror. 'My dad thinks I'm pregnant?'

'I'm afraid so. Mind you, nobody believed him! Jim Brady danced with Alison one night at the Orpheus and he swore he never touched you.' But I did, he inwardly lamented. His teeth gnawed at his lower lip as he tried to frame the next question.

'Jim Brady knows I'm pregnant?' she cried, aghast. 'Ah no, no!' The very idea of him knowing filled her with a great sorrow. What must he be thinking?

In spite of her efforts at self-control, she started to tremble and low moans escaped her lips. Frantically he watched for a lay-by to stop the car in. To his relief one came up right away and he drew the car into it and turned to her. 'Susan, don't let it upset you so. No one knows you're pregnant. It was just an idea your dad came up with. A reason for you not coming home.'

Images of Jim Brady filled her mind, his dark, handsome face full of disgust at her downfall. What a low opinion he must have of her. All the same, he should find it easy enough to believe. Hadn't she thrown herself at him, and hadn't he pushed her away?

Graham reached for her hands and clasped them tightly. Blindly she turned to him for consolation. Then, with an exclamation of dismay, she pulled herself free, all thoughts of Jim fading from her mind at Graham's touch. The dark warmth of the car's interior brought to mind another time spent in similar circumstances – and look where that had led. Would she never learn? Still, how she longed for the comfort of his embrace. Anybody's embrace, for that matter. Just to be held by him would be wonderful. Just to be held by someone, with no strings attached, would be soothing to her tortured soul, but she couldn't take that chance. What if she blurted out everything into his sympathetic ear?

Feverishly she groped for the door handle. The heat in the car was stifling; she needed to get out of here, needed fresh air, or she was likely to faint. A heavy mist had descended and the air, with an agricultural taint, was far from fresh, but still she gulped great mouthfuls of it into her lungs. The cold dampness hit the back of her throat, making her splutter and cough.

He was out of the car and beside her immediately. 'Susan, please get back in the car. I'm not going to touch you.'

'You're dead right, you're not,' she gasped indignantly between coughs.

'Please, Susan, don't be so bitter. If only you knew how much I regretted that night. If only I could turn back the clock, I would do so. Can't you forgive me?'

'I forgave you a long time ago, Graham. It was just one of those things. We were both to blame.'

Instinctively her hand rested on her stomach and he was quick to notice. 'It was my fault! I knew you were vulnerable, but I couldn't help myself, Susan. You're very lovely, and so sensual. I was gobsmacked when I realised you were a virgin.'

Sensual? He thought her sensual? Why couldn't Jim have thought so? She pushed this thought away and latched on to the rest of his words. 'Why?' she cried accusingly. 'Why were you gobsmacked? Did I come across to you as an easy lay? Did you think I'd been sleeping around?'

'Of course not!' he retaliated, alarmed at her reaction. 'Just, you and Jim were so close I felt sure you must have been intimate.'

'Hah! I'll have you know he wouldn't so much as lay a finger on me. That's how intimate we were.'

'That's because he loved you.'

She was quick to note the past tense. 'You said "loved". Is there someone new in his life now?'

He shrugged his shoulders and spread his hands wide in frustration. 'How would I know? I never see him these days.'

She stood with bowed head and he sensed that she was crying, though not a sound came from her. He should go away and leave her in peace. But he had to find out the truth. A sob escaped her lips and, thrusting a handkerchief into her hand, he persisted in his quest. 'Susan, you were a virgin that night . . . Is this my child? I may as well own up, that's the real reason why I'm here this evening. The business in Newcastle was just an excuse to get over and see you. And I want a truthful answer.'

She recoiled from him in horror. How had he guessed? 'What on earth makes you think that?'

'Alison only let slip that you might be pregnant on New Year's Eve. She had never mentioned it before or I'd have been over here long ago. It struck me immediately that, if Trevor was right, I might be the father. I haven't been able to think of anything else since. Only, if it is, I can't see why you didn't tell me. Is it mine? Is it, Susan?'

'No! No, it's not yours.'

'Susan.' His voice was slow and deliberate. He must make his position clear. 'I'd be more than willing to marry you, you know. You need have no qualms about that.'

Willing to marry her. What a wonderful recipe for a happy marriage! Everyone talking and pointing the finger. A heartbroken Alison in the background. Even for the sake of the child he would be unable to hide his love for her sister. The child would have its father's name, but everything else would be a disaster.

Looking him straight in the eye, she said, 'Believe me, you are not the father.'

'Then who is? You have to tell me, so I can go home with a clear conscience.'

'Graham, listen to me. If I had wanted to wash my dirty linen in public, I'd have gone home. I'm not proud of the position I'm in, you know! Far from it, but it's nobody's business but my own and, if I can help it, it won't be talked about in the dance halls of Belfast. You can go home and marry Alison with a clear mind.'

Still unsure, he probed, 'Are you telling me the truth?'

'Yes. Now will you please take me back. I'm cold.'

She climbed awkwardly back into the car, but he knew better than to try and assist her. On the journey back she sat crouched against the car door, the picture of misery, and he regretted adding to her worries. Still, he had to be sure. After all, he was engaged to her sister. They were just drawing up to the house when the heavens opened and rain fell in a sheet.

The door was opened quickly. 'You just made it in time.'

Susan wryly examined her soaked coat and replied, 'I don't know about that.'

'Take off your coat, Graham, and hang it up there.' Edith nodded to a rack in the hall. 'I'll fetch you a towel for your hair in a jiffy.' She helped her niece off with her coat. 'Are you all right, love,' she whispered.

'I'm fine, Aunt Edith, just cold. My, you have been busy,' she exclaimed when she entered the sitting room. All the cartons and tea chests had disappeared, and the settee and chairs were in position against the wall and close to the coal fire that now burned brightly in the grate.

Billy laughed. 'You should see the state of the living room and kitchen. Meanwhile, we can be comfortable in here for the rest of the evening.'

'Where is everybody?'

'Jack and Margaret had made arrangements for tonight, so Donald offered to run them home. Donald's coming back for his tea. Sit over here, love, you look like death warmed up.'

Relieved to know that Margaret wouldn't be there watching every move with those inquisitive eyes, Susan sank into the armchair closest to the fire. Billy soon had a conversation going with Graham, and Edith disappeared into the kitchen. Susan sat and gazed into the leaping flames, her thoughts in a whirl. The cat was well and truly out of the bag now. When they heard about her predicament – shame or no shame – her parents would expect her to return home. No matter how hateful it might be to her father, he would demand that she come home and face the music. If she didn't, he would wash his hands of her for ever.

With a start of surprise she became aware of sounds coming from the kitchen. Rising to her feet, she addressed Graham. 'Will you excuse me, please? I must help Aunt Edith.'

Without waiting for a reply, she joined her aunt. 'Thank God you came in,' Edith greeted her. 'I'm standing here deciding what to do for the best. Do you want to be alone with Graham? Will I get Billy in here on some pretext or other, then you and Graham can have a good old chinwag?'

'No! I know I must try to persuade him to hold his tongue about me, but not at the moment. I'm too mixed up and weepy, and the last thing I want to do is bawl in front of him.'

Reaching for her, Edith held her close. 'You really should go home now, love,' she said gently. 'He will face a barrage of questions when he gets back. You can't expect him to cover up for you.'

'I can try.' She clung tightly to Edith. 'Why, oh why, did he have to come over? I was managing so well. Now what am I going to do?'

'What about trusting him? Eh, love? Tell him the truth. Explain who the father is and why you don't want anybody back home to know. Perhaps then he will cover up for you.'

Drawing away from her, Susan said, 'You don't understand. I can't do that.'

'You're being silly. You know what they say? A problem shared . . .'

Susan shook her head. 'You don't understand.'

'You can say that again. I've noticed you've taken off the wedding ring.'

'I'm wrapped up in so many lies and half-truths that sometimes I don't know myself what's right any more. But one thing's for sure – he's not going home with the idea I'm married. If I have to go home eventually, I'll have enough explaining to do, without everybody asking questions about an imaginary husband.'

'Mm, I see what you mean.' Edith nodded to the pots bubbling away on the cooker. 'I've had these simmering for ages. It's almost ready, love. Away and tidy yourself up a bit. We'll work something out between us.'

Graham watched covertly as Donald lavished care and attention on Susan during the very appetising meal Edith had managed to conjure up at such short notice. Later, as they sat conversing by the fire, Donald shared the settee with Susan, murmuring now and then into her ear. Not enough to be intimate, but just enough to make it obvious he cared for her.

The rain continued to pour down and the wind was gathering strength. He would have to make a move soon, but he still needed another private chat with Susan. In a dilemma, he flailed about in his mind for an excuse to be alone with her. It was Edith who gave him the excuse to extend his stay.

'Graham, that's a terrible night to be on the road. Can you not stay overnight? What time is your flight tomorrow?'

'I think you're right, Edith. I'm not too sure of the road back to the airport. I'd be more comfortable driving in daylight and my flight isn't until noon. When I was looking for your house earlier on, I noticed the Traveller's Rest Inn nearby. Perhaps they will have a room.'

'You can stay here!' Edith exclaimed. 'I know it's all a mess at the moment, but the settee is comfortable. Or, if you don't fancy sleeping here, I'm sure Donald will put you up in his house.'

All eyes turned on Donald. Not knowing what Susan would want him to say, he met her eyes. She give a slight nod. This way she would be able to see Graham before he left in the morning and beg him not to reveal her secret.

'That's fine by me,' he agreed.

To their surprise, Graham accepted Edith's offer. 'Thanks very much, Donald, but if it's all right with you, I'd be glad to sleep on the settee.' He looked towards Edith. 'If you're sure it's no bother?'

'No bother at all. While you were out in the car with Susan we put up the two beds, and I have left some bedclothes out for the settee.'

Billy rose to his feet. 'In that case I don't see why we can't have a drink. I refrained from offering you one earlier, Graham, because I thought you would be driving back to Newcastle tonight.'

'What about Donald? He'll be driving,' Edith exclaimed.

'He can walk down to the village later on and phone a taxi,' Billy pointed out reasonably, and leaving the room he returned with a bottle of whiskey and some cans of beer. 'Will you get the glasses, love? I've no idea which box they're in, and there's a bottle of wine somewhere for you, and maybe Susan will have a small glass.'

The drink loosened their tongues and the evening passed pleasantly. Susan questioned Graham about all her friends back home and listened in rapture as he related all about the engagement party. 'You should have been there, Susan,' he chastised her gently. 'You were sadly missed. Everybody was asking about you.'

'Ah well, you can see how it is.' Her hand patted her stomach in a futile gesture. Regret made her voice sad.

Graham looked at her and wondered, if she had come home in that condition, would the engagement have taken place? He was far from convinced that he wasn't the father.

At half-past ten, Donald rose to go home. 'It's been a long day and I'm sure you're all tired. I'll go now and let you get to bed. I'll call up tomorrow night after work and see if I can give you a hand with anything.'

'Thanks, Donald. We'll be glad to see you.'

He turned to Graham. 'You're sure you wouldn't prefer a bed?'

'No, thanks all the same, I'll be fine on the settee.'

'I'll run away on then.'

He held Susan's eye and she responded. 'I'll see you out, Donald.'

They opened the front door and gazed out into the torrential rain. 'You'll be soaked. Take my umbrella.'

He smiled wryly. 'I think not. It would be blown inside out in no time.' He moved close and lowered his voice. 'Did I do the right thing back there, letting him think we were a couple?'

'You did the right thing,' she agreed. 'And thank you.'

Before she could move he had his arms around her and, when she looked up startled, his mouth covered hers. She stood passive – after all, it was just a good-night kiss. However, he persisted gently and against her will her lips, as if of their own volition, moved hungrily under his.

Dragging her mouth away, she covered his with her fingers. 'This will never do, Donald. There is absolutely no need to put on an act out here.'

'It's no act! Surely you realise that I care?' She shook her head despairingly and he confessed, 'I have to admit I'm frightened, Susan.'

'Frightened?'

'Yes, there's something about the way that guy looks at you. As if he had a claim on you. Is he a friend of your husband's, by any chance?'

'You're imagining things, and no, he isn't a friend of my husband's. I wish you wouldn't harp on about my husband.'

'I can't help it. And there's nothing wrong with my imagination. He acts too possessive towards you. Don't let him persuade you to go home, sure you won't? Your place is here with us. Now, away in and close the door. It's freezing out here. I'll see you tomorrow night.'

The rain battered against the window panes and the wind was fiercely relentless in its buffeting pursuit of admittance. Tired and weary in body and spirit, Susan tossed and turned, but her mind was too active to let sleep claim her. No matter what direction her thoughts took, she could find no way to persuade Graham to cover up for her. At last, in despair, she left her bed and, donning her dressing gown, quietly descended the bare stairs to the kitchen. She was pouring herself a cup of tea when Graham's voice came to her.

'Is there another cup in that pot?'

Silently, she opened the cupboard door and lifted down a mug. Filling it with tea, she nodded to the sugar bowl and milk jug. 'Help yourself.'

He added a little milk and two spoonfuls of sugar, and then, wrapping his hands gratefully around the mug's warmth, held it to his cheek. She had so far avoided looking directly at him. Now, noting that he was stripped to the waist, she exclaimed in concern, 'You must be freezing. Can I fetch you an old shirt of Billy's?'

'It's okay, I'll be warm enough. I've plenty of blankets in there. I heard someone come down and hoped it was you. We must talk, Susan.'

'I know.' She led the way into the sitting room and he followed her. Without meeting his eyes, she said tentatively, 'Graham, I have a great favour to ask of you.'

His eyes were wary, but he said, 'Fire away.'

'Please don't tell anybody I'm expecting a baby.'

'You're asking the impossible, Susan. I can't do that.'

'Why? You say you came over here on business? Well, tell them you never got down to see me, then they won't question you.'

'But why, Susan? They have to know some time.'

She was sitting hunched over the dying embers of the fire. Now she rose and, placing her cup on the mantelpiece, approached him. 'It's very important to me that no one knows.' She placed a hand on his chest and gazed appealingly at him. 'Please do this for me.'

Placing his own cup on the mantelpiece, he rested his hands on her shoulders and gazed down into her eyes. 'Susan, even if I'm not the father, I'd be willing to take the responsibility and marry you.'

She gazed at him, startled, her mouth gaping slightly. 'Don't be ridiculous! You love Alison.'

Afraid to declare his love for her – after all, it would

look as if he was stringing her sister along, and wasn't he? he derided himself – and at a loss for words, he said weakly, 'I also care for *you*.'

She shook her head in bewilderment. 'You don't know what you're saying, Graham. I don't want your pity.'

'Pity? No, not pity. Far from it! I care deeply for you.' His arms slipped around her and, receiving no resistance, gently drew her close to his body. For the second time that night she found herself in a man's embrace. He clasped her closer still, one hand pressing her cheek against his bare chest, his lips ruffling her hair. Mesmerised, she stood immobile listening to the thudding of his heart; aware of his rising passion. The memory of the pleasure that this man's hands and body could do to her sent a wave of sensual longing through her. Her response to him was swift and sweet, and she savoured it and pressed closer still. Cupping her face gently in his hands, he raised it for a kiss. His lips were more urgent than Donald's and passion heightened swiftly between them. Dismayed at her fiery reaction, she tried to break away, but, weakened by longing, her effort was feeble and went unnoticed, and the kiss intensified.

They were on the settee when she came to her senses. What on earth kind of woman am I, she thought, aghast, that I could go from one man to another and respond so readily? It was because I was hungry for affection, that's why, she consoled herself. With a mighty shove she pushed him away. He rolled off the settee and, arms around his knees, sat gazing up at her, bereft. It had been wonderful holding her close, even with the child between them; it had felt like coming home. It strengthened his resolve. He was now more than ever convinced that the child was his.

'I'm sorry. I got carried away. Again! You have that effect on me, Susan. I do care deeply for you, you know.'

'It's infatuation, and it's wrong, Graham. You're engaged to my sister. She loves you!'

'Does she? I'm not so sure about that. And, as you well know, engagements can be – and often are – broken. You need me more than she does. Alison will survive. You know that as well as I do!' He was on his knees now beside the settee. 'And it's not infatuation. I think you care more than you realise, Susan, or you would never have lost control like that. I didn't force you.'

She turned away in despair. 'I'm aware of that! No need to rub it in. It's because I'm lonely. That's all it is.'

'I don't believe that. You wanted me as much as I wanted you.'

'Graham, I don't understand your reasoning,' she cried in frustration. 'We were never meant for each other. I never noticed you back home. I was besotted by Jim Brady; still am, as a matter of fact. And you know that's the truth. That episode with you was an accident. It should never have happened.'

'But it did happen! If the baby is mine, I want to . . .'

'Hold on a minute!' she curtly interrupted him. 'Get that idea out of your head once and for all. You're not the father.' Crossing her fingers out of sight, she lied, 'Donald is going to make an honest woman of me. I just don't want everybody back home to know until I have a ring on my finger. Then they need never know it was conceived outside matrimony. You know what

Mam and Dad are like. Will you do this for me, Graham? Please?' she pleaded.

'Susan . . . How can I tell your family a pack of lies?'

'At least think about it. Please, Graham. I'd be indebted to you. Come on, get up off that and let's finish our tea.'

They sat each side of the hearth and finished their tea in silence. At last she decided he'd had enough time to think and rose to her feet.

'Well?'

He had been trying to think of a reason to persuade her to go back home with him, and now raised a startled glance. 'Well, what?' he asked, a bewildered frown on his brow.

'Oh, men!' she cried and, forgetful of her sleeping aunt and uncle, she thumped up the stairs.

Edith and Billy left the house very early next morning and a sullen Susan prepared breakfast for Graham. Determined not to make any promises he might later regret, he ate the bacon and eggs in silence.

'There's plenty of hot water if you would like a bath,' she informed him.

'Thanks, but I'll have a quick shower at the hotel.'

'Do you not think it's time you were making a move?'

A glance at his watch brought him to his feet. 'You're right. I'll just visit the bathroom and then I'll be on my merry way.'

Dressed for the road, he stood tentatively in front of her. 'Have you had time to think what you intend doing?' she asked, her eyes beseeching him.

He shook his head. 'No, I'm afraid not. Is there any

way I can get in touch with you and let you know what I decide?'

'The phone is being installed today, but I've no idea what the number will be. Can I call you?'

'If you like. At the office, please.'

He wrote his number on the pad she handed him. 'Tomorrow morning. I'll go to the office in the morning.' He sighed. 'The die will be cast, one way or the other by then.'

'Thank you. And safe journey home.'

A quick hug and he left her standing at the door in tears.

The tears continued to fall as she cleared up the breakfast dishes. In the bathroom she brushed them angrily away. She must get control of her emotions; she had a job to go to, and customers expected a bit of pleasant chitchat. Time enough for tears if Graham blew the whistle on her and she had to return to Belfast.

Chapter Seven

Graham drove carefully up to Newcastle through the heavy mist and rain, struggling with his conscience all the way. He was sorry he had been unable to reassure Susan before he left that morning, but how could he deceive Alison and her parents? There was no way he could see himself telling lies about Susan's welfare. He would never be able to keep up the pretence and would trip himself up in the process. Her silent reproach had been unbearable. Those beautiful, big grey eyes had almost swayed him. However, he had managed to stand firm, although it had pained him to see her looking hurt and tearful. Did she not realise just what she was asking of him?

Suppose he did pretend not to have seen her, and something went wrong at the birth and she died – how could he live with himself? And these things did still happen, in spite of the advancements of medicine. On the other hand, he could see her point of view. If he kept his mouth shut, she could come over later in the year, married to Donald, and no one would dare question the date of their wedding. The very idea of her married to someone else was like a knife turning in his breast. One thing he had learnt from the meeting. It had been brought home to him in no uncertain terms that he could not possibly marry Alison. Not feeling as he did about her sister.

To his dismay, while he was showering, a knock on his door informed him that the flight was delayed due to severe weather conditions at Aldergrove. He was in a dilemma. He couldn't even phone Alison and let her know of the delay! She would be wondering why he didn't ring sooner, but if he did, she would be sure to inquire after Susan and he had yet to decide what to do. What a mess! He was beginning to wish he had never come over here; better to have lived in ignorance than have this decision to make. But it was too late for those kinds of regrets. What could he say to Alison? If only he knew what to do for the best. If he followed his instincts and spoke out, would Susan ever forgive him? He might just drive her into marriage all the quicker. Donald seemed a nice enough guy, but he couldn't bear the idea of her marrying him. Especially if, as he was inclined to believe, the child was his.

It was late afternoon before it was judged safe to take off and, after tedious hours prowling about the airport, he at last boarded the plane, still undecided. As usual, as they neared Aldergrove airport, the pilot told them what kind of weather to expect. They were warned to take care on the roads. Apparently there had been heavy snow during the night in Northern Ireland and the roads were treacherous.

It was dark when they eventually landed and, after picking his luggage up, Graham walked to where his car was parked in the long-stay car park. He cleared the snow from it and placed his suitcase in the boot. A Jaguar, the car was in perfect nick and the engine fired at the first turn of the ignition. Carefully he edged it out of the car park into the slow-moving traffic. As had been forecast, the roads were still treacherous and, to make matters worse, snow was starting to fall again.

His windscreen wipers were soon having trouble in their fight to keep a space clear for his vision. He sat hunched over the steering wheel, peering ahead through the swirling snow, carefully keeping a safe distance from the car in front. The needle never passed the thirty mark, but although impatient to get home, in these atrocious conditions he was not tempted to go any faster. To his astonishment he saw in his side-mirror a Mini car pull out to overtake him. On the brow of a hill? The man must be a lunatic. They both saw the headlights come over the top of the hill at the same time. In an attempt to avoid hitting the oncoming car, the Mini driver came close to the Jaguar, clipping the front wing. Graham swung the car towards the side of the road and automatically slammed on the brakes. The wheels locked and the rear swung sideways, hitting the Mini and sending it spinning into the path of the oncoming car. Then he crashed through a hedge. The trunk of a great oak tree came rushing to meet him through the snow.

Alison sat by her mother's bedside, gently caressing her hand and whispering words of comfort to her. 'The ambulance will be here soon, Mam. You're going to be okay.' Words her mother could not hear.

But was she? Alison was frantic with worry. Was Rachel going to be okay? What had brought this on?

She had heard her parents arguing in their bedroom but had been unable to distinguish what was being said. This was nothing new; her father had a nasty tongue sometimes and seemed to save its sharpness for her mother. Susan had been on the receiving end of it before going off to England, but she had been able to face up to him.

Two hours they had been waiting now. With the heavy snow there had been a pile-up on the motorway and some accidents involving broken limbs on the slippery footpaths, with the result the ambulance service was under acute pressure. When her mother had collapsed, the doctor had diagnosed a stroke. He made her as comfortable as possible before calling the ambulance.

Her father's voice, fraught with anxiety, reached her from where he hovered in the hall. 'They're here, Alison.'

'Thank God.' Poor Dad was out of his mind with worry; was probably blaming himself. What on earth would he do if Mam died?

Descending the stairs, she was in time to hear her father ask the ambulance man, 'Where are you taking her?'

'The Mater.'

'No, you are not! I want her taken to the Royal Victoria Hospital.'

'Look, mister. Sorry and all that, but the doctor was lucky to get her a bed anywhere. Believe me, this weather is causing havoc on the roads and the hospitals are stretched to the limit.'

Seeing her father was about to argue, Alison cried, 'Dad! Mam needs attention *now*. It doesn't matter which hospital she goes to.' With these words she pushed him aside and preceded the ambulance men upstairs.

Still unconscious, Rachel was lifted gently and carried downstairs. Trevor and Alison followed her into the ambulance. At the hospital they waited impatiently while she was put to bed and examined by a doctor. Alison sat huddled in a chair and Trevor paced the floor. At last they were allowed in to see Rachel.

She lay with eyes closed. One side of her face was slightly twisted. Alison reached for her hand, which also lay twisted on the bedclothes, and stroked it gently. Her eyes sought her father's. 'Do you think she'll be all right, Dad?' Her voice broke on a sob.

Trevor gripped his daughter's shoulder tightly. 'I hope so. Oh God, I hope so. How could we manage without her?'

It was some hours later and, having been assured that Rachel was in no immediate danger and that things looked hopeful for a full recovery, they agreed to go home and return next day.

The phone was ringing as they entered the house and Alison rushed to answer it. 'It's sure to be Graham, Dad. I expected him home long ago.'

Trevor watched her eyes widen and her face take on a shocked expression.

'When did this happen? Why didn't you let me know? Of course, I'm sorry. I've been to the hospital as well. My mother was taken into the Mater today. Dad and I are just home from there this very minute. Yes. Yes, of course I'll come right away. Bye. See you soon.'

She dropped the phone in its cradle and ran to her father. His arms held her close. 'What's wrong, Alison?'

'That was Mrs Robson. It's Graham. He's been in a car crash. He's in the Royal.'

'Is he badly hurt?'

'They don't know how bad his injuries are. I'm meeting his parents at the hospital in half a hour. Will you run me over?'

'You should have something to eat first, Alison.'

'I'd rather go now, Dad. Food's the last thing on my mind at the minute.'

He released her gently. 'All right. If that's how you feel, let's go.'

Susan replaced the public phone, installed at the bottom of the market, on its hook and hurried back to the stall with an apologetic look at Vera. This was the third time she had attempted to get in touch with Graham, but to no avail. Apparently he was on holiday and had not returned to work yet. But he had said he'd be in the office today. Perhaps he would be in this afternoon – she could try then, or should she leave a message?

It being Holy Week, Vera had asked her to work the full week. 'I'm sorry about this, Vera, but I did promise to phone and find out how things are.'

'Never worry. We're not exactly rushed off our feet at the moment. Feel free to phone when you get a respite.'

In spite of many more calls, the reply remained the same: Mr Robson had not yet returned from holiday. In despair, Susan asked for his home number, but was refused it on the grounds that the staff were forbidden to give out personal numbers. What was Graham playing at?

That night, on the pretext of letting her family know

their newly acquired telephone number, Susan rang home. One way or the other she had to find out if Graham had blown the whistle on her. Here she also had difficulty making contact. After numerous attempts, she finally got through.

The phone was answered by her sister. 'Where on earth have you been?' Susan asked, highly indignant. 'I've been trying to get hold of you for ages.'

'Susan? Is that you, Susan?'

'Of course it's me. Don't you recognise my voice?'

'I'm sorry. It's just that I didn't expect it to be you. We – Dad and I – were thinking of sending you a telegram.'

'A telegram? What on earth for? What's happened?'

'Mam's had a stroke. She's in the Mater hospital. Please come home, Susan.'

So this was probably the reason why Graham wasn't at the office. He had obviously decided to keep his mouth closed about her. Or . . . dear God, was the bad news he had disclosed the cause of her mother's stroke? No! Alison would not be so calm if that was the case. She would be ranting and raving. Graham had probably decided she had no choice but to come home now; that's why he was keeping quiet. Well, he was wrong! Unless her mother was in immediate danger she would stay put.

'Susan? Susan, are you still there?'

'Yes. I'm still here. Look, I'll ring you back tomorrow and find out how things stand. Okay? We're very busy in the market. I might not be able to get the time off.'

'Susan, how can you?' Alison was aghast. 'Mam's unconscious. We need you here.'

Susan had no intention of being rushed into doing anything hasty. There was too much at stake. 'I'll phone tomorrow night, when you have more news.'

'You should come home in the morning, if you have any decency in you at all. Don't you understand? Mam's had a stroke. You should get the first possible flight over here. How am I supposed to attend two hospitals every day? Eh? Tell me that.'

Alison's voice had risen hysterically. 'Hush, calm down. Two hospitals? I don't understand. Is Dad ill, too?'

'No . . . . Oh God, didn't I tell you? Graham's car crashed on the way home from Aldergrove on Monday. He's in the Royal in a critical condition.'

Susan's knees buckled and she sank down on to the nearest chair, unable to believe her ears. 'Graham's injured? How badly?'

'He has concussion and broken ribs. He's unconscious and his spine is damaged, and God knows what else is wrong with him. They won't know for some time whether or not he'll walk again. It's awful watching him lying there. Oh, Susan, I'm going out of my mind with worry. Dad's useless. He blames himself for Mam's condition and he's fit for nothing. You've just got to come home.'

'And is Dad to blame?' Susan asked, an edge to her voice.

'Of course he isn't! They had an argument, but that's nothing new, as you well know. Susan, please . . . please, come home.'

Susan's lips tightened as she digested this information. She knew only too well how arguments went between her parents. Her mother was too soft! She let him bully and jeer at her and ended up in tears. Mam would need her. Whether she liked it or not, she had to go home.

'All right. I'll book a flight tomorrow and let you know what time it arrives. Good night, Alison.'

Alison stared blankly at the receiver as the disengaged tone purred. Susan hadn't even given her a chance to say good night. But then she must be terribly upset. Thank God she was coming home.

Trevor had come into the hall and listened to Alison's side of the conversation. 'Well? What had *she* to say for herself?'

'She's coming home tomorrow.'

Needing time to think before she blurted out her decision to Edith, Susan grabbed her coat and scarf from the rack in the hall and headed for the door.

'I'll be back soon, Aunt Edith,' she called out and was through the door before anyone had a chance to question her.

As she stormed along West Auckland Road anger was uppermost in her mind, followed closely by despair. She was angry that, after all her planning and plotting, the decision whether to go home or stay was being taken out of her hands. Then shame smote her as she pictured her poor mother lying ill in a hospital bed. How bad was she really? There was only one way to find out and that was to go over and see for herself.

And what about Graham? It would be awful if that fine man never walked again. She remembered the strength of his arms, the passion he had aroused in her, and felt like weeping. Life was so unfair. It would be such a waste if he was crippled. He would need someone strong to support him. Would Alison be able to face up to marrying a cripple? Her sister could be very selfish at times. Hopefully she would be a comfort to Graham, but Susan had her doubts.

She walked for a long time, into the countryside. It was a cold, crisp evening and in the comparative quiet, calm entered her soul. Whatever lay in front of her had to be faced up to. It was as simple as that. It wouldn't be pleasant, but the decision had been taken out of her hands, so . . . so be it. At last, with a deep sigh, she turned tail and headed home.

Donald's car was drawing up to the kerb as she approached the house. Deciding that she may as well break the bad news to him first, she motioned him to stay in the car and climbed in beside him.

One look at her face and he was all concern. 'What's wrong, Susan? You look awful. Are you ill?'

She shook her head. 'Let's go for a short drive. I need to talk to someone. Clear my brain. Just stop anywhere, Donald.'

Once out of the built-up area, in the quiet of the countryside, he drew the car to a standstill on the grass verge and turned to face her.

'What's happened that has upset you so much?'

'I'm going home tomorrow.'

Reaching across, he gripped her hands. 'You can't! I won't let you.'

'I've no choice! My mother's ill. She's had a stroke and she'll need me. Our Alison will be absolutely hopeless in a sick room.'

His grip tightened. 'Ah, Susan.'

Her eyes were bleak. 'I just hope when she sees this bump,' her gaze rested sadly on her stomach, 'it doesn't finish her off. As for my dad, he might very well show me the door. Then where will I go?'

'What about your husband? Is there any chance of you going back to him?'

He sounded so worried that she wanted to blurt out the truth, but what good would it do at this late stage? Donald might take her confession as encouragement – a sign that she cared for him – and she had enough on her plate at the moment without fending him off.

'There's no chance of that.'

His sigh was heartfelt. 'Thank God for that, at least!'

'Will you take me back now, please? I haven't told Edith yet.'

Edith and Billy were about to get into a taxi when they arrived back at the house. 'We didn't know you were coming up tonight, Donald, or you could have saved us the taxi fare,' Billy exclaimed.

'Jack phoned about fifteen minutes ago,' Edith explained. 'Margaret's in labour, so we're in a hurry down to Greenbank Hospital to lend him support. Will you keep an eye on the dinner, Susan? I put it on hold, not knowing where you'd run off to.' There was a query in the words, but Susan pretended not to notice. No need to upset Edith at the moment with her own bad news. 'Now you're here, you can finish off that pie in the oven. About another half-hour should do it. When it's ready, you have yours and give Donald some. There's plenty to go round. Just stick ours in the oven till we get back. I'll ring as soon as there's any news.'

'Give them my regards.'

'I will, love. Bye for now.'

Susan waved them off and entered the kitchen. A look at the steak-and-kidney pie and she too judged it would be another good half-hour before it was ready. The turnip was already cooked and strained and set to one side. She lit the gas under the potatoes.

Donald was watching her closely as she went about these chores. Her hands were shaking, and every now and then tremors passed through her body. Edging her gently to one side, he lowered the gas under the pots. Then, taking her by the arm, he led her into the living room. Pushing her into one of the armchairs, he poured some whiskey and thrust it into her hand . . . 'Here, drink up.'

She tried to push the glass away. 'I don't want . . .'

'Drink up.' He stood over her until she had drunk some of the whiskey, and then, taking the glass from her, placed it on a nearby coffee table. Pulling her up into his arms, he cradled her against the warmth of his body.

'I dread going home, Donald. My dad will do his nut when he sees me.'

'Then don't go!'

'I have to. I must go and find out just how bad my mother is.' Suddenly Graham entered her mind. 'I forgot to tell you. Graham was involved in a car crash. He's badly hurt.' She felt guilty. Imagine forgetting about Graham.

'Good God! When did this happen?'

'On the way home from the airport. It was snowing heavily at the time.'

'Poor Graham.'

'I know. And poor Alison. She was almost hysterical on the phone, and no wonder, with Mam and Graham both in hospital; she doesn't know whether she's coming or going. I'm afraid I was no comfort to her whatsoever. All I could think about was my own predicament.' He heard her out in silence. Glad of his understanding, she relaxed against him for some moments, then gently pushed herself free. 'I'll finish off the dinner and after we've had ours, perhaps you'll take me somewhere quiet for a drink?' He nodded and she continued, 'Edith will be upset when she hears the news. We'll let her get over the birth of her first grandchild before breaking it to her.'

Leaving a note for Billy and Edith, telling them their whereabouts, they walked down to the Traveller's Rest. In a quiet corner of the lounge Donald gripped her hand tightly. 'Listen, Susan, I've been thinking. How's about I go home with you, and you introduce me as your boyfriend. Then everybody will assume the baby is mine and your secret will be safe.'

She looked at this dear, caring man and wished with all her heart she could take him up on his offer. He would make a good, loving husband and father for some girl, but not for her. No, not for her. He deserved someone better. Still, to go home with him there to support her would be heaven. Squeezing his hand, she pushed temptation to one side. 'Donald, you really are a good man. But can't you see? That would only start up a new pack of lies. Besides, you have your job to consider.'

'It's coming up to Easter, I can easily get a few extra days off.'

'Thanks, Donald. I really appreciate your concern. But it wouldn't work out. If I have to . . . can I pretend we are close friends?'

'You don't have to pretend. We are close. I wish you were divorced, then I could propose to you – you know, put a ring on your finger.' He lifted her left hand and rubbed the ring finger. 'I've noticed you aren't wearing your wedding ring. Could that possibly mean your divorce is through and you're not saying?'

She was saved from answering him by the boisterous entry of someone through the lounge door of the pub. It was Billy. A wide grin on his face, he approached their table, obviously bursting with pride. 'I couldn't wait to tell you. It's a girl. Six pounds six. Our first grandchild. What do you think of that?'

Rising to her feet, Susan gave him a warm hug. 'That's wonderful, Uncle Billy, congratulations. And so quick, too! I'm sure Aunt Edith is thrilled to bits. Is Margaret all right?'

'She's exhausted, but glad it's all over. It wasn't all that quick. Seems she's been in labour since last night, but they knew we would be busy at the market and didn't want to worry us.'

Donald thrust out his hand and Billy gripped it. 'Congratulations, Billy. May you live long to enjoy your granddaughter. What would you like to drink?'

'Thanks, Donald, but if I start drinking now, God knows what time I'll get home and I've an early start in the morning.' He glanced at their almost empty glasses. 'Shall I wait for you? Are you ready to come back to the house?'

'Not yet, Uncle Billy. We have something to talk over.

We'll be up shortly. I'm sure you're hungry. Away and get your dinner before it's all dried up. The pie's delicious.'

'See you later, then.'

Later that evening, when all the good wishes for their little granddaughter were over, Billy fetched a bottle of fine wine. 'I've been saving this for an "occasion". And I think this is a big occasion.'

The wine was duly poured, but as they raised their glasses to toast the baby, Susan felt tears run down her cheeks. Donald put an arm across her shoulders and gave her a hug.

'What on earth's the matter?' Edith cried. 'You haven't started, have you?'

'No! No, God forbid I'd be this early.'

It was Donald who explained. 'I'm afraid Susan has had some bad news.'

A sob in her voice, Susan took over. 'Mam has had a stroke, Aunt Edith. She's in hospital. And Graham crashed his car on the way home from the airport yesterday. He's in a bad way, so you see I have to go home as soon as possible.'

Edith groped for a chair and sat down. 'Oh, my God. I can't take it in. Rachel's a young woman in her mid-forties. What on earth caused it?'

'I don't know.' The tears fell faster and the fear uppermost in Susan's mind rushed into words. 'Perhaps she was worrying about me.'

'Ah, don't say that, Susan. We all worry about our children.' Edith glanced at her husband. 'I'll have to go over with her, Billy.'

'But . . .' Billy stopped short. What he was about to say could not be said in front of Susan. It would sound so callous.

She smiled through her tears. 'It's all right, Uncle Billy. I know you can't do without her at a busy time like this. And Margaret will need her help with the baby.' She turned to Edith. 'Tell you what. You can come over later on in the year, when you're not so busy.'

'If she's very bad you'll let me know, won't you, Susan? I'll come right away, market or no market.'

'I'll phone and let you know how things stand when I find out for myself.'

'Billy.' Edith turned to her husband. 'Could you spare me for a few days when the market is closed after Easter?'

'I'll manage, love. But what about Margaret? Will she not need you?'

'Margaret will be out of the hospital by then. Once back home, she will be okay.'

Billy looked dubious but held his tongue. It was only right that his wife should go over and see for herself how her only sister was. Margaret was a young woman; she would manage. She'd just have to!

Susan booked a very early morning flight and Donald insisted on driving her to the airport. He was grim-faced as he helped her with her luggage. When the flight number was called, he gathered her close. 'Promise you won't do anything foolish.'

'What do you mean, foolish?'

'I don't really know what I mean. But don't think you're alone and be forced into something you don't want. Do you hear me? Remember I'm here if you need me. A phone call will have me on the move in no time.'

'I'll have to go now. Thanks for everything, Donald.' Gently she released her hands and with a final 'thank you' joined the queue heading through the security gate.

How she dreaded the next few hours. Would her father put her out? Her grandparents on her mother's side now lived in Enniskillen; they would be tolerant of her plight, but lived too far away to be of any use to her, while her father's parents were very strait-laced; they would frown on her wantonness, and that she could do without. She would need somewhere in Belfast to stay. Perhaps Ruth would be able to suggest somewhere. But that would mean everybody knowing her business. She would just have to play it by ear.

The flight to Aldergrove was short, but today it seemed shorter still. In no time they were told to fasten their seatbelts and soon they were taxiing along the runway and Susan prepared to meet her father's wrath.

Heart in mouth, she descended the steps from the plane. She hoped Alison would be with her father. What if her sister was unable to come? After all, she had two patients to visit every day. It must be a terrible strain on her. Susan dreaded this first meeting with her father. In her big, loose winter coat her pregnancy was not immediately obvious. She hoped they wouldn't notice until they were in the privacy of their own home.

The minute she entered the arrival lounge, Alison, with a cry of delight, swooped down on her and gripped her close. Her brows gathered together as she hugged her. Drawing back a little, she whispered, 'So it's true! You *are* expecting?'

'Yes. Be careful. I hope Dad doesn't notice until we get home.'

'Ah, Susan. He'll go berserk, so he will.'

'Do you think I don't know that? Why do you think I didn't want to come home in the first place? Hush now. Here he comes.'

Trevor nodded briefly at his eldest daughter and reached for her suitcase. Then, without a word, he led the way out of the lounge and headed for the car park.

Although he held the passenger door open and motioned for Alison to sit in front with him, she declined. 'I'll sit in the back with Susan. Bring her up to date on how things are.'

The car door closed with unnecessary force and Alison grimaced as she climbed in beside Susan.

'How is Mam?'

'She has regained consciousness and recognises us, which is a good sign. They say it's only a minor stroke and expect her to make a complete recovery.'

'Poor Mam. I can't remember her ever being ill before.'

'We popped in to see her before coming here and I told her you were on your way home. She looked so pleased.'

'What about Graham?'

'He has also gained consciousness, but he's in pain and they're keeping him sedated. He has hardly spoken at all. His parents are devastated.'

'And you? How do you feel?'

A tear escaped and ran down Alison's cheek. With a warning glance at the back of her father's head, she whispered, 'Not now. Later. We'll talk later.'

* * *

It was brought home to Susan, on the journey to Belfast, just how different her life had been for the last few months. She would miss Darlington! Over there she had been accepted for what she was; she had been taken at face value. Especially by Donald. He had been a true friend. Here tongues would wag and the finger would be pointed at her. She would be in disgrace.

She quickly left the car and hurried up the steps to her home. The confrontation with her father was imminent.

'I'll make a pot of tea and then we'll go and see Mam.' With these words Alison removed her coat and headed for the kitchen.

Slowly Susan followed her example and, hanging her coat in the cloakroom, went after her. The big clock adorning a prominent place on the wall showed it was still only eleven o'clock in the morning. 'Will we be allowed into the hospital this early?' she queried.

Alison glanced over her shoulder to reply, then swung round in amazement to gaze at her sister's bump. 'Oh, God. You're quite big, aren't you?' she whispered, her dismay apparent. 'I didn't realise . . .' Her voice trailed off. 'Dad will do his nut when he sees you.'

Not wanting to be reminded just how her father would react, Susan repeated tersely, 'Will we be allowed into the hospital this early?'

'We can visit any time we like at the moment. It's the same with Graham; although he's off the critical list now, we can still go in any time. His mother haunts the hospital. She disapproves of me because I don't do likewise. But I had Mam to think about and Dad to look after. I couldn't sit in the Royal all day. Besides, he slept most of the time and it frightened me to see him so helpless. It will be easier now you're here.' Her eyes were still fixed on the bump. 'Is it . . . is it Jim Brady's?'

'No! It's not, and I wish you'd give Jim a rest. I don't want to hear his name mentioned again.'

'When are you due?'

'I'm not sure. End of June or beginning of July.' Susan silently prayed she would go that length of time, but it was more likely to be early May. Hearing footsteps crossing the hall, she whispered warningly, 'Hush. Here's Dad.'

Susan turned to face her father as he followed them into the kitchen, a defiant tilt to her head.

His eyes raked her from head to toe and the look in them said everything. 'I knew it! You're nothing but a dirty wee slut.' He turned on his heel and left the kitchen.

'Oh, Susan, don't look like that. He doesn't really mean what he says half the time. He'll come round.'

Fighting back tears, Susan said, 'Well, that was short and sweet. I'm not really bothered what he says to me. It's those looks of his – he can make you feel so small. And as to him coming round? I don't care whether he does or not. I am only here because of Mam. He can go to hell for all I care.' A tear escaped and she brushed it impatiently away with the back of her hand. 'I suppose I should be glad he didn't order me out of the house. I'll have to watch my p's and q's and not give him any excuse to throw me out.'

At the hospital it was a quiet period. The patients had been prepared for the consultant's visit and the nurses were busy getting the wards ready for the great man's arrival. Rachel shared a small ward with an elderly patient. This woman was asleep, but Rachel lay, eyes fastened on the doorway, awaiting the arrival of her eldest daughter. Her eyes met and clung to Susan's when she at last came through the door.

Sinking to her knees beside the bed, Susan pressed her cheek against her mother's. 'Mam, Mam, I'm so sorry. Is this all my fault?'

Concern clouded Rachel's eyes and she gripped her daughter's hand tightly with her own good one and shook her head.

Glad that her mother's mind seemed unimpaired, and wanting her to know the bad news before her father arrived, Susan whispered, 'Mam, I've some bad news. I'm expecting a baby.'

Rachel's eyes sought Alison's. She understood and answered the unspoken question. 'Yes, Dad knows, and he isn't very happy about it.'

The grip on Susan's hand tightened and Susan cried, 'Don't you worry about me. I can handle Dad. Thank God, you're not as bad as I imagined you'd be. Once we get you home, we'll soon have you on your feet again. And what do you think? Aunt Edith is coming over to visit for a couple of days next week. Also, you are a great-aunt now! Jack's wife had a baby girl yesterday.'

Rachel smiled her crooked smile. It faded as she glanced over her daughter's shoulder. Turning her head to see the cause, Susan saw that her father had entered the room. Ignoring her, he bent over his wife.

'Are you feeling any better today, dear?'

She nodded, her eyes wary.

'No thanks to her!' Trevor continued with a glare at Susan. 'What do you think of all this, eh, Rachel? Our daughter's nothing but a common little slut.'

Rachel's hand clawed agitatedly at the bedclothes and, afraid he would upset her still further, Susan rose quickly to her feet. Kissing Rachel on the cheek, she whispered, 'It's great to see you, Mam. I'll be back later.'

Their next visit was to the Royal Victoria Hospital. Not waiting for their father to come out and give them a lift over, they walked down Crumlin Road to Carlisle Circus and caught a bus into the city centre. From there they got another one up the Falls Road.

During the journey, each remained lost in her own thoughts. It wasn't until they left the bus and were walking down Grosvenor Road that Alison spoke of her anxiety. 'You'll find a change in Graham. He's so thin, he seems to have shrunk, and I'm worried about the results of his X-rays.'

'What if it's bad news, Alison? What will you do?'

'I don't know. I'm terrified at the idea of being married to a cripple.'

'As long as you love him, you'll see it through.'

Panic in her voice, Alison cried, 'That's just it! I don't think I love him enough. What if I can't go through with it? What then, Susan? I'm out of my mind with worry.'

'Whatever you do, don't make any decisions yet,' Susan warned. 'Wait until you know how bad he is. You can't let him down now. That would be cruel. It could even set him back no end. He needs assurance that you'll be there for him.'

Blinking back tears, Alison led the way up some stairs and down a corridor. She motioned towards a doorway. 'He's in here.'

Graham had a small ward to himself. He lay flat on his back, his legs hidden by a blanket-covered cage, his arm in plaster. His bed was close by the high, narrow window and he was gazing blankly out at the heavy grey clouds that obscured the sky. His mind was as leaden as the sky. What was to become of him? His face in repose was very sad; a droop to the lips, thick eyelashes shadowing pale cheeks. He was unaware of them until Alison spoke. 'Look who's here to see you, Graham.'

His head swung slowly in their direction, and a smile lit his gaunt features when he saw Susan. 'You came home after all then?'

'I had no choice. I came because of Mam's illness, Graham.'

'Rachel's ill?' He looked askance at Alison. 'You never told me.'

'You were too ill! This is the first chance I've had. How do you feel, love?'

'Oh, not too bad, considering. I'll survive.'

'I'm surprised your mother isn't here.' Alison peered fearfully around as if expecting Alma Robson to pop up from nowhere.

Guessing the line of her thoughts, Graham smiled. 'She was! I made her go home. I know she means well, but she was driving me round the bend with her fussing.' He smiled at Susan. 'I'm glad you decided to come home, no matter what the reason. Your place is here with your family. You need their support at this time.'

Alison was indignant and showed it. 'You knew she was pregnant and you never said?'

'I never got the chance. Remember, I was out cold most of the time. But as I said to her, and repeat yet again. Your place is here with your family.'

'What about the baby's father? If it's not Jim Brady, who is it and why isn't he here to support her? That's what I'd like to know,' Alison cried.

Graham was quick to get his oar in. 'I'm sure the father would be only too willing to support her, given the chance.'

Avoiding his accusing eye, Susan retorted, 'I wish you'd all mind your own business! All will be revealed in due course.'

'Will it, Susan? The truth and nothing but the truth? We'll see about that. Is Donald with you?' Graham asked diffidently.

'Donald? Who's Donald?'

'A friend of mine,' Susan informed her sister. 'No, Graham. He wanted to come, but I put him off. He sends his regards, and so do Edith and Billy. Jack's wife has had her baby. It's a little girl.'

Relieved that Donald wouldn't be hanging around, Graham said, 'I'm glad to hear that. She seemed a nice girl.'

'Huh! That's a matter of opinion.'

'Graham, you have obviously met all these people, so why did you not ring and tell me about them?'

'That was my fault, Alison. I tried to persuade Graham to keep quiet about this.' She grimaced down at her stomach. 'I don't think I succeeded, though, did I?' She glanced in Graham's direction. 'You were going to blow the whistle on me, weren't you?'

'To be truthful, I really don't know what I would have done, Susan. I was in a dither, and once that tree came rushing at me, I was out for the count and remembered no more.'

'What's the latest news on your back, Graham?'

'I don't know, Alison. They took more X-rays, but they're more likely to tell my parents or you the results, than me. But enough about me. Tell me, what's the matter with Rachel?'

'The same morning you were tangling with that tree, Mam had a stroke. But thankfully, it's only a minor one and she's expected to make a full recovery.'

'Thank God for that.'

'Graham, we came straight from the Mater and I'm here empty-handed,' Susan confessed ruefully. 'Can I bring anything the next time I come to visit you?'

'I've everything I need, Susan. Just bring yourself, I'll be glad to see you.'

He was smiling foolishly at her, unable to hide his delight at her presence. Embarrassed, she glanced at her sister, but Alison seemed unaware of his reaction. Relieved, Susan said, 'It's been a busy morning, Graham. Now I've seen for myself that you're on the road to recovery, I'd better go back to the house and unpack. No need for you to come, Alison; stay and keep Graham company.'

To her dismay, Alison was on her feet in an instant. Susan had not wanted to take her away. Indeed, her intention was to leave them alone. 'I'll come with you. I've some shopping to do. You don't mind if I go now, do you, Graham?'

With a wry smile, Graham agreed, 'Not in the slightest, Alison. You'd be bored stiff sitting here. Goodbye, Susan.'

'I'll come back tomorrow, Graham. I hope you have some good news by then. So long for now.'

'Come with Alison tonight, Susan.'

'Will your parents be here?'

He nodded. 'Probably.'

She smiled wryly. 'I had better not.'

'You will have to meet them sometime, you know,' he said gently. 'After all, one way or another, we are to be related.'

She flashed him a warning look. One way or another! Was he going to make things awkward for her?

Unaware of the undertones, Alison assured him, 'I'll bring her with me tonight, Graham. We'll go to the Mater first to see Mam and then come up here. See you then, love.' She kissed him on the cheek and followed Susan out of the door.

Graham gazed bleakly after them. With each day that passed he was slipping further and further into despair. So far he had been able to hide his misery, but how much longer would he be able to conceal this terror that plagued his mind? Never to walk again? How could he bear it? To be confined to a wheelchair for the rest of his life. How could he tie a healthy young woman to a cripple? Would he now not be able to father a child? His mother was already lamenting the fact that she would probably never have a grandchild. Had the doctors hinted at this, or was she jumping the gun? Whatever the result of the tests, as soon as he was able he would release Alison from her promise to marry him. Even if he should recover completely, he knew he could not now marry Alison. No, it was Susan whose face was forever with him. If he recovered fully he would do all in his power to win her over. *If he recovered fully!* He wasn't very optimistic.

Susan and Alison decided to walk down Grosvenor Road into the town centre. Silence reigned for some time. A covert glance at her sister revealed the worry and tension that Alison had managed to hide so far. Pushing her own troubles to the back of her mind, Susan slipped her arm through Alison's and pressed it close to her side.

'Let's go round to the Ulster Milk Bar and have a cup of their wonderful coffee, and you can tell me all about it.'

Sensing her sister's urgent need to talk, Susan propelled her past the stores with their eye-catching window displays advertising their Easter wares, and straight to the milk bar on the corner of Castle Place. They sat at a secluded table and sipped at the frothy coffee. 'Come on now, tell me what's bothering you,' Susan said gently.

To her dismay, tears gathered in Alison's eyes. She blinked furiously to contain them. 'Oh, Susan, I'm devastated. I can't even sleep at night trying to picture how I'd manage to look after Graham. I'd be hopeless looking after an invalid. Bad enough if Mam was bedridden, although thanks be to God she isn't, but a *man*?'

'Aren't you being a bit premature? Graham might very well make a full recovery.'

'What if he doesn't? Eh? How will I manage?'

'He has money! He would build a house to suit his needs. Nurses would come daily to attend to him until he can look after himself. You're lucky it's only his lower limbs that . . .'

'Lucky? Are you daft?'

'I'm just pointing out that it could be a lot worse. Lots of people confined to wheelchairs live full, active lives.'

'I'd still have to help him to bed. Lie beside him every night. Would he expect to . . .' There was dread in the look she bestowed on her sister. 'You know? Indeed, will he even be able to?'

'You sound very selfish, Alison. Forget about your feelings for a minute and put yourself in his place for a change. You cared enough to become engaged to him so you must have some deep feelings for him.' Struck by a sudden thought, Susan asked fearfully. 'Have you met someone else?'

'No. There's no one in particular. To be truthful, though, before his accident I think Graham had also changed his mind.'

'I don't understand. If you were both in doubt, why get engaged?'

'It was my fault. I insisted. I knew Dad was expecting us to, and with you refusing to come home and him being so annoyed, I didn't want to disappoint him as well. Also . . .' she added shamefacedly, 'I didn't want to lose face where my friends were concerned, and they were all waiting for me to produce a ring. Mind you, Mam had reservations. I know she thought I was too flighty.'

'By the sound of it she was right. Just don't do anything rash, eh? Take each day at a time and wait and see what happens. If he recovers, your worries will be over, and if you're still in the same frame of mind, you can eventually break off your engagement later on. But until then, for goodness sake hold your tongue.'

The sensation that someone was watching her caused Susan to turn her head slowly and scan the café. Jim Brady was on his feet instantly and, leaving the tall stool at the bar, wended his way between the tables towards them.

'I thought I recognised the back of your head, Susan. When did you get home?'

'Hello, Jim. How are you?'

He leant closer. 'All the better for seeing you. You look wonderful! May I join you?' Without waiting for assent, he sat down, sure of his welcome, a delighted grin on his face. 'Hello, Alison.' The greeting was thrown in her direction without wasting a glance on her.

Alison acknowledged him with a nod. She was in a dilemma. Would Susan want her to stay put, or would she prefer to be alone with him? A slight shake of the head warned her not to go.

Jim leant across the table, his eyes devouring Susan's face. 'Are you just home for Easter or for good?' He couldn't believe she was here, sitting facing him.

'I came home because my mother is ill, Jim.'

'Oh, I'm sorry to hear that. So . . . you won't be staying?'

'That depends on circumstances.'

His attention was riveted on Susan, and Alison felt invisible. Perhaps she should go? His next words brought her to her feet. 'Susan, you will never know how I regret that last evening.' This was private! She had no right listening in on this.

'Look, Susan, I've something to do. It's two o'clock. I'll meet you at the bus stop at half past. Okay?' Susan looked at her blankly and Alison repeated, 'Right! Half an hour at the bus stop?'

The words sank in and Susan nodded. 'All right. I'll be there.'

At the door Alison looked back to wave, but Jim was gripping Susan's hands and talking earnestly to her. Neither spared her a glance.

Eyes aglow with happiness, Jim cried, 'I can't believe this is happening. I'm so glad to see you. No one would give me your address. They said you forbade them to. Why would you not let me write to you?' In his happiness the words tumbled out in a rush.

Susan couldn't take in what he was saying. If he had cared so much, why had he rejected her? Glad that the table hid her shape, she said, 'Because there would have been no point. We have nothing to say to each other. Remember, you yourself made that very plain, Jim.'

'I was stupid. A fool. Please don't make me suffer for my stupidity.' He swung his head from side to side at the memory. 'But I thought I had no choice. I couldn't see any future for us, and I didn't want to be wasting the best years of your life. But what do you think?' His eyes shone and his voice shook with excitement as he explained. 'Things have changed. Ma has got herself a fellow. Imagine! I couldn't believe it when she told me. Although why I'm so surprised I don't know. After all, she's still a young woman. She met this man just before Christmas. He's a widower with a comfortable income and they're to be married on Easter Monday. How does that grab you? He's a grand man and he's going to look after the girls' education. I'm free to do as I please.'

Her heart thumped wildly in her breast as she drank in his beloved features. At his words she smiled wanly at him. 'I'm very pleased for you, Jim.'

A puzzled look crossed his face; apprehension dampening his happiness, he stressed, 'Can't you see what this means? We can be married. I've always loved you, Susan. You must surely know that? I haven't changed. There'll never be anyone else for me. I'll marry you anywhere you like.'

A deep sadness engulfed her. If only she hadn't been so foolish, she could now have her heart's desire. 'Jim, you don't understand. It's too late for us. Much too late.'

'Have you met someone else?'

'No.'

'I don't understand. How is it too late?'

'I can't explain. Just take my word for it, it's too late. There's no going back. There's no *us* any more.'

He glanced at his watch and then out the window. 'Look, there's my mother waiting outside. I was here to meet her, but I was early, so I came in for a coffee. I couldn't believe my eyes when I spotted you. Ma's taking me to see her new home. Would you like to meet her? I'll call her in, shall I?'

'No! Please don't.' He had made to rise, but at the panic in her voice he sat slowly down again. He frowned, strong white teeth gnawing at his lower lip for some seconds, then he said softly, 'I understand. You don't want to meet her just yet. But you will see me again, won't you? Promise.'

Glad that he would be leaving the café before her, and wouldn't have to see her waddle out, she promised. 'Give me a ring and I'll meet you sometime next week. Go on. Away you go now.'

Reluctantly he rose to his feet. Still doubtful, he repeated, 'At home? Is it all right to ring you at home?'

'Yes. At home.'

Still uneasy, he repeated, 'You're not just putting me off? You will meet me, won't you?'

'Yes, if you still want me to, I promise to meet you. Look, your mother has spotted you. Go out to her.'

'There's something wrong, Susan. I know there is. Tell me, please.'

'I'll explain everything when I see you again. Okay? Please go.'

With an abrupt 'I'll ring you tomorrow', he left her.

She watched mother and son greet each other and then Jim took his mother's arm and, with a final glance over his shoulder into the café, led her away. Only then did Susan relax; his presence had kept the adrenaline pumping through her body, making her feel more alive than she had for many long months. He still had the power to thrill her. Now, his presence removed, she slumped down into her chair, a mass of quivering nerves.

She had hoped to avoid any contact with Jim while she was at home, but here she was, less than a day in Belfast, and he was one of the first people she bumped into. He obviously didn't believe she was pregnant. Why on earth had she promised to see him again? She couldn't possibly meet him in her condition. What explanation could she give him? She would have to make some excuse when he rang. How she wished things were different and they could take up where they had left off. Lost in thought, she sat on, imagining how it might have been; forgetful that Alison was waiting for her.

Chapter Eight

Alison had arrived at the bus stop at twenty-five past and now, twenty minutes later, she was stamping her feet and swinging her arms in an attempt to keep out the cold. What on earth was keeping Susan? At last, in despair she headed back to the Ulster Milk Bar, praying all the while that her sister wouldn't take a different route to the bus stop and that they'd miss each other. She needn't have worried. Susan was sitting where she had left her, the empty coffee cup in front of her and a look of misery on her face.

She came out of her reverie with a start of surprise when Alison stopped at the table. 'I'm sorry. Is it time to meet you?'

'Well past it.'

Susan started to rise, but Alison with a hand on her shoulder said kindly, 'Sit where you are. I'll get us another coffee.'

The warm liquid brought a little colour to Susan's cheeks and she apologised. 'I'm sorry. I completely forgot about the time.'

'What had Jim Brady to say for himself, and why did he leave you in such a state – and you in your condition? He should be horsewhipped.'

'You've got it all wrong! Thank God he didn't notice my condition.' She patted the table. 'This hid my bump. He was meeting his mother. When she arrived he wanted to introduce her to me, but I managed to put him off by promising to meet him next week.'

'Surely that wasn't enough to upset you?'

'No. He asked me to marry him.'

'Why, that's wonderful news . . .' The look of derision cast in her direction caused Alison to come to an abrupt halt. 'I . . . I thought you loved him!'

'I do. At least I think I do. But so much has happened I don't know whether I'm standing on my head or my heels.'

'But you will accept his proposal?'

'Don't be daft! How can I?'

A bewildered expression crossed Alison's face, then she said slowly, 'So he really isn't the father?' She smiled wryly. 'You know something? I didn't believe you.'

'I know you didn't. But now you know!'

'Then . . . who on earth is the father?'

'Look . . . if it becomes necessary, and only if it becomes necessary, I'll tell you who the father is. Until then you're wasting your breath asking.'

'Well, drink up. We'd better head home. Dad will be starving. Do you know something? That man won't even get up off his backside to make himself a bite to eat. Mam has him spoiled rotten. She waits on him hand and foot.'

'More fool she! Let's get going, then. We wouldn't want him to fade away to a shadow, now would we?'

* * *

Rachel was discharged from hospital on Good Friday, on condition that she rested completely. They had given her a brain scan and were pleased with the results. She was to return to the hospital for therapy twice a week. The stroke was a warning, the doctors tried to instil into her. She was very lucky, they said, that although still a bit shaky on her feet, she could walk. Speech therapy would in time probably give her full recovery of her voice, and meanwhile, although her speech was slurred, she could communicate quite well. The future looked very promising, but she mustn't take any unnecessary chances.

Glad to be home and in her own bed, she silently vowed to obey the doctors' orders to the letter. After all, she was soon to be a grannie and didn't want to miss out on that pleasure. Propped up on pillows, she smiled happily at her eldest daughter. 'I'm so glad you're home, Susan.'

Placing a tray across her mother's knees, Susan replied, 'I'm glad you're coming on so well. Now I want you to eat all your lunch. I'll stay with you in case you need a hand.'

Rachel's left hand was still very weak – almost useless – but as she was right-handed she was able to feed herself if the food was cut into small pieces. However, she soon indicated that she'd had enough and, pleased at the amount she had managed to eat, Susan removed the tray. 'I'll bring us both up a cup of tea and we'll have a nice little chat. I won't be long.'

This was their first time alone together and as they sipped their tea, Rachel attempted to question her.

'Mam, don't strain your voice. I know you must be

worried about me, but don't overdo it. I'll try and fill you in on how things stand. First, Dad acts as if I've been sleeping around, and I want you to know that I haven't. Honestly! I've only ever been with the baby's father.'

Although it was slurred, Susan had no difficulty understanding her mother's next question and answered as honestly as she could. 'No, I won't be marrying him. He's already engaged to someone else. Come on now, you've talked enough. Finish your tea. It's time you were having a nap. We can have another chat later.'

Rachel gripped her arm with her strong hand and managed to say in her slow, indistinct way, 'You'll stay at home, won't you?'

'Mam, that depends on a lot of things. As you can imagine, Dad's not exactly over the moon to have me here in this condition. He never speaks directly to me, and it will probably be worse when the baby comes. So let's just wait and see what happens. Okay?'

'I suppose so. You know, Susan, he can't help how he feels.'

'Oh, can't he?'

'One day I'll explain and you'll understand.' The tablets Rachel had taken with her tea began to take effect and her lids drooped towards sleep. Pulling the bedclothes over her mother's arms, Susan gently touched her cheek. 'Yes, Mam,' she whispered. 'I'll stay if I possibly can, and God help me dad if he annoys you,' she vowed. 'I'll swing for him.'

Susan examined herself in the full-length mirror and sighed. She was dressed for outdoors, but even the loose coat now failed to hide the fact that she was pregnant. Alison sat on the bed watching her.

'You should have warned him on the phone what to expect,' she chided. 'He's bound to get one hell of a shock when he sees you.'

'I tried to put him off, but he wouldn't take no for an answer.'

'He might have, if you'd told him the truth.' Alison tilted her head inquiringly. 'In your heart, are you maybe hoping he will say it doesn't matter and he still wants to marry you?'

'Huh! Chance would be a fine thing.'

'I still can't believe you let this happen to you. I would have thought you'd be the last person to let a man take advantage of you.'

A harsh laugh escaped Susan's lips. 'You'd be surprised how things can happen. Indeed, you would be very surprised.'

Agog with excitement, Alison pleaded, 'Well, tell me! I'm near dead to know! Help me to avoid the pitfalls.'

'That's just it. We can only look out for ourselves, and I failed miserably.'

Jim Brady was a bundle of nerves as he waited for Susan at the corner of Castle Street. When he had phoned on Wednesday she had done her damnedest to put him off. Offering all kind of excuses, from her mother's illness to needing time to herself. Only the threat that he would come to her home had made her relent and agree to meet him. He stood to attention when he saw her hurrying along towards him, dark curls lifting in the breeze and cheeks glowing pink with the cold. She looked wonderful. Absolutely wonderful. How he had missed her!

A frown puckered his brow as she drew closer; she had put on a lot of weight. Shock coursed through him as comprehension dawned. Good God! So it's true. She really is pregnant . . . his Susan.

Susan stopped in front of him and met his accusing gaze.

'Are you . . .' His voice trailed off.

She tossed her head and looked him straight in the eye. 'Yes, I am. Do you want me to pass on by, or are we going to the pictures as planned?'

At a loss for words, he simply looked her up and down in amazement. After bearing his scrutiny for some moments, she turned and started to retrace her steps. He was instantly beside her.

'I say . . . I'm sorry. You took me by surprise. Why didn't you tell me?'

She shrugged. 'Perhaps I wanted to see the shocked expression on your face when you finally got the message.' Her lips tightened and her eyes scorned him. 'I certainly wasn't disappointed.'

He took her gently by the arm and drew her to a standstill. 'If we're going to the Ritz, we're going in the wrong direction.'

'Are you sure you want to go?' She was at a loss now over what to do. 'I honestly never thought of the position I was placing you in. Suppose someone sees us and gets the wrong idea. What then?'

He shrugged. 'Too bad! I never was one to care what anyone thought, so let's get going or we'll miss the start of the big picture.' A grin showed his even white teeth.

'Now that would annoy me,' he assured her, and led her along Donegall Place in the direction of the Ritz.

She could feel him giving her covert glances but was unable to think of anything to say. His futile attempts at conversation petered out for lack of support and the journey across town was conducted in comparative silence.

They joined the queue that was already wending its way into the auditorium and were soon settled in their seats. In the darkness of the cinema he was very aware of the bulk of her sitting next to him. He remembered how slim she had been not so long ago. How he had slipped his arm around her and held her as close as the arm of the plush-covered seats allowed, revelling in the passion she could so easily arouse in him. Now he had no inclination at all to hold her. This attitude dismayed him. Was he being fickle? After all, this was the same girl he had courted and asked to marry him. The girl he still dreamt of every night. But, to be fair on himself, she *was* carrying another man's child, and by the look of her it must have happened shortly after she had offered herself to him. Had he had a lucky escape? Was she really that promiscuous?

Susan could imagine the drift of his thoughts and tears smarted her eyes for times lost. What had she done so wrong in her short life that one lapse had left her pregnant and her life in ruins? One mistake – one! – had ruined everything. In the dark, warm intimacy she longed for him to hold her hand, to show he still had some feelings for her, but he sat rigid, as if afraid of accidentally touching her arm.

The film seemed to go on for ever, but at last to her

intense relief it was over and they left the cinema. March was certainly living up to its reputation and going out like a lion, with sharp winds penetrating through to the very bone. Shivering, she pulled her coat closer around her and on the pavement faced Jim with a bright smile. 'Thank you for a lovely evening. I was glad to get away from the house for a few hours. As you can imagine, my dad is far from happy with me. To be truthful, I'm surprised he allowed me to stay at home.'

'He probably knows when he's on to a good thing. He knows you will look after your mother hand and foot.' He took her hand. 'Susan, I apologise for hounding you the way I did. I had no right! But I had no idea. Oh, I was told you might be pregnant . . . Indeed, Alison even accused me of being the father, but I couldn't take it in. I thought there must surely be some mistake. I just couldn't believe it was true.' He paused as if the enormity of it still confounded him. Then he asked tentatively, 'Do I know him? Have you set a date for the wedding?'

Ignoring the first question, she said, 'There isn't going to be a wedding. At least, not for me. Just think, Jim. I'll be the lowest of the low, an unmarried mother. Alison and Graham got engaged at Christmas, but they haven't set the date yet, what with Graham being in hospital.' She watched him digest these words. Which would catch his attention most? Graham's plight or her own? Graham won.

'Graham's in hospital?'

'Yes, he was involved in a car crash last Monday. I believe the weather was terrible here last weekend.'

'It was indeed. A lot of heavy snow! The road conditions were atrocious.'

'Well, Graham was over in England last week . . .'

'Visiting you?' he interrupted suspiciously.

Fear squeezed her heart. Hadn't she known Jim was no fool? 'No. Why would he visit me? As it happens, he was over in Newcastle on business and, on his return on Monday, on the journey home from Aldergrove his car was caught up in a collision with two other cars. I don't know the ins and outs of it, just that Graham and another man were badly injured and a man and woman were killed.'

'Thank God Graham survived.'

'Indeed! He was very lucky. The car was a write-off.'

'That beautiful Jag? That must have hurt more than the injuries.'

'Wrong again. They don't know if he'll ever walk again, let alone drive. He must be in a terrible state, but he's putting a brave face on it. Look, I'll have to go, Jim. Remember, times have changed.' Her smile was strained as she admitted, 'I'm in no condition to be running for the last bus.'

'Ah.' He sighed audibly. 'Those were the days, eh, Susan? I prayed they'd last for ever.'

'So did I,' she echoed sadly. 'So did I.'

'I'll walk to the bus stop with you.' Reluctantly she fell into step beside him, loath to prolong the agony, wanting to lick her wounds. After a short silence he continued, 'Do you know something? I also got promotion at work. I thought life was smiling on me for a change. I pictured us living happily ever after, but now this . . .' He gestured vaguely at her bump, then cried in anguish, 'Why, Susan? Why the big rush? Could you not have waited a while? Was that act so important to you? I thought you cared for *me!* I can't believe you rushed to someone else right away. By the look of you, you can't have waited any length of time.'

Hearing the hurt and bewilderment in his voice, she cried, 'I can't explain, Jim. It wasn't like you think. You wouldn't want to hear how foolish I've been.'

'Try me.'

She shook her head. 'Least said, soonest mended.'

'Why won't this guy marry you?'

'He has offered, but he isn't free. There would be a terrible scandal and I couldn't do that to my parents. It's bad enough as it is.'

They were nearing the bus stop, where a queue had formed, and he drew her to one side. 'A married man? I don't believe it!' he cried incredulously. 'You rushed into the arms of a married man? You would never be that stupid.'

Afraid he might put two and two together and guess the truth, she nodded. It was best if he thought a married man was responsible. 'These things happen, Jim.'

Jim pondered on her words. It saddened him to think that she must have been seeing this other man when she was dating him. There was no other explanation. 'And if he wasn't married, would you marry him?' he queried.

'If he was free I might, for the sake of the child. Look, here's my bus. Thank you once again for a lovely evening.'

Against his better judgement he gripped her arm. 'I'll come with you.'

'That won't be necessary,' she cried in alarm. Tears were threatening and she was determined that he wouldn't see her break down. He ignored her plea.

'I want to. To tell you the truth, I'm finding it hard to make the break.'

He paid the fares, but when he would have hustled her upstairs, she declined, saying the climb would be too much for her, and chose a seat near the front of the bus where private conversation would be impossible. He was finding it hard to make the break! These words warmed her heart and helped her get a grip on her shaky emotions.

At the corner of the street, in the shadow of the hedges, she cringed with shame when she recalled their last encounter there. She felt degraded. How could she have been so wanton? So shameless! But she had loved him. Was so sure her love was returned, she had thrown caution to the wind. Was he remembering too, and thinking she had loose morals? How could he think anything else, with her a short time later the size of a house! In a voice choked with emotion she said, 'Thanks again for a lovely evening, Jim. Now I really must go. Me dad will be wondering where I am.'

Once again a hand on her arm delayed her. 'Susan, we can't just part like this. I feel at a loss. Can't we remain friends? See each other at least now and again?'

Her heart raced wildly and her thoughts went into overdrive. If they could remain friends, then once the baby was born and she was slim and attractive again, perhaps she would be able to win him back. Was there hope for her yet? Common sense prevailed. It would be foolish for them to see each other again and give food for idle gossip. It wouldn't be fair to him.

She shook her head. 'It wouldn't work out, Jim. Who knows, perhaps once the baby is born and the dust has settled, we might run into each other again. Until then, it's better if we don't see each other. So please, Jim, let me go. I've enough on my plate without worrying about you popping up.'

Taking her face between his hands, he gazed into the beautiful, haunted eyes and whispered, 'I wish with all my heart that things were different. I can't believe we have no future, Susan, but I see what you mean. At the moment I would be an embarrassment to you. Perhaps later.' A gentle kiss was pressed on the trembling lips and he left her gazing tearfully after him.

Cold and windy though it was, Jim decided to walk home. His mind was in turmoil. If only he hadn't rejected her all those months ago, they would be in a position to marry now. But he had rejected her advances, and curtly. He would be the first to admit that it could have been handled better. But he had been afraid of taking advantage of her! Still, someone else had done just that, and obviously without taking precautions. If she had really cared for him, could she have turned for solace to someone else so quickly? No! She must have known this other man. They must have had some kind of a relationship going, whilst she was seeing him. There was no other excuse for her actions.

Did he still hope to marry her? He was still very much attracted to her, but did he want her for his wife now? He was too confused to tell. After the baby was born perhaps they could take up where they had left off. But . . . what about the baby?

* * *

To cool her emotions, Susan went for a walk along the silent avenues. The rain from the wet hedges blew on her face and she welcomed the coldness. She felt in a fever. Oh, Jim, Jim, what have I done? she lamented.

It was late when at last she quietly entered the house. Her father came out from the lounge and faced her. 'Where have you been?'

She wanted to tell him to mind his own business, but bit on her tongue, afraid to agitate him. 'I was at the pictures.'

'Till this time of night?' he cried in disbelief. 'Who with?'

This time her tongue would not be stilled. 'That's none of your business.'

His lips tightened and his nostrils flared. 'What you do while living under my roof is very much my business. For a start, you'll keep decent hours! You've disgraced us enough already.'

Again her tongue would not be stilled. Stretching her arms wide, she stuck out her stomach even further. 'Look at me, Dad! What do you think I was doing in my condition?'

'Huh! I couldn't make a guess. If I live to be a very old man, I'll never understand you. You're not in the least like your sister.'

The temper drained from her. She couldn't afford to antagonise her father any further. 'You're right,' she agreed sadly. After all, she was unlikely to be out late again, so why get her dad's hump up. 'I was out with an old friend. It was a one-off. It won't happen again. Is Mam asleep?'

'I doubt it! She's lying up there worrying about you.'

'Oh, I am sorry. I'll go up and say good night. Set her mind at rest.' She climbed the stairs, glad to have avoided a confrontation.

The worried look on her mother's face saddened Susan. She must watch her step where her father was concerned and not cause her mother any more distress. 'Can I get you anything, Mam?'

'No. Now I know you're home I can take my tablets and maybe get some sleep.'

'Mam, you're exhausted. You mustn't wait up for me.'

'I wouldn't normally, but your father has been acting a bit strange lately and I don't want you two at each other's throats.' Rachel struggled to raise herself on an elbow.

'Here, let me give you a hand.' Placing an arm gently around her shoulders, Susan tenderly raised her mother up sufficiently to put the tablets in her mouth and assisted her in washing them down with a drink of water sitting ready on the bedside table. Then, fluffing the pillows, she settled Rachel down for the night. 'Good night, love. See you in the morning.'

'Susan.' Rachel beckoned her down and, when she leant over, with her good hand gently touched her daughter's hair. 'Susan, I'm worried. You never talk about the baby – you do want it, don't you?'

'Of course I do.' Susan was nonplussed, but realised that her mother had hit the nail on the head. She never mentioned the baby. Indeed, she tried not to think of it. Time enough for that when it was born. She shrugged negatively. 'I suppose it's because I've had an easy pregnancy and so many other things to worry about.' She smiled reassuringly at her mother. 'I have made some plans, you know. I've a drawer full of baby equipment over in Darlington. I suppose, now I'm home, I don't want to rub me dad's nose in it.'

'You should see the doctor, Susan. After Easter you really would need to get booked into the hospital.'

'I'm already booked into Greenbank Hospital over in Darlington. After all, I don't know whether I'll be here for the birth.'

Alarmed now, Rachel cried, 'But you said you'd stay here.'

'I know, Mam. I know! Please don't get upset. I have to play things by ear. You know yourself that Dad's not too happy about me living here in my condition. It's bad enough now, but what will it be like when the baby comes along, eh? When the neighbours have an excuse to stop me in the street and inquire after its health and try to find out who the father is. If it proves too much hassle for Dad, I'll have to go. I wouldn't wish that on either of you. Aunt Edith really does make me feel at home, so you needn't worry. I'd be happy staying with her.'

'While there's breath in my body, you will always be welcome here. It is your home too, you know! I'll have a quiet word with your father.'

Hearing footsteps on the stairs, Susan whispered, 'But not tonight, Mam. Promise you'll leave it for a while. It will be better for all concerned.'

Seeing the wisdom of her words Rachel nodded her head. 'All right. Now away to bed.'

'Good night, Mam.'

Susan was never to learn what her mother said to her

father, but things took a sudden change for the better. Trevor didn't go out of his way to speak to her, but neither did he ignore her completely or constantly find fault and the atmosphere over Easter weekend was quite amicable.

Her mother insisted on talking about the baby. Lamenting the fact that she was unable to knit for her first grandchild, she phoned and arranged for an exclusive shop in town to send her a catalogue of all their baby clothes and nursery ware. From this many clothes were selected, until Susan cried out in despair that one baby would be unable to use so many outfits. A beautiful cradle was also ordered, and Susan gasped when she saw what it would cost and tried to talk her mother out of buying it, but in vain. Nothing would be too good for her first grandchild.

Names were often discussed and there was much laughter as some outlandish ones were suggested and then discarded. Susan was at last able to think of the baby she carried. It was great not to worry too much about the future; not with her mother behind her. Her only real worry now about having the baby in Belfast was . . . who it would look like.

To Susan's amazement, her father made no outward objections to all the plans her mother was making, and she began to look to the future. Should she ring her boss, Mr Kennedy, and find out how things stood at work, and whether there would still be a position for her after the baby was born? She decided it would be worth a try. It would be nice if she had a job to go back to.

* * *

Edith's arrival on the Tuesday of Easter week brought great excitement to the household. Ideally, Susan would have accompanied her father to the airport to meet her, but Trevor made it obvious that he would prefer Alison's company, so Susan remained at home to keep her mother company. However, the minute the car stopped in the driveway, Susan was there gripping her aunt close.

'It's wonderful to see you again, Aunt Edith. I've missed you so much. How's everyone back in Darlington?'

'And I've missed you too, love. Everybody's fine! They all send their regards.'

'Look here!' Trevor said tersely. 'I'll put Edith's case up in the spare room. Don't keep her standing in the cold, Susan, or your mother will be out here, too.'

Tired of waiting, Rachel had indeed ventured to the door. Edith quickly climbed the steps to the house and the sisters eyed each other at arm's length. 'You look great,' Edith exclaimed. 'I expected an invalid.'

'I'm coming along fine, except for this.' Rachel motioned towards her left arm.

'I'm glad to see you looking so well.'

'You look wonderful too, Edith. And how's that big husband of yours?' Rachel had always had a soft spot for Billy Devine. He had the ability to make her laugh – something Trevor seldom did.

'The same as usual. Wouldn't hurt a fly. By the way,' Trevor was descending the stairs and, with a twinkle in her eye, Edith informed him, 'Billy sends his best regards, Trevor.'

Knowing full well that she was taking the mickey, he

ignored her remark and growled, 'Will you all come inside and close that door before we freeze to death'.

They moved into the hallway and, closing the front door, Susan edged them towards the lounge. 'Let's get you two settled. You can have a long natter while Alison and I make some lunch.'

Sitting on the settee, Rachel said fondly, 'Susan tells me you have a stall in the market, Edith.'

'Yes, and we're doing very well, I'm happy to say.'

'I'm glad for you. Billy has the right disposition for dealing directly with the public. So do you, for that matter.'

'I was a bit doubtful at first, you know. Didn't want to risk using our savings, but Billy talked me round to his way of thinking. Now we're doing so well I'm glad he did. I'm sure Susan told you we've bought a new house?' Edith lifted an eyebrow and, receiving a nod of confirmation, continued, 'Well, we have also just last week invested in a brand-new van. What do you think of that?'

'That's wonderful news, Edith.' It was Trevor who answered her. 'About time Billy gave you some kind of a decent life.'

Greatly affronted, Edith cried, 'I beg your pardon? I'll have you know that I've never wanted for anything in all the years I've been with Billy Devine.'

'Are you trying to tell me you don't regret running off with a married man? Cutting yourself off from family and friends. Huh! For a Catholic into the bargain?'

'I can honestly put my hand on my heart and say I've never had a day's regret.'

'Hmm! Are you still living in sin, then?'

'Oh, don't be so old-fashioned! Besides, it's none of your business, Trevor Cummings, but for your information, Billy and I got married years ago, after the death of his wife.'

'Poor woman. You probably sent her to an early grave.'

In spite of herself Edith's voice rose shrilly. 'No. She died of cancer. We had nothing whatsoever to do with it,' she informed her brother-in-law with a glare. He was going too far!

During this discourse Rachel had tried to make her voice heard, but in vain. Trevor seemed determined to insult Edith. Catching sight of her sister's anguished look, Edith joined her on the settee.

'Don't pay any attention to us, Rachel. You know what we're like when we get together. It's just a bit of banter, isn't it, Trevor?'

Her brother-in-law had the grace to look ashamed as he became aware of his wife's distress. 'Of course it is! Don't upset yourself, love. Would you like a glass of sherry before your lunch, Edith?'

'That would be lovely, Trevor. How is your business doing in the present climate?'

'Not bad. Not bad at all.'

To the relief of all, Alison put her head round the door and announced that lunch was ready. In the dining room the tension eased as the conversation became general. Relieved, Rachel inquired about Edith's new granddaughter.

'She's a wee beaut, so she is. They have named her Angela because she looks like a wee angel.'

'Hah! There speaks the doting grandmother,' Trevor said drily.

'Just you wait and see. You'll be exactly the same when Susan's baby is born,' Edith assured him.

'I don't think so. It will be a wee bastard, after all. So how could anyone in their right mind be proud of that?'

Shock struck them all dumb. Susan kept her head bent over her plate to hide the tears that threatened to fall. She willed someone to say something. Anything to break the tension. It was her mother who broke the ghastly silence.

'Well, I for one will be more than proud to welcome my grandchild and it will live here in this house with its mother, as long as Susan wishes to stay,' she cried with a defiant look in her husband's direction.

Edith waited until Trevor looked up, and then, catching his eye, she upbraided him. 'Do you know something, Trevor? You are a nasty bully. You miss out on so much with your false puritan ways. Because we know you're not as good as you make out to be, don't we? You were a Jack-the-lad in your younger days. Weren't you?'

Colour flooded his face and a sneer twisted his mouth. 'No matter what you may say, this child is a bastard. There's no getting away from that!' Crumpling his napkin into a ball, he threw it on his plate and, pushing his chair away from the table, left the room.

Later that day, when Rachel was having her afternoon nap, Edith expressed the desire to take a trip into town to see all the changes that had taken place since her last visit. Declining a lift from Trevor, who was in the doghouse since his remarks at lunchtime, she and Susan headed for the bus stop. Alison accompanied them on her way to visit Graham.

'I was sorry to hear about Graham's accident, Alison. Coming on top of your mother's stroke, it must have been very traumatic.'

'It was, Aunt Edith. I can assure you, I didn't know whether I was on my head or my heels. You met Graham, didn't you?'

'Yes, and I found him a very nice young man.'

'Oh, yes, he's that all right,' Alison agreed with her. 'Every parents' idea of a perfect son-in-law. But I'm a bit annoyed with him. He never even phoned to say he had managed to get down to see Susan.'

'I think he got a bit of a shock when he did see her,' Edith said soothingly.

'No matter! We're engaged to be married. He should have let me know.'

They had reached the bottom of Castle Street, where Alison was leaving them to catch a bus up the Falls Road to the hospital.

'Will it be all right if I come up to see Graham, after we've had a walk round town? Would I be intruding?' Edith asked tentatively.

'Of course you won't be intruding. I'm sure he'll be glad to see you. Will you come too, Susan?'

'All right. You can wait with Graham and come home with us.'

'Not if his mother's there, I won't,' Alison said with a grimace. 'If she's there I won't stay long.'

They left her and headed for the big stores. As they went from shop to shop Edith tried to lift the gloom that had enveloped her niece since her father's remarks at the dining table. 'Don't pay any attention to your dad, Susan. He won't be able to resist the baby once it's born.

Nobody can resist a wee baby. Especially when it's their own flesh and blood.'

'Still, he's right in what he says. It's what everyone else will be saying behind my back. It's not fair to the baby, either, not having its father's name.'

'If it's going to worry you, love, come back to Darlington with me. Mind you, there will be those over there who will call it a bastard as well, you know. My daughter-in-law, for one, although I don't think you will worry about the likes of her.'

'I certainly won't. Has she been taking my name in vain then?'

'Only if Donald is there. She tries to make him admit he's the father and says he should make a honest woman of you before the child is born. She's just winding him up. However, she had better watch her step. I think our Jack's getting a bit fed up with the way she taunts Donald.'

'And what has Donald to say about all this?'

'He says he would be only too willing to marry you, but you won't have him.'

'Dear Donald, he's too kind for his own good.'

'He really cares about you, Susan.'

'I know he does. But we're just very good friends, that's all. We're not in love with each other.'

'Sometimes that's the best basis for a happy marriage.'

'Not for me and Donald. It wouldn't be fair to him. Does Margaret see much of him?'

'Not to my knowledge. But then I'd be the last to know, wouldn't I? Besides, where would she get the time, what with the baby and all?'

'She's still very fond of him, you know.'

'Yes, I'm aware of that. But thank God we both know where his interest lies. You could do a lot worse, Susan. He's more than fond of you.' Receiving no answer, she continued, 'I wish our Jack would put his foot down. Billy's forever warning me to keep my nose out of their affairs, but I don't want to see Jack hurt again.'

Susan wasn't too sure where Donald's affections lay. Without her as a buffer against Margaret's wiles, who knew what might happen? But she couldn't add to Edith's worries by mentioning this to her. 'I'm sure Margaret realises how very lucky she is to have you for a mother-in-law. She won't want to do anything to alienate you.'

'I can only do my best. Margaret isn't an easy person to get close to.' Recalling Alison's remarks about Graham's mother, Edith asked, 'Does Alison not get on with her future mother-in-law?'

'Well, I don't really know. I think it's them being confined in the hospital ward together for long periods. Alison has got a couple of weeks compassionate leave off work on account of Mam, so it will probably be easier when she returns to work. Graham's mother expects too much of her. He's an only child and his mother haunts the hospital. They're bound to get on each other's nerves.'

'It must be awful for his parents watching him lying there. How's he coming on?'

'I'm not sure. He seems to be progressing favourably, but they still don't know whether or not he'll walk. I'm sure he's worried sick, but you wouldn't think it to look at him. He puts a brave face on it.'

* * *

Later that afternoon it was with apprehension that Edith followed Susan into the small private ward now occupied by Graham at the Royal Victoria Hospital. The idea of a strong man like Graham lying helpless tugged at her heart strings. She was also wary of meeting his mother. The poor woman must be devastated. She could imagine how she would feel if it was her Jack. What did one say to his mother? A quick glance showed that Graham's mother wasn't present and she breathed a sigh of relief. But neither was Alison.

Clasping her hand between both of his, Graham cried, 'Edith! It's kind of you to visit me, and you only here for a few days.'

'It's a pleasure to see you, Graham. Billy and Donald sent their best wishes. Where's Alison?'

'She's nipped down to the hospital shop to get me a box of tissues. She won't be long.'

'Where is this shop? I wanted to buy you something in town, but Susan said you would be annoyed if I did. But I really would like to.' She flashed her niece a reproachful look. 'Is there anything in particular that you'd like, Graham?'

'I wouldn't mind a bottle of mineral water, Edith, if it's not too much bother.'

'Of course, it's no bother at all.'

'The shop is on the next floor up. You can't miss it, so I'm told. It's near the head of the stairs.'

'No doubt I'll find it. Is there anything else you need?'

'No, thank you.'

Edith quickly left the room and Susan looked at Graham in amazement.

'I know! I know what you're thinking, and normally

I wouldn't ask anyone to trek to the shop to buy me anything, let alone a visitor from England. But this is a God-sent opportunity. I couldn't let it pass. Do you realise I haven't had one minute alone with you since you came home? Please come closer, I want to talk to you.'

Slowly she approached the bed. Before she was aware of his intention, he reached for her hand and gripped it tightly. 'Susan, I can't stop thinking about you.'

'Graham, this will never do! You're upset. You don't know what you're saying. It's because you're lying here with all different wild ideas running through your mind. Ideas that have no foundation whatsoever.' She struggled to release her hand, but he clung on desperately.

'How come I don't believe you?'

'Well, it's the truth! And I've done all I can to convince you.'

'In vain, I'm afraid. I still don't believe you.'

At her wits' end, her voice rose shrilly. 'Nevertheless, it's the truth.'

'Susan, I should never have got engaged to Alison. It's you I want. Even if the child isn't mine.'

Angry now, she snapped, 'Let go of my hand. They'll be back any minute.'

Her tone of voice brought him to his senses and he relaxed his grip. 'I'll let go if you promise not to run away.'

Hearing footsteps approaching she whispered, 'I promise.'

Reluctantly he let go of her hand and she quickly put some distance between them.

The footsteps passed and he said softly, 'Alison told

me Jim Brady has asked you to marry him.' She nodded, but didn't bother to inform him that that was before Jim knew about the baby. He continued, 'Susan, please don't do anything rash. I feel so helpless lying here. I beg God every day to grant me the power of my legs that I might be in a position to pursue you.'

Alarmed, Susan whispered furiously, 'Graham, stop this nonsense! You have no right to speak like this.'

'Are you going to marry Jim?'

'What I do is none of your business. You're engaged to Alison! I don't understand why you're acting like this. But no, I'm not going to marry Jim, if it makes you feel any better.'

'Please don't be angry with me, Susan. I can't bear it when you're cross.'

'Well then, behave yourself!'

To appease her, he quickly changed the subject. 'What do you think? Dad has had his study turned into a bedroom for me. He's arranged for a therapist and a nurse to come in every day, so that I can go home. I'll be glad to get away from this place. They're letting me out on Saturday. You'll visit me at home, won't you?'

Beside herself with worry, she hissed, 'Not if you behave like this, I won't.'

'I promise to be good.'

'I wish I could believe you. Hush,' she warned as he opened his mouth to answer her. 'Here they are now.'

Edith came in first with a huge bunch of flowers and a bottle of mineral water.

Embarrassed, Graham chastised her. 'Edith, they're beautiful, but you shouldn't be spending all your money on me.'

'I'm glad to.' She looked vaguely around the room. 'What will I do with them?'

'I'll show you where the sluice room is,' Alison volunteered, and to Susan's dismay she was once more left alone with Graham.

'Susan, come a bit closer. I don't mean to annoy you, but I feel so helpless lying here.'

Remaining where she was, she said, 'Graham, keep your voice down, for goodness sake. How can you go on like this? You're not being fair to Alison. She's desperately worried about you.'

'I know she is! And I feel such a traitor. I've offered her her freedom, you know, but she won't hear tell of it. So what else can I do? As for keeping my voice down . . . How can I, when you insist on standing away over there? Come a bit closer.'

'If you're sure you don't love Alison, and it's not just this silly obsession you have, then make her listen to reason.'

'Can I tell her the truth? You know . . . about the baby? That would make her sit up and take notice.'

'Don't you start that nonsense again!' she cried, tears of frustration filling her eyes.

'Start what again?' Alison asked as she entered the room holding the flowers. Placing the vase on the bedside locker, she looked inquiringly at her sister. 'Mm?'

Susan's heart was in her mouth. Edith was eyeing her with a quizzical expression on her face. Just what had been said? What had they heard? She couldn't think straight. Graham came to her rescue.

'She was chastising me. I was going on and on about

hating this place. You will all be glad to hear they are letting me go home on Saturday. I think they're glad to get rid of me and my constant whining.'

Diverted, and with a gasp of relief Alison sat on the side of the bed. 'Why, that's wonderful news, Graham, so it is. But how will you manage?'

'Dad has had the study converted to suit my needs and the hospital is lending me a wheelchair. I want to buy one of my own, but they insist I wait a while. They seem to think it might not be necessary.'

'That's good news, Graham. It means they think you might be able to walk again. Oh, I can't tell you how pleased I am to hear this.'

He hit the top of his thigh with a fist. 'I find it hard to believe, with these two useless things lying here. But enough of that! Time will tell.' He gave all his attention to Edith. 'Susan tells me you have some snaps of Jack's baby. Did you bring them along to show me?'

Susan had told him no such thing and stood silent, amazed at his ingenuity.

'I sure did.' With a pleased smile Edith plunged into her large handbag. Alison leant forward to adjust the collar of Graham's pyjama coat, and while the two women were so occupied Susan took the opportunity to give Graham a warning look above Alison's head. He just gave her a cheeky wink in return. Obviously he thought he had the upper hand.

It was raining heavily when they left the hospital and they decided to take a taxi home. Whilst waiting for it to arrive, Susan was very aware of the speculative looks her aunt was giving her. She had been afraid that Alison might ask embarrassing questions, but was thankful her sister apparently had not picked up on Graham's remarks. Of Edith she was not so sure, but to her relief nothing was mentioned.

It dismayed her the attitude Graham was taking. He seemed determined to make her admit the truth. She wished with all her heart that she had not visited the hospital today. By her foolishness, she appeared to have set things in motion and who knew where they would end? It appeared that Graham was willing to throw discretion to the winds, and she couldn't take a chance. It looked as if she would have to return to Darlington. If she didn't, Graham would keep on trying to wear her down and a scandal would be unavoidable. It was her mother's health that worried her most. She must break the news gently to her. Rachel was doing so well; was avidly looking forward to the birth of her grandchild. What if it set her back or caused another stroke? It didn't bear thinking about! To have that on her conscience would be unbearable. But wouldn't hearing that the baby was Graham's be an even greater shock?

Susan decided to have a word with her father, get him to explain to her mother that she must return to England with her aunt. He would be glad to be shot of her. If it meant her leaving the house, she could depend on him to win his wife round to their way of thinking. It was difficult to get him alone, but at last the opportunity presented itself. After dinner that night, declaring, to no one in particular, that he must examine the summer house and see what would be required to make it habitable for the summer months, he left the house and headed for the bottom of the garden.

Waiting until the others were otherwise occupied, Susan saw her chance and, leaving the house via the French windows, stealthily made her way down to the summer house.

Trevor had examined the roof of the structure; no sign of leaks. It appeared in good condition and, with a pleased smile, he turned his attention to the windows. If he was surprised that Susan came seeking him, he managed to conceal it admirably.

He frowned in her direction and said, 'I think we'll get away with a lick of paint this year.'

'That's good news.'

There was silence for some moments, as he continued his examination. At last, satisfied that he was right and only very minor repairs were required, he smiled wryly at her. 'Come over here and sit down.' When she had obeyed, he said, 'I imagine you have a reason for following me out here?'

'Yes, Dad. I've a favour to ask of you.'

'Yes?'

'I would like to return to England with Aunt Edith, but I'm afraid of upsetting Mam. Will you break it gently to her?'

To her amazement his face flooded with colour and appeared to swell with anger. He actually stuttered when at last he attempted to answer her. 'Ho-w d-dare you! How dare you waltz over here and worm your way back into this house. Against my better judgement I allowed you to stay, and now you throw my goodness in my face. Why are you going back to England? I suppose it was that Edith who's persuaded you to leave here?'

Unable to hide her amazement, Susan cried, 'Aunt

Edith has nothing to do with my decision. She doesn't even know I'm talking to you.'

'Why then? Eh? Why are you going back with her?'

Completely confused at his reaction, Susan said, 'I thought you'd be glad to see me go.'

'Oh, don't think for one moment I wouldn't be glad to see the back of you! It's your mother I'm thinking of. This news could cause a relapse and she might not be so lucky next time.'

'I know. That's what's worrying me,' she said mournfully. 'That's why I want you to break the news to her.'

'Well then, if you're really worried, don't go. Stay! Have the baby here. Give her something to look forward to. She hasn't looked this happy since you left the house last year. Besides, the damage is done. Everybody now knows you're about to give birth to a bastard, so why go now?'

'Don't, Dad, there's no need to use that word. It sounds so awful.'

'I'm sorry, Susan, but you know I believe in calling a spade a spade, and I'm only speaking the truth. What I'm trying to say is, there's no reason for you to leave now that the cat is well and truly out of the bag.'

'I'd love to stay, Dad. But it's a bit complicated.'

'I suppose the father has shown up and is threatening to make himself known. Eh, is that the situation?'

Surprised at his intuition, she agreed, 'Something like that.'

Once again her father astonished her. Leaning across, he gripped her hand. 'Susan . . . can you not marry this guy before the baby is born and give it his name? You're not being fair to the child.'

'I can't! You don't understand. The scandal would be terrible.'

'Who the hell is he, then?' He turned aside in disgust and growled, 'A Taig, no doubt.'

'No, actually you're wrong. He's a Protestant.'

'What's the problem, then? Will he not have you?'

'He's not free,' she whispered.

'Ah, I see. A married man. How could you, Susan? How could you be so bloody stupid?'

Susan sat with head bowed, unable to defend herself. After a short pause, he continued, 'Ah, Susan, Susan. It breaks my heart to see you in this situation. You've spoilt your whole life, so you have.' To her great amazement he put his arm around her shoulders in a comforting gesture. 'Well, we will just have to make the best of it. But you must stay here. Your mother's welfare must come first. Okay?'

'Okay. If you think I should.'

'I think you should.'

Edith spent the next two days at Enniskillen visiting her parents. Thus she was able to curb her curiosity during the remainder of her stay and it was the morning that she was returning to England when, on the pretext of borrowing a pen, she cornered her niece in her bedroom. Susan looked at her, surprised at her request; there were pens lying about all over the place. Reaching for one on her dresser, she turned to find Edith closing the bedroom door and standing with her back against it.

'I want a few minutes alone with you, girl,' she declared. 'I've a question to ask you, and I want the truth, mind.' She lowered her voice before continuing. 'Is Graham the father of your child?'

Sinking slowly down on to the bed, Susan whispered, 'How on earth did you guess?'

'I heard! That day at the hospital I heard enough to make me suspicious. And now you have just confirmed those suspicions. How on earth Alison didn't twig that day, I'll never know. She is very naive, unless of course she doesn't want to face the truth. What on earth are you playing at, girl?'

'You've got to believe me, Aunt Edith. I wasn't carrying on with him! It's like I told you. It just happened on the spur of the moment.' She patted her stomach. 'And this is the result.'

'Does Graham know the truth, or . . .?'

'No. He guesses. When me da suggested that maybe I'd run away to England because I was pregnant, he put two and two together and came over to see for himself. But I convinced him he was wrong. At least, I put doubts in his mind. If I'm lucky enough to go over my time, he might be convinced I met someone over there and got carried away. That's why I didn't want to come home. I wanted to be in a position to lie, if necessary, about the baby's age. I don't want to cause a scandal. Especially now, with Mam being the way she is.'

'Would you not be better coming home with me then?'

'It's me mam. She's so looking forward to the birth of her grandchild. It's all she talks about. If I go she might have a relapse. And . . . believe it or not, me da wants me to stay.'

Edith's eyes stretched in surprise and she cried, 'Wonders will never cease.'

Susan grimaced and shrugged her shoulders. 'I know. I was surprised, too.'

'Is Graham in love with you?'

'At the moment he thinks he is. He's all mixed up.'

'Surely he won't marry Alison, in these circumstances?'

'He tried to break off the engagement, but she won't hear tell of it. To be truthful, she as good as admitted she doesn't love him, but she is probably feeling noble and feels she must stick by him.'

'Dear God, it's a vicious circle, isn't it?'

'You can say that again.'

'Well look, you know I'll always be there for you. You can come over to Billy and me any time. No matter what the circumstances. Remember that!'

They were in each other's arms, their tears mingling. 'Thanks, Aunt Edith. I don't know how I'd have managed without you these past months. I don't deserve your help.'

Embarrassed at all this emotion, Edith gave her a gentle push. 'Ah, get away with you. I must go and finish packing. Take care, love. And remember I'm there for you.'

Chapter Nine

Susan clasped her precious bundle close to her breast as she carried it up the two staircases to the attic rooms. Once she was certain she was staying at home for the birth, she had asked her parents' permission to be allowed to decorate these two rooms for herself and the baby. She was pleased with the result. Her bedroom was painted in cool shades of grey and lemon with a suite, consisting of wardrobe, chest of drawers and long elegant headboard, of pale ash toning in nicely with matching bedding and curtains. The nursery was decorated in various shades of blue, ranging from powder blue to a ceiling so brilliant it lit up the whole room. Watercolours of nursery rhymes adorned the walls and an assortment of soft cuddly toys were scattered about on shelves. She paused on the threshold, drinking in all this beauty, and couldn't believe how fortunate she was.

Rays of May sunlight seeped through the slats of the venetian blinds on the wide dormer window, giving the nursery a misty fairytale aura. Her shoulders heaved as she sighed with contentment. Crossing the soft carpeted floor, she laid her son in the brand-new cot presented by his grandfather (much to Susan's surprise). He was beautiful; the loveliest wee baby in the whole wide world. She laughed softly at the very idea. Didn't all mothers think that? Still, right from the beginning, except for the slight blue bruises on his temple where the doctor had delivered him with the aid of forceps, his features had been perfect; pale and interesting, with great big, dark eyes. Not in the least bit red and wrinkled like other babies she had seen.

Intently she examined these features now, but could see nothing of Graham – or herself for that matter – in him. Her mother was convinced he was the picture of Trevor and had hinted that he would be ever so pleased if the baby was named after him, but Susan shied away from this idea. Trevor was not one of her favourite names. Born a fortnight ago today, her son had been two weeks early, throwing all her conniving plans into disarray. She who had hoped to last until at least the middle of June had produced a baby two weeks premature. Her father had been sceptical, saying that the baby looked big enough to him and asking if there was any particular reason why she was claiming it was premature? Noticing her mother's discomfiture, Susan had indignantly cried, 'No, why should I? What reason would I have to claim he's premature if he was full-term? Not that two weeks makes much difference.'

'In some cases it can make a lot of difference. I've heard tell some women do that to pull the wool over their husband's eyes. But then, you don't have a husband to deceive.' His shoulders were slumped as he left the room.

Susan glanced at her mother in bewilderment and

was amazed to see red spots of embarrassment in her cheeks. 'What was all that about?'

'Just a wee bee your father has in his bonnet.'

Digesting these words, Susan suddenly reached a conclusion. 'Was I premature?'

Rachel sighed. 'I suppose you may as well know. You're old enough now not to agitate your father by mentioning it. Yes, you were a couple of months premature.'

Again Susan took her time answering, sifting through the muddled thoughts racing through her mind. 'But . . . why would he be agitated?' Her eyes widened as comprehension dawned. 'Are you trying to tell me Dad thinks I'm not his daughter?'

'Just sometimes . . . Silly things, like baby William coming early, for instance, trigger off these doubts.'

Mesmerised, Susan gazed at her mother long and earnestly. It explained so many things. Why sometimes, out of the blue, her father suddenly seemed to dislike her without any justification. Why every now and again he was nasty to his wife.

'Is he . . .' She paused in confusion. This was delicate ground she was treading. She had no right to probe. Or did she?

With a harsh laugh Rachel anticipated her question. 'What do you think? It's mainly because you don't look like any of us. Never have! But that's not unusual in a family. Most times he believes, but every now and again I don't know what gets into him, but the doubts creep back. It can be very upsetting, I can tell you.'

'I'll bet it can. And you've had to put up with this torture all these years?'

'Mm, what else could I do?'

Going to her, Susan gave her a hug. 'Ah, Mam. Poor Mam.' It was only much later she realised her mother had neither confirmed nor denied whether Trevor was indeed her father.

Now that the child was born, Susan had time to reflect on the past months. She was amazed at the extreme lengths to which she had gone to hide her pregnancy. Disrupting everyone by running over to Aunt Edith, instead of facing the music at home. But if she had stayed, wouldn't Graham have guessed right from the beginning and let the cat out of the bag? Then all hell would have broken loose. Her father would most definitely have kicked her out on to the street for her betrayal of her sister, no matter what her mother said. Alison would have hated the very sight of her, and what about Graham? Would he have been so eager to claim responsibility at that time?

No, she had done the right thing and the father's name had remained her little secret. So long as it stayed that way, she didn't care about anything else. This was a wonderful feeling of release. What did it matter what people thought of her? Sticks and stones and all that! To think she had been daft enough to worry about the likes of that! All that mattered to her now was the welfare of this beautiful wee baby. Her son! She would work her fingers to the bone for him. If anybody got too nosy, she would tell them to take a running jump. No one could take this wonderful gift away from her. The only blot on the landscape at the moment was that a father's name would not appear on her son's birth certificate.

The doctor who had delivered him had been called Dr William McCartney and so, recalling her mother's hints and to avoid any arguments, Susan had said the baby would be christened William after this young doctor, who had relieved her of pain and delivered her son safely into the world. William was also her grandfather's name and so her mother wasn't too disappointed. William Cummings. She turned her mind away from what his name should really be, and the inheritance she was denying her child. In the circumstances, that couldn't be helped!

A shadow fell across the cot and she glanced over her shoulder as her mother joined her.

'Mam, I was so engrossed in William I didn't hear you come up. You shouldn't have climbed all those stairs,' Susan chastised her.

'I just wanted another little peek at him. I don't know why you want to keep him away up here, anyway,' Rachel said grumpily.

'Ah, Mam, you've been nursing him for the last half-hour. You still have to be careful, you know, not to overtire yourself,' Susan reproached her. 'And you know very well why I chose these rooms – it's because I want him to disturb the household as little as possible. I'm very grateful that you and Dad are accepting him and I don't want any regrets. Up here, if he's restless at night you'll hardly hear him.'

Rachel hung over the cot admiring the pink chubby cheeks fanned by thick dark lashes. 'He's beautiful,' she enthused. 'Look at those eyelashes. And you know something, Susan, we don't expect him to be quiet for ever. It wouldn't be natural.'

'I know, but remember, Dad and Alison still have to get up early for work, so they need a good night's sleep. The less bother he is, the better for all concerned.'

'I suppose you're right.'

'Don't worry, you'll see plenty of him. We're still in the same house after all, not miles away, and he will be downstairs most of the day. You'll soon be sick of him.'

'No, never,' Rachel vowed softly. For some seconds they stood in silence and paid the baby homage. Then Rachel whispered, 'He doesn't look in the least premature. Are you sure he is? Perhaps you got your dates wrong?'

Susan shook her head sadly. 'He's premature all right. No mistake about it. I only wish he had hung on until sometime in June.'

'Why?'

'So that certain people wouldn't get the wrong idea.'

'Who? Who might get the wrong idea? Oh, Susan, why must you be so secretive?'

'Because you wouldn't understand.'

'You'd be surprised. Try me. You know I can hold my tongue when required. I've had plenty of practice over the years. You'd be amazed at the things I can't let pass my lips. I know a lot of secrets.'

Susan laughed. 'Well, this is one secret you won't have to keep, because I'm not telling you anything.'

'Ah, well, if that's how you feel. While he's sleeping, you take a wee rest. You'll need to build up your strength. After all, he is only two weeks old, and I agree with you, there's bound to be some sleepless nights ahead. So rest every chance you get. I'm so excited, Susan. I can't believe he's so beautiful. By the way . . .

Graham said he would be over tonight to see him.'

Knowing the dismay that she felt must be written all over her face, Susan bent and fussed over the cot, adjusting the blankets, to hide it. 'Is he well enough?' she asked.

'I forgot, you haven't seen him lately, sure you haven't?' This realization made Rachel frown. 'How come?'

'Oh, you know how it is. I felt large and ungainly and didn't fancy seeing his parents in my condition in case they thought I was flaunting myself. You know what it's like? I didn't want to start their tongues wagging.'

'The Robsons? Never! They're too refined for that kind of nonsense.'

Susan laughed aloud. 'Now, Mam, you know there isn't a woman on earth who can resist a bit of scandal, and I'm sure Alma Robson is no exception.'

Her mother smiled and said, 'I suppose you're right.'

'You can take my word for it.'

'Mm. Well, Graham is doing remarkably well and can get about on sticks now. It's like a small miracle. They say it was the shock to his nervous system that caused the paralysis, but in time he should make a complete recovery. But you must already know all this. You've surely heard us talking. You'll see tonight for yourself how well he's doing. Now take a lie down, and I'll keep an eye on William.'

'I don't feel in the least sleepy, Mam. I'm too tensed up. I'll connect the intercom and then come down and sort out those wonderful presents that arrived this morning from Darlington. People are too kind! Even Donald has spent far too much on William.'

'Okay, if that's what you want. I'll put the kettle on, and we'll have a nice wee cup of tea first.'

Feverishly now, Susan re-examined the features of her son. As far as she could see, there was nothing to cause anyone to exclaim and say, 'Doesn't he resemble Graham?' But then what was she thinking of? Why should they? They wouldn't be looking for signs of Graham in him. After all, he was engaged to her sister. Except for Graham, that is! He would certainly be looking to see if there was any family resemblance.

Entering her own room, she stood by the wide window and looked down on the garden. The borders were a riot of colour with May flowers, and the smooth, green lawn, mowed in opposing stripes, swept down to the newly painted summer house. Their house was set in beautiful surroundings. She could hear birds twittering in the hedgerows and a red squirrel scampered along the lower branches of the oak tree. Was she going to be forced to leave all this splendour and go back to Darlington just to avoid Graham?

She hadn't seen Graham since that fatal afternoon at the hospital; had made all kinds of excuses to avoid going visiting with Alison. She could imagine how he must resent her attitude towards him, but she had felt unable to face any more interrogations. Now tonight he was coming to see the baby. God grant that he would be reasonable and wouldn't make things awkward for her. Wouldn't make insinuations in front of the family. This was no bump any more! It was living flesh and blood; beautiful flesh and blood. Graham would be more determined than ever to lay claim to him. Given the chance, she must convince him once and for all that he wasn't William's father. But how? He was so stubborn.

Everything had been working better than she had dared hope. Her father was more affable towards her since the birth, and positively doted on his grandson, bastard or not. Her boss was saying that her position would be open for her so long as she didn't delay too long. The knowledge that she would be in a position to give her son a good life had gladdened her heart. At last she could see some kind of a future before her. A light at the end of the tunnel, so to say. She wasn't going to let Graham spoil her dream!

Her mother's voice reached her, bringing her out of her reverie. A last look at the sleeping child and she descended the stairs and joined Rachel in the kitchen.

'What kept you? Is William all right?'

'Yes. He's in a sound sleep. I just couldn't tear myself away.'

'I don't blame you. We'll have to start advertising for someone to help me look after him when you return to work.'

'Mam, there's plenty of time yet. I've another few months before I go back,' Susan exclaimed, a laugh in her voice.

'You may well laugh, girl, but not just anybody will do, you know. For a start they'll have to have good references, and those ones won't be hanging around waiting for you to advertise for their services. So the sooner we start looking, the better.'

'I suppose you're right,' Susan readily agreed. 'But let's wait another few weeks, eh, love?'

* * *

Susan stood beside her mother and looked from the window of the lounge as Graham's father assisted him from the car, watched anxiously from the back seat by his mother. He looked much better. In the six weeks or so since she had last seen him, he had put some weight back on and his face had lost its grey pallor. His father made to help him up the steps to the house, but Graham shrugged him aside and manoeuvred up the steps slowly and deliberately, but quite capably on his own, with the aid of his walking sticks. Alison stood waiting at the door for him, patiently curbing the urge to go and put a supporting arm around his waist to help him. His father declined her invitation for him and his wife to come inside. They were going to a business dinner, he explained, and would pick Graham up at about eleven o'clock.

Slipping an arm through Graham's, Alison tenderly led him slowly into the lounge. Trevor was on his feet at once and, offering his hand to Graham, exclaimed, 'Welcome, son. It's great to see you back on your feet again.'

When Alison would have guided him to the nearest chair, Graham resisted her efforts and, shrugging off her hand, walked slowly and obviously in some pain across the lounge to where Rachel and Susan hovered over the cradle. The reproachful look he cast in Susan's direction as he leant painfully over to gaze on the baby was not lost on Alison and she was quick to come to her sister's defence. 'Now, Graham, as I explained, Susan has been very busy, and with that little rascal coming early, she hadn't time to visit you. Anyway, she's under no obligation to you. So don't start giving off to her.'

Her words were lost on him. He was gazing avidly at the sleeping child. With his free hand he gently touched the soft pink cheek. 'He's beautiful.' He raised his head and met Susan's eyes. 'Congratulations, Susan.'

The emotion that gripped Susan as Graham looked on his son for the first time took her unawares. The enormity of what she was doing suddenly struck her and a great ball of pain gathered in her throat, threatening to choke her. She was depriving this man of the right to his son and heir. But what else could she do? It was out of her hands. If only things had been different, she silently lamented. If only Alison wasn't involved. But her sister must at all costs be shielded from their terrible betrayal. Swallowing the lump in her throat with difficulty, she mumbled, 'Thank you.'

Something of the anguish she was feeling must have been reflected in her face because his eyes clung to hers pleadingly. The silence stretched and, to her relief, Alison broke it. 'We all agree with you on that score, Graham. He is beautiful,' she said fondly. She put a hand gently on his arm to help him towards the settee. When he would have resisted, she insisted softly, 'Shouldn't you sit down, Graham? You mustn't overdo it. You know what the doctors said about doing too much too soon. Why take unnecessary risks?'

He waved her away. 'I'm all right.' His eyes once again met Susan's and saw the anguish there. With a sigh he allowed Alison to help him.

Once settled in an upright posture with cushions supporting his back, he said, 'You're looking well, Susan.'

'I feel great. Just tire easily. You're looking much better

yourself. It's wonderful to see you walking again. Can I get you a cup of tea or coffee? Or a drink?'

'A cup of coffee would be most welcome, thank you. And yes, I should be running about in no time.'

'That's if you do as you're told,' Alison warned. 'I'll make the coffee,' she volunteered and left the room.

'While you and Graham catch up on each other's gossip, I'll prepare some snacks – nothing too heavy,' Rachel said. 'Trevor, will you give me a hand and then see to the drinks for later on?'

He followed his wife from the room and Graham gave a rueful smile. It couldn't have worked out better if he had planned it. He and Susan were alone.

He patted the settee. 'Come and talk to me, Susan.'

Afraid to antagonise him, she reluctantly crossed the room and sat down.

His eyes scanned her face, taking in the bloom of luminous skin, the shining hair and worried eyes. No one would ever guess she had just had a child. He longed to reach for her but managed to control the impulse. 'Motherhood certainly agrees with you, Susan.'

'Thank you. Graham, I apologise for not visiting you at home but you wouldn't listen to reason and you're so wrong. So *very* wrong,' she stressed. 'I didn't want you giving everybody the wrong idea.'

'Am I wrong, Susan? Do you know what I think? I think you were afraid to come, in case the truth would leak out.' He lowered his voice. 'Am I right?'

She closed her eyes tightly and raised her face towards the ceiling in frustration. 'No, you're not right! Oh, Graham, how can I ever convince you?'

He reached out and covered her hand with his. An involuntary thrill ran through her and her eyes shot open wide in amazement. Jerking her hand away, she whispered, 'Don't do that!'

A triumphant smile lit his face. 'You see? You have feelings for me after all.'

'That's where you're wrong! To me, you're just my sister's fiancé. Nothing else!'

He spread his hands wide. 'Seeing is believing.'

Desperate now, she beseeched him. 'Don't do this, Graham. Don't spoil things for me. Don't drive me across the water again. Much as I like Darlington, I want to stay here.'

Fear plucked at his heart. Would she really run away again? Surely not. Still, he couldn't resist the temptation to find out the truth. He had to take the chance of maybe driving her away for ever. 'Susan, I can't just stand by and watch you ruin all our lives.'

A tear spilled over and ran down her cheek. Brushing it angrily away with the back of her hand, she whispered, 'You're being very foolish. My sister is a lovely girl. You should be delighted that she's going to marry you.'

'I know that! And God knows I wouldn't hurt her for the world, but it's you I want. Why can't you listen to reason? We could get this all sorted out. The scandal would be short-lived and then we could get on with our lives.'

Despair gripped her. So much for convincing him. He was as obstinate as ever. And could she blame him? To her great relief, William started to whimper and, glad of the respite, she rose eagerly to her feet. Graham reached out and gripped her arm. 'This isn't over, Susan. Not by any means. We must talk.'

Knocking his hand aside, she crossed the floor and lifted the child. 'He's hungry. I'll have to give him a feed.' Without another glance in Graham's direction she left the room.

As William nuzzled contentedly at her breast, Susan tried to analyse the effect Graham's touch had had on her. She had been amazed at the thrill of pleasure that had shot through her; had been taken completely unaware and been unable to hide her reaction from him. He had been surprised too, and how he had gloated! God, what a mess she was in. She would have to do something drastic, to put a stop to all this nonsense. She would confess that she intended seeing Jim Brady again, with marriage in mind. Not that she really thought marriage would be in his mind, but one never knew.

A large bouquet had been delivered to the hospital the day after William's birth, from Jim. How he had known, Susan had yet to find out. Probably through Ruth, whom she had been meeting every Wednesday in town on her day off from the supermarket where she worked.

Ruth had proved a staunch friend. As soon as she heard that Susan was back home she had phoned to make arrangements to see her. They met in the city centre and at that first meeting, when Ruth saw her condition, she wept openly in sympathy with her.

'Ah, Susan, Susan, my heart goes out to you.'

Susan shrugged and admitted, 'I've been foolish, but I'm not the first and I certainly won't be the last.'

'Ah, Susan. And to think I believed Jim Brady when

he denied all knowledge of it,' she cried indignantly. 'I really did!'

Susan shook her head in frustration. 'For heaven's sake don't you start.'

Ruth's eyes scanned her face, 'You mean it isn't his?'

'That's exactly what I mean.'

Susan had watched different expressions flit across her friend's face and could imagine the trend that her thoughts would take. She would be thinking back over the time after Jim and she had split up; would be trying to fit another face in the frame. Unsuccessfully, of course.

At last Ruth smiled ruefully. 'But . . . I don't understand. Who else was there?' she asked in confusion.

'Believe me, you wouldn't want to know,' Susan assured her.

'You're wrong! I do want to know. Every single gory detail.'

Linking her arm through her friend's, Susan said firmly, 'Well, you're not going to. So let's find somewhere we can have a coffee and you can tell me all your gossip.'

Ruth brought her up to date on all their friends and acquaintances. She shyly admitted that she was in love with Dougie and was hoping he felt the same and would ask her to marry him. A twinge of jealousy plucked at Susan's heartstrings at this news. Why had she been so foolish?

During the following weeks Ruth had tried to wheedle the father's name out of her friend, but eventually gave up in despair. She kept Susan up to date on all the gossip and casually mentioned that Jim Brady was on the scene again, but didn't seem interested in any one particular girl. Eventually Susan confided in her that Jim had asked her to marry him. Round-eyed with wonder, Ruth hung breathlessly on her every word. Susan told her of running into Jim in the Ulster Milk Bar, and of how the table had hidden her condition and he had proposed marriage. She made a big joke of how, later, when she gave into his pleas and met him to go to the pictures, he apparently changed his mind when he saw her big bump.

Ruth listened in silence to all these disclosures, tears in her eyes at the futility of it all. 'Ah, Susan. I'm so sorry. Why on earth didn't he ask you to marry him before?'

'There were family problems.' She shrugged. 'Or, who knows, perhaps it wasn't meant to be.'

They sat sipping their coffee, pursuing their own lines of thought, and then Ruth asked, 'How did your dad take all this?'

'Can't you imagine?'

With a grimace, Ruth said, 'Yes, I think so, but obviously he's come round or you wouldn't still be living at home. How is he now?'

'Not too bad. He thinks I've made a complete mess of my life.'

'You can't blame him for that,' Ruth said softly. 'Mm?'

'I know. You're right of course. Still, these things happen, but life goes on. I'll work something out.' Suddenly she bent over, clasping her stomach in obvious pain. 'Ouch! That was a funny sensation,' she gasped.

Ruth panicked. Rising to her feet, she shrieked, 'What will I do, Susan? Shall I call an ambulance?'

'Believe me, Ruth, even if it is starting, it will be a long time before anything really happens. Besides, I'm not due yet, I've weeks to go. Sit down and finish your coffee.'

Reluctantly Ruth sat down, anxious eyes fixed on Susan's face. When another pain gripped her friend and could not be ignored, she was on her feet again instantly. 'No buts about it! I'm phoning for the ambulance now.'

'No! Hold on a minute.' When the pain had subsided, digging into her handbag Susan brought out an address book. 'Here, look for my dad's office number and ring him. He'll come and fetch me.'

Fifteen minutes later she was on her way to the Royal Maternity Hospital. Ten long, torturous hours later, her son was delivered into the world.

Alone in the lounge, Graham rested his head back against the top of the settee and, closing his eyes, tried to recapture and put a name to the expression he'd caught on Susan's face as he looked at the baby. Pity? Compassion? But it had been too fleeting and had eluded him. However, her reaction to his touch hadn't been so elusive. It had been both startling and satisfying, and had filled him with great joy. Surely she must care to react like that?

Rachel wheeled a trolley into the room and Alison followed her, carrying a tray laden with a large coffee pot, teapot, sugar bowl and milk jug. Seeing the expression on his face she asked, 'What are you looking so pleased about?'

'Am I?'

'Yes. You're like the proverbial Cheshire cat with that

big, foolish grin on your face. I suppose it's William. He has that effect on everybody. One does tend to smile inanely when he's about.' She peered into the empty cradle. 'Where is he?'

'He was crying . . .'

'Never,' Alison interrupted him teasingly. 'Our William never cries.'

His grin widened. 'Well, whinging a little then, and Susan took him away to feed him.'

'Mm, yes, maybe a little whinge.' She poured him a cup of coffee and smiled tenderly as she handed it to him. Rachel asked him what he would like from the selection on the trolley.

'He really is a lovely baby, isn't he?' she said as she put the sandwich he asked for on a plate and handed it to him.

Graham readily agreed and did a bit of probing. 'Doesn't anyone know who the father is?' he asked tentatively.

Regretfully Rachel shook her head. 'No. Whoever he is, he's a fool. He doesn't know what he's missing.'

'Perhaps he doesn't know he has a son?' Graham suggested.

'Well, all I can say is, he must be very stupid not to have guessed.'

'Perhaps Susan is deliberately keeping him in the dark?'

Rachel's brows rose. 'Why would she, if he was free and willing to give the child his name? If he's married he definitely won't want to know.'

'Hush, she's coming back!' Alison hissed.

Susan was aware, by the sudden silence and embarrassed glances in her direction when she entered the room, that she had been the topic of conversation. Serenely she crossed the floor and gently laid the sleeping child in his cradle, then turned to face them all. 'That coffee smells delicious. May I have a cup, please Mam?' Thus setting them all at ease.

Alison helped herself from the trolley and settled next to Graham on the settee. 'Just think, Graham, if you hadn't been in that accident, we would be sitting here planning our wedding for next month.'

'Oh, if only you were. It would be great to be up to one's neck in wedding plans,' Rachel cried. 'Have you thought of another date yet?'

'No!' Graham said abruptly. 'It won't be this year, I fear. Not the state my legs are in.'

The look that Alison turned on him was full of amazement. 'But we talked about a Christmas wedding,' she cried. 'Your mam has her heart set on it.'

'I know! But to be truthful, I'd like to walk down the aisle completely cured. Not shuffling along on a stick. Surely you can't blame me for that? There's no big hurry, is there, Alison?'

Alison's shrug was dismissive. 'So long as you can convince your mother how you feel, it will be all right with me. But please get her off my back, Graham. She thinks I'm the one holding back.' With a disgruntled look on her face she pushed herself free of the settee and, with a muttered excuse, left the room.

Graham gazed after her in bewilderment and made futile efforts to rise.

'Don't you be getting up, Graham. I'll make sure she's all right.' Susan found her sister sitting at the kitchen table, head buried in her hands.

'Alison, don't think I'm interfering, but do you not think it better to wait until the spring to get married?'

Pushing her hair back from her face with a tired gesture, Alison cried, 'To be truthful, I've reached the stage where I don't care if we never get married. Since his accident Graham is getting on like a zombie. He never shows any affection. As for his mother! She's changed her tune. Before the accident I got the idea I wasn't good enough for her precious son. Now she can't get us married quickly enough.' She fell silent for some moments, then cried in a rush, 'Sometimes I wonder if Graham will ever be really well. Maybe he will be lame all his life. What if she knows something I don't?'

'I doubt that, Graham wouldn't deceive you.'

'But what if he doesn't know? Or, what if he does know and that's why he's postponing the wedding?'

'Nonsense! The doctors wouldn't keep him in the dark about anything that serious. As he said, he wants to be really fit before he gets married.'

Alison looked unconvinced. 'I don't know about that.'

Pulling a chair away from the table, Susan sat down beside her sister and gazed earnestly at her. 'Listen, Alison. If you're unsure of your feelings, if you feel you don't love Graham enough, take my advice and agree to a separation for a time.'

'Love? What's love? I'm very, very fond of Graham. I know we can make a go of it. So if we're going to marry, the sooner the better.'

Susan slumped in her chair, woebegone. She had thought that if her sister and Graham had a trial separation, Graham would have no excuse to frequent their home. But by the sound of it, he would soon be part of the family. He was no match for Alison *and* his mother.

It was a beautiful day, the middle of June and the sun shone brightly, throwing down a heavy heat. Cherry trees were in full bloom along the avenue where Susan was walking with her pram. She had been to the park and William lay spreadeagled, a parasol protecting his little arms and legs from the direct rays of the sun. Turning into the driveway she pushed the pram around the house to the back garden and parked it in the shade of the oak tree. Covering it with a protective net, she entered the house in search of a cool drink.

Her mother met her in the hall. 'Someone rang a short time ago. He said he would call back later.'

'Did he give a name?'

'Of course. How silly of me. He said to tell you that Jim Brady had called and would ring back later.'

Rachel watched as delight lit up her daughter's face with a rosy hue. 'Do you know him, then?'

'Yes, yes, I know him.'

'Is he . . .' Her voice trailed off.

Anticipating the question, Susan shook her head. 'No, he is not William's father.'

'Is he important to you?'

'He's just a friend, Mam, but I do like him a lot.'

Worry puckered Rachel's face. 'You will be careful, won't you?'

Susan laughed. 'Mam, it's only a phone call, so it is. And he probably just wants to ask after my and William's welfare.'

'Just be careful, love. Won't you?'

Annoyed at her mother's persistence, Susan answered curtly. 'Don't be silly, Mam. I'm not likely to make the same mistake again. What time did he phone?'

Rachel glanced at her watch. 'About an hour ago.'

Just then the phone rang and Susan hurried through the kitchen and into the hall to answer it.

'Hello?'

'Is that you, Susan?'

'Yes. Who's speaking, please?' As if she didn't know. But she intended playing it cool.

'Jim . . . . Jim Brady. How are you?'

'Oh, hello, Jim. It's nice to hear from you. I'm fine. What about you?'

'I'm all right. I've been thinking a lot about you.' There was a pregnant pause as he waited for her to return the compliment. For the life of her she couldn't. What with caring for William and fighting off Graham, he hadn't been on her mind all that often, lately. 'Are you still there, Susan?'

'Yes. Yes, I'm still here, Jim.'

'Can we meet?'

'I'd like that, Jim. I'll have to arrange for a babysitter, of course. When suits you?'

'Let's make it Saturday night, shall we? There's a big band playing at the Orpheus and I thought we could go there. Is that all right with you?'

'Yes, sounds great. I'd like that. I'm sure my mam will look after William.'

'Smashing! I'll pick you up at half-past seven. Goodbye till then.'

'Pick me up?'

'Yes, I've got a car now, a Hillman Minx. Nothing

great, but it gets me from A to B. See you on Saturday then.'

'Right! Goodbye, Jim.'

Fearing the sensual feelings that his voice had aroused would be evident on her face, Susan hurried upstairs. She didn't want her mother to see and worry about her. In the bathroom she gazed at her reflection in the mirror and was surprised to find that, except for a brightness in her eyes, she looked no different. With a rueful smile she retraced her steps and went to join her mother.

'Well, was that your friend?' Rachel asked.

'Yes. Mam?' A raised brow invited Susan to continue. 'Jim has asked me to go out with him on Saturday night. Is there any chance of you babysitting? I promise not to be home late.'

'You know I'll be only too glad to look after William any time, Susan.'

'Thanks, Mam. Oh, I think I hear him. He'll be hungry. I'd better go out before he starts yelling the place down.'

Susan's milk was drying up and the nurse at the clinic had advised her to wean him on to the bottle, before it disappeared completely. Placing her crochet work to one side, Rachel rose to her feet. 'I'll make him a bottle. I'm glad he'll not be depending on you for a feed when you return to work. It will make it easier all round.'

Susan met Ruth as usual the next day, a Wednesday. Ruth was waiting at the bus stop to help her off with the pram.

'You're looking very smug today,' Susan greeted her friend as she adjusted the pram and, reaching for her son, settled him in it.

'Oh, he's lovely, and awake for a change. That's the first time I've actually seen his eyes.'

'Stop changing the subject. What's that look in aid of?'

A hand was thrust towards her displaying an engagement ring.

Susan gasped, delighted for her friend. 'Oh! It's beautiful! No wonder you look so smug. Congratulations. I take it Dougie bought it?' Her eyes twinkled teasingly.

'Of course! Who else would have me?'

'Oh, now, there are plenty who'd have you, and you know it. When's the big day then?'

'We haven't decided yet. Probably sometime next year.'

'That's an event to look forward to. Would you like to take a walk around the shops today, Ruth? I've decided to treat myself to a new dress.'

'Oh . . . for any special occasion?'

'Not exactly. However, I am going to the Orpheus with Jim Brady on Saturday night, and if I get something nice I'll wear it then,' Susan informed her casually.

Ruth's smile widened. 'You're joking me, aren't you?'

Susan suppressed a laugh at her friend's expression. 'Cross my heart and hope to die.'

'That's wonderful news, so it is.'

'Don't read anything into it. It's only a date, for heaven's sake.'

'Huh! He must still be keen all the same, or he wouldn't have bothered. What with the baby and all.'

Susan had been thinking along similar lines herself, but she wasn't going to let Ruth know her thoughts. 'Time will tell,' she said.

'I noticed when I passed on the bus earlier on, there's a sale on in the London Mantle Warehouse. Let's walk up there and see what they have to offer.'

'Good idea.'

They walked along Donegall Place and up Castle Street to the long, narrow shop with the grand name, which stood on the corner of Chapel Lane. Susan examined the window displays and was not impressed. 'That was a wasted effort. There's nothing there to lure me inside,' she decided.

'I know what you mean. It's all a bit old-fashioned-looking, isn't it? You want something special to make Jim sit up and take notice.'

'I wouldn't go as far as to say that. No, it's not just for Jim's benefit. Anything I buy I'll have to really like. It will have to last a long time. I can't afford to be extravagant any more. I've William to think of now.'

They headed back down towards the centre of town, stopping to look in shop windows along the way.

In Fountain Lane Ruth stopped in front of a small boutique. A solitary dress was displayed in the window, with no sign of a price tag. 'Isn't that classy, Susan?'

'It certainly is. Let's move on.'

'They've got a sale on.'

'Believe me, sale or no sale, it will still be too expensive for my budget.'

'It would suit you down to the ground, so it would.'

'That's neither here nor there. I simply couldn't afford it.'

'How do you know? It costs nothing to look.'

Susan looked intently at the dress. Draped against a black velvet background, its deep ruby colour seemed to glow; the design was simplicity itself, the material soft and clinging. With breast-feeding William and exercising to strengthen her muscles, she had regained most of her figure and could picture herself in this creation. Oh to be rich and not have to count the cost. Once she was back at work things would be different, but for now she must be careful with her money. There was always the chance Graham would make it impossible for her to stay in Belfast and she would need her savings to settle in Darlington. With a sad shake of the head she walked determinedly on. Reluctantly Ruth followed her.

They had afternoon tea in a café where there was room for the pram, the Ulster Milk Bar being too narrow and confined. Ruth was very quiet and Susan was worried about her. Lifting her friend's left hand, she examined the ring. 'Why so quiet, Ruth? Are you worried about getting married?'

'Don't be daft! Dougie is the best thing that ever happened to me. It's you I'm worried about. I want you to knock Jim Brady sideways on Saturday night. I want him to propose to you again.'

'And do you really think a dress will make all that much difference?'

'Not to Jim, but it will make you feel a lot more confident.'

Inwardly Susan agreed. Ruth saw her wavering and urged, 'Just try it on. If it looks awful then nothing's lost.'

'What if it looks good, what then, eh?'

'Just to please me, at least try it on.'

'Oh, come on then. But mind you, nothing will induce me to buy it if it's too expensive, okay?'

* * *

They retraced their steps to Fountain Lane and, with trepidation, entered the small shop. A tall, very thin woman hurried towards them frowning disdainfully at the pram. 'I'm very sorry, but prams are not allowed on these premises.'

Looking politely around her, Ruth asked in her best posh voice, 'And where does it say so?'

The woman's nostrils flared and she stretched taller still at the audacity of this young woman. 'It doesn't, but surely it's obvious that such a small establishment cannot cater for prams?'

Susan began to edge out backwards, but with a hand on the pram Ruth stopped her. 'As you can see, the child is sleeping. We shall not take up too much of your precious time.' With these words she headed towards the rear of the shop to a rail with a sale sign on it.

Flashing an apologetic look at the woman, Susan left the pram inside the doorway and followed Ruth. Only two dresses on the rail were her size. One she disliked immediately and quickly replaced. A glance at the price tag on the other one caused her to gasp aloud and make to hang it up again.

'Try it on,' Ruth whispered furiously. 'I won't please her,' with a nod in the assistant's direction, 'to let her know we can't afford her creations.'

'But I can't afford it! Besides, I don't even like it.'

'How do you know? It might look lovely on.'

'No!' Susan was adamant. 'I don't like the colour. It's just not me.'

'Oh, Susan!' In despair, Ruth approached the woman

and peered at the name tag attached to her jacket. 'Ah, Lynette, what size is the dress in the window?'

'Twelve.'

'Is it in the sale?'

An abrupt nod confirmed it was indeed in the sale.

'Can my friend try it on, please?'

'I'm afraid I'm not allowed to interfere with the window display.' Lynette was looking down her nose from her superior height, causing Ruth's temper to rise.

'That's all right, I'll remove it for you.' She had the access door to the window display open before a horrified Lynette could intervene.

'Here, you can't do that.' Lynette grabbed her arm. 'Only Mrs Donovan can do that.'

'And who, may I ask, is Mrs Donovan?'

'The proprietor.'

'And where is she?'

'She's off work for a few days.'

'And are you not in charge while she's away?'

'I am, yes, but . . .'

Ruth interrupted her. 'If you're in charge, you can take that dress out of the window and let my friend try it on.'

Lynette's more-superior-than-thou attitude was quickly evaporating and she was practically wringing her hands with indecision. 'I'm afraid . . .'

'Well, don't be,' Ruth interrupted. 'If it doesn't suit I will help you to drape it round the stand again. And if it does suit my friend,' tongue-in-cheek she said, 'you will have made a cash sale and Mrs Donovan should surely be pleased.'

With more than a little reluctance, the dress was carefully taken from the window. Lynette took great pains to remove all the pins that kept it tucked into shape. Reverently she placed the dress over Ruth's outstretched arm. 'Please be careful with it.'

'We have tried on dresses before, if I may boldly inform one,' Ruth assured her in her continuing posh accent. 'And without any accidents, if I may add.' She motioned Susan into the small cubicle and, following her, drew the curtain across.

Quickly removing her blouse and skirt, Susan pulled the dress over her head and, smoothing it down over her hips, surveyed her reflection in the mirror. She was amazed at the transformation before her eyes. The dress was cut low at the front and even lower at the back. Her shoulders rose above it in creamy splendour. The deep ruby red of the dress darkened the grey of her eyes and her skin seemed to glow. Only the offending straps of her bra spoiled the effect.

Ruth gazed at her in awe. 'Take your bra off!' Susan tucked the straps out of sight and Ruth whispered, 'You look absolutely gorgeous. I told you it was you! You just have to buy it, Susan.'

'I'm afraid to look at the price,' Susan wailed. 'It's bound to be too expensive.'

The tag was hanging on the back of the dress and, with trembling fingers, Ruth turned it over.

'Well . . . it's not as dear as the other one,' she said. 'And it does look lovely on you.'

'Just give me the bottom line, Ruth, and get it over with,' Susan ordered, only to gasp in dismay when her friend told her.

Feverishly she started to remove the dress. 'Hold on

a minute, Susan. At least let me get another look at you before you take it off. You'll never look so lovely again.'

Gazing at her reflection in the mirror, Susan agreed with her. Twisting her hair into a knot on top of her head, she pouted and sighed at her image. 'I really do suit it, don't I?'

'You look absolutely gorgeous in it. Can you not possibly afford it?'

'It would take up a big chunk of my savings. I can't justify buying it. It would be a sin to waste all that money.'

'It's a pity, though. Jim Brady wouldn't be able to keep his hands off you in that outfit.'

'Can I be of any assistance to you ladies?' Lynette's voice reached them.

Pulling aside the curtain, Ruth gestured towards Susan. 'Doesn't she look wonderful, Lynette?'

Lynette clasped her hands together and gave out a suppressed exclamation. 'Oh, madam. Oh, madam,' she whispered.

Susan smiled wryly at her. 'Thanks for letting me try it on, but it's much too expensive for me.'

William started to stir and she hurriedly closed the curtain and quickly removed the dress. She put on her clothes and left the cubicle, handing the dress to Ruth. 'Help Lynette return it to the window, Ruth. I'll need to attend to William. Thanks again for letting me try it on.'

'Madam? If I may be so bold?'

'Yes?'

'That's last year's model. I have the authority to lower the price if necessary.'

Both girls gazed at her in wonder and at last Ruth asked, 'How much?'

'I can reduce it by a further twenty pounds for a cash sale.'

The two girls looked at each other. 'Susan?'

'Well, now . . .'

Her hesitation was enough for Ruth. 'She'll take it,' she cried, settling the matter.

Between them they managed to scrape up the required deposit and Susan arranged to collect the dress on Saturday morning. Outside the shop she gazed in bewilderment at Ruth. 'I can't believe I've just bought that dress! I must need my head examined.'

'You'll be glad on Saturday night when you see the look in Jim's eyes. He won't be able to resist you. He'll be fighting off all the single guys. You wait and see.'

Still undecided, Susan bit agitatedly on her lip and lamented, 'Perhaps I should go back and cancel it? Eh?'

'You'll do no such thing! You'll never get the chance to own a dress like that again. And it's so simple it will never date. Believe me, you got a bargain there, so you did. It's a real gem. You won't regret it.'

'I hope you're right. I feel guilty spending so much money.'

'Trust me. Everything will be all right. I might even get Dougie to give his beloved Club Orchid a miss and come and see the attention you get on Saturday night.'

Not at all pleased by this idea, Susan informed her, 'You can't! It's a ticket-only dance.'

Ruth was not to be so easily put off. 'It will run late then?' she queried.

'Midnight! But I won't be able to stay till the end. Mam will be babysitting.'

'Nevertheless I'll get Dougie to walk me round there after we leave the Orchid. Will that be all right with you?'

Still unhappy at the idea, Susan nodded her consent. It would be ungracious to do otherwise.

Chapter Ten

Saturday started out a beautiful day, bright and sunny with a light breeze keeping the heat in check. Susan spent the afternoon in the garden with William. He was becoming very aware of all around him and followed the toy that she dangled about in front of him, with big bright eyes and groping fingers. She had hoped his eyes would change colour, and become grey like hers, but they remained blue.

Rachel watched from her easy chair under the tree. To her great delight, she had discovered that therapy had strengthened her damaged arm enough for her to manage a crochet hook. She was now busy working on some matinée coats for her grandson. 'What time are you going out tonight, Susan?'

'Jim's picking me up at half-past seven.'

'After tea give yourself plenty of time to get ready. I'll see to William's needs.'

'Are you sure, Mam? I was going to bathe him before I got ready. What about your arm?'

'I'll manage fine, so don't you worry your head about me. It's surprising what I can do now. I've been very lucky, you know.'

'You have indeed, Mam! And we're all very pleased for you. I'll be delighted to leave William in your tender care. You're an angel, so you are. Thanks a lot, Mam.'

'My pleasure. I love having that wee rascal all to myself. I think Alison has persuaded Graham to take her out tonight too,' she mused. 'I'm so glad for her. She's young and has her whole life ahead of her. She should get out more often before she gets tied down to married life.'

'Oh.' For some reason Susan felt apprehensive. 'Did she say where?'

'No, she didn't mention it at all. I was in the lounge, but she was so delighted to be going out that she was shouting with excitement and I couldn't help but overhear. I wasn't eavesdropping, mind, so I didn't hear any particular venue being mentioned.'

Susan mulled over this information in her mind. One thing was sure: Graham, although walking with just the aid of one stick now, was still very shaky on his legs. Even he would hardly have the gumption to go to a dance in his condition. On the other hand, if her sister had mentioned that Susan was going to the Orpheus with Jim Brady, he would be contrary enough to do just that.

She gave herself a little shake and warned herself not to be paranoid about him. Besides, it was a ticket-only dance and even Graham would have difficulty obtaining tickets at such short notice.

After tea that evening her mother cradled her grandson in her good arm and shooed her daughter upstairs to get ready for her date. When Susan would have demurred, Rachel cried, 'Away you go! I can cope all right. My arm's not as bad as you think. Besides, if I need any help your father will be here.'

The dress, collected that morning, hung on a hanger from the back of the bathroom door. It had got slightly wrinkled, but the steam from the bath should soon resolve that problem. She still fretted about how much it had cost, and no way was she going to put an iron to it. With her luck she was likely to scorch it.

As she lay soaking in the bath, she eyed the dress. It really was beautiful; the material soft and clinging and the rich ruby suited her colouring perfectly. But . . . was this creation not meant to be worn for someone you cared dearly for? Someone you were committed to and were sure of? Someone you loved and who loved you in return? Did she want Jim to be so bowled over by her in it that he would be unable to keep his hands off her, as Ruth had suggested? Did they not need to take things easy, one step at a time; see how they felt about each other now that a child was involved? What if he did get carried away – would she be able to resist him? She certainly should! Once bitten, twice shy was going to be the motto of the day. However, it was so long since a man had held her and kissed her that she would be vulnerable. She would have to be very, very careful tonight.

Putting the finishing touches to her make-up, she was still undecided about the dress. Brushing her thick, freshly shampooed hair until it glowed with chestnut highlights, she secured it with clips on top of her head in a crown of curls, emphasising the geometry of her face: high cheekbones, widely spaced grey eyes, perfect nose and small, determined chin. She moved her head from side to side, pouting at her reflection, and her full, sensuous lips spread into a wide smile at the antics of herself. Next she turned her attention to the dress.

To avoid messing her hair she stepped into it and carefully wriggled the soft material up over her hips and into place over a strapless bra purchased for this very purpose. She had thought that perhaps it had been the dim, coloured lights in the shop that had made her look so good in it, but no! Here in the bright lights of her bedroom she studied her image reflected in the full-length mirror and felt and looked every bit as glamorous. There was still a slight heaviness about her hips, but the drape of the dress hid this.

She let out a long sigh and eyed her reflection apprehensively. It was make-up-your-mind time. Should she or shouldn't she wear it? After some thought she slowly removed the dress and hung it reverently on a hanger. It just didn't feel right to wear it tonight. It wasn't the right time. Perhaps if Jim and she became close she would wear it for him alone. She put a dustsheet over it and hung it at the back of the wardrobe, glad that she hadn't mentioned it to any of the family.

A shout from her father alerted her to the fact that Jim had arrived. Vexed with him for being early, she hurriedly changed her bra and, selecting another snug-fitting velvet dress, quickly pulled it on. She had meant to be ready to leave as soon as he arrived, and not give her father a chance to question him. She descended the stairs in a rush and crossed the hall, aware of voices coming from the lounge. Her father's deep tones were recognisable and she sighed. She had hoped to avoid this meeting. Her father would be giving Jim the third degree.

Surprise slackened her features as she entered the room. Both Graham and Jim were holding a conversation with her father. Jim gave her a broad grin of welcome, indicating that he was getting on all right with Trevor. Graham acknowledged her with a wave of his hand.

Alison hurried towards her and whispered, 'Do you mind if we accompany you to the Orpheus?'

The dismay she felt must have shown, causing Alison to continue quickly, 'I'm so sorry. Graham and I were going to the pictures, but when Jim arrived and said you were going to the Orpheus, Graham asked if we could tag along. Say you don't mind, Susan. Please? I'd be ever so glad to get out to a dance for a change.'

'But you can't! Didn't Jim mention it was a ticket do?'

'Yes! Jim did explain that, but Graham still wants to give it a shot. You know how it is. If any tickets are returned they sell them at the door. He thinks we stand a good chance of getting in.'

Susan had forgotten about being able to buy returned tickets. Still unable to hide her annoyance, she asked, 'Will he be able to dance? You'll be bored stiff if you have to sit and watch all evening.'

'He thinks he will be able to manage a few slow dances. And I hope you would let Jim give me a couple of dances. Ah, come on, Susan. I'd do the same for you, and you know it.'

Rachel appeared in the doorway, William cradled in her arms. He was rosy from his bath and dressed for bed. 'I just wanted to tell you not to leave the dance too early, Susan. Your father can carry William's cot into our room so that he can sleep with us tonight.'

Putting her arms around both her mother and child, Susan said gratefully, 'Thanks, Mam. Thanks, Dad. I'll phone later and make sure he's not playing up on you. I was going to come and see him before I went out.' She ruffled her son's wispy hair and planted a kiss on his cheek. 'Mam, have you met Jim yet?'

'No, I've been seeing to William. How are you, son?'

'I'm fine, and very pleased to meet you, Mrs Cummings,' he replied, rising quickly from his chair.

'Are you all going out together?' Rachel asked, surprised to see Alison and Graham still there.

'It looks like it.' Susan's voice was dry and her mother gave her a sharp look. 'I think it's nice to see you all getting out together,' she said softly. 'You know, a family affair? I'm sure you'll enjoy yourselves. Now, if you'll all excuse me, I'll take this little fellow upstairs.'

The others gathered round to kiss William good night. Only Jim hung back, looking ill at ease. At last Rachel was free to leave the room and, bidding Trevor and her good night, the four of them left the house and, with admiring comments about its make and colour, climbed into Jim's new car. Although he tried to hide it, Susan noticed that Graham was in pain as he eased himself into the car.

'Sit in the front, Graham, you will have more room.'

'No, thank you, Susan, for your concern, but I'll be fine here.' His voice was abrupt, causing her to take umbrage.

'Suit yourself.' He had no right going to a dance, and him hardly able to walk, let alone dance.

* * *

In the cloakroom at the Orpheus Alison turned to her sister in despair. 'Look at me! I'm not dressed for dancing. I should have nipped upstairs and changed my clothes before I came out.' She grimaced down at her skirt and blouse. 'I'm sure they'll all be dressed to kill in there tonight.'

Glad she had decided against wearing the new dress, which would have caused speculation, Susan smoothed her hands over her empire-line velvet dress and sadly agreed with her sister. 'No, you're not. But never mind. You won't be doing much dancing, will you? Tonight you'll just be a spectator. It wouldn't be fair on Graham if you were to dance with someone else and leave him sitting alone.' If she could possibly avoid it, she was determined not to sit out any dances keeping Graham company. She was in no mood for his snide remarks and subtle threats.

Alison looked at her sister through narrowed lids. 'You're still annoyed with me, aren't you? Why are you being so unreasonable, Susan? It's not like you.'

'Well, I'm sure you can appreciate that I would have liked to be alone with Jim. It's been a long time and we have a lot of catching up to do.'

'When Graham suggested we come along and Jim didn't raise any objections, I was so pleased to be going to a dance I wasn't going to argue about it. Even though I had an idea you might not want our company. I don't understand why, Susan. Surely it won't make that much difference whether we're here or not?'

'No? Well, that's neither here nor there. What's done is done, so let's join the men and make the best of it.'

Susan felt Alison's acute bewilderment at her attitude, but for the life of her she couldn't shrug off her displeasure.

They found their partners seated at a table near the edge of the dance floor. The bandsmen, resplendent in their dress suits and bow ties, were already in place and testing their instruments. Soon the first dance, a foxtrot, was announced. Jim rose immediately and with a slight bow asked Susan to dance.

She was so stiff in his arms that he frowned down at her. 'Is anything bothering you?'

'As if you didn't know,' she muttered. 'Did you have to ask them along?'

'I thought you knew all about it!' he cried defensively. 'The way Graham put it, I thought my say-so was already taken for granted. Do you think *I* wanted them along?' He gathered her closer. 'I've thought of nothing this past couple of days but having you all to myself tonight.'

Mollified, she relaxed in his arms. 'Just please don't leave me sitting with Graham, or I might say something to offend him. He had no right tagging along – and him hardly able to put one foot in front of the other.'

Jim frowned. 'You're putting me on the spot, Susan. I'll have to give Alison a few dances. Surely you can see that? It's only common courtesy to ask her.'

Knowing he spoke the truth, she replied mournfully, 'I know. I'm talking a lot of nonsense. It's just that I'm annoyed at his cheek, asking to join us. But let's make the best of it and enjoy ourselves.'

'Yes,' he agreed. 'We'll have plenty of time in the future to get to know each other again,' he whispered in her ear and let his lips trail over her cheek and neck, sending thrills of pleasure coursing through her.

They danced the next dance together and sat the next one out talking to Alison and Graham. The following one, with an apologetic glance at Susan, Jim asked Alison to dance. She was on the floor like a shot and Susan felt ashamed because she begrudged her sister a little bit of pleasure. Prepared to excuse herself and retire to the cloakroom, she glanced across at Graham. The excuse died on her lips when she saw the misery reflected in his eyes.

'Are you in pain?' she asked anxiously. 'Can I get you anything?'

'Hah, so you have decided to forgive me?'

Mystified, she queried, 'Forgive you for what?'

'For spoiling your reunion with your precious boyfriend. You haven't spoken directly to me all evening.'

Her lips tightened in anger. 'So it was deliberate, then?'

He shook his head as if weary of arguing. 'Not really. The occasion arose during the conversation and I couldn't resist it. You should have seen your sister's face when Jim said you were going to the Orpheus. I couldn't deny her the pleasure of at least watching the dancers, if it was at all possible. But you're spoiling it all for her, begrudging her a dance with Jim. I wouldn't have believed you'd be so selfish.'

Hot colour blazed across her cheeks at the insult and she glowered at him, nostrils flaring in anger. He thought she had never looked more lovely. 'What about me?' she cried. 'Eh? Doesn't it matter that my night is ruined?'

'And why is it ruined? Because I'm here?' His voice

was bitter and his eyes showed distaste. 'I never thought of you as a selfish person, Susan, but I'm getting an eye-opener tonight. Alison is a much better person than you'll ever be.'

'For once I agree with you! And you're a very lucky man that she's still willing to marry you, after the way you've been behaving lately. Getting on like a spoilt brat. Don't you realise that if she got an inkling of how we betrayed her trust, she would drop you like a hot potato?'

Suddenly alert, he leant forward only to fall back as the sudden movement caused a spasm of pain. 'Perhaps that's the best thing that could happen?' he hissed through clenched teeth.

'Oh, don't be ridiculous! You'd be spoiling everyone's happiness just because you can't accept the truth.'

He lapsed into silence and she waited breathlessly for his response. If only he would believe her.

She was silently urging him to speak and at last he did. 'Don't get me wrong, Susan, I'm still convinced William *is* my son. I can even see a likeness to my family in him.'

Fear gripped her heart. 'That's wishful thinking, and you must surely know it,' she cried in anguish.

'I don't think so. However, he was conceived in a moment of lustful madness that we've since regretted. We will both have other children, so forget I exist, if you must. I'll never trouble you again.'

Shame was consuming her, making her bitter in return. 'I'm glad you're convinced at last. Now maybe you'll get out of my life and leave me alone. I'm sick to the teeth of listening to your insinuations. Do you hear me?'

Tears blinding her, she rose from the table and hurried to the cloakroom. How dare he talk to her like that, she fumed inwardly. He was treating her as if she were some naughty schoolgirl. Whereas he was the one who was behaving irrationally. How dare he! Well, at least she was shot of him at last. Hopefully he would never bother her again. But would it spoil things for Alison? Did her sister really want to marry him? Would she be happy married to Graham? And how would it be to have him for a brother-in-law, constantly watching William grow up, with suspicious eyes.

Oh, dear God, it would be an awful way to live. But on the other hand of course, if Jim did ask her to marry him, she would be living at the other end of town. That should help matters. She repaired her make-up and, when she could delay no longer, made her way back to the ballroom.

At the table Jim rose to his feet and eyed her with concern. 'Are you all right, Susan?'

She nodded, aware that all eyes were on her. 'Can we dance, please?'

Wordlessly he led her on to the dance floor. Tenderly holding her close, he pressed his cheek to hers and was dismayed to discover that it was wet with tears. Drawing back, he looked down at her. 'What on earth's the matter?'

Thankful that the dimmed lights hid her tears from the other dancers, and ashamed that she was unable to control them, Susan buried her head against his chest and muttered, 'I'm sorry. It must be the aftermath of having a baby that reduces me to tears for nothing. Having a baby upsets the hormones, you know. I think maybe I'm suffering from postnatal depression.'

'Come off it. Baby or no baby, you're not stupid enough to cry for nothing. Did Graham upset you?'

'It doesn't matter.'

'Oh, but it does matter. What happened?'

'Forget it, Jim. Please? It was my own fault. I didn't try to hide the fact that I resented their company and Graham took exception to it and we had words.'

'But, he had no right . . .'

'Please, Jim, don't let me spoil our first evening back together. I just need time to get a grip on myself.'

'Okay. Let's stay away from the table for a while. Give you a chance to pull yourself together. Shall we have a drink?'

She nodded gratefully and he twirled her in and out of the dancers until they were close to the bar. While they waited to be served she felt calmer and her conscience began to plague her. 'Jim, I feel guilty leaving them sitting there.'

'They're not our problem, Susan. After all, we didn't invite them along.'

'Still . . . I feel I am mostly to blame. Can we bring them back a drink and let bygones be bygones?'

Undecided, he eyed her through narrowed lids. 'Are you sure that's what you want to do?'

'Yes.'

He shrugged, obviously still perturbed. 'All right! If that's what you want.'

'How do I look? Would you know I've been crying?'

Jim eyed her intently. 'No. No, you would never guess. Now take a deep breath and give me a big smile, then we can go back to them.'

Graham saw them approaching the table and his heart lifted. He thought he had blown it. He regretted his outburst to Susan. Watching her plastered against Jim Brady as they circled the dance floor had made him so jealous that he had lost control of his reason and, when given the chance, had lashed out blindly with his tongue. He had said some terrible things to her. Now he gratefully accepted the glass of beer Jim handed him. 'Thanks, Jim.' He raised it to Susan. 'Cheers.'

Susan raised her glass of orange juice in reply. Holding his eye, she asked, 'All friends again?'

Alison was looking from one to the other of them in mystified surprise. Deciding to give them a chance to resolve their differences, Jim placed his beer on the table and said, 'Would you like to dance, Alison?'

'Only if it's not going to upset anyone.' She looked apprehensively at her sister.

'Please, be my guest.'

Alone at the table, Graham and Susan eyed each other. 'Can we call a truce?' she asked apprehensively.

'With pleasure. But first I would like to apologise. I said some unforgivable things to you.'

'Yes, you did.'

'I'm very sorry, Susan. I realise now that I have been very unreasonable where William is concerned. I promise I won't harass you again. If at any time in the future you should change your mind and wish to talk to me concerning him, I'll be only too willing to listen. Meanwhile, he's your son and I wish you both the best of everything.'

Susan couldn't believe her ears. He was letting her off the hook. 'Do you mean it? No more insinuations?'

'I've been a fool. Instead of trying to win you over, I've driven you away. I realise now your heart belongs to Jim.'

'Can we be friends, Graham?'

He grimaced. 'That won't be easy.'

'What about Alison? If you marry her we will be family.'

He shrugged. 'I admit I'm very fond of her and intend marrying one day. So why not her? Believe me, if we do marry, I'll do all in my power to make her happy. She will want for nothing. But don't you worry about it. I'll keep out of your hair.'

The rest of the evening passed without incident, until near the end, when Ruth swooped down on them followed by an embarrassed Dougie. Stopping in front of Susan, she gaped in confusion. 'Dougie knows the doorman and he let us in for the last couple of dances,' she explained. Her eyes roamed over her friend's dress and then rose questioningly to her face.

Glad that Ruth had the sense not to question her openly in front of the others, Susan advised her friend, 'You had better get on the floor then and sample this great band.'

With a wry smile at them all, Ruth turned to her partner. 'Come on, Dougie, let's not waste any more time.'

During the course of the evening Graham had managed to dance a couple of slow waltzes with Alison. Now he gestured towards the dance floor and said, 'May I have this waltz, Susan?'

Silently she allowed herself to be led on to the floor;

it would be unkind to refuse, but she wished he hadn't asked. She entered his arms and he drew her close. 'I hope you don't mind me asking you to dance? It will only be a bit of a shuffle, you know.'

'No!' Her voice was curt and she repeated more gently, 'No, why should I?'

'Well then, relax. I won't bite you.'

She was afraid to relax in case she gave him the wrong impression. She was remembering how, when he had stayed overnight in Edith's house, she had got carried away at his closeness. But then, hadn't she that very same night almost succumbed to Donald's charms? It seemed she was just too easily seduced. He winced and, concerned, she asked, 'Does it hurt you to dance?'

He smiled wryly. 'Believe me, the pleasure is worth the pain.'

She glanced up and saw the dark shadows under his eyes; the pain he tried so hard to hide. 'Look, Graham, there's a couple of empty chairs over there along the wall. Let's sit down.'

'Promise you'll stay with me, not run away.'

'Of course I'll stay. What kind of a person do you take me for?'

He opened his mouth to speak, but closed it again.

'What were you going to say?' He looked so forlorn that she wanted to put her arms around him and press his head to her breast. Comfort him as she would a child. God, what was she thinking of? That was Alison's responsibility.

They reached the chairs and he sighed with relief as he sank carefully down on to one of them.

Undecided, she hovered in front of him. 'You look

awful! Can I get you anything? Some painkillers perhaps?'

He shook his head. 'Just sit down and keep me company for a wee while.'

She obeyed and asked speculatively, 'What were you going to say, back there?'

Before he could answer her question, Alison and Jim stopped in front of them. 'Are you all right, Graham?' Alison asked anxiously.

He shook his head. 'No, I don't feel so good. Sorry for spoiling your night, love, but I'd like to go home now. Please phone for a taxi.'

'I'll run you home.'

'You'll do nothing of the kind, Jim. The dance will soon be over.'

'I insist . . . In fact, I'm sure Susan won't mind if we all leave now?' He glanced questioningly at Susan.

Quickly Graham cried, 'I won't hear tell of it! I've been a big enough nuisance for one night. Please phone for a taxi, Jim. Perhaps you will be kind enough to take Alison home?'

'Of course.' Seeing that he was at the end of his tether, Jim said, 'I'll ring for a taxi now.'

'Thanks, mate.'

The rush of late-night revellers going home had yet to start and the taxi arrived in no time at all. Leaving Alison at the door to say good night in private to her fiancé, Jim and Susan bade him farewell and returned to the ballroom.

'He must love Alison a lot to suffer as he did tonight, just so that she could have a dance,' Jim mused. 'I'm not sure I'd have the guts to do it.'

'Mm, indeed he must.'

Her voice was tinged with irony and he questioned her, 'Do you know something I don't?'

'Such as?'

He shrugged. 'I can't even hazard a guess, but I know this much: something isn't right between you two.'

'Will you excuse me, Jim? Ruth has just left the room alone. She must be going to the cloakroom. I want to speak to her. I'll be back in a jiffy.'

In the cloakroom Ruth faced her friend in indignation. 'What on earth are you playing at?' she cried. 'What happened to that beautiful dress you bought?'

Hustling her into a corner, away from the other two occupants in the room, Susan hissed, 'Hush. Alison will probably be in here any minute. She's seeing Graham into a taxi.'

'You didn't show it to her?'

'No. As a matter of fact, I didn't show it to anyone.'

'How were you able to resist?'

'I only collected it this morning, remember?'

'Well, put me out of my misery! Why didn't you wear it tonight? Did you spill something on it? Is that it?'

'No. I'm saving it for a better occasion. Perhaps Christmas.'

Ruth's eyes lit up. 'He's proposed, hasn't he?' she gasped in delight. 'You're going to get engaged at Christmas and that's why you're saving it.'

'Do you know something, Ruth? You could write a book with that imagination of yours. Jim hasn't asked me to marry him and I'm not getting engaged.'

'Watch my lips, Susan. After paying all that money,

why are you not wearing the dress tonight? That's all I want to know.'

She shrugged negatively and confessed, 'I felt too grand in it. Overdressed, you know, for this kind of a dance. And I'm glad I didn't wear it. No one else is wearing an off-the-shoulder dress here tonight. I'd have stuck out like a sore thumb.'

'A very attractive sore thumb. If I looked half as good as you did in that dress, I wouldn't care about anybody else. I'd be in my glory. Showing off.'

'I'm different from you. I prefer to keep it for a special occasion. So there.'

Ruth glanced over Susan's shoulder. 'Hi, Alison. Did Graham get away all right?'

'Yes, the taxi came in no time. I shouldn't have asked him to come here tonight. It was selfish of me. It was too much for him. He's exhausted, poor dear.'

'Never mind. Did you enjoy yourself?'

'I did, Ruth.' Alison glanced at her sister. 'In spite of everything, I enjoyed myself.'

Sensing a mystery, Ruth looked from one to the other. Her mouth opened to speak, but Susan forestalled her. 'Come on, there must surely only be a couple of dances left. Let's not waste any more time in here in idle gossip.' She left the cloakroom and the others were obliged to follow, with Ruth silently vowing to get to the bottom of the mystery next time she met her friend.

When the car drew into the driveway, Alison, who had remained silent throughout the journey home, leant forward from her seat in the back, and patting Jim's shoulder, said, 'Thank you very much for the lift home and for tolerating our company at the dance, Jim. It was very kind of you.' Without a glance in her sister's direction, she said, 'Good night, Susan' and hurried from the car.

They watched her climb the steps and disappear through the door. 'She's still very annoyed at you,' Jim mused.

Tight-lipped, Susan argued, 'I'm the one who should be annoyed.'

'Yes, I suppose so.'

'What do you mean, *suppose*? I'm very disappointed in you, Jim. I thought you, at least, would be on my side.'

'Here! Hold on a minute. I'm not on anybody's side. My mind boggles just trying to make sense of it all.'

Realising that he must be bewildered at her attitude towards Graham, she apologised. 'I'm sorry. I didn't mean to spoil everyone's night. It's just that I'd been so looking forward to it and I'm afraid I couldn't hide my disappointment. It's as simple as that. No other reason. Anyway, thanks for putting up with me, Jim. Good night.'

She was out of the car so quickly that for a moment he sat, taken aback. Bounding from his seat, he caught hold of her at the bottom of the steps. 'Hey, hold on a minute. Why the big rush?'

'I thought you'd had enough of me for one night.'

'Don't be silly. Get back in the car, I want to talk to you.'

Fearful of eyes watching them from the house, she said, 'It's a lovely night, let's go for a walk.'

Obediently he followed her down the driveway. They

headed on up the Old Cavehill Road and he was amazed when, a few minutes later, the Cave Hill loomed before them.

She heard his gasp of surprise and agreed, 'It does come as a bit of a shock the first time you see it. This is what I call the gentle side of the hill. It's easier to climb than the rest of it.' He still seemed dazed and she teased him, 'You didn't realise I literally lived at the foot of the Cave Hill, did you?'

'I knew it was a long trek back the nights I walked home in the winter months, but I didn't realise you lived so far out.'

She slipped her arm through his and they climbed the twisting path until all the houses were out of sight. 'It's too late to climb any further. Shall we sit down for a few minutes?' She closed her eyes tight in despair as she realised how this might sound to him. Would he think she was about to throw herself at him again, and take to his heels?

To her relief, without any hesitation whatsoever he removed his jacket and spread it on the grass. They sat side by side in companionable silence. It was eerie by the light of the pale moon; all shadows and animal sounds. An owl hooted somewhere close and she shivered at the sound, pulled her cardigan closer around her body and hugged herself. Jim put his arm around her waist and pulled her close. They were sitting thigh-to-thigh and hip-to-hip, but to her surprise she wasn't in the least bit physically aroused. She certainly had no great desire to ravage him. Remembering the agitated state she had been in the last time they were alone like this she felt a little confused, but glad to be in control of the situation. She felt very much at ease with him. Was this how it would be if they were married? Feeling his gaze, she turned her head and met his eyes. His lips hovered close and then claimed hers. He kissed her passionately – on the lips, the throat and cleavage – and she returned his caresses with warmth but no great passion. She was glad he wasn't trying to take advantage of her and she was quite happy to respond to his kisses. At last he pushed her gently away and rising to his feet, pulled her upright.

They stood face-to-face and, cupping her chin in his hands, he kissed her once more. 'We'd better go now. It's getting late.'

At the door he asked, 'Can I see you tomorrow night?'

Regretfully she shook her head. 'I couldn't expect Mam to babysit two nights in a row. She isn't fit enough, and William can be a right handful at times.'

He smiled wryly. 'I keep forgetting that you're a mother. It will take a bit of getting used to. When can I see you?'

'Give me a ring during the week and we'll fix something up.'

'Okay.' A light kiss on the lips and he climbed into the car and was away.

Susan made sure all the doors were locked and barred for the night. Climbing the stairs, she paused outside her parents' door and listened. All she could hear was the regular snoring of her father. Gently turning the doorknob, she quietly opened the door and peeped in. The cot was empty, but William took up most of the wide bed, arms and legs outstretched while her mother and father hung precariously on the edge of their respective sides.

She debated whether or not to lift William and bring him to her bed, but decided it would be a shame to disturb everyone. With a smile she gently closed the door. This was something that mustn't become a regular habit. The young rascal must be taught to sleep in his own cot or he would get used to the company and she would have trouble later on when she returned to work and needed to get a good night's sleep.

As she creamed off her make-up she went over in her mind the events of the evening. She admitted to herself that she had been a right nasty bitch. Still, it would be worth being thought a bitch if Graham really did stop pestering her. She remembered his strained face and her heart went out to him. If only he and Alison were closer. It was her fault that they weren't! How she regretted that night of lust! If she hadn't been so stupid, her sister and Graham would be married by now and she would probably be engaged to Jim. It hadn't been all her fault, she lamented. Graham had wanted it, too.

Was there any truth in the old wives' tale that everything happened for a purpose? Surely not. What advantage could there be in the sin that she and Graham had committed? Not that they had planned it – no, it had been the result of a series of occurrences.

Try though she did to recapture the comfortable feelings she had experienced with Jim, it was Graham's face she carried into her unsettled dreams.

She dreamt he was pursuing her towards the edge of a high cliff. She shook with terror as she peered over the edge at the angry waves crashing against the jagged rocks far below. Seeing no way of escape, she squared her shoulders and bravely turned to face him, but he wasn't there. She awoke lathered in sweat, her heart pounding against her ribs. The feeling of panic stayed with her for a long time, making sleep almost impossible.

For six wonderful weeks Susan was very contented with her lot; life could not be better. William was coming on like a house on fire. Bright as a button, he viewed the world around him with gurgles and smiles. She was due to return to work at the beginning of September and was looking forward to it. The weather continued to be fine and warm with just the odd dull or wet day. Graham had had a relapse after the night out at the dance. He was confined to bed for three weeks and Alison spent a lot of time at his home. Once he was on his feet again, she went about with a smug smile on her face like the cat who had stolen the cream. It appeared to all concerned that her every wish was Graham's command. He certainly appeared to be living up to his promise to make Alison happy and stay out of Susan's hair. What more could she ask?

She saw Jim twice a week; he wanted to see her more often, but tentative efforts to get him to include William in some outings so that they could go out on a Sunday afternoon, for instance, had so far failed. This worried her somewhat, but she convinced herself he needed time to get accustomed to her being a mother. Hadn't he said, 'It will take a bit of getting used to'?

To her joy she received a letter from Donald Murphy. Being a maintenance fitter, he had to work during the annual summer holiday, which in Darlington was the last week in July and the first in August. Now he wrote to inform Susan that, starting the second week in August, he was thinking about visiting Northern Ireland to see for himself some of the places she had told him about. He intended travelling up through Scotland to Stranraer and crossing on the ferry to Larne, and wanted to know if he could possibly call and see her and her wee son while he was over? He also asked if she could recommend a good guest house. He would have a three-week break.

As it turned out, Alison was accompanying Graham and his parents to Killarney the first two weeks that Donald would be in Belfast and she was quick to suggest that he could have her room, as it was much bigger than the spare room. It was with trepidation that Susan approached her father and asked if she could offer Alison's room to Donald for a fortnight.

'And what has Alison got to say about that?'

'It was her suggested it, Dad. And Donald was a true friend to me when I lived in Darlington. I could always rely on him.'

Trevor's eyebrows gathered in a frown. 'Is he . . .'

'No,' she anticipated his question. 'He's not William's father.'

'Then by all means invite him to stay.'

Inwardly she marvelled at how her father had mellowed in his attitude towards Catholics. There had been a time when he would not have allowed one over his doorstep, let alone hold a civil conversation with one. Now he and Jim got on quite well together. She gave into her instinct to hug him. He released himself quickly from her embrace, but, although embarrassed, she could see he was nevertheless pleased.

She replied that day to Donald's letter, assuring him of a good Irish welcome, and informed him that he was to stay at her parents' home. Once he knew dates and times, he was to be sure to let her know immediately what ferry he would be on and when he would arrive, so that she could arrange for someone to meet him at Larne harbour and pilot him to Belfast, him being a stranger to the Emerald Isle.

During her stay in Darlington, Donald had endeavoured to teach her how to drive and had been quite pleased with her efforts. Now she regretted not keeping it up. It would be so handy to be able to drive. Her father's car often sat unused in the garage at weekends because neither she nor Alison had a driving licence. Perhaps Jim would give her some driving lessons if she asked him? Men were not very forthcoming where women learner drivers were concerned, but perhaps if she worked on him, he might just agree to teach her.

Her excitement bubbled over when she told Jim about Donald coming to visit. They had been to the cinema and were sitting in the car outside the house talking when she told him the news. At first she didn't notice his withdrawal as she babbled on about how good Donald had been to her. Eventually she broached the subject of learning to drive.

'Maybe you'll give me some driving lessons, Jim. Donald will be so surprised if I can drive. He warned me to keep it up or I'd just lose all my confidence. I was coming along great, too. Then I got word about Mam and I had to come home. Will you help me, Jim?'

It was some seconds before she realised he was not responding to her. She turned in her seat and eyed him warily. 'Is anything wrong?'

'You seem very excited at the idea of meeting this bloke again.'

'I am.' She warned herself to be careful; not to give Jim cause for jealousy. 'He was a very good friend to me when I was over at Aunt Edith's. I'd have been lost without him.'

He still refused to meet her eye. 'Is he William's father?' he asked flatly.

To her surprise she found that she wanted to lash out at him and tell him to mind his own bloody business. After all, she at last despairingly admitted to herself, he had shown very little interest in William so far, so what did it matter who the father was? Then she remonstrated inwardly. He had the right to know the truth, but it was something she could never tell him. If anything was to come of their relationship, he would have to take her at face value.

'No, he's not!' Her tone of voice brooked no further questions.

He ignored her reticence and suddenly reached out and gripped her hands tightly. 'Susan, it would be easier all round if you would only tell me the father's name. Surely you can trust me not to broadcast it?' His tone deepened. 'Can't you see? I need to know,' he cried in anguish.

If she were to confess to him now, she could imagine how he would react the next time he saw Graham. There was no way he could act normally and all her conniving would be in vain. Leaning towards him, her eyes beseeched him. 'Jim, I can't! I can never tell anyone.'

'Why not?' he cried in bewilderment. 'You make it sound like a virgin birth! Did you not realise what was going on until it was too late, or something? Is that why? Did he take advantage of you?'

She remembered the intensity of her brief union with Graham, the pain and the pleasure, and cried, 'No! No, far from it. I can never accuse him of that. It was by mutual consent.'

He threw her hands from him in disgust. All the doubts and dark thoughts he had harboured for a long time erupted. They came into his mouth and, without thought of the consequences, he spewed them out in despair. 'You must have been seeing this guy while you were dating me all those months ago,' he accused. Ignoring her wild shake of the head and the piteous moans of denial coming from her lips, he continued. 'Were you, Susan? If we had done it that night, would you have palmed William off as mine? Eh, Susan? Is that why you were so keen? Was I intended to be the fall guy? When I didn't play ball, is that why you ran off to England?'

The enormity of this tirade was like an icy wind blowing through her, leaving her numb to the core. She gaped at him in horror, eyes and mouth stretched wide. How could he think that of her? All these weeks while he dated her he had been harbouring these terrible dark thoughts. Distraught, she cried, 'How can you think that?'

'Why not? Can you blame me? You certainly have never shown such passion since,' he muttered bitterly.

Slowly a hot rage consumed her at his audacity. How

dare he! All this time he had been waiting for her to throw herself at him again. Who did he think he was? Well, he would have a long wait! Never again would she risk rejection such as she had been subjected to at his hands. Her tongue was sharp when at last she found her voice and upbraided him, 'Shall I tell you why that is?' she hissed. 'It's because I'm afraid that maybe this time you might think I'm easy prey and that I'll let you have your way with me and then run away again, perhaps leaving me with another child. Besides which, you're not exactly the world's most passionate lover yourself, you know! It's not too hard for me to control my emotions when I'm with you. We may as well be an old married couple for all the passion you show.' Aghast at the effrontery of her remarks, she fumbled for the door handle. The close confinement of the car was becoming unbearable. She must get away before he insulted her further, in retaliation. He would never forgive her for attacking his ego like that. But it was true! There had been no great moments of passion between them, as once there had been. Even at the dances when they had danced close together, there was no great awareness; no longing to be alone. Not on her part, anyhow. He must have noticed it too. She had been foolish enough to think it was out of respect for her.

Before she could open the door, his hands suddenly gripped her shoulders, shook her and roughly pulled her towards him. 'You want a display of passion, do you? Eh? How about this?' His lips were brutal as they crushed against hers, and she tasted blood as she frantically tried to escape his savage kiss. 'And this!' She struggled to be free, but he held her firmly in one arm and his free hand was relentless in his endeavour to hurt. He tore wildly at her blouse. It was of flimsy material and the buttons gave easily under his attack. Pushing her bra roughly to one side, he cupped her breast and kneaded it with sharp, cruel fingers. 'Is this how you like it? Eh, Susan? Is this how it was with him? Do you like it rough?'

With one last desperate push she managed to free herself from his grasp and this time her groping hand found the door handle. Gripping the ends of her blouse together with one hand to hide her nakedness, she grabbed her bag, stumbled from the car, almost falling, and raced blindly up the steps. With hands that shook she had the key out, the door open and was through it before he had time to get out of the car.

He gazed after her in stunned silence. Dear God, what on earth had possessed him to attack her like that? He, who had never once lifted a hand or raised his voice in mock anger at his sisters when they were disobedient? He looked down at his hands; they were trembling, and no wonder! He was shaking all over. He started to get out of the car – he had to beg her forgiveness, explain how her silence had been tormenting him all these weeks. He must somehow get her to understand that he was only human and needed to know the truth. Then he sank back in his seat in defeat, his hands washing over his face in anguish. She could never have a rational conversation with him now. Not the state she was in. And who could blame her! How she must hate him. He might wake the whole household if he went after her. He cringed when he pictured how Trevor would react if he saw her torn blouse. Head in hands, he sat for some time regaining control of his shaking body, then slowly set the car in motion and drove away.

Passionless! Did you ever hear the like of it? She thought him passionless. He wanted to weep at the very idea. If only she knew the times he had wanted to ravage her; arouse her to awareness such as she had known before and, declaring his love, ask her to marry him. Well, why hadn't he, he ranted inwardly? Because he wasn't sure how she felt towards him. What if he was unable to arouse her? The emotions they used to ignite in each other at the slightest provocation were no more. He had hoped to rekindle them. Now it was too late. He had ruined everything by losing his self-control like some wild beast. Besides, now there was the child to consider. He found he couldn't work up any great enthusiasm for this other man's offspring. Perhaps if she had trusted him enough to tell him the father's name he might have felt differently. Then this would never have happened. Surely he had the right to know his identity, if they were to marry.

Susan stood trembling with her back pressed against the door in the dark hall, willing him to go away. What if he came to the door and created a scene and woke her father? There would be hell to pay. At last she heard the engine start up and, with a sigh of relief, pushed herself away from the door. It was too early to lock up for the night. Alison couldn't be home yet. They had made arrangements to leave their door key on the hall-stand so that the last one in would know to lock and bar the door. There was no sign of Alison's key. Wearily, she climbed the stairs. Perversely, now that Jim was gone, she derided him for not following her. He must surely have known how upset she was; why hadn't he tried to put matters right? Offered some kind of apology for his bullish behaviour? But then, could she ever forgive him?

She paused outside her parents' bedroom, but all was silent, except for the usual rhythmic snoring from her father. William must be in his cot. Continuing on up the stairs she entered the nursery. She had managed to get William into a routine whereby he slept in his cot most of the night and had insisted that her parents bear with her and use the intercom when babysitting. He lay in his usual spreadeagled position with the bedclothes kicked off. Bending over the cot, she gently caressed his small head and pulled the blankets back over him before entering her own room and quickly undressing.

She had just pulled on her pyjama coat when she heard light footsteps on the stairs. A tap on the door and her mother entered the room, holding the other half of the intercom.

'I thought you might need this, Susan,' she whispered.

'Thanks, Mam, but really, you shouldn't have got out of bed. You should have just turned it off. After all, he's right next door to me, I would have been sure to hear him.'

'It's still quite early. Your father is snoring away, but I was reading.' She peered intently at her daughter. 'Are you all right, love?'

'Yes! Why wouldn't I be?'

'I have a confession to make. I was on my way to the bathroom and I glanced out of the landing window earlier on and I saw you leave Jim's car. You seemed in a big hurry to get away from him. Have you two had a tiff?'

Suddenly it all proved too much for Susan and, covering her face with her hands, she sank down on the bed. 'Oh, Mam. I don't know what to do. Jim doesn't want William.'

Quickly crossing the floor, Rachel sat down beside her and put a comforting arm across her shoulders. 'Perhaps he just needs time?'

'You must surely have noticed, Mam, how we never take William out with us? Even when Jim's in the house he pays little attention to him. He's yet to hold him.'

'You can't very well take him to a dance or the pictures, Susan,' Rachel reasoned gently.

'He wants to see me more often, but I've tried to get him to take me and William out at weekends. You know, to the park or the beach, even over to the zoo. Just to let him get to know what a lovely baby William is, but Jim never takes the hint. He just doesn't want to know.'

'From what I've heard, he seems to be a nice, hard-working, caring lad. Even your dad likes him, and you know how he feels about you girls dating Catholics. Not many men would support their families like Jim has, since his father died. Perhaps that's why he's reluctant to take on someone else's responsibilities. Don't be too rash, Susan. Give him more time.'

'Time won't change anything. You see, he insists on knowing who the father is.'

'Ah, now, Susan. He has the right to know. Surely you can at least confide in *him*?'

'That's just it! I can't, Mam! Once he knows, his

opinion of me would be so low, he'd walk away for ever. So I'd be daft to tell him.'

This revelation left Rachel aghast. 'Ah, love,' she muttered in despair. 'What's going to become of you? No matter who you meet, they will want to know the truth.'

'Yes, I know! And there's those I could tell, and they would respect my wishes and it wouldn't make any difference to them. But not Jim! Mam, I wish I could explain. It's all such a sorry mess. I only wish I could tell the truth. Get it off my chest. Indeed, it would be a relief! But too many people would be hurt.' Tears continued to flow.

Bewildered, Rachel gathered her close, at a loss how to comfort her daughter. Who on earth was this mystery man? 'Don't take it so much to heart, love. If he's the one for you, he will marry you in spite of everything. If not, you'll meet someone else. You're young! You've your whole life ahead of you.' She rocked her daughter gently until at last the sobs petered out and the tears stopped.

Dabbing her eyes with the corner of her pyjama jacket, Susan said, 'You're right, Mam. But if he comes back tomorrow – not that I think he'd have the audacity, but if he does – I don't want to see him. You'll make some excuse for me, won't you? I need time to think.'

'All right. I'll do my best,' Rachel promised sadly.

Next morning Susan was appalled to see bruises on her upper arms and breast. She hadn't realised Jim had been so brutal. But then, she did bruise easily, she reminded herself, only to cry in retaliation that he had no right to abuse her at all! No right whatsoever!

She had to get out of the house in case he returned. There was no way she could face him at the present time. She would phone Ruth and see if she was free, and if so, perhaps they could go to the park for a picnic. This plan, however, was quickly abandoned. Ruth would guess right away that something was wrong and would wheedle the truth out of her, and she didn't want to make any confessions she might later regret.

At breakfast Alison gazed at her in concern. 'You look awful this morning, Susan! Are you ill?'

'No, William was restless during the night. I didn't get much sleep.'

'Was he? I didn't hear him. But of course I was home late and was out like a light as soon as my head hit the pillow.'

Rachel came to Susan's rescue. 'I was thinking that perhaps your father . . .' An eyebrow was raised towards the foot of the table, where Trevor was scanning the morning paper as he ate breakfast.

Aware of the sudden silence, he glanced up. 'Did someone speak to me?'

'I was wondering if you would run us all down to Enniskillen to visit my parents today. They haven't seen William since shortly after he was born. They would be so pleased.'

'I don't see why not. But it will only be a flying visit, mind. I don't fancy driving home late at night. I'd probably fall asleep behind the wheel.'

'That will be fine. Eh, Susan, don't you agree?'

'I'd love that, Mam.' Susan shot her a grateful glance. 'I'll go and prepare all I need to bring with me for William.'

'I'm afraid you'll have to count me out,' Alison said, suppressed excitement in her voice. 'I'm going over to Graham's house today.'

'So what's new?' Rachel said drily. 'You practically live there now. I take it you and Alma have resolved your differences by now?'

'She's not a bad old soul once you get to know her,' Alison assured her mother. 'And, what do you think? We're going to look at some houses today. If we find anything suitable, there might be a Christmas wedding after all.'

'Is Graham well enough?' Rachel asked in concern.

'Not really. It will have to be a very quiet affair in a registry office.'

'Ah, Alison, would it not be better to wait and have a nice big church wedding?'

A very definite shake of the head disputed this idea. 'Graham wants to get away from his mother's fussing as soon as possible.'

'That's no reason to rush into marriage. Don't you rush into anything just to suit everybody else!' Rachel admonished. 'Is this what you want?'

'The sooner we're settled in our own home, the better. Everything will be all right then.'

Then? Did that mean that everything wasn't all right now? Rachel was worried and tried to get her husband's opinion. 'Did you hear that, Trevor? There might be a Christmas wedding after all.'

Coming from the depths of his newspaper, Trevor muttered, 'Eh? What's that? Did anyone speak to me?'

Tut-tutting, Rachel sighed. Trevor could be very irritating at times. If he had been listening, instead of lost in that silly newspaper, he might have come up with something constructive. She repeated, 'Alison and Graham might get married at Christmas after all. What do you think of that?' Silently, she willed him to question the wisdom of it.

But no! A grin split her husband's face in two and to her disappointment, he cried, 'I think that's a grand idea!'

'And I have another bit of news for you,' Alison announced.

They waited patiently for her to continue. She kept them in suspense for some moments until at last Rachel cried, 'Well? Go on, tell us.'

'I'm learning to drive. I've put in for my test and, if I pass, Graham is going to buy me a car. Isn't that wonderful?'

'I hope you realise how lucky you are, Alison. See and show Graham the respect he deserves,' Trevor warned.

'Oh, I will. Believe me, Dad, I will.'

Susan felt a twinge of jealousy. Not, she assured herself, because her sister was marrying Graham. Or indeed because she was learning to drive – a desire that had brought things to a head between herself and Jim. But because everything seemed to fall into her sister's lap without much effort on her part, whilst nothing seemed to go right for her.

The trip to Enniskillen was most enjoyable. When their eldest daughter Edith had run off with a married man, a Catholic, William and Jane Wilson had managed to weather the furore that followed. The scandal had threatened to ruin their marriage. William had been bitter and unforgiving, but Jane had sided with her daughter, saying that she must follow her heart. Most of their neighbours had been understanding, knowing they had no control over events. Others had condemned them as weaklings for having no control over their daughter. A year later Rachel had somewhat redeemed their standing by marrying Trevor Cummings, a wealthy Protestant businessman.

With Rachel's marriage, William and Jane were free to get on with their lives and had left their Shankill Road enclave and, using most of their savings, had retired to a little village on the outskirts of Enniskillen, a move they never regretted. Their cottage was set well back from the lane in a garden still abundant with late summer flowers, whose perfume permeated the air. The hills in the background were ablaze with pink and purple heathers. They were sitting in the garden awaiting the arrival of their daughter and family, and ushered them inside for a cup of tea before taking advantage of the good weather and retiring to the conservatory at the back of the cottage.

Both grandparents were captivated by baby William and not a word of censure or curiosity was passed on how he had come about. He was their great-grandson and that was all that mattered. To Susan's surprise, her grannie found an opportunity to have a quiet word in her ear.

'I don't want to pry, love, but you seem to be unhappy. Can I help in any way?'

'Ah, Grannie, I didn't mean to be a wet blanket.'

'Don't be silly, girl! It's been a pleasure having you

here. I just sense a deep, hidden unhappiness. Am I right?'

Susan sighed and confided in her. 'It's just . . . well, the man I love doesn't appear to want William.'

'Not want that beautiful wee baby?' A stern expression settled on her grannie's face. 'You're better off without him, love,' she assured her granddaughter. 'Any man who wouldn't want that lovely wee baby must need his head examined. He's not worth his salt!'

Susan laughed outright at her grannie's words. 'Do you know something, Grannie? You're probably right.'

'Remember, Susan, if you need to get away from it all for a while, bring William here. Okay? I know we get harsh winters, but nevertheless this house is warm and comfortable. We'd be delighted to have you.'

Tears brimming on her eyelashes, Susan hugged the slight figure of her grannie close. 'Thanks, Grannie. You're a dear. Actually, everybody has been very supportive, considering how I've fallen from grace. I've a friend coming over from England on a visit in a few weeks' time. Perhaps I could bring him here for a few days and let him sample some of this lovely countryside?'

'Just you do that! That would be wonderful, love. We'll be glad of the company.'

It was quite late when they returned to Belfast. When they turned off North Circular Road and rounded the corner of Old Cavehill Road, the first thing to catch Susan's eye was Jim's car parked on the opposite side of the road near the house. Pretending not to notice it, she turned her head away, and when her father drew to a halt in the driveway she hurried from the car and quickly entered the house. Perhaps if she continued to ignore him, Jim might get the message and stay away. To complicate matters still further, a taxi pulled up behind her father's car and Alison jumped out, followed more cautiously by Graham.

In the hall, under the harsh glare of the electric lights, Susan gasped in concern when she saw how ill Graham looked. Dark rings under baggy eyes and a pallid face that looked as if it had caved in. He noted her reaction and smiled wryly. 'I'm not as bad as I look. I just did too much too soon.' He paused to gaze down at the sleeping child in Susan's arms. When his eyes met hers again the bleakness within their depths caught at her heartstrings.

'You shouldn't have gone to the Orpheus that night, Graham,' she admonished. 'It was an unnecessary risk you took and it's set you back months.'

He shrugged. 'Not quite unnecessary,' he disagreed wryly. 'It cleared the air and showed me where I stood with you.'

'What are you two whispering about?' Alison asked gaily. Putting a possessive hand on his arm, she drew him away. 'Come in and sit down, love.'

A knock on the door sent Susan hurrying to climb the stairs, clutching William in her arms. 'I'll just put him in his cot.' Feeling all the surprised eyes on her, she explained, 'He's out to the world. It's been a long day for the poor wee soul.' She had a good idea it would be Jim at the door.

She was right! Out of sight at the head of the stairs, she paused and strained her ears. Her father's voice reached her. 'Come in, Jim. Susan has just gone up to put William to bed. We've been to Enniskillen and the good fresh air there has knocked him out. She shouldn't be too long. Come in and join the rest of us in the lounge.'

Tears blinded her as she gave her son a quick wash, put on his nightclothes and laid him in his cot. Locked into his night's sleep, he barely stirred during her administrations. Gazing down on his rosy cheeks and parted pink lips, she agreed with her grannie. Any man who turned away from this wee bundle of joy did indeed need his head examined. She delayed as long as she dared and at last reluctantly descended the stairs.

'Ah, there you are, Susan. Jim's been waiting for you,' her father greeted her.

Jim's eyes met hers across the room and she saw the regret and anxiety in them. He rose and crossed the floor to her. 'Can we go for a short walk, Susan?' he said quietly. 'We need to talk.'

'I'm very tired, Jim. And William might wake any minute looking for his bottle. Perhaps we could meet tomorrow night and talk?'

He hesitated, then nodded in agreement. 'Where?'

'Let's meet outside the GPO about seven and take it from there. Eh?'

'Yes, that would be fine.'

Soon after he made his excuses and left the house.

Chapter Eleven

Jim waited twenty anxious minutes outside the GPO gazing blindly at the passing pedestrians. Convinced that Susan wasn't going to show up, he was about to go home in despair. Relief flooded through him when he saw her dodging in and out of the crowds on Royal Avenue towards him, brown hair lifting in the light breeze and cheeks pink with exertion. His heart lightened at the sight of her. Would she ever forgive him? He had said some awful things to her in the heat of the moment. If she did forgive him, would he be able to persuade her to his way of thinking?

She halted in front of him, breathless. 'I'm sorry to be so late, but William was restless and I couldn't very well leave Mother to cope with him. I had to stay until he settled down.'

He forced a smile to his lips. This was something he would have to get used to if he was to further their relationship. The child would always come first now. If only it were his child, it wouldn't be a problem! In fact if the truth be known, he would be delighted. But it wasn't his and, as things stood, he would have to be more resilient if he wanted to win her over. 'You don't have to apologise, Susan. Where would you like to go?'

She had noted the smile and guessed the trend of his thoughts. Her child had to be loved, not tolerated. Why didn't he give himself a chance to get to know William? She shrugged and his spirits dropped at her apparent indifference. 'I've no idea. Somewhere quiet where we can talk.'

'Mooney's lounge bar is quiet on a Monday night, shall we head there?'

'Great! That sounds fine.' In her opinion it was great. She didn't want to be completely alone with him, in case her heart overruled her head.

They walked along Royal Avenue and she was very aware of his height and breadth. Crossing Castle Junction, they headed for Cornmarket where Mooney's pub graced one corner. The public bar was crowded as usual, but as Jim had predicted the lounge was practically empty. A few girls chatting noisily at a table in the middle of the room and a couple gazing dreamily at each other over their glasses at a side table. Once inside, he led her to a corner table.

'What would you like to drink?'

'I'll have a Pernod and lime with ice, please.'

Conversation had been sparse between them so far, and Susan couldn't think of any excuse he might come up with that could possibly put things back on an even keel, in her eyes. Her heart was heavy as she watched him standing at the bar. She admired his long, lean body, broad shoulders and dark good looks. He was so handsome! Her idea of the perfect partner. Had she been describing him in writing, she would have labelled him Adonis. She had thought they were well matched. As if aware of her scrutiny, he turned and met her glance, a slight smile playing at the corners of his mouth. Confused, she looked away, embarrassed colour lighting up her face.

Blinking hard to contain the tears that threatened to fall, she gazed blindly down at her hands clasped on the table in front of her and thought of the high hopes she'd had of a future with Jim. What a fool she'd been! While she had convinced herself that he really cared, he'd been harbouring awful doubts about her. As if she would ever have tried to con him into accepting another man's child as his. He could never undo the harm he had caused to her self-esteem.

Slipping into the seat opposite her, he placed her drink close to hand. She lifted the glass and without looking at him said, 'Thank you. Cheers,' and sipped at the pale-green liquid.

When he had acknowledged her salute with raised glass, he gently removed hers and placed it to one side, then tightly gripped both her hands within his own. In spite of the warm atmosphere, they were icy-cold and trembled in his grasp. Her gaze remained downcast.

'Look at me, Susan,' he whispered.

Reluctantly, great tear-filled eyes were lifted to his and he was full of remorse at how much pain he was causing her. 'What I did was terrible and unforgivable, Susan. I know that! And I'm ashamed of myself.' His head swayed in distress. 'I can't believe I acted like that. It shows the stress I've been under these past weeks. I've tried and tried, until I think I'm going round the bend, to put a face to the father of your child, but it's beyond me. No one I know fits the bill. I can't remember you showing interest in any other man. But I swear I will never act like that again. Do you think you could ever find it in your heart to forgive me?'

'I realise I was partly to blame,' she conceded. 'And I do forgive you. But I honestly think it would be better if we didn't see each other again, Jim. There's no way I can see a future together for us.'

'Listen, Susan.' His voice was urgent. 'I want to explain something to you.'

Wordlessly, she gazed at him. Could he possibly put matters right? She doubted it, but nevertheless a flicker of hope kindled deep within her.

'First, I want you to know that I love you dearly. There has never been anyone else as far as I'm concerned. Since I met you I've never looked at another woman, let alone touched one. Never wanted to. Do you believe me?'

She did not answer; just gazed fixedly at him. Could he really love her, yet treat her like he had? She wasn't sure, so she remained silent.

Desperate to get his point across, he pleaded, 'Susan, please believe me. I really do love you. That's why I was so gobsmacked when I saw you were pregnant. It didn't take much arithmetic to figure out you had been seeing him at the same time you were dating me. And I never guessed! I just couldn't take it in. I wanted to walk away! Put you out of my life for good. What with Mam getting married and all, I'd such great hopes for us. Then you turned up big with another man's child and it was as if you were a different Susan from the one I knew. Still, if I'd been more understanding that night, things might have turned out different. But I didn't understand your desperate need. I could only feel this deep need to possess *you*. And to realise that you were mine for the taking? I couldn't take advantage of you like that. That's why I treated you with scorn and walked away. Fool! I was a fool. I wish now I'd stayed! Just how much I wish I'd stayed you'll never know. Then none of this would have happened. But you see, I thought I was doing you a good turn. I never dreamt that someone else was involved. Someone who wouldn't show you the respect you deserved. And he didn't, you know. No matter what you say. Whoever he is, he took advantage of you.'

Jim fell silent and she thought of her brief time with Graham. He hadn't taken advantage of her. It had been mutual. She opened her mouth to defend him, but Jim was continuing.

'However, I was totally out of order when I accused you of trying to implicate me. You're too decent a person to do anything underhand like that.'

Sifting through his words, she was able to see his point of view, but could not understand why he had never contacted her, later, before she was aware that she was pregnant and had run away in despair.

She voiced her thoughts. 'Why did you never get in touch with me again? I mean, you must have known I was ashamed of my carry-on that night.'

'I couldn't, Susan. Ma's auld fellow hadn't come on the scene then and I was in no position to offer you marriage. In my opinion, nothing else is good enough for you. That's where I'm different from this other bloke. I do love you dearly. Too much to use you for my own needs.'

She desperately wanted to believe his protestations of

love, but found that she couldn't. Had he not been harbouring awful doubts about her for weeks? Had he not mauled her? How could he do that if he loved her? When they were together she had imagined they were happy enough – not as wildly happy as they had formerly been, but a quiet, settled happiness. Had these doubts been festering away in his heart? He had practically confessed that he had been waiting for her to throw herself at him! If she had, would he then have thought her a slag? There was no way she would ever know. She could never comprehend the way his mind worked. And she must never for one minute forget that he *had* cruelly manhandled her. There was no excuse for that.

Sadly she shook her head. 'It wouldn't work, Jim.'

'Could we not give it a try?'

'I can't tell you the name of William's father. And you won't be happy otherwise.'

He sighed. 'I've been thinking about that, and I realise you must have very good reasons. I think perhaps I could learn to live with it.' He gripped her hands tighter still. 'Listen, our firm is sending two workers over to the parent company in California for a year's training in some new design methods. I've been offered the chance to go.'

These words killed off the last shred of hope. She tried to sound pleased for him. 'That's a wonderful opportunity for you.'

'For us, Susan! For *us!* I want you to come with me.'

'Me? I don't understand.'

'I would be going out in about three months' time. We could be married quietly in the registry office before then. Think about it, Susan. A honeymoon in America!'

'You're forgetting about William.'

'No, I'm not! But we would be better on our own. The other fellow who's going is single.'

'Would you not be better going as a single man?'

'I want you to come with me. I told the boss I wanted to get married and he said, "No problem! What better place for a honeymoon than America?" Think of it, Susan . . . A honeymoon in California. Could William not stay with your parents? It's obvious they dote on him.'

'And you didn't think to mention that I had a son?'

'I thought we'd be better on our own, Susan,' he admitted. 'And I don't think a child would be permitted. I mean, I am going out there to work. It's a bonus them letting you go along.'

'Let me get this straight. You want me to marry you and go to America with you . . . but without my son? You must know I could never leave William behind, no matter what the circumstances were.'

Aware that he wasn't convincing her, he nodded slowly, his eyes wary.

'And what about when we come back? What then, Jim?'

'I have to confess I haven't thought that far ahead, Susan.' He felt the colour rise in his face and he hoped she wouldn't notice. Because he *had* given it a lot of thought! He pictured Susan's parents rearing William. After all, they could afford it and he would want for nothing. Susan and he would hopefully have children of their own one day. Susan was far from stupid and he felt she must be aware of his duplicity. He was not surprised when she rose swiftly to her feet, almost upsetting the drinks.

She gazed sadly down on him. 'What kind of person do you think I am, Jim? Do you really think I could turn my back on my beautiful wee son? I thought you knew me better than that.'

Tight-lipped, he replied, 'Why not? His father obviously did!' He regretted the words the instant they left his mouth, but it was too late. Would he never learn?

He didn't see her hand coming and received the full strength of her wrath, as it made contact with his cheek with such force that it drove his head back on his shoulders.

'I can't believe how rotten you are, Jim Brady! You're certainly making a career of insulting me. This much I can tell you! William's father would marry me tomorrow if I gave him the go-ahead. What do you think of that?'

'Then why don't you marry him?'

'Hah! I'll tell you one of the reasons why. Because, poor fool that I am, I actually believed I still loved you. But you certainly hit that on the head once and for all. I don't want to see you ever again. Do you hear me?' Tears blinded her as she hurried from the pub. How could she ever have thought him Mr Wonderful? He was nothing but a selfish, two-faced pig.

Jim sat sipping his pint, aware of the covert glances directed at him. What did he care what anyone thought? He smiled slightly as he gingerly fingered his throbbing cheek. Susan could certainly pack a wallop. It looked as if he would be going to America on his own after all. If he had put in a bigger effort to show willingness where the child was concerned, he might have been able to persuade her that everything would be okay when they returned. No good thinking along those lines now. He loved kids and couldn't understand why he couldn't warm to William. His aversion to the child disturbed him somewhat. How could he be a good, loving father to him, feeling the way he did? The idea that Susan had cared enough to have a relationship with another man hurt him beyond measure. Especially since it must have been while she was professing to love him. Still, surely he could overcome his dislike and learn to love this child. He drained his glass and rose slowly to his feet. He cordially saluted the people who were now smiling openly at him. One young girl even shouted, 'Hey, gorgeous, we'll be here next week if she doesn't come back to you.' Another, 'Good luck, mate.' A cheer went up as he left the bar.

Locked in misery, Susan was unaware of the concerned glances that came her way as she queued for the bus. As she paid her fare the conductor, an elderly man with daughters of his own, asked kindly, 'Are you all right, love?'

She nodded and attempted a smile, but failed miserably. Climbing to the upper deck, she sat with bowed head and tried to get a grip on her emotions.

The journey home seemed endless, but at last she was at her own front door. Her mother was crossing the hall with William in her arms when Susan let herself into the house.

A glance in her daughter's direction brought Rachel to an abrupt halt. 'Susan, what's wrong, love?'

Taking the child from his grandmother's arms, Susan

clasped him close to her breast. 'You should hear the plans Jim Brady has in mind for us,' she wailed and at last the tears fell like rain and she wept bitterly, great drops falling down unchecked on William's head.

Concerned, Rachel patted her shoulder consolingly. 'Look, I was just about to heat William's bottle. Take him into the lounge and, when it's ready, I'll come and you can tell me all about it.'

A few minutes later she found her daughter sitting on the edge of the settee rocking back and forth in a distraught state. William was howling in sympathy with her. Reaching for the child, Rachel spoke soothingly to him and admonished her daughter. 'Stop that racket, for heaven's sake. You're terrifying the poor wee soul.' When William's sobs petered out, she wiped his blotched face and offered him his bottle. He snuffled, still in distress for another few seconds, then with a sigh snuggled close and sucked contentedly.

Only then did Rachel give her full attention to her daughter. 'Now, tell me about these plans Jim Brady has in mind for you.'

Rachel heard her out in silence, her mind digesting her daughter's words of woe. Unable to bear it any longer, Susan gulped back a sob and cried, 'Well, what do you think of that? Isn't he just one cruel, heartless bugger?'

'Hush, we'll have less of that language in this house, if you don't mind.'

'Sorry, Mam. It's just . . .' She shrugged dejectedly. 'I'm so disappointed.'

'Let's get one thing straight. Do you love Jim Brady?'

'Yes! God help me! He'd need to, I can't help myself.'

Rachel looked down at the now sleeping child. She could not comprehend how this child had come about if her daughter loved Jim Brady so much. A sudden thought entered her mind, to be pushed away in horror. If Susan had been raped she would not have covered up for the man. Unless . . . it was someone close. Someone they all knew. Hadn't she said that to tell his name would cause one hell of a scandal? Impossible! No one they knew would do a thing like that.

Susan noticed the worried expression flitting across her mother's face. 'Mam? What are you thinking? Good or bad, I want your opinion. What do you think I should do?'

Rachel tried to free her mind from the dreadful thoughts that swirled around in it. 'I'm thinking,' she said slowly, 'that it might be a good idea if you married Jim. That is, if you're absolutely sure you love him?'

'Mam! Whether I love him or not doesn't enter into it!' Susan was horrified that her mother could even think of her leaving William. 'How can you condone him asking me to leave my son behind?'

'Because obviously it would be the proper thing to do. It would give you a chance to enjoy married life together, without Jim having the constant reminder of your infidelity. Once he was sure of your love he might feel differently towards William. And . . . you know yourself that William would be well looked after by your father and me.'

Susan was looking at her mother, mouth agape. 'I can't believe I'm hearing this. From you of all people, Mam.'

'Well, you did ask my advice. You've got to be realistic,

Susan. You say you love Jim! He wants to marry you! So go for it! I bet when you come back he won't be able to resist William and everything will work out in the long run.'

Scandalised, Susan retorted, 'Don't you realise that babies' memories are short? William will have forgotten me in a year's time.'

'A year's nothing in a baby's life, Susan. As long as he's loved and cared for, I admit he won't necessarily miss you. But he will quickly get to know you again.'

Susan stood rooted to the spot for some moments. She wanted to scream in frustration, grab her son and rush from the house, but common sense prevailed. Where could she go? Instead she gave her mother a baleful glare and, turning on her heel, left the room.

A short while later Rachel heard the front door slam and sat motionless, feeling that she had failed her daughter. But if Jim persuaded Susan to marry him, there was no way Rachel was going to encourage them to take William with them. For a whole year? No way at all. He had become too precious to her.

Some thirty minutes later Trevor found her still clasping the sleeping child and rocking gently to and fro. 'Is he poorly?' he asked in concern.

Great haunted eyes gazed up at him. 'Jim Brady wants Susan to marry him.'

Perplexed, Trevor asked, 'Is that not a good idea? Oh, I know he's a Catholic and normally the idea would upset me no end, as you well know, but all children need a father and Jim seems a reliable kind of bloke.'

'His firm is sending him and another chap to America on a training course and he wants Susan to marry him and go with him. They'd be away for a year. He wants her to leave William with us.'

Still feeling very much in the dark, Trevor asked softly, 'And do you not feel well enough to look after him? Is that why you look so worried? You know I'd do all I can to help, and I'm sure Alison would pull her weight too. We can even employ a nanny if need be.'

'No! Susan won't go unless she can take William with her. What will we do if Jim agrees to take him? They could like America so much that they might even settle over there.'

Slowly Trevor sank down on to the settee beside her. Now he could see only too well why she was so worried. 'We can't let that happen, Rachel.'

'I know. But it's out of our hands. I advised Susan to marry Jim and go, but she acted as if I was a traitor.'

'Is she upstairs?'

'No. She ran out of the house as if the devil himself was after her. Oh, Trevor, I feel I've let her down badly.'

He slipped to his knees beside her, the better to see the sleeping child. In the months since he was born this wee fellow had wormed his way into his grandfather's heart. Their whole life seemed to revolve around him. In the midst of her worries, Rachel felt joy creep into her heart as she gazed at them both, so close together. 'Look, Trevor,' she whispered, 'look at him!'

Bewildered, he examined his grandson's features. 'What am I looking for?'

'Can't you see? He's a smaller version of yourself. You must surely see the resemblance?'

Slowly Trevor examined his grandson feature by feature. He couldn't believe William's nose was like his, but then it would be on a smaller scale. And definitely not the eyes. Although they were closed, he knew they were a different colour entirely from his. However, as the child moved restlessly in his wife's arms he saw what she meant. The shape of the brows, the contours of the face . . . why, it was a miniature of the face that looked out of the mirror at him every morning when he shaved.

'Well?' Rachel's voice throbbed with urgency.

Trevor placed an arm around his wife and pressed his cheek to hers. 'I see what you mean, and I'm sorry I ever doubted you, love.'

Rachel closed her eyes and sent a prayer heavenwards, thanking God for his mercy. Now she could forget that mad fling she had indulged in shortly before her marriage. What had possessed her she would never know. He had been a handsome man, it was true, but she hadn't loved him. Love had never entered into it. Trevor had been away at the time and she had agreed to go to the Plaza with the girls she worked with in Gallaher's tobacco factory.

All the armed service men who came into Belfast harbour frequented the Plaza ballroom, soldiers and sailors alike. Hans had been a Norwegian sailor and she had agreed to go out with him. One date had led to another. She had been vulnerable at the time, missing Trevor, and Hans' compliments and gentle caresses had persuaded her it would do no harm – he would take care, he assured her. One night his attentions and soft words of persuasion had aroused her so much, she had let lust rule her head. Once the deed was done, however, she had been riddled with guilt and had refused to see Hans again.

To her dismay he had actually sought her out, coming to her workplace in York Road and hanging about outside, waiting for her. Trevor was due home soon and, terrified he would find out, she had begged Hans not to mess up her life. At last she had persuaded him that he really would ruin her life if he carried on in the same way. He had given in to her wishes, but, professing to love her, had insisted that she take his address in case she changed her mind.

When Susan had been premature and had resembled none of the family, Rachel had been terrified, especially in the face of Trevor's suspicions. Because of her guilty secret she hadn't blamed him for doubting her. There had been moments in their marriage when she had fought the desire to tell him about Hans and clear the air once and for all. Now she was glad she hadn't. There could be no doubt now that Susan was Trevor's daughter. He need never know her well-kept secret.

Suddenly her heart contracted with fear as shameful thoughts entered her mind. There could be another reason why William resembled him so much; why Trevor gave in so easily and accepted Susan and her child back into the family home.

Cupping her cheek with his hand, Trevor turned her face towards him. 'I really am sorry for doubting you, love.'

Eyes full of dread met his. How could she think these terrible things about her husband, Susan's father? But was he responsible? She was very much aware that these things did happen. Remembered such a case happening in the street where she grew up. There had been a terrible scandal. It had broken up the family! The father had eventually been arrested and imprisoned. But he had been an unsavoury character. Nothing at all like Trevor.

'It doesn't matter, I understood your fears,' she whispered. But when, above the sleeping child's head, he sought her lips, she turned her head aside. She would have to question Susan closely and insist on knowing the man's name. Her daughter was making life impossible for them all by her obstinate silence.

'I'll make it up to you, love. I promise.'

'I know you will. Just give me time.'

Susan's mad rush sent her up the side of the Cave Hill at a gallop. Halfway there she had to pause for breath, sitting on the trunk of a fallen tree and wiping the tears from her face. A man walking his dog passed her and bid her the time of day. She returned his greeting and then let her thoughts hold sway. Imagine her mother, of all people, advising her to leave her son behind. She would never have believed it possible if she hadn't heard it with her own two ears. Her own mother! She couldn't get over it. Had the whole world gone crazy? After she had regained her breath, more slowly now, she continued on up the hill until she was standing on the brow looking out over Belfast Lough.

A heat haze made everything ethereal and she felt ghostly spirits must surely be hovering about observing her. 'Is anyone I know out there,' she whispered softly. 'Any spirits of dead friends or relatives? If so, please help me to do what's right.' Suddenly memories of nights when much younger came to her, when she and her schoolfriends had gathered together on the hill to tell ghost stories and see who could terrify the others the most, as they sat in a ring, clasping hands. Shivers ran down her spine as the memories unfolded. It was alleged that caves hidden below the brow of the hill were used for satanic meetings. What if there was any truth in the rumours and she was calling on the wrong kind of spirits for help? Could you unwittingly make a pact with the Devil? With a last fearful look around she hurriedly retraced her footsteps, glancing apprehensively over her shoulder now and again until she reached the foot of the hill and civilisation.

Feeling more at ease, her thoughts turned to Donald. She was glad he was coming over on a visit. He would be a pleasant change from Jim and Graham. They had been very close friends, so perhaps she would feel able to confide in him and find out what he thought about her marrying Jim Brady and going to America for a year without William. Good God! What was she thinking of? Was there even the slightest of chances that she might marry Jim? Of course not. She could never leave William behind for a whole year. Why, she would miss out on so much: the cutting of his first tooth; his attempts to crawl; maybe even his first unaided steps.

Against her will Jim's words came back to tempt her. A honeymoon in California with the man she loved would be out of this world. It was a wonderful opportunity. Too good to be missed. Was there any way he could be persuaded to bring William with them? No! Not after the way she'd reacted to his proposal, slapping his face in public like that. He would never come anywhere near her again. She had surely burnt her bridges.

All day Sunday she moped about the house, barely speaking to her parents. Rachel tried to work up the courage to confront her daughter, find out the truth once and for all. Seeing his wife's distress, Trevor thought her worry was in case Susan went to America and took William with her. He warned her not to try and soft-soap Susan, but to let things take their own course.

Three days later Susan was proved wrong about Jim's intentions. On Tuesday morning there was a letter in the post for her. The handwriting was only slightly familiar and her thoughts flew to Donald. Was he cancelling his holiday? It was with trepidation that she opened it.

Colour rushed to her face when she saw it was from Jim. It was so unexpected; she had thought she would never hear from him again. All eyes were on her and she pushed it unread into the pocket of her skirt and continued to eat her breakfast.

'Aren't you going to tell us who the letter's from?' teased Alison. 'Have you a secret admirer.'

'It's none of your business, Alison.'

'You're blushing so much I just had to ask.'

'Did no one ever tell you that curiosity killed the cat?'

'Ah well, I suppose all will be revealed soon enough.' A glance at the clock brought Alison quickly to her feet. 'Is that the time it is? I'll have to run or I'll be late. See you all tonight.'

Trevor was as usual lost in the morning paper and hadn't noticed anything untoward. Susan studiously avoided her mother's eye and Rachel knew better than to pursue the matter. The writer of the letter would be revealed when – and only when – her daughter thought fit.

As soon as she was free, Susan locked herself in the bathroom and, sitting on the edge of the bath, pulled the letter from her pocket. It was quite brief. In it Jim expressed his sorrow at the way things had turned out on Saturday night. He took all the blame for failing to impress her, saying he had been insensitive in the extreme and did not blame her for slapping him on the Monday. He asked if they could please be friends and offered to give her some driving lessons before her friend arrived from England. Suggesting Wednesday evening as a starting date, he said he would be outside the gates at seven o'clock. If she failed to show he would understand and wished her all the best for the future.

Susan sat gazing into space for some time debating what she should do. Feeling as she did about him, could they be just good friends? It was worth a try. After all, not all friends became lovers – look at her and Donald, for instance. She might be only too glad of Jim's friendship one day. So what had she to lose?

Hearing William gurgling, she left the bathroom and went to attend to him. He always wakened in a happy mood, but if he was ignored for too long he would soon give off. Her mother cornered her later, whilst she was bathing William.

'Susan, I'm going to ask you a question and I want you to tell me the truth, mind.' Rachel was so agitated that she was wringing her hands in apprehension.

From her position kneeling beside the baby bath, Susan sat back on her heels and gazed at her in amazement. The state her mother was in, if Susan said 'Boo',

Rachel would probably have fainted on the spot. She held her tongue and waited.

'Were you raped?'

Susan couldn't believe her ears. 'Pardon?'

'You heard me.'

Susan's mouth dropped open. 'Catch yourself on, Mam.'

'Well, were you? Are you covering up for some man?'

'Look, Mam, believe me, I'd never be so noble. If I'd been raped, you can bet your sweet life everybody would have known all about it. Do you think I'm daft or something? I'd never let any man get away with the likes of that.'

'Why be so secretive then? Why not speak out and set everybody's mind at rest.'

'Because, as I've said time and time again, it's nobody's business but mine, and too many people would be hurt. Why are you suddenly so hot and bothered?'

'You would tell me if you'd been raped, wouldn't you?' Rachel persisted. 'Even if it is someone we all know?' Her voice was ragged with worry and Susan gazed at her in bewilderment.

'Mam, believe me, I wasn't raped!'

'Convince me, please. Tell me the man's name.'

'Mam, what's got into you? I wasn't raped. You'll just have to take my word for it.'

Hand pressed to her mouth to stifle a sob, Rachel turned and left the room.

Pulling a towel from the hot rail, Susan lifted her wriggling bundle of joy out of the bath and carried him to the nursery. She was confused beyond measure; could not comprehend what her mother was getting at. Did she suspect Graham was the father and thought her sister should be informed? Well, tough! She had no intention of opening that can of worms. Not even to please her mother.

The first meeting with Jim was an awkward affair. On Wednesday evening she watched from the landing window and saw him arrive dead on seven o'clock. Tightly gripping her handbag, she quickly descended the stairs and was out the door without anyone detaining her.

When he spotted her coming down the drive, Jim left the car and came round to open the passenger door for her. 'Thank you for coming. I don't deserve it.'

'After what I did? I'm sorry I slapped your face in public like that,' she said ruefully. 'Were you very embarrassed?'

He shrugged. 'Just a bit, but I got over it. Actually, it got me a lot of sympathy from those girls. They cheered me when I eventually left the bar.' He had opened the car door but was blocking access to it. 'How well do you drive, Susan? I've no idea. Would you like to start now?'

'Oh no,' she cried in alarm. 'Let's go somewhere there isn't a lot of traffic, please. I'm sure to be very rusty.'

He laughed and opened the door wide for her.

He drove up to the zoo car park and stopped the car. 'This should do the trick.' He turned in his seat to look at her. 'Susan, what happened between us lately can't be ignored. I just want to say I'll be going to America in three months' time and so far the firm thinks you are coming with me. If you feel you care enough to marry me, let me know. Meanwhile, I'll be only too happy to teach you to drive.'

'Thank you, but don't count on it, Jim. William must always come first.'

'I realise that now.' He squeezed her arm gently. 'Let's swap seats. I want to see how well you drive.'

Donald left his car in the garage at Cockerton to get it serviced and walked up West Auckland Road to tell Edith he was going over to Ireland for a holiday. 'Why, that's wonderful news!' she cried. 'Will you be anywhere near Belfast?' she asked excitedly.

'Not only will I be near Belfast, but I'll be staying there.' He laughed happily as he informed her, 'Susan has invited me to stay in her home. What do you think of that?'

'That's marvellous!' She nodded wisely. 'They'll see that you have a good time while you're with them, so they will. If I get some wee presents for them all, will you take them over for me? That is, if you're driving over?'

'I am, yes, taking the car, and of course I'll deliver your presents.'

'I wish I was going with you,' she lamented.

'Now that's an idea, Edith. Why don't you come with me? I'd be glad of the company and there's stacks of room in the car. And you know they'd be glad to see you.'

Edith's voice was sad. 'If only I could, but we're too busy at the moment. This good weather is bringing so many visitors to Darlington. Not just on market days, but every day. It wouldn't be fair to leave Billy to cope on his own. Especially at weekends.'

'Would Jack not help out at weekends?'

'Can you see Margaret letting him? She gripes enough as it is because he can't afford a car to squire her about. That wee girl wants to run before she can walk. There's no way she would let him give up his free time to help out. And mind you . . . we wouldn't ask him to do it for nothing.'

'Put it to Billy anyhow,' Donald urged. 'See what he says.'

'No. No, it wouldn't be fair putting the onus on him. He would only insist on me going with you. Perhaps in the autumn when we're not so busy, he and I will get over for a week. That wee baby of Susan's looks lovely in the photographs she sent over. I'd love to see him. But forget about me. Do you need anything, son? How are you off for money?'

'I couldn't take your hard-earned cash, Edith! But it's more than generous of you to offer.'

'It would be a loan, but you could take your time paying it back.'

'Not even for a loan! Cash flow is most important in business. You need a little capital behind you in case of the unexpected. Thanks all the same, but I'll manage.'

'Quite the little businessman,' she laughed. 'But if you should need help, sure you won't be too shy to ask?'

'Thanks, Edith, you're a pal. I'll bear it in mind.'

'Hush, here's Billy now. Don't mention me saying I'd like to go to Belfast.'

'Look who I picked up along the way,' Billy cried as he stood, still hidden from view, behind the open living-room door.

A little head came around the door, face alight with laughter.

'Why, it's a little angel.' Edith swooped on her granddaughter and, taking her from Billy's arms, hugged her close. 'How's my little darling today?' she crooned.

Margaret followed Billy into the room, her eyes brightening noticeably when she saw Donald. 'She's a bit off-colour. We had taken her out for a breath of fresh air when Billy spotted us, and insisted we come home with him. I didn't notice your car outside, Donald?'

'It's in getting serviced.'

Jack followed her into the room. 'We won't be able to stay too long, mind,' he warned when his eyes fell on Donald.

'Well, I'm sure you can all at least take time to have a cup of tea,' Edith reasoned. 'I've a lovely fresh Madeira cake.'

'You've convinced me, Edith,' Donald chuckled.

'I second that,' Margaret agreed, and planked herself down on the settee beside him. So close it wasn't decent. He squirmed as Jack glared at him. Why was he glaring at him? Why didn't he control his wife, instead of taking it out on him? He wanted to upbraid Jack, but what good would it do? He moved as far away from her as possible, but she edged along after him and patted the space on the other side of her, as if they were making room for her husband. Jack looked at her and wasn't fooled. The venom in his eyes was almost tangible as his eyes raked their faces. For a moment Donald braced himself, convinced that Jack was about to lunge at them in a rage, but with a stifled oath he turned on his heel and left the room. They heard the front door slam and Margaret, with a smug smile, snuggled closer to Donald.

'Isn't this nice,' she whispered.

They were alone, Billy having taken Angela out to see the birds in the back garden, while Edith was in the kitchen making the tea. With a contented sigh, Margaret wiggled her body along the length of his, pressing closer still; rubbing her cheek against his sleeve.

Appalled at her effrontery in her mother-in-law's house, Donald growled, 'You're asking for trouble, girl.'

She smiled sweetly at him. 'No, you're reading the signs all wrong, Donald. It's a bit of lust I'm after. Just good, old-fashioned sex, you know! God knows, my life is so drab I could do with a bit of excitement in it.' Daringly she placed a hand on his thigh and gently caressed it.

He pushed it away. 'You're shameless!'

'No. Wrong again. Just bored. You know, you could put a stop to my boredom, Donald. And then everybody would be happy. And the best of it is, no one need be any the wiser. We could be very discreet about it.'

'You don't know the meaning of the word.'

'Oh, but I do. You'd be surprised.' The hand was back and she laughed softly when she saw the effect it was having. 'It's very obvious to me you still find me attractive, Donald, and it would do no harm to give in to your urges. I promise never to tell anyone.'

He was on his feet and away from her caressing hand and the unwanted effect it was having on him. 'Are you actually looking for a divorce?' he hissed into her face.

'Jack dotes on Angela. He'd never divorce me,' she said confidently. 'Unless of course I forced him to.' A speculative look came into her eye. 'Would you be interested, Donald, if I was free?' Her mouth twisted in a wry grimace as she assured him, 'You needn't worry about Jack. I can manage him. He's putty in my hands.'

'More fool him! Do you know something? You're sick! You don't know when you're well off.' With these words, Donald left her and went off to join Edith in the kitchen.

Edith eyed him covertly as he gazed blindly out of the window. 'Is Margaret up to her old tricks again?'

He turned a look of surprise on her. 'What do you mean?' he asked apprehensively.

She laughed sadly. 'Do you think I'm blind, son? I know what's going on. It will do you good to get away from her for a while, before she wears you down.'

'What I don't understand, Edith,' he cried in frustration, 'is why Jack doesn't put his foot down. Show her who's boss.'

'I think he's afraid! If they have a showdown, he doesn't know whether you'll be waiting to take her on. Will you, Donald?'

He puffed out his cheeks and expelled his breath loudly. 'I've had enough of Margaret to last me a lifetime, thank you.'

'I'm glad to hear that, son. To be truthful, I wasn't sure. She's a very attractive woman – and a very determined one at that. She likes to get her own way.'

'I suppose, if I had any sense, I'd get out of Darlington. Give their marriage a chance.'

'Why? Why should you be the one to move? This is your home town. You've always lived in Darlington, and I for one would be sorry to see you go. As for your mother? Why, she'd be devastated. Here, take this tray in, son. Let Margaret make herself useful for a change, being mother. I'll give Billy a shout when I cut this cake, and follow you in.'

They hadn't heard Jack return, but he sat at the opposite end of the settee from Margaret, looking the picture of misery.

'Edith says will you pour, Margaret?'

'Sure.'

Her pale hair swung down around her face as she bent over the tray, casting mysterious shadows around her eyes and mouth. She really was lovely to look at. A pity her demeanour wasn't as nice. Still, Donald could understand why Jack put up with her tantrums. His eyes ran down her body, lingering on the curve of her hips. Yes, she still had the power to arouse him, in spite of the fact that he didn't like her any more. He could understand why Jack was so besotted with her. Raising his head, he met Jack's baleful glare and blushed with shame at the road his thoughts had taken. He really would be glad to get away from them both for a while.

Edith passed the plate of Madeira cake around and, feeling the tension hanging in the air, sought to break it. 'Has Donald told you he's going over to Ireland in a couple of weeks' time?'

Margaret's head reared back. 'No, he hasn't mentioned it. My, but you're a dark horse. When did you decide on this, Donald?'

'Just lately.'

'Are you going over to Susan?'

'Yes.' He didn't elaborate and she gazed down at her plate. With Jack sitting there she didn't dare show too much concern; he was upset enough already.

Billy broke off putting small morsels of cake into his

granddaughter's mouth. 'Did I hear you right? Is Trevor Cummings actually letting you stay in his house?'

Looking apprehensive, Donald nodded his head. 'Is there any reason why he shouldn't?'

'No, no. But he must have changed his spots. There was a time he would hardly pass the time of day with a Catholic. Or perhaps he doesn't know you're a Catholic. Is that it?'

Seeing a worried frown gather on Donald's brow, Edith admonished her husband. 'Stop teasing, Billy. You're worrying the lad. Don't you listen to him, Donald. If Susan says you can stay in their house it must be all right.'

'Are you going over to make an honest woman of her, Donald?' Margaret asked maliciously.

'Not really, but I'll tell you this much: if I think there's a chance she'll have me, I'll certainly ask her to marry me. You couldn't meet a nicer girl.'

'Huh! That's a matter of opinion.'

'I think most people like her, Margaret.' Donald drained his cup and rose to his feet. 'That was worth waiting for, Edith. The cake was delicious. I'll have to be shoving off now.'

Margaret came to the door of the kitchen as he placed his cup in the sink. 'I would like to send something over for the baby. Will you call in and see us before you go, Donald?'

Not wanting to give her an excuse to follow him over to the sink and make a fool of him again, he joined her at the doorway, where they were in full view of the others. 'I will surely, Margaret. As soon as I know when I'm leaving I'll give you a tinkle and you can leave your gift with Edith. I'll be picking some things up from here before I go.' He had raised his voice just loud enough for everyone to hear.

'I'll buy something tomorrow.' She looked meaningfully at him. 'Perhaps we'll have a drink with you before you go? Wouldn't that be nice, Jack?'

No answer was forthcoming from her husband, but undeterred she continued, 'We'll see you before you go, Donald.'

Not if I can help it, Donald thought and, bidding them all good day, left the house.

On a fine Saturday morning two weeks later Donald left Darlington early in the morning on his journey up to Stranraer and the cross-channel ferry. He was booked on a late afternoon sailing, but never having been to Scotland before wanted to take his time and see all the beautiful scenery Susan had raved about. Billy had also warned him about all the small villages and towns he would pass through, which would slow his journey down somewhat; especially Dumfries, where the traffic was usually bumper-to-bumper on Saturdays.

The further he got away from Darlington, the more relaxed he became. In spite of all his best endeavours to elude her, Margaret had at last caught up with him the night before. He had been collecting the gifts that Edith was sending over to all her family when Margaret arrived with her present for Susan's baby, just as he was about to leave. Edith had apologised for letting her know he was coming, but as she pointed out, Margaret had phoned knowing that Donald was leaving the next morning and had asked if she could come over with a present for Susan's baby, so what could she do but agree?

Jack was on the late shift, Margaret explained when she arrived, and so, wanting to catch Donald, she had left Angela with her neighbour for a while to come over with her present for the baby. 'You're a hard man to catch,' she said and eyed him reproachfully, knowing full well that he had managed to elude all her attempts to waylay him en route from work.

Glad that her gifts were already packed into the boot, Edith asked, 'Have you time for a cup of tea, Margaret? Billy will be out some time yet, but if you can wait he'll give you a lift home as soon as he gets here.'

'I don't want to impose on my neighbour by being away too long. If I do stay for a cuppa, will you give me a lift home, Donald? It would save me waiting for a bus. They're few and far between at this time of evening.'

Reluctantly he agreed, and fifteen minutes later they left Cockerton and headed over to Albert Hill. She was very quiet and this worried him. Just what was going on in that conniving little mind of hers? he wondered.

He drew the car up in front of her house but made no attempt to get out. She turned in her seat and those big, dark eyes of hers mocked him and the full, sensuous lips pouted seductively at him. With a rueful smile she shook her head. 'I do believe you're afraid of me, Donald Murphy. I wonder why? Could it be that you don't trust yourself?'

'Good night, Margaret. I'll see you when I get back.'

'Ah now, Donald. You're not getting off as lightly as that.' A key was thrust at him. 'Here, open the door while I fetch Angela.'

Before he could object she was out of the car and he had no option but to follow her. Planning to leave the minute she came back with the child, he opened the door and entering the small hall waited there. He had to admit that Margaret had hit the nail on the head. He didn't trust himself and had no intention of being manoeuvred any further into the house. To his dismay, in spite of his determination, he had to move into the living room to allow a young man who returned with Margaret, carrying a sleeping Angela in his arms, to enter the house. He looked surprised when he saw Donald and acknowledged him with an abrupt nod.

'In here, Joseph.'

Joseph hesitated. 'Don't you want me to carry her upstairs, Margaret? She's getting quite a weight, you know.'

'No, in here will be fine, Joseph. Lay her on the settee, please. If need be, Donald can carry her upstairs before he goes.' She introduced them. 'Joseph, this is Jack's friend. Donald, this is my next-door neighbour. He lives in the house you used to rent.'

The men exchanged nods and then Joseph, with a quizzical look at Margaret, took his leave.

'Sit down, Donald.'

'I'm afraid I'll have to be going now, Margaret. I've still a lot of packing to do.'

'Why do I not believe you? In my experience, men just throw their belongings together at the last minute, especially when travelling by car. As a rule they don't worry about packing the way women do.'

'I must be the exception to the rule then. Good night, Margaret.'

'You must hold on for a minute or two, Donald. I can't leave Angela on her own in case she rolls off the settee. I need to get her nightclothes down.'

It was on the tip of his tongue to offer to carry the child upstairs, but he caught the words back in time. Look where that could lead.

As if she had read his mind Margaret laughed aloud. 'For heaven's sake sit down, Donald. I'm not going to eat you! I won't be a minute.'

He sat on the edge of the settee and watched the sleeping child. With her golden curls and rosy cheeks, she looked a picture. If things had worked out differently that could be his daughter lying there. If they had married as planned, would Margaret still be discontented with her lot? He imagined so. She would always want what she couldn't have. He'd had a lucky escape.

Was life already laid for you? A matter of whatever will be, will be? Was there someone out there waiting for him? What about Susan Cummings? Who knows? He had questioned Edith about Susan's marriage. Had tried to find out if she was divorced or in the process of being divorced. Edith had been very evasive and had advised him to speak to Susan about it when he was over there. Well, he'd do that! It would be nice to get married and have children of his own. Perhaps one day he and . . .

His thoughts were interrupted by Margaret returning to the living room. She had changed into a loose garment – Donald wasn't sure, but he thought it was called a housecoat. It was of fine material and clung to her full breasts. It was obvious that she had nothing on under it. She had also taken time to brush her hair and, although dusk was falling, it still caught the light that filtered through the window and moved like quicksilver around her face and shoulders.

His breath caught in his throat at the beauty of her and as desire made itself felt. He rose quickly to his feet. 'I'll have to be going now.' His voice was shaky and silently he cursed himself. He knew she was aware of his agitation.

'Bear with me another few minutes, Donald.'

She disappeared into the kitchen and reappeared with a bottle of whiskey and two glasses. 'Remember, I promised to share a drink with you before you left. I wanted Jack to invite you out for a meal with us, but he wouldn't hear tell of it. I can't think why. So . . .' She placed the glasses on a small table and half-filled them with whiskey. 'I believe in keeping my promises.' A glass was thrust at him. 'Safe journey over and back,' she said softly.

Feeling it would be churlish to refuse, he said 'Thanks' and raised the glass to his lips. Darkness was closing in on them and he reached for the light switch.

Quickly setting down her glass, Margaret was there before him, covering the switch with her hand. 'Don't, Donald.' She was so close her breath was fanning his face and her perfume was wafting around him. 'Don't fight it! No one will ever know. You want me. I know you do. So why not? Eh, why not? I made a mistake, but there's no need for us to suffer for ever. We were meant to come together.' She moved closer and raised her face for his kiss.

Feeling his control slipping, he tried to move away but relentlessly she followed, all the while subtly using her body to excite him. Distracted, he thought: why not indeed? He was a mug trying to resist her. After all, you never missed a slice from a cut loaf. As she frequently pointed out, no one need ever know. Susan's face rose before his mind, but he ignored it. No promises had been made there. All she had ever offered him was friendship and for all he knew her marriage may have been reconciled. She had never willingly discussed it with him, but she had said there was a man she was in love with. So why was he letting thoughts of her trespass on this passionate moment?

Margaret was in his arms now; warm and willing. Only a fool would push her away. He crushed her close and his lips trailed her face and neck before savagely covering her mouth. Her lips were soft and moist and worked hungrily under his. He opened her housecoat and caressed her full breasts. The child stirred on the settee and settled down again, but he had been distracted. He raised his head to gaze at her in bewilderment. What was he thinking of? Well, that was obvious enough! But why? Why was he coveting his mate's wife? Jack Devine, God help him, had enough on his plate without him adding to his worries. She pulled his head down towards her and whispered urgently, 'You can't stop now, Donald.'

'I can't do this to Jack.'

'Why not? He did it to you.'

'Two wrongs don't make a right, Margaret. And who knows? I'm beginning to think he did me a good turn. Besides, I don't want to join a queue, and that Joseph guy next door seemed to know his way about here earlier on.'

'Joseph means nothing to me. You must believe that. It's you I want. I've always wanted you.'

Gripping her arms, he put her firmly from him.

'You fool! You stupid fool!' she cried. 'It's only an act after all. A bit of excitement.'

'No, Margaret. In most people's books it's a betrayal.'

In one last desperate attempt to delay him, opening her housecoat and arms wide she cried, 'Look! Look what you're missing.'

A quick glance was all he needed to warn him he must get out of here before it was too late. Roughly pushing past her, he opened the door and hurried to his car. As he eased it away from the kerb, he wasn't surprised to see Joseph, in the rear mirror, leave his house and approach the one next door. Nor was he surprised to see him being admitted. He smiled wryly. Ah, well . . . that's the way the cookie crumbles, he thought. Was he a fool to turn down what was being offered on a plate, so to speak?

Pushing all thoughts of his old flame from his mind, he concentrated on the road ahead. At this hour of the morning it was clear. Dawn was breaking, the sun a fiery ball rising behind him and giving a pink blush to fields and hedges as it rose slowly in the sky, like an artist's brush creating a scene in watercolour. He had never seen anything like it in his life before. He drove through Barnard Castle and over Bowes Moor, before stopping in a lay-by to enjoy all this peaceful beauty. He delayed for twenty minutes looking out over the moors; watching the transformation, with only the wary sheep for company. Then, with a sigh of contentment, he continued over the moors until he reached Penrith, where he left the scenic route for the more mundane motorway towards Carlisle, one of the signs he had been told to watch out for. Half an hour later he passed Carlisle and was crossing the invisible border into Scotland.

Soon he came upon a road sign pointing off the dual carriageway, indicating Dumfries and Stranraer, his ultimate destination. Following these directions, he was surprised to come across another road sign pointing to Gretna Green. Doing a quick calculation of the time it would take to reach Stranraer from here, he decided he was well ahead of schedule, so he made a detour to take a walk round Gretna Green. He was enthralled by the different stories displayed around the blacksmith's shop: some sad, some downright hilarious, but all with the same theme – romance. Stories of lords and ladies eloping to marry their true loves. Stories, too, of girls and boys, considered by law to be too young to marry in their own countries, eloping to Gretna Green to take their wedding vows. As in days of old, some even got married over the blacksmith's anvil. All too soon he had to leave this romantic setting behind and continue on his way.

He was delayed slightly driving through Annan due to the Saturday traffic and shoppers. Feeling a bit peckish as he neared Dumfries, he remembered Billy telling him about one of the fish-and-chip shops where he wouldn't be disappointed with the fare. Finding a car park by a river, he went in search of the shop. Billy was right of course. The fish and chips were delicious and were washed down with a Coke. A glance at his watch warned him that he had better get cracking and go at a steady pace from now on, just in case of any unforeseen hold-ups. He passed through lots of beautiful villages and along the twisting road with the sea shimmering in the bright sunlight below on his left, until he finally arrived at Stranraer harbour with a little time to spare. He booked in at the terminal and was directed into a line of cars.

Locking the car, he went to the terminal café and ordered some sandwiches and a pot of tea. Thus refreshed, he settled down to await the call for all motorists to return to their cars, reflecting on his journey so far. He would certainly give the west coast of Scotland some priority when he next considered taking a holiday.

Chapter Twelve

The short crossing over on the ferry to Larne had been pleasant. So calm and warm Donald had spent all two and a half hours on the upper deck watching Scotland receding in the distance and the shores of Ireland eventually appearing on the horizon. Susan had phoned the night before and explained she would be waiting in the lorry park at Larne harbour and to be sure to watch out for her. As soon as the first vehicle rolled down the ramp she would get out of the car and watch for him.

He pictured her as he had last seen her, anxious and stressed and big with child, and wondered how she would look now. The PA system interrupted his musing, informing drivers to return to their vehicles and foot passengers to gather at some point or other. With a last appraising glance at the fast-approaching Larne harbour, Donald joined the other drivers and passengers and descended the iron companionway down into the bowels of the ship. Waiting for the great iron doors to open and release the cars and vans and wagons, he sat, his thoughts occupied with Susan. Would her husband be with her? Would she be foolish enough to think he would be glad to hear her marriage had been salvaged?

God forgive him, but he hoped a divorce was in the pipeline. There didn't seem much substance to this shadowy husband and Susan deserved a real man. But he could be wrong. Perhaps when he met the guy he would be impressed by him. Only time would tell! Twenty minutes later he was bumping noisily down the ramp on to *terra firma*.

Donald's first sight of Susan brought to the surface all the latent feelings she had once aroused in him. He remembered when he had first become aware of her sensuality on High Row and his pulse quickened. She looked beautiful in a white sleeveless top and brief white shorts, her limbs a golden honey colour. Her figure was neat and trim and the sun caught the chestnut highlights in her hair. Suddenly, to his surprise, he recaptured the feel and smell of her in his arms as if it were yesterday. To his dismay, however, she was accompanied by a tall, dark-haired man. He was deeply tanned and wore a white sports shirt and shorts. Donald smiled as it crossed his mind that the pair of them would make a good advertisement for Persil. Was this the husband?

He steered the car out of the flow of traffic and, leaving it, joined Susan and her companion on the pavement. 'You look wonderful, Susan,' he exclaimed and dared to kiss her on the cheek. To his delight she threw her arms around him and hugged him close.

'It's great to see you again, Donald.' She swung away from him but stayed in the circle of his arm. Indicating her companion, she said, 'This is my friend, Jim Brady. Jim, you must feel you already know Donald, since I've talked of nothing else since I knew he was coming.'

Jim thrust his hand at Donald and wryly agreed. 'I do indeed. Susan thinks the world of you. Apparently you were there for her when no one else was, and for that I am grateful to you.'

Donald gripped the proffered hand and inwardly lamented this man's handsome good looks. Jim's words had a possessive ring to them and this dismayed Donald even more. 'Pleased to meet you, Jim,' he said, his voice pleasant, his demeanour neutral.

'Donald, you'll be glad to hear that Jim has been giving me driving lessons. I drove all the way here,' Susan announced proudly.

A delighted grin split Donald's face. 'I'm glad to hear that! That's very good news. You were doing very well before you left Darlington.'

'She's a natural! She'll have no bother passing her test.' Jim's words of praise warmed her heart. He really had been making an effort these past few weeks. Why couldn't she just forgive and forget?

'Jim will lead the way back to Belfast, Donald, and I'll go in your car. Then you can bring me up to date about everybody across the water.'

'Right!' Jim took control. 'Donald, my car is over in the lorry park. Give me a few minutes and then Susan will direct you to me and we'll get on our way.'

Jim strode off, admiring eyes following his progress. Donald gazed thoughtfully after him, feeling pale and insignificant compared to Jim. And to imagine that he had thought he had a tan! He glanced down at arms that now appeared yellow in the face of the other man's tanned limbs.

Susan tugged at his sleeve to get his attention and

gazed smilingly up into his face. 'I really am so pleased to see you. Mam is looking after William, and Dad is mowing the lawn. All in your honour. They're looking forward to meeting you, and Mam will have a meal ready for us.'

At once all his attention was hers. After all, tanned skin didn't make the man, and she and Jim didn't appear to be all that close. 'Billy Devine had me a bit worried about your dad. Said he wasn't too fond of Catholics. Mind you, Edith didn't contradict him, but she assured me that you would look after me.'

Susan laughed aloud. 'I've discovered lately my dad's bark's worse than his bite. Don't worry about it. Everything's going to be just fine. You're even having our Alison's bedroom while you're here. It's much bigger than the guest room. She left for Galway this morning with Graham and his parents.'

'How is Graham?'

'I don't see very much of him these days. But I hear he's still a bit wobbly on his legs. They say he will eventually get back to his old self. It looks like a Christmas wedding is on the cards.'

Donald eyed her closely, wanting to ask her how she felt about this. He held his tongue. Perhaps he had just imagined that Graham was interested in Susan, after all. If that were the case, he was hardly likely to be planning to marry her sister, and Susan certainly didn't seem in the least perturbed.

'I think we've delayed long enough. Let's go find Jim, eh, Donald? In case he thinks we've got lost already,' she laughed.

When Jim saw Donald's car coming along the lane

between the high container lorries, he eased slowly into his path and Donald fell in behind him. The journey to Belfast had commenced. In his rear-view mirror Jim could see Susan chatting away to Donald and he was worried. Were they closer than Susan had led him to believe? He had thought he was making headway with her these past weeks, and would maybe be able to persuade her to marry him, but seeing how well she and Donald were getting on, he felt uneasy. This guy would be living under the same roof as Susan for the next three weeks; how could he further his own cause while Donald was there?

In the car Susan sat twisted in her seat to gaze at Donald. 'How is Edith and Billy?'

'Doing very well, as far as I can make out. Edith would have liked to come over with me, but they're far too busy. She wants to see your wee son in person.'

'Oh, I wish she had come with you,' she said wistfully.

'She said her and Billy would probably come over in the autumn.'

'Good! Mam will be so pleased.' A smile creased Susan's face as she asked after her cousin and his wife. 'How is Jack and the wonderful Margaret?'

'Jack should put his foot down where that girl's concerned,' he retorted. 'She's far too brazen, that one!' He squirmed in his seat as he remembered how he had almost succumbed to temptation with her the previous night.

'Ah! So she's still making passes at you, mm?' Susan queried knowingly. Watching the red colour rise from his collar to hairline, she felt sad. 'Don't let her ruin your life, Donald. She's not worth it. You deserve better.'

'What about you? Is Jim your estranged husband?'

She laughed ruefully, 'Oh, Donald, there's so much I must explain to you. And I will, I promise. But not now. Later! We have three whole weeks to talk. That is, if you don't mind me trekking about with you?'

'I'll be very glad of your company, Susan. Remember, I've never been to Ireland before, so I'll need a guide to show me around.'

Contented, she relaxed back in her seat with a sigh and started pointing out places she thought might be of interest to him during the rest of the drive.

When they arrived at the house Jim declined her invitation to stay for a meal, saying he needed to have a shower and a change of clothes if they were to go to the Orpheus that night.

Clapping a hand to her mouth in dismay, Susan cried, 'I completely forgot to mention the dance. Perhaps you're too tired to go, Donald, after travelling all day?'

Her eyes questioned him and he was quick to respond. 'Not too tired to see this famous dance hall of yours.' He had a feeling Jim would expect Susan to go, whether he went or not, and he had no intention of losing out.

'That's smashing! Jim and I go every Saturday night.'

'I'll pick you up then, a bit later than usual, eh, Susan? Give you both a chance to get ready. Say about half-eight?'

'That'll be fine, Jim. And thanks for all your help and for letting me drive your car to Larne.'

'No problem.'

Without another glance she climbed the steps, as her mother appeared at the door with William in her arms and her father hovering in the background.

Donald watched her, a slight frown on his brow, feeling that she was being very abrupt with Jim. 'Thanks for all your bother, Jim. See you tonight,' he said before following Susan up the steps.

'Donald, this is my mother and father.' She reached for William as she introduced them.

'Come in, son.' Rachel stepped aside and motioned him inside. 'I'm very pleased to meet you at last.' Seeing Jim turn away, she said in surprise, 'Are you not coming in, Jim?'

'No, I'll see you and Mr Cummings later. Bye for now.'

Trevor gripped Donald's hand. 'Glad to meet you, son.'

'The pleasure's all mine, Mr Cummings. Thanks for putting me up.'

'Uncle Billy had him a bit worried about you, Dad.'

'No doubt! We never did see eye to eye. How is Billy and Edith?'

'Well! Very well. They send their regards. And this must be William.' Tentatively Donald touched a chubby arm and was rewarded with a toothless grin. 'He's beautiful, Susan. The photographs you sent over don't do him justice.'

'Tell me, why do we always stand about in the hall when someone visits?' Trevor complained. 'Come into the lounge, Donald, and sit down. Would you like a lager before your meal?'

'That would be appreciated, Mr Cummings.'

'While you pour the drinks, Trevor, I'll check on the

dinner.' Rachel bustled off in the direction of the kitchen.

'While Mam and Dad are busy, fetch your bags in and I'll show you up to your room,' Susan offered.

Donald disappeared and returned loaded down with parcels. 'These are all presents. Most of them are from Edith and Billy. A small gift from me for the baby and a box of Thornton's continental chocolates for your mother. Edith says you can't get them over here?'

'No. Maybe some day they'll open a shop over here, but not so far. Mam will be delighted.'

'That one in the blue wrapping paper is from Margaret and Jack.' He glanced at Susan and they shared a smile.

'Just leave them all on that coffee table in the corner there, Donald,' she said, suppressed laughter in her voice. She could imagine Margaret making a big thing out of getting the gift to Donald. 'We'll enjoy opening them after dinner. It'll be like Christmas, so it will. Meanwhile, get your bags in and follow me.'

Ascending the stairs behind her, he couldn't keep his eyes of her slim, tanned thighs and well-rounded calves. She turned on the landing to await him and he blushed as she caught his appraising glance.

A smile played about her wide, sensuous mouth. 'In here.' She threw open the bedroom door and stood aside for him to enter.

He gazed around Alison's room in admiration. 'This is lovely. Are you sure your sister won't mind?'

'Not in the slightest. You will be more comfortable here than in the guest room. It's much bigger. As you can see, I've put on plain bedclothes. I trust you won't be too overwhelmed by the flowered curtains and pink carpet, will you?'

He moved closer and whispered, 'It's a secret fetish of mine, to be surrounded by feminine things.'

Eyes wide, she whispered back, 'Don't tell me you wear women's underwear as well?'

'No, I'm fighting that urge. But I think I'm slowly losing the battle.'

They enjoyed a good laugh together and she was struck anew by how easy he was to get on with, and by just how much she liked him. 'We had better go down or your beer will be flat and Mam will be getting worried in case the dinner spoils.'

He held out his arms. 'Let me carry William down for you, he looks a right handful.'

She handed the child over and Donald hugged him against his chest. Her heart was sad as she watched him cuddle her son. This was no act put on for her sake! It was obvious he was genuinely fond of children. If only Jim could be more like Donald it would solve a lot of her problems.

After dinner her parents disappeared into the kitchen and, rising to her feet, Susan said, 'Alas, time marches on. I'm afraid I won't have time to open the presents now. Mam and Dad can go ahead and open theirs if they like. Donald, I'm sorry about this. I should have realised we'd be pushed for time, but I can't let Jim down. Would you prefer to stay here and rest yourself?'

'To be truthful, I'm looking forward to the dance. The presents can keep until tomorrow. Shouldn't I offer to help with the dishes?'

'They just have to be loaded into the dishwasher and Mam will have all that organised by now. Here she is now. Mam, if I leave William's things out, will you get him ready for bed? We're running late.'

'You know I will! You two away and get ready.'

'Thanks, Mam. Donald, come on and I'll show where everything is and you can have a shower while I decide what to wear. I think we can just about make it for half-eight. So let's get a move on.'

Jim arrived on the dot and Trevor crossed the hall and admitted him as Susan came down the stairs looking flushed and happy. Donald joined them from the lounge, where he and her parents were getting to know each other.

'I'll just say good night to William and then we'll go.'

'Here he is!' Rachel came from the lounge with William in her arms. 'Donald was nursing him and he's almost asleep.'

They all kissed the sleepy baby, except Jim, who was aware of Donald's appraising look but was unable to do anything about it. Lately he had made tentative attempts to include the child in outings with him and Susan, but she didn't seem to notice. As for suddenly becoming all loving towards him in front of her parents, that was beyond him. They'd only think him a hypocrite.

To his relief they were at last outside and climbing into the car. The Orpheus was packed, but the doorman recognised Jim and Susan as regulars and allowed them through.

Claiming priority over her, Jim asked for the first dance. With a smile of apology at Donald, she followed Jim on to the floor. 'You look lovely tonight, Susan.'

'Thank you.'

'You suit that colour.'

She wore a pale primrose-coloured cotton dress. Short-sleeved and full-skirted, it showed off her tan and called attention to her slim legs. Glancing down at it, she smiled. 'One of last year's, I'm afraid. I have to be careful with my savings now I've William to think about. I can tell you, I'll be glad to get back to work and earn some extra cash. That's another thing, Jim. If I was to consider your proposal, I'd forfeit all right to my job. There's no way they would keep it for another year.'

'But if we were married, you wouldn't need to work.'

'With William not being yours, I'd always feel the need to be independent.'

'You're talking nonsense now, Susan. When we marry I'll be responsible for him.'

'*If* we marry!' she reminded him. 'Please don't be counting on it, Jim,' she warned.

A frown puckered his brow. 'Susan, I'll still see you while Donald is here, won't I?'

'I don't see why not. Donald is unlikely to want me hanging around him every night. I shall show him the sights during the day and we'll be going to Enniskillen to visit Grannie and Grandad for a couple of days. Edith has sent presents over for her parents. But other than that, I'm sure Donald will want to do his own thing.'

Jim wasn't so sure about this. 'Will you make a point of seeing me as usual on Tuesday and Thursday for your driving lessons?' he asked anxiously. 'You won't want to miss out now that you're doing so well.'

'I don't think you need worry about my lessons, Jim. I'm sure Donald will let me have a go behind the wheel when the roads aren't too busy.'

'You know that's not what I'm worried about! I must see you, Susan, on a regular basis, otherwise how can I hope you will change your mind and marry me?'

'I never made any promises, Jim,' she cried in dismay. 'You said we could be friends.'

Before he could reason with her the music ended and she quickly left his arms and headed to where Donald was waiting. The next dance was a foxtrot and Donald, with a flourish, led Susan on to the floor. Jim watched bleakly as they executed the steps together in perfect harmony. So much for hoping that Donald had two left feet. He was as good a dancer, if indeed not better, than himself.

They danced in silence for some minutes, giving themselves up to the joy of the music. Susan found that she wanted to move closer to Donald and this confused her. She was inclined to keep Jim at arm's length now, not wanting to give him any false impressions. But surely, if she loved Jim, she would be unable to resist contact with him?

To resist the urge, she broke the silence. 'Well! What do you think of the Orpheus, then?'

'It's not what I expected. From the way you spoke of it, I thought it would be more like the Pali.'

'No, that's the Plaza ballroom you're thinking of. Here and the Club Orchid are where we usually dance.'

'Ah, I remember now. The Plaza is where all the servicemen go. Isn't it?'

'That's right.'

The music once again drew to a halt and she reluctantly left Donald's arms and crossed the floor towards Jim.

Jim noted her reluctance and greeted them abruptly. 'Would you like a drink?'

'Yes, please. Excuse me while I go and powder my nose.'

The two men headed for the bar. 'What would you like to drink, Donald?'

'Allow me, please. What will you have?'

'Just an orange juice, thank you. Remember I'm driving.'

'What about Susan?'

'She usually has a pineapple juice.'

Donald ordered the drinks, and whilst they waited for them to be poured, he said tentatively, 'Look, Jim, if I'm in the way, tell me. I don't want to trample on anyone's toes.'

'I'll give it to you straight, Donald. I go to America in about nine weeks' time. I've asked Susan to marry me and accompany me to the States. We were once very close, but I'm afraid I made a mess of it. However, I'm still hoping she'll change her mind and come with me.'

'I see.'

'I hope I can depend on your cooperation?'

'Is she divorced, then?'

'Divorced? What are you talking about?'

'I was under the impression she was married and seeking a divorce.'

Susan caught the tail-end of this sentence as she joined them. Red-faced, she said, 'Hi! I'm here. Is that my drink?'

Donald lifted the drink from the bar and handed it to her. His eyes questioned her, but she refused to meet them. Jim watched them both, completely in the dark. What was Donald talking about? Surely Susan couldn't have married over in England? Was her lover English? Impossible! William was conceived while she was dating him. Of that he was certain!

During their next dance together, Jim showed his bewilderment. 'What on earth's Donald talking about? He seems to think you're married.'

'I know. I'll have to explain to him later on. You see, Aunt Edith thought it would look better if I wore a wedding ring while living with her. Just to keep tongues from wagging. It made no difference to me what people thought, but since I was living in her house I wore it to please her. And it had its purposes. It kept Donald from thinking of me in a personal way. If you know what I mean.'

'Was he interested?'

'No. He was suffering from a broken heart. The girl he was to marry ran off with my cousin Jack. Donald was devastated. He was lonely and so was I. We were good company for each other.'

His voice tight, Jim asked, 'Was that as far as it went?'

Taken aback by his forthrightness, she retorted, 'Not that it's any of your business, but there was never anything but friendship between us.'

He nuzzled his face in her hair and his voice was heartfelt. 'Thank God for that! I don't think I could bear for you two to be under the same roof if you had ever been intimate.'

Thinking how close it had been many a time, she allowed Jim to continue to hold her close. She was afraid of him seeing the guilt she knew was written all over her face, even though she and Donald hadn't actually gone the whole way.

The next dance she forestalled Donald when he opened his mouth to question her. 'Donald, I'm well aware I owe you an explanation. But this isn't the time, or the place. I promise I'll tell you all when we get home tonight. All right?'

Noting how close she and Jim had been dancing, he was inclined to think he had unwittingly been the cause of this and was annoyed, and showed it. 'I suppose it will have to be!' he said abruptly.

She didn't blame him for being annoyed and said soothingly, 'I promise to tell you all I can tonight.'

'That sounds as if I'm not going to learn everything?' he grumbled.

'No. Not quite everything. As I say, I'll tell you as much as I can.'

The house was in darkness when they arrived home. Jim had been very quiet since her disclosure about the wedding ring and now Susan asked tentatively, 'Are you coming in for a cup of coffee, Jim?'

Aware that she had no intention of lingering outside with him for a while, like she usually did, he considered her offer. He was cold sober, but Donald, although far from drunk, had sunk a few beers. He didn't particularly want to go in and watch them together. It was obvious that Donald thought a lot of Susan, and if he happened to do or say anything in the least out of place, Jim knew, the mood he was in, that he would be likely to punch him. However, he decided he had better accept Susan's offer of coffee or she might think he was in a huff. And who knows, perhaps after what he had told Donald about hoping to marry Susan, Donald might retire and leave them alone. Jim was doomed for disappointment.

Inside, Donald slumped into a chair and showed no intention of going to bed. He felt quite tipsy. That was because he was tired to start with, after all the travelling. Then the heat of the Orpheus and all that dancing hadn't helped him relax. On top of all that, a few pints were enough to intoxicate him.

Jim followed Susan into the kitchen and watched as she poured milk into a pot to make the coffee. 'I'm afraid it will have to be instant coffee. I like mine made with milk – what about you?'

'That's fine by me.' He stood drumming his fingers on the table. 'Donald's quite drunk. Will it be safe to leave you alone with him?' he asked apprehensively.

Turning from the stove, she gaped at him in amazement. 'He only had three pints.'

Ah, so she'd been counting! 'Sometimes if you're tired, as he obviously must be after all that travelling today, even one pint is enough.'

'I don't understand? Enough for what?'

'I think you know what I mean! What if he tries it on?'

'He won't! But even if he does, it takes two, you know.'

Jim shrugged his shoulders slightly in frustration, but she took offence at what she thought he was implying. Moving closer to him, she hissed into his face, 'You really do have a very low opinion of me, Jim Brady! You must think I have the morals of an alley cat.'

'Susan, I think nothing of the kind! Do you think I'd want to marry you if I thought that?' He wrapped his arms around her and gripped her close. 'I love you,

Susan, and I'm afraid to leave you alone with him. It's obvious he likes you.'

'That shows how much you trust me.' The milk boiled over on the stove and, breaking away from him, she ran to rescue it. 'Now look what you've made me do.'

'Can I be of any assistance?' Donald stood blinking in the doorway. Although unable to hear what was said, he had been aware of the heated whispered conversation in the kitchen and had forced himself alert to deal with anything unexpected.

Jim threw him a look that verged on loathing. 'No, I was just about to leave. See you Tuesday night, Susan.' Without another word to Donald he left the house.

'What's got into *him*?'

'Jealousy.' Susan's voice was grim as she mopped angrily at the overflow of milk.

'I should have gone on up to bed and left you two alone.'

'It wouldn't have made any difference! I never bring him in on a Saturday night. I do love him, you know, and I don't want to be tempted to do something I might later regret. If I ever do marry him, it will be because I'm sure he wants to be a father to William, not because I was frustrated enough to lose my self-control. We say good night in the car and that's as far as it goes.'

'He told me earlier on he wants to marry you, soon.'

'Oh, did he indeed? And what brought that on?'

'I think he realises I care for you and was warning me off.'

'That was stupid of him! I told him you and I are just good friends.'

'He has eyes in his head, Susan, he can see that I care for you a lot.'

'But that's just it. You don't!'

'I do.' The words were said quietly, yet filled with conviction.

'I see.' Her voice was sad as she spooned instant coffee into the cups and poured the milk. Handing a cup to him, she preceded him into the lounge. 'I think I'll soon change your mind about that. Come on, it's time I removed your rose-tinted glasses once and for all and put you in the picture.'

She perched on the edge of the settee and Donald sat down beside her, but sank back into its depths. Choosing her words carefully, Susan began her narrative.

She told him the whole rigmarole of meeting Jim at the Club Orchid ballroom and how, in spite of warnings from her friend Ruth, she had fallen in love with him. For some months everything had been rosy. Then, when Jim had tried to break it off, she had accused him of having met someone else. Of course she knew in her heart this wasn't so, she stressed, for they were so very much in love. He'd convinced her there was no one else, saying that he was thinking only of her and didn't want her to waste any more of her youth on him. There was no way he could ever marry her.

'He's Catholic and I thought it was because I was a Protestant, and I even offered to go and live with him. He explained he had too many commitments to his family.

'I was distraught when I discovered I was pregnant.'

Donald stirred restlessly beside her when he heard these words and she hurried on before he could interrupt. 'Aunt Edith seemed the only solution. I took the easy way out. I left my parents a note and went over to Darlington. Aunt Edith was wonderful. She hated deceiving Mam, but allowed me to stay. Later, when she suggested I should wear Billy's mother's wedding ring, I agreed to please her – and the rest you know.'

Donald heard her out in silence. The silence stretched and she glanced round at him, thinking that perhaps he had fallen asleep. But no, his gaze was bright and alert.

'Did you understand all that, Donald?'

'I'm still digesting it. However, I'm a bit confused. You forgot to say how or when you got pregnant. According to your story, only Jim could be the father, but why then does he resent the child?'

'He isn't the father, and I won't tell him who is. That's why he resents William.'

Donald ran his fingers through his hair in frustration. Was it the drink that was making him feel thick and stupid? 'I can't say I blame him, Susan. You appear to have been pulling the wool over everyone's eyes. Am I right?'

She nodded and bent her head in shame. Put like that, it did sound disgraceful.

'Susan, do you realise if I had known you were free, things would have been very different back in Darlington?'

'No, they wouldn't! Don't forget you were, and probably still are, in love with Margaret.'

'Not any more I'm not. Even then, with a bit of

encouragement, I could have fallen in love with you. But you kept putting up all these obstacles between us.'

'Well, for a start I was pregnant! And I really do love Jim. There has never been anyone else for me but him.'

'I don't believe that! I don't know what it was like before, but now, as far as I can see, there's a great big void between you and him. Whether you're aware of it or not.'

'I'm very well aware of it. Do you think I'm stupid? But that's only because he wouldn't accept William.'

'And now?'

'He says if we get married he'll make William his responsibility.'

'Responsibility? Is that good enough for you, Susan? I've only been here a few short hours, but I noticed that he seemed to steer clear of the boy.'

'If we married, it would be different. He wouldn't be able to help loving William.'

'You really believe that? You don't think he might always resent him?'

'Of course I believe it. Even Mam thinks everything would work out all right.'

'You've asked your mother's advice about something as important as this?'

'Yes,' she whispered, close to tears now. How could she ever have expected Donald to understand and advise her? She had even thought she would have his blessing.

He put his arm around her and pulled her back against the warmth of his body. 'Listen, Susan. It seems to me everybody is looking out for their own selfish ends, here. Your mother, for instance, obviously doesn't want to lose contact with her grandson, so thinking you love Jim Brady, she will encourage you to marry him with an easy conscience. Then she will have William to herself for a whole year. And she can be sure that you won't be tempted to stay in America, while William is over here. She and your father dote on the child. Much as they love you, it's William who will come first. I've seen the same situation over at Edith's. She and Billy will put up with anything – anything at all – in order to keep Margaret sweet so that she won't leave Jack.'

She jerked her head back to look up at him. 'Do you think she might?' she gasped, eyes wide in apprehension.

'How would I know? She's bored and finds anything in trousers attractive.'

'But you wouldn't . . .'

'Let's get something straight, Susan. I'm no saint. I'm flesh and blood, and remember we can all be tempted.'

'We managed to build up a strong friendship between us,' she reminded him.

'Ah, come off it, Susan. We came close to making love a number of times and you know it!'

'And why do you think I put a stop to it, eh? It was because Jim was always there in my mind, and you – huh! – were obviously still besotted with Margaret.'

He frowned. 'Do I detect a note of complaint there? At that time I had reason to think your husband was the obstacle . . . Hah! What a sham that was. Eh, Susan? Was it Margaret all along? Is that what you're saying?'

His hands were gently caressing her shoulders and arms, trying to ease the tense muscles.

She tried to break his hold. 'I don't know what you mean.'

'I think you do. Even though you were pregnant, if you hadn't pretended to have a phantom husband in the background, we might very well have become lovers and eventually married.'

She tried to rise, but his hands tightened on her shoulders. 'I think we've rambled on long enough for one night. Let's go to bed.'

His arms gathered her close and a rueful smile twisted his lips. 'I wish you really meant that, Susan.'

She lifted her head to chastise him and his lips were there, waiting. She willed herself to look away, but was lost and without further ado he kissed her. It went on and on, and all the emotions she had been bottling up since William's birth were there crying for release. Gently his lips left hers and he put her away from him.

'Listen to me, Susan. Don't marry Jim unless you're absolutely sure you do love him. It won't be an easy commitment if he finds he can't love William. The child will always come between you.' She opened her mouth to assure him she did indeed love Jim Brady, but recalling the longing in her just now, in Donald's arms, she closed it again.

He continued, 'I'll be here for the next three weeks and if I can win you over, I think we could make a go of it. I've always thought we'd make a great match. If not, Jim will have a further six weeks to plead his case. So be prepared! All's fair in love and war! Now, let's go to our separate beds before I forget I'm a gentleman.'

'Donald . . .'

'Let's play it by ear. Eh? But I warn you! Be prepared, because I'll be hugging and kissing you every chance I get.'

She pressed her lips firmly closed. Imagine! She had just been about to say that she couldn't think of anything nicer. She really did like playing with fire.

The next few days passed in a happy blur. Sunday started off wet but warm and Susan, much to the displeasure of her father, attended Mass with Donald in St Patrick's Church on Donegall Street. Afterwards she gave him a tour of how Belfast looked on a wet, quiet Sunday morning.

Rachel had an Ulster fry-up ready for them when they returned and Trevor had obviously been warned to hold his tongue where Mass was concerned. Susan hid a smile at his endeavours to be amicable. Then the presents were opened and a few tears were shed by Rachel and Susan at the goodness of the people over in Darlington. Vera Crabtree had also enclosed a gift for William with Edith's lot. In the afternoon they visited Belfast Castle and Bellevue Zoo, Donald insisting on taking William along with them, which pleased Susan no end.

The evening was spent quietly at home and Susan watched as Donald lay on the carpet and amused her son with soft toys and rattles. He also used all his considerable charm on her parents. Becoming aware that this young man just might be interested in his daughter, Trevor started asking questions about his future prospects and was pleased at what he gleaned from Donald. Warning bells, however, rang loud and clear in Rachel's head as she took stock of all this information. She realised that if Donald and Susan were to marry, they might settle down in England. She buried her fears within her, assuring herself it was unlikely to happen.

Didn't her daughter love Jim Brady? And nice as Donald was, he couldn't hold a candle to Jim in the good-looks stakes.

Monday was spent touring the Antrim coast. They had passed through Glenarm, Glenariff, Cushendall and Cushendun and stopped for a cup of tea in Ballycastle before reaching Bushmills, where Donald purchased a bottle of the famous Black Bush whiskey at the distillery to take home to Billy Devine.

On the way back they stopped at Carrickfergus. Susan was amazed at how much Donald knew about the history of Carrickfergus and some of the towns and fishing villages they had passed through.

'You never cease to amaze me! I'm ashamed to say, you know more about the local history than I do. And I live here for heaven's sake.'

He laughed at her awed expression and informed her, 'I was very good at history when at school. It was my favourite subject and I've read a lot of books about Ireland.'

'Are you enjoying yourself then?' she asked diffidently. 'I mean, you would say if you would prefer to be alone, wouldn't you? You aren't bored with me and William trailing along?'

They were sitting in a sheltered spot in the grounds of the castle overlooking Belfast Lough, eating the picnic lunch prepared by Susan. William was asleep in his carrycot, exhausted by all the fresh air according to Susan. There was no one else about and it was as if they were cut off from civilisation. Moving closer, he put his arm around her shoulders.

'I can honestly say I'm far from bored.'

'I'm glad to hear that. Okay then, tomorrow we'll . . .'

He put a finger to her lips. 'Tomorrow, we won't travel far. I think you owe it to Jim to see him and go for your usual driving lesson. I don't want to take unfair advantage of him.'

With laughter in her voice, she said, 'I thought you said all's fair in love and war?'

'I still think that, but I feel sorry for him. I fear he's fighting a losing battle and there's not much he can do about it.' A finger under her chin, he tilted her face towards his. 'For instance, he's not in a position to do this.' His lips were soft and tender on hers. She squirmed, wanting more, but he again put her gently from him. At her frustrated sigh he smiled and said, 'All in good time.'

Tuesday night she was ready when Jim came to collect her. He breathed a sigh of relief.

Opening the driver's door, he said, 'In you go. I think we'll go straight into town tonight. It's time you learnt to drive in the city traffic for a change and it won't be too busy at this time of night. We'll get you used to the traffic lights and do a bit of hand signalling on the way.'

'Oh, no!' she cried aghast as she slid behind the wheel. 'There are plenty of car parks and quiet streets about. I'd be too nervous to go anywhere else.'

'You're a very good driver, Susan. You could do anything you set you mind on. It's all about confidence. Remember that when you take your test.'

'There will be no hurry with that.'

'Not if I have my way and you come to America with me.'

'Jim . . .'

'I know. You don't want to talk about it. But I can hope, can't I?' Her expression was glum and he promised, 'No more talk about America tonight. After you've conquered the town, you can drive me out to the Chimney Corner Inn. I've booked a table for dinner.'

She smiled. 'If I've to conquer the town first we'll never get there. You might very well starve.'

'Look, Susan, think positive. Now prepare to turn right at these traffic lights coming up.'

She immediately tensed. She hated taking right-hand turns.

'You can do it, Susan. You've done it before. Just relax.'

To her relief, she managed the hand signal and manoeuvre without any difficulty and his words of praise warmed her heart. Nevertheless she was glad when at last her lesson in town was over. Ten minutes later they were passing through Glengormley on their way to the Chimney Corner. She was feeling more relaxed now and enjoying the driving. She even managed a perfect reverse into a parking spot in the car park.

After they had perused the menu and ordered, he inquired after Donald. 'Well, have you been squiring Donald around the sights?'

'Not really. We visited the castle and the zoo on Sunday and yesterday we went along the coast road as far as Bushmills. We went into the distillery and Donald bought a bottle of Black Bush to take home to Billy. On the way back we stopped at Carrick castle for a picnic. He thought the scenery was out of this world.'

'That's nice. The weather's holding out rightly for him. Does he intend going down south?'

'Yes. He's taking off tomorrow for Dublin. I left him and Dad poring over road maps. I wouldn't be a bit surprised if Dad takes a couple of days off and goes with him. They get on remarkably well, you know . . .'

'You're not going to accompany him then?'

'No, William has a touch of the sniffles and I want to keep him indoors for a couple of days. It's probably all that sea air that brought it on.'

The relief Jim experienced was profound. At last he had something to be thankful to William for. And better still, Susan didn't appear in the least bit disappointed not to be accompanying Donald. 'Then I'll see you as usual on Thursday night?'

She nodded and he asked tentatively, 'Can we go to the pictures or somewhere after your driving lesson?'

'I would like that, Jim, because I won't be able to see you on Saturday night. As I've already told you, Aunt Edith has sent over some presents for her parents, and when I phoned Grannie she said to come down at the weekend, when there would be a sing-song in one of the local pubs and we would enjoy it.'

He swallowed his disappointment and smiled gamely. 'I must admit that time is dragging for me at the moment. I hate the thought of you two being together so often. But still, he will only be here a few weeks, and he's well aware you're my girl. Isn't he?'

She nodded and agreed with him. 'Yes, he is.' However, she didn't meet Jim's eyes and the arrival of their starters put an end to the topic.

Back home, when he drew the car to a standstill in the driveway, Susan turned to him. 'I enjoyed myself tonight,

Jim. Thank you very much. Would you care to come in for a coffee?' Her eyes teased him. 'After all, you didn't get the last one.'

'I'm sorry about that. It was very childish of me.'

'Never mind.' She made to get out of the car, but a hand on her arm stopped her. For some unknown reason, the last time he had tried to stop her leaving the car entered her mind and she went rigid. He immediately let go his hold. 'Susan? Surely you don't . . .'

'I'm sorry. I don't know what came over me just now. I honestly haven't even thought of that night in a long while.'

'I was just going to say I wouldn't come in for coffee. Stay and talk to me for a while, like you usually do.'

'I can't. Donald will know we're here and he'll wonder why you aren't coming in.'

'If Donald is any kind of a man at all, he will know very well why I want to stay out here with you.'

Sensing that he was feeling hurt, she relaxed and put her hand on his arm. 'I'm sorry. Of course I'll stay . . . for a short while.'

With a sigh of relief he put his arm around her.

For all his warnings, except for that one time at Carrickfergus, Donald hadn't hugged and kissed her. Just the odd peck on the cheek, leaving her wanting more. Now Jim was nuzzling her neck and whispering endearments in her ear and she found it quite pleasant. More than pleasant! She turned in his arms and returned his caresses. Sensual longing was apparent in her hands and mouth. It was a half-hour later when she sighed and said that she must go in.

Delighted at her show of passion, which had been

sorely lacking of late, Jim reluctantly released her from his embrace. 'Good night, my love. See you Thursday night.'

To her dismay, Donald had retired when she at last entered the house. Only her mother was downstairs. 'Would you like a cup of tea or coffee?' she asked.

'No, thank you, Mam. I'm tired, I'll go on up to bed.'

'Your dad and Donald are off early in the morning – that's why they went to bed early.'

'Is Dad going with Donald, then?'

'Yes, I'm glad to say. He deserves a break. Did you enjoy the meal?'

'Oh, it was so-so.'

'But you enjoyed being with Jim.'

Bewildered, Susan nodded.

'You do still intend marrying him, don't you?'

'Now, Mam, I never said I was going to marry him! I said I'd think about it.'

'You love him, so what's there to think about?'

'William! Remember him? Your grandson?'

Hesitantly Rachel said, 'Promise you won't let Donald sway you.'

'If I let Donald influence me, it will be because I'm not sure of my feelings, and it wouldn't be fair to marry Jim unless I'm sure of how I feel.' Seeing a worried frown gather on her mother's brow, Susan said, 'Don't worry your head about me, Mam. I'm a big girl and I'll do what's best for all concerned. Now away you go to bed. I'll lock up.'

'Good night, Susan. I only hope you know what you're doing.'

Donald heard Rachel climb the stairs and debated

whether or not to go down and have a chat with Susan. Unable to bear the long wait while she said good night to Jim, he had made his excuses and retired to his room. What on earth were they doing out there? As if he didn't know! On the landing he paused to look out and, through the partly misted car windows, could just about see them. The figures in the car were in a tight embrace. Appalled at the intense jealousy that engulfed him, he regretted the plans he had made to go south with Trevor the next day. What if he returned to find Susan engaged to Jim?

Donald came back from the south full of the wonderful architecture of Dublin and the fantastic scenery they had encountered on their travels. They had spent the first day visiting the most popular attractions in the capital, going into museums, cathedrals and the like – and of course the pubs, 'for a wee drop of the cratur'. They had a stroll around St Stephen's Green and even managed a quick visit to Trinity College. Darkness was falling when they eventually got to their hotel, exhausted but happy with their day's adventure.

Next morning, after a hearty Irish breakfast, they travelled across country to Galway. Trevor drove while Donald acted as navigator, stopping along the way at Athlone for coffee and to stretch their legs. They arrived in Galway town late morning and parked the car. It was a warm, bright sunny morning as they stood by the bay looking out over the calm, shimmering water. As they stood admiring the view Donald couldn't resist humming 'Galway Bay', bringing a loud guffaw and a friendly punch on the shoulder from Trevor.

'I didn't hear you singing yesterday when we passed through Drogheda,' chided Trevor.

'Should I have?' Donald was somewhat mystified.

'Well, you were humming 'Galway Bay' here.'

'So?'

'*The Boyne* runs through Drogheda.'

'I think you're losing me, Trevor.'

'Oh, never mind. I was only joking anyway. Where's your sense of humour?'

Donald was slightly offended. 'Here, hold on a minute, Trevor. I've a very good sense of humour if you must know. It's just that I don't understand what you're going on about. I do remember passing through Drogheda, and I do know the River Boyne runs through it. So what?'

'Listen, son. Did you ever hear of William III, known over here as King Billy?'

At last the penny dropped. 'Oh! Now I know what you're going on about.' Donald laughed. 'You're talking about the *Battle of the Boyne*, where William defeated King James II. Why didn't you say that in the first place?'

'God, give me strength.' Trevor was looking skywards, shaking his head in mock frustration. He was nevertheless impressed that this young Englishman would have knowledge of this bit of information. But then again, hadn't Susan mentioned this very fact to him and Rachel – just how knowledgeable Donald was of Irish history.

'Let's go for a short drive along the coast, before we look for somewhere to eat,' suggested Trevor.

'I'm all for it,' replied Donald, and they headed back to the car.

* * *

They drove slowly along the coastal road as far as Clifden before returning to Galway for their lunch. They found an upstairs steak house on the main street and had to wait some time before being served. They both agreed the meal, complemented by a fine red wine, was well worth the wait. After lunch they took a stroll around the town, stopping for a short while to listen to the buskers in the square. Later, as they sat on a bench watching the world go by, Trevor had a sudden thought.

'Look, Donald, do you remember that John Wayne film . . . *The Quiet Man*?'

'This isn't another one of your "guess the song" games, is it? Of course I remember it. I don't think there'd be too many people who wouldn't. Why do you ask?'

Trevor was getting a little bit excited now. 'If my memory serves me right, there's a village not a stone's throw from here called Cong. And that was the outside location for the shooting of that very film. Now then, what do you think of that?'

'Well, I have to admit, Trevor, I don't know what to think.' Donald was beginning to get on Trevor's wavelength at last and waited for his reply.

'Do you fancy taking a drive up to have a look? You never know, we might even run into Barry Fitzgerald with a bit of luck.' They both had a good laugh at his wit.

'Not to mention Ward Bond,' suggested Donald.

'Ah yes, Ward Bond.'

'I said not to mention him,' laughed Donald. 'It must have been that wine we drank, giving us a fit of the giggles.'

'Okay, let's get back to business. If we go to Cong we

can always go home that way, instead of going back through Dublin. What do you think?'

'I think that's a brilliant idea, Trevor. That way we'd be able to see more of Ireland, instead of backtracking through places we've already seen,' he said as he eagerly dug out his trusty map of Ireland and proceeded to pore over it, with Trevor looking over his shoulder.

'There's Cong, there, at the top of Lough Corrib,' said Trevor, stabbing at the map with a finger.

Donald traced the road further north. 'We could then go up through Castlebar and further north to Sligo,' he exclaimed running his finger up the map. 'Where do we go from there?'

'We'll cut across to Enniskillen and from there it's plain sailing all the way back to Belfast, so to speak.'

'Enniskillen? That's where we're going on Saturday isn't it?'

'Yes! But we won't call in on Susan's grandparents. It would only spoil the women's pleasure. You know what they're like! So we'll pass on through.'

'You know what's best, Trevor.'

'Right then, we'd better be getting a move on if we want to have a look around John Wayne country before it gets too late,' said Trevor, getting to his feet and giving his back a good old stretch.

An hour later, after a leisurely drive through some lovely scenery, they were standing outside the large gates of Ashford castle.

'It's in there where that big fight between Big John and Victor McLaglen took place,' said Trevor with an all-knowing tone. 'Let's take a walk around the village and see if we can get a cup of tea. Or maybe you'd like a pint of the black stuff, Donald, eh?'

'Thanks, but tea will be fine. I'm already getting too much of a liking for the Guinness over here and I'll probably take over the driving on the way back, now I know in which direction we're heading.'

They hadn't gone far when they found a little corner café and sat down, 'to take the weight off our feet,' said Trevor as they waited for the tea and home-baked cake. The walls were lined with framed photographs of some of the locals posing with the crew and cast of *The Quiet Man*. Donald, seeing them for the first time, got up and walked around the café scrutinising each and every picture, passing comments to Trevor in the process. Feeling more refreshed they went for a stroll through the village, which didn't take very long. They stood on a bridge watching a pair of swans feeding lazily on a pond and then made their way back to the castle gates and into the castle grounds. Feeling a bit tired from the stifling heat of the day and from walking about, they planted themselves down under a large chestnut tree and sat there for some time in companionable silence, each – more than likely – imagining Maureen O'Hara being dragged bodily across this beautiful countryside, or maybe the horserace down on the shore, or the highlight of the film – that big fight. Who in their right mind could ever forget that?

It was Trevor who intruded on their tranquillity. 'Look, Donald, if we sit here any longer daydreaming, I'll fall asleep. We'd better pull ourselves together and get a move on if we want to find somewhere to stay the night, before it gets dark.'

Reluctantly they left the idyllic Cong in their wake as they headed north towards Castlebar, where they booked into a B&B and went out to find somewhere to eat. And perhaps 'a wee dram', suggested Trevor with a smile. He was really enjoying this young man's company.

Next morning they were heading up towards Sligo and then across to Enniskillen, passing alongside the beautiful Lough Erne, on the final stage of their travels. As they travelled along the motorway to Belfast, Donald thanked Trevor for his company and remarked on the places they had passed through and visited. 'We certainly saw a lot of places in such a short time,' he remarked. 'I'd love to take more time out and tour around the south for, say, a couple of weeks. It was a fantastic couple of days. Wasn't it?'

'You can say that again, Donald. On second thoughts, don't bother, son.' Another loud laugh. 'Seriously, though. Do you know something? This is the first break I've had in five years and I really needed it. I've enjoyed it every bit as much as you. And do you know something else? I enjoyed your company tremendously,' he confessed. 'And do you know something else, son? I'm going to make damned sure, pardon my French, that me and Rachel take a holiday every year from now on. What's the use of slogging yourself half to death, six days a week, fifty-two weeks a year, and not getting any enjoyment out of it? You can't take your money with you when the Big Man calls, you know. Oh no, I've had a right eye-opener this last couple of days. From now on I'm going to be a changed man. Take things a lot easier and not drive myself into an early grave.'

Donald had listened in silence to every word as they approached the end of the motorway, before he finally spoke in a very solemn voice. 'Okay, that was a very good confession. Now, for your penance I want you to say three Hail . . .'

They both had a good old laugh at that and were still laughing as they pulled into the driveway of Trevor's home.

Chapter Thirteen

Trevor had assured Donald he would enjoy himself in Enniskillen and it certainly lived up to his expectations. Susan's grandparents welcomed him so warmly that he immediately felt at home. He particularly liked Jane, as she reminded him of his own mother.

It started to rain as they travelled along the motorway on Saturday morning. 'It would have to start raining now,' grumbled Susan.

'I'm not complaining. It's only a shower. I've been very lucky with the weather so far. Two light showers in a week? Your dad couldn't get over us having no rain at all while we were down south.'

She smiled at him. 'You're right, of course, but I did so want you to see Enniskillen at its best.'

'I've a confession to make, Susan. We passed through Enniskillen on the way home yesterday, so I've already seen it bathed in sunshine and it looks a grand town. Don't you worry! With you for company, I'll enjoy myself, rain or shine.'

They shared a smile. They hadn't had a chance to talk since he had returned with Trevor the night before. He was anxious about how things had progressed between her and Jim. Now, diffidently, he ventured to ask, 'How are you and Jim getting along?'

She shrugged nonchalantly. 'Oh, the same as usual.'

'He hasn't yet persuaded you to marry him, then?'

'Not yet, though sometimes I think it would be for the best. Other times I worry about leaving William behind and that puts me off.'

Much relieved to hear this, Donald tried to be fair towards his rival in love. 'At the moment I'm cramping his style. When I go home next week things will be different.'

'Oh? So you've decided *we* wouldn't be suited after all?'

Surprised at this question, he debated whether to admit seeing her and Jim in the car on Tuesday night; it sounded as if he'd been spying on them. And so he had! He shrugged inwardly. May as well come clean and clear the air. 'I saw you and Jim in the car on Tuesday night and you seemed to be getting on all right.'

She turned in her seat and gaped at him. 'Were you spying on us?' she asked, aware that she was blushing, as the memory of Tuesday night's episode crossed her mind.

'No! No, I wasn't! I just happened to glance out the landing window on my way to bed.'

'Huh! Do you expect me to believe that?' Receiving no reply, she dared to ask, 'And just what did you see, eh?'

He smiled wryly as he admitted, 'As a matter of fact, very little. The windows were all steamed up and, since it wasn't a very cold night, my imagination went into overdrive.'

'Did it indeed? Well, I'll have you know that we did have a good old cuddle. Any objections?'

'No, why should I?' His voice was abrupt. So much for being honest. 'You're a free agent after all.'

'Do you know something? I enjoyed it. A girl likes to be kissed now and again, you know. Not being promised hugs and kisses that never materialise. Some people are just all talk! No action. Know what I mean?'

Aghast at this outburst, her face blazed with colour. Now he would think she was throwing herself at him.

Noting her high colour, he said gently, 'Give me a chance, Susan. I didn't want to rush you. But, believe you me, all that's about to change. I'll have you screaming for mercy before we leave Enniskillen. You mark my words,' he promised.

She was saved from replying by sounds from William, whose carrycot was strapped to the back seat. He soon settled down again, but the conversation was not pursued, as Donald was by now commenting on the countryside as they cruised along towards County Fermanagh.

Donald had insisted on buying her grandparents some little token to show his appreciation of their kindness, so after a hearty lunch they spent a few hours in the town centre shopping and looking at buildings of historic interest that Susan thought would be of interest to him. She mentioned there was a pottery up near the border which produced the world-famous Belleek china and Donald jumped at the chance, suggesting they should visit it while they were in the region.

'I might even get a gift there for Edith,' he said.

They travelled up alongside the Lough Erne, a route that was by now becoming quite familiar to Donald.

'This is the road your dad and I came down on our way home from Cong yesterday,' he said nodding towards Upper Lough Erne. 'Isn't that view something else? You could spend your whole holiday on one of those cruisers.'

'Well, that's what a lot of tourists actually do,' Susan replied. 'And it is a lovely view. Mind you, I wouldn't fancy being out on the lough if it were raining.'

'I suppose if you were really into boats, you wouldn't care what the weather was like,' Donald replied.

Before long they were in Belleek and followed directions to the factory. They spent an hour browsing over the magnificent displays of china.

'Look at some of those price tags,' said Susan. 'They'd take your breath away. Wouldn't they, Donald?'

'They sure would, but I'm just admiring the craft.'

'You men! You never see the important things, do you?'

He just smiled at her and shrugged his shoulders. He did, however, manage to afford a pair of delicate china candlesticks for Edith.

'She'll be delighted with them. I noticed some china ornaments in her display cabinet, when I was over there,' Susan enthused.

On their way out of Belleek, Susan noticed that one of the pointers on the road sign indicated Bundoran. 'Do you fancy a visit to the seaside before we return to Grannie's? It's only a short distance over the border.'

'Why not! We've plenty of time.'

A short time later they were sitting by the seaside, each enjoying a bag of fish and chips.

* * *

Donald was suitably impressed with his day's travels and his praise of Enniskillen and the surrounding countryside, when they returned to the cottage, pleased Susan's grandparents.

That night William and Jane shooed them out of the house and down to the pub while they pampered baby William; warning them not to hurry back, as they would give William a bath and put him to sleep in the carrycot.

Susan and Donald sat in the corner of the olde-worlde pub and sang along with the rest of the customers to the traditional music played by the two fiddlers. He kept her in the circle of his arm, hugging her close and kissing her every now and again. It was with reluctance that they rose to go. The bar was still open, though it was after one o'clock in the morning. As for the fiddlers, they looked as if they could go on playing all night.

Nearing the end of August, it was still quite warm outside. The rain had stayed at bay, bright stars studded the clear sky and the air smelt fresh and earthy. Putting an arm around her shoulders, Donald pulled Susan close as they made their way back to the cottage.

She eased away from him. 'You don't have to overdo it, you know, Donald.'

'Overdo what?'

'You know rightly what I'm talking about,' she admonished him. 'All that kissing and hugging. I know it's all a big show after what I said earlier today.'

They were now at the cottage, which was in darkness. He secured the gate and followed her up the path in silence, but when she would have unlocked the front door, he closed his hand over hers and, pulling her against him, kissed her in a long satisfying kiss.

They were both breathless when he eventually released her. 'That's what I call a real kiss, Susan. I've wanted to do that constantly, but felt I was betraying Jim's friendship. See what I mean?'

'Not really.'

'I mean, have I your permission to court you? Is there any chance you might consider marrying me? Otherwise it would be a waste of time continuing like this, and might cause bad feeling all round.'

Her look was appealing. 'How can I know, Donald? Eh, tell me that. How can I know if you don't try?'

'Fair enough. Jim Brady will just have to look out for himself, then.'

Once more he drew her into his arms and she willingly lifted her face for his kisses.

After that it was no holds barred and Susan felt loved and desired. He didn't overstep the mark once, but during their stay at Enniskillen his attention was passionate and loving, and all thoughts of Jim Brady melted into insignificance, at least for the time being.

Her grandmother gave Susan her blessing. When they were making their farewells on Monday morning she whispered in her ear, 'I hope to hear of a wedding in the not too distant future, girl. Donald is a fine young man and it's obvious he cares for William as well as you, and that's most important for your future happiness.'

Whether Susan put Jim wise to the situation, Donald did not know nor did he care. She went for driving lessons with Jim as usual during the week. On Tuesday night Trevor took Donald to Dunmore Park to the greyhound racing and on Thursday night they visited a few of the city-centre pubs. Thus he was out late both nights and returned when Jim had long departed, so he was not tempted to spy on Susan and Jim in the car again.

Donald was quite confident about his chances with Susan. The only snag, as far as he could see, was that he would be here such a short time, while Jim would have much longer to win her over. How would Susan react if they all went to the Orpheus on Saturday night? Donald smiled at the idea. She would probably flirt with both of them and he would be none the wiser.

Donald was alone with William when a car pulled up to the front of the house on Friday. Trevor was at work and Susan and her mother had gone shopping in preparation for Alison coming home the next day, leaving Donald babysitting. Lifting the child up in his arms, he entered the hall and waited for a knock on the door. To his surprise a key turned in the lock and a young blonde girl with big sparkling blue eyes stepped inside. She set down the suitcase she was carrying and beamed at him.

'Hello. You must be Donald,' she said. 'I'm Alison, Susan's sister.'

Donald was struck dumb, such was the effect this girl was having on him. Shifting William on to his left arm, he clasped the small, firm hand offered to him and, unable to find his voice, nodded in greeting, still holding her hand.

Embarrassed at his reaction, Alison gently withdrew her hand and gave her attention to the child. 'And how's my lovely wee nephew?' she crooned and stretched out her arms for him, hugging him close. 'Oh, how I've missed you.'

To Donald's relief Graham staggered in, weighed down with parcels. 'Hello, Donald. Nice to see you again. I do declare Alison has brought twice as much back with her as she had going.' Dropping the parcels, he approached Donald with hand outstretched.

'You're looking well, Graham,' Donald greeted him.

'You too, Donald. You too.'

'Ah, but I haven't been in a car crash and, may I say, what a car to crash in!'

Graham grinned, displaying a flash of even white teeth set in a tanned face. 'Thank God it was the car that was a write off and not me. It was touch and go for a while, you know, whether or not I'd ever walk again. But I must admit this holiday has done me all the good in the world. The weather down south was marvellous for a change and we spent most of the time lying about in the sun. We did, however, manage a tour of the Ring of Kerry. The scenery was out of this world. Is there no one else at home?'

'Susan and her mother are in town doing a bit of shopping. They weren't expecting you until tomorrow.'

'That's Alison's fault. She wants me to take her to the Orpheus tomorrow night, now that I'm steadier on my feet. If the truth be known, I think it's just so she can show off her tan. Will you be going to the dance?'

'As far as I know, we are going to a dance in somewhere called the Floral Hall.'

'Oh, that's up at Hazelwood, near the zoo. Is it a ticket do?'

'Yes, it was Jim who got the tickets.'

'I'll give him a ring and see if he can get another two. But look, Donald, I'll have to rush on now. I've Mam and Dad waiting in the car. I'll see you when I come back later for Alison.'

'I look forward to it.'

The door closed on Graham, and Donald drew a deep breath before joining Alison in the lounge. She was kneeling on the floor playing with William and his heart lurched in his breast at the beauty of her. He should have been prepared for this, he chastised himself. Hadn't Susan intimated that her sister was beautiful?

'Is anything wrong?' she asked, a puzzled frown ruffling a smooth brow. 'You needn't worry about giving up your room, you know. I'll be staying at Graham's while you're here.'

Glad that she had given him an excuse for his awkwardness, he smiled. 'Are you sure it'll be no bother?'

'No bother at all! There's no shortage of rooms in his house.'

William started to whimper and Alison asked anxiously, 'Is he due a feed?'

A glance at his watch and Donald cried, 'Lord, yes. I'll just heat a bottle for him.'

'You look after him and I'll attend to the bottle.'

As if drawn by a magnet, he followed her into the kitchen, William in his arms.

She glanced over her shoulder at him. 'Are you enjoying yourself here?'

'Yes, I'm having a marvellous time. I've been all over and seen some wonderful places. Of course there's lots I haven't seen, but time goes by so quickly. Last weekend we visited your grandparents in Enniskillen. We had a great time.'

'I enjoy going there too. What did you think of the country pubs? I love them.'

'I enjoyed them immensely. We have working men's clubs over in England and I must say they put on some marvellous acts in their concert rooms. A lot of Irish groups and comedians are very popular. The two fiddlers playing in the pub last Saturday would go down a treat over there. They'd have the women up dancing on the tables. I thoroughly enjoyed the Irish music and the sing-songs. It was smashing.'

'I'm glad you enjoyed yourself.' She tested the bottle on the inside of her wrist. 'There you are. Will you give it to him, while I unpack and sort out some fresh clothes to take to Graham's house tonight?'

He held William out to her. 'First, let me carry those cases upstairs for you.' He was already halfway across the hall, but paused when struck by a thought. 'Where will I put them?'

'Just dump them in the spare room at the end of the landing for the time being.'

Once away from the effect her presence was having on him, Donald sat on the edge of the bed in the spare room and tried to justify his behaviour. What was he playing at? He had practically convinced Susan they were meant for each other and here he was drooling over her sister. And that very same sister was engaged to Graham, and Jim was still clinging to the hope that Susan would marry him. Even if she did decide to marry Jim, that wouldn't clear the way for him and Alison; there was still Graham to consider. Why would she look at him anyway? He was hardly God's gift to women. What a mess! He had better get a grip, before he made a complete idiot of himself. Rising to his feet, he drew a deep breath and exhaled slowly to steady his nerves, before descending the stairs.

Now that he had his emotions under some semblance of control he found Alison easy to get on with. She kept the conversation going, asking after her relatives in England and how her grandparents were faring in Enniskillen, and how he was getting on with her father. Donald was not to know that Alison was usually very quiet and reserved and it was nerves that put her in such a talkative mood. This big fellow made her feel uneasy; albeit in the nicest possible kind of way, she still felt uneasy.

After dinner that evening, Susan sat on the bed and watched her sister pack some things to take to Graham's. 'Did you have a nice time?' she asked.

'Very quiet, but I enjoyed myself. It gave me and Graham a chance to get to know each other.'

'With his parents there?' Susan's voice was sceptical.

'Don't sound so surprised, Susan. They were very understanding and took themselves off for hours at a time. And the hotel was marvellous, great food and plenty of entertainment each evening. I think Graham and I will be very happy together.'

'What about Graham? Is his walking getting any better?'

'He's coming along fine. He even manages to shuffle round the dance floor now. Are you going to the Orpheus tomorrow night?'

Susan shook her head. 'We're going to the Floral Hall. Victor Sylvester and his orchestra are playing there, and Jim and I thought it would . . .'

Alison's eyes widened. 'Oh, is the big romance back on again?'

'I'm not sure yet, but in the meantime he has been giving me driving lessons.'

'I see.' Alison smiled wisely. 'Is this dance a ticket-only do?'

'Victor Sylvester? What do you think? However, Donald says that when Graham heard about it, he said he would ring Jim to see if he could possibly get two extra tickets.'

'You won't mind us tagging along?'

'Not in the slightest. Anything new on your wedding front?'

'No date set yet, if that's what you mean, but it'll be in the not too distant future. Graham wants a place of his own.'

'Will it be before Christmas, do you think?'

'I really don't know. Why all this sudden interest?'

'Well, you see, I've also had a proposal of marriage . . . two, actually.'

'Huh! Two? You're not letting the grass grow under your feet, are you?' Alison sat down on the bed beside Susan and gazed at her wide-eyed.

Susan laughed at her sister's amazement. 'Yes, two. Jim is going to America on contract for his firm and he wants me to marry him and go with him. He would have to leave here in about six or seven weeks, so my wedding would be a hurried affair in the registry office. I don't want to spoil your plans, so what do you think?

Do you think it would interfere with your wedding plans if I were to marry soon?'

'Don't you worry your head about me! There's no chance of us getting married in a couple of months' time. Having said that, I don't want it too near Christmas, either. But I'm sure Graham won't mind waiting until the spring. Easter would be nice, so it would. But I'll say this much: we'll all sure as hell miss William. We kept talking about him the whole time we were away.'

This admission surprised Susan. 'Did you indeed?'

'He's so quiet that you might find this hard to believe, but Graham is very fond of him.'

Hiding her concern, Susan replied, 'That's the snag! Jim wants me to leave William with Mam and Dad. It will only be for a year.'

'Huh! He's a gag! There's no way you'll leave William for a week, let alone a year. Why, as far as a baby is concerned, it's a lifetime. I know I wouldn't chance it! Although, mind you, Graham and I would be delighted to help out.'

Susan's heart dropped. Her sister was just confirming all her own misgivings.

'You said you'd had two proposals?' Alison prompted her.

'Yes, Donald thinks we could make a go of it, and I must say he is more attached to William than Jim is.'

Alison rose to her feet and, crossing the floor, opened a drawer and rummaged unnecessarily about in it. Why did the mention of Donald make her blush? Had Susan noticed? When Susan and her mother had returned from town she had stayed as far away from him as she could, for he made her feel so uncomfortable. During dinner she had been aware of his frequent probing glances and now Susan had intimated that she might marry him. Could she bear to have Donald for a brother-in-law? Turning to face her sister, she said, 'But you love Jim, don't you?'

'I don't really know any more. To tell you the truth, I'm all mixed up.'

'For heaven's sake, Susan, you used to be nuts about him! When you first fell out I thought you'd die of a broken heart. He was all you ever talked about.'

'I know, but he was my first love and I always imagined your first romance is always in Technicolor, as it were. You must know what I mean? Graham's *your* first love. You see, I've grown up now. I'd never let a man get a grip like that on me again. I'm also very attracted to Donald. He's one of the best, and such fun to be with.'

Alison was at a loss to understand her sister's reasoning. She didn't know what she meant about your first love being in Technicolor. All she knew was that she had envied the deep, sensual magnetism between her sister and Jim Brady. It had been there in the air all around them. She wished she could feel that way about Graham, but so far it hadn't happened. As yet the ground hadn't even shivered – let alone moved – when she was in his company.

'Just be careful, Susan,' she warned gently. 'You and Jim were very committed to each other at one time.' The sound of the doorbell brought her to attention. 'That'll be Graham. Will you go down and talk to him till I finish off here?'

It was reluctantly that Susan left the room and descended the stairs. She had seen Graham just once since that awful night at the Orpheus and he'd looked dreadful. How would he look now? More importantly, how would he behave? Would he still live up to his promise? It was her mother who crossed the hall and opened the door.

Giving him a warm hug, she said, 'Graham, it's wonderful to see you. You do look so much better.'

'Thank you, Rachel. I must confess I do feel much better now. Almost back to my old self, as a matter of fact.'

'That's good to hear, son. Come into the lounge, Donald and Trevor are there.'

'Thanks, Rachel. I'll just have a quick word with Susan first.'

He stood at the foot of the wide staircase and watched Susan descend, a sad smile on his face. She looked lovely to him, and putting a hand on each shoulder he kissed her lightly on the cheek. 'You're looking very attractive, if I may say so.'

She smiled into his eyes, seeking reassurance. 'You can pay me compliments like that any time you feel like it.'

His hold on her tightened. 'Ah, Susan, there's so much I would like to say to you. If only . . .'

Dismayed, Susan whispered warningly, 'Graham, remember your promise . . . please.'

Slowly he released his hold on her. 'Forgive me and don't worry. I don't intend breaking my word. It hasn't been easy, you know, staying away. It's so long since I last saw you.' Seeing that she was becoming agitated, he said gently, 'Don't look so worried. I'll behave. Where is that lovely wee son of yours?'

'He's asleep, so he is.'

Unheard by Susan, Alison was descending the stairs. Her voice reached them. 'Are you staying for a while, Graham?'

'I certainly am. I want to renew Donald's acquaintance, and I'm hoping Susan will let me have a look in on her son.'

'Of course she will. I can see a big difference in him in just two weeks and it's much longer since you've set eyes on him. Take him up, Susan, and I'll make some coffee.'

Slowly Susan retraced her steps, followed by Graham. 'You've lost a bit of weight,' he admonished her.

'Just a little. I want to be slim if I decide to get married.' She had reasoned that the sooner he knew her plans, the better. Shock made his step falter and he gripped the banister tightly. Concerned, she swung round to face him. 'Are you all right? Is it your back?'

Pain in his voice, he retorted, 'Do you care?'

'Look, Graham, you know I don't wish you any harm.' She had reached the door of the nursery and gently pushed it open. He preceded her into the room and stood looking down on his son.

He was overcome at the sight of the chubby, pink cheeks and long, curly lashes. 'Alison's right. He has grown. It's not fair, you know, Susan. You're breaking my heart with all this secrecy.'

'Look, for the last time he isn't yours.' Fear of being overheard made her keep her voice low, but it was tight with anger and he hastened to pacify her.

'Don't worry. I'll stick to my word.' With a gentle touch on the baby's head he pushed abruptly past her and descended the stairs.

Susan stood by the cot looking blindly down at her child, her mind in turmoil. How could she ever contemplate leaving William to grow under Graham's suspicious, probing eye for a whole year? She hadn't even considered that angle! All she had worried about was William forgetting her. There was no way she could marry Jim. She had been daft even to consider it. She must tell him at the first possible opportunity; not keep him waiting and hoping in vain. Good! That was one decision taken out of her hands. She would tell him at the dance tomorrow night, in case she was tempted to change her mind if she waited much longer.

Having made up her mind about Jim, Susan felt bereft. She realised now that she had intended marrying him all along. If that was the case, why was she stringing Donald along? As insurance against unforeseen hitches? Besides, she did care a lot for Donald! As he had implied, they would make a good couple. If they did marry, she would make him a good, faithful wife and William would be reared over in Darlington, well out of harm's way. But not too far away for her parents to visit any time they felt like it.

Jim managed to get another two tickets for the dance. It was a special occasion, with Victor Sylvester and his orchestra playing. A big enough occasion for Susan to wear her new ruby dress. She tried it on once again. Tonight, as she examined her reflection in the mirror, she didn't feel in the least bit attractive in it. She had hardly slept a wink the night before, and there were dark shadows under her eyes. She felt depressed and dreaded telling Jim the bad news. Slowly she removed the dress. What a waste! Would she ever wear it? Perhaps at another time in the future she might feel more comfortable in it and wear it for Donald. But not tonight! Not when she was sending her beloved Jim away for good; never again to feel his strong arms around her. Thank God Donald would be there to console and support her. What would she do without his understanding? He was her mentor indeed.

When Jim arrived Donald offered to drive them to the Floral Hall, insisting that it was Jim's turn to have a few beers. Outside the white, round-shaped building, Susan stopped and waited for Donald's reaction.

'Well? What do you think of it?'

He seemed to come to with a start. 'Well, it certainly looks wonderful from here.'

Taken aback by his lack of interest, she entered the building with the two men and excused herself to go and deposit her wrap in the cloakroom, while they went to the men's room.

They had agreed to meet Graham and Alison inside. The ballroom was packed and the men were delighted to discover that Graham had already secured a table by the windows overlooking the duck pond. As she approached them, Susan noted how well Donald and Jim looked in dark lounge suits with crisp, white shirts and black bow ties, but she had never seen Graham look so handsome. Usually he dressed in pale colours, greys and blues, but she thought with his fair colouring and fine physique he carried off his dark suit and white shirt with such panache!

Alison had bought a new dress whilst in Cork. Of pale blue silky material, it fitted her like a glove, made her eyes glow like sapphires and she exuded sensuality. The dress had narrow shoulder-straps and the men's eyes were drawn like a magnet to her tanned cleavage.

Susan now regretted not wearing the ruby dress; she felt quite frumpy in a white sheath, little knowing that it complemented her dark looks and showed off her long, slim legs. Graham caught her appraising glance and winked, with a hint of a smile playing at the corners of his mouth. Embarrassed, she instinctively moved closer to Donald.

This move upset Jim and when Victor Sylvester announced the first dance of the evening, with a slight bow in her direction he said, 'Would you like to dance, Susan?'

Reluctantly she left Donald's side and followed him on to the dance floor.

As if under compulsion, Donald immediately turned to Graham. 'Is it all right if I ask Alison for this dance?'

Taken aback, Graham stretched out a hand, palm upward. 'If Alison doesn't mind?' He glanced at her. She did mind! The affect Donald was having on her frightened her. But what could she say? A slight nod of the head gave her consent. Graham shrugged. 'Be my guest, Donald.'

He watched them take to the floor, a bewildered look on his face. What was Donald playing at? He had noticed Susan's movement towards Donald and Jim's quick intervention. Was that why he had rushed on to the floor with Alison? Did he want to keep a close eye on Susan?

With a shake of the head Graham dismissed the idea and turned his thoughts to his own problems. Now that he had seen William again he was regretting his promise to Susan. If only he could talk it over with someone? But who? No matter to whom he confided his doubts, the cat would be out of the bag and Susan would never forgive him. Besides, he had no real proof that William was his. No proof at all! Just a gut feeling! Only Susan knew the truth. The old adage that sprang to mind was really true. You could always be sure of the mother, but the father could be open to speculation.

Embarrassed at his impulsive gesture, Donald was stiff and awkward as he led Alison around the dance floor. Mortified, he glanced down at her only to discover that she was eyeing him covertly from under long, golden lashes, a slight smile on her face at his discomfort. He apologised. 'I'm sorry. I'm not usually so impetuous, but I might not get another chance to dance with you tonight.'

She wanted to ask him if it mattered, but was afraid of what his answer might be. Before they left the house Susan had confided in her that she had made up her mind not to marry Jim after all. Seeing Alison's reaction had only reinforced her own feelings, that it would be wrong to leave William for such a long time. Did that mean Susan was going to accept Donald's proposal?

He grimaced in apology as he trod on her toes. 'Believe it or not, I'm no country yokel, you know. I can dance as well as the next one.'

'Perhaps if you just relaxed a little and led me around, instead of pushing me away from you, we'd manage better,' she teased.

A chuckle started deep within him and erupted. She

joined him in laughter and, before she knew it, he was sweeping her in and out of the dancers, their steps in perfect harmony.

She was light as a feather in his arms and he gave himself up to the exultation of holding her close. He had never experienced emotions like this in his life before. And he had actually thought he loved Margaret McGivern? He shook his head at the very idea. How could he have been so stupid?

Alison's heart was racing so fast she thought he must surely hear it. What on earth was the matter with her? Donald was only a man, after all. All too soon the dance was over. She thanked him and, withdrawing from his arms, headed back to the table. She felt as if there were gentle electric currents pulsating through her.

He danced the next dance with Susan. It was a slow foxtrot and as they swayed to the rhythm of the music she confided in him. 'I've decided that it would be wrong to marry Jim and leave William behind.'

His heart sank. 'Have you told him yet?'

'No, I can't find the right words to let him down as lightly as possible.'

'Don't be too hasty. Be sure it's what you want, Susan.'

A bewildered frown puckered her brow. 'I thought you'd be pleased.'

'I want what's best for you and the child, Susan.'

'Don't you want me any more?'

'Of course I do. I promise I won't let you down.'

She moved closer, her face almost against his chest, hiding her expression. What did he mean, he wouldn't let her down? It sounded as if he was making some kind of sacrifice for her sake.

They finished the dance in silence and over her shoulder Donald's eyes found and followed Alison. As if under some hypnotic charm, her eyes were drawn to his. They gazed at each other and she had difficulty tearing her glance away. His mother had always told him that some day he would meet a girl and he would know right away that she was the one for him. He had laughed at the very idea of it, but she had said, 'You mark my words, son!' Now it had come about, but too late for him. He was practically engaged to her sister.

Later on in the evening Jim waltzed Susan out into the grounds of the dance hall. Leading her away from the building to one of the benches strategically placed for viewing Belfast Lough, he waited until she was seated, then sat close beside her. They gazed down over the lough for some moments in silence.

'It's beautiful, isn't it?' she whispered.

'It is. We'll miss Belfast when we go away. America will be a completely different kettle of fish for us.'

She squirmed restlessly. Now, she must tell him, *now*. Before she could form the words to break it gently, he spoke again.

'What's wrong, Susan? You've been like a cat on a hot griddle all evening.' He put his arm around her and tilted her face towards his. His kiss was hungry, and to her dismay she found herself reciprocating. It would be wonderful to marry him. If only they could take William with them. If only he would accept the child. When his hands started to explore her body, with a strangled groan she found the strength to push him away.

He recoiled, gazing at her in hurt bewilderment.

Reaching for his hand, she clasped it between her own. 'Forgive me, Jim, and please try to understand. I've something to tell you,' she whispered in a shaky voice.

'From your expression I assume it's bad news?'

'I can't come to America with you. Please understand. I can't leave William for a whole year. It wouldn't be fair on the child, especially at such a young age. He needs me now!'

'Your parents would look after him well. You know that. There's no sweat there, and he's young enough not to miss you.'

'That's not what I'm worried about.'

'What then?'

Deciding to be truthful, she said, 'I'm afraid if I decide to go, his father will make himself known. Not deliberately, but it could happen and I'm not willing to risk it.'

'I wish I could understand why you're so loyal to this guy,' he snarled. 'You must love him, Susan, to shield him like this.'

'Don't be silly! It's not him I'm shielding.'

It was on the tip of her tongue to tell him the truth. After all, once he knew it was Graham, he would see her for the slut she was and want nothing more to do with her. He would go away quietly. Who was she kidding? He would go straight back in and give Graham the length of his tongue. He'd make all kinds of accusations. That's what he'd do! There would be no stopping him! And it would snowball out of all proportion. Then what would her sister and her parents think of her and Graham? They'd be scandalised! The shame of it, the humiliation! She couldn't bear ever to let that happen.

Jim was eyeing her intently. 'Whether you believe it or not, Susan, I think you're in love with this guy and you don't even realise it.'

Tears shone in her eyes as she tried to convince him. 'I'm not! I tell you, I'm not.'

'All right. If you say so. Don't get yourself all upset. Now listen to me, Susan. Please don't rush into anything with Donald until you're absolutely certain. Sure you won't? I'll be here for a while yet, so if you change your mind just let me know. All right?'

She nodded and he kissed her briefly on the lips. 'You're getting cold! Let's go back inside.'

Their table was empty. 'Would you like a drink?'

'Yes, please. I'd like a Coke.'

Jim had barely left when Graham appeared. 'Dare I ask you for this dance, Susan?'

With a nod she rose to her feet and followed him on to the dance floor. 'Where's Alison?'

'Dancing with Donald. She seems to have made a big impression on him. I haven't seen much of you tonight – or her, for that matter.'

'I was out in the grounds for a while with Jim. I've told him I can't go to America after all.'

He successfully hid his relief. 'And what did he have to say about that? Has he asked you to wait for him?'

She shook her head despondently. 'No. He thinks I'll change my mind.'

'And what do you think, Susan?'

'I don't know what to think. I'm so confused.'

He saw the tears glistening on her lashes, threatening to fall. 'Let's get out of here.'

She found herself outside again, on a different bench and with a different man holding her. It had become quite cool and she shivered slightly. Removing his jacket, he placed it around her shoulders and gathered her tightly against him.

She tried to oppose him. 'No, Graham. I can't take your coat, you'll be cold.'

He wanted to say 'I've got my love to keep me warm', but she might take umbrage and storm off, so he remained silent. She felt safe and warm in his arms and instinctively snuggled closer. He was so tender that she longed to experience again his sweet lovemaking; that feeling of oneness. If only . . . Aghast at her line of thought, she lifted her head and gazed at him.

Her expression puzzled him and he said, haltingly, 'What is it?'

She shook her head, bewildered at the thoughts flitting across her confused mind. 'Nothing. Just a passing thought.'

'I must confess, Susan, I'm glad you're not going to marry Jim Brady. I think you'd be doing the wrong thing.'

'What difference does it make whom I marry?'

'Because, while we're both single, I can hope for a miracle.'

'Oh, Graham, Graham.' An urge to offer him her lips was so strong it almost overwhelmed her. She struggled from his embrace, leaving him holding the empty coat. 'I'll have to go inside and repair my make-up.' She was off before he could say another word.

He watched her go with bleak eyes. Why did life have to be so complicated?

In the cloakroom Susan powdered her nose and the dark shadows around her eyes. She looked as awful as she felt. Thank goodness the dim lights in the ballroom would help to camouflage her unhappiness. She practised putting a bright smile on her pale face, then decided to go in search of Donald. She was disappointed in him. He had not lived up to her expectations as a comforter and mentor. She had hardly seen him all evening.

Earlier, Donald had casually asked Alison to show him the grounds around the Floral Hall. It was with trepidation that she allowed him to whisk her off the dance floor and through one of the open French windows. Putting an arm around her shoulders, he walked her to the edge of the lawn and stood gazing over the lough in amazement. 'I can't understand Susan not mentioning this view to me.'

'She can't remember everything, and besides she has a lot on her mind tonight and you're not exactly looking after her, if you don't mind my saying so.'

He did mind! He minded very much any criticism from those lovely, sensuous lips. 'I don't know what you mean.'

'Don't you? She told me you had also proposed marriage?'

'Yes, I did. I thought we were well suited,' he admitted. 'But that was before I met you.'

She twisted round to face him and he immediately put his other arm around her, circling her waist. 'What on earth do you mean? What have I got to do with it?'

His heart sank as he gazed down on her lovely

features. His emotions were so strong that he had been certain she must feel the same. Surely these intense feelings that gripped him could not all be one-sided? He gave in to temptation and kissed her. Shock coursed through her and then a wonderful feeling of release as she returned his kiss. Terrified at the wave of emotions that raged through her at his touch, she angrily pushed him away.

'Don't you dare kiss me like that,' she cried, angrily dabbing at her bruised lips with the back of her hand. 'You've no right at all.'

'I thought there were two of us sharing that kiss,' he chided gently.

'You were taking advantage of me! That's what you were doing.'

'Don't you feel anything at all for me, Alison?' he cried.

'No. Why should I? I hardly know you.' She was being far from honest. The affect Donald was having on her frightened the life out of her. She had never experienced anything like it in her life before, but she had no intention of admitting it. She didn't want any disruptions in her life right now. She was happy with it as it was. Graham could give her everything she ever wanted.

'I don't believe you don't have some feelings for me,' he insisted gently and reached for her again.

Fright, and the need to get away from him, made her speech strong. 'You're one arrogant English bastard, so you are! Practically engaged to my sister and now trying it on with me. Are they all like that over there?'

If she had struck him with her clenched fist Donald couldn't have looked more taken aback. 'I'm sorry. You're right of course.' He stepped quickly away from her. 'I had no right to assume you felt the same as me.' With these words he turned on his heel and left her.

Tears blinding her, she sought solace in the cloakroom. She bumped into Susan on her way out. One look at Alison's face and her sister followed her back in.

'What on earth's wrong with you?'

Blowing her nose, Alison replied, 'Nothing! I was outside. The air is very cold. I think it's a touch of hay fever. What would be wrong with me?'

Hay fever at this time of night? Not for one minute taken in by her lame excuses, Susan said bluntly, 'You look awful, so you do.'

Alison was repairing her make-up and was refusing to meet her sister's eyes in the mirror. She spared her a fleeting glance and retorted, 'You don't look so good yourself.'

'I've a good excuse. I've just told Jim I can't marry him.'

'And what about Donald? Do you love him?'

'I care deeply for him, but it's not the same as love.'

'But is it enough for marriage?'

'Well, you see, Donald is also in love with someone else, so I suppose we understand each other.'

Startled, Alison gaped at her in the mirror. Had Donald confessed his feelings for her, to her sister? Surely not. 'Did he say who this someone else was?'

'He didn't have to. You see, I saw for myself. The girl he really loves married our cousin Jack.'

Rage rose in Alison's breast. He really was an arrogant bastard! There now, he had reduced her to swearing again. Who would want to take on a man like that? He must make a pass at all the girls. Thank God she hadn't succumbed to his advances. For a moment it had been touch and go, she admitted, because whether she liked it or not, Donald was capable of awakening unwanted feelings deep within her.

Controlling her temper, she said curtly, 'Then you are well suited.'

'What do you mean?'

'Both nursing broken hearts? That's a great basis for marriage, so it is. Taking each other on the rebound.' Returning her compact to her purse, she turned to face Susan. 'Thank goodness I have Graham. He can be depended upon, so he can.'

'Oh, can he indeed?' Susan's temper flared and she railed at her sister. 'Let me tell you something, Alison Cummings . . .' Horrified at her outburst, she took a deep breath and finished lamely, 'No man can be relied on. They only think of themselves. "What's in it for me" is their motto. You remember that! Even your wonderful Graham is no different.' She turned aside, dismayed to think she had almost blurted out the truth.

'No, not Graham,' Alison stated with confidence and left the cloakroom with an exaggerated flounce.

Susan wanted to call her back and wipe the smug look off her face, but how could she without letting the cat out of the bag? After all the sacrifices she had made to keep her great secret, she had no intention of doing that.

Graham and Alison were taking to the floor when she arrived back at the table. The other two men were sitting with faces as long as wet weekends. Wearily Susan joined them. 'What a miserable night this has turned out to be. Such a waste! Victor Sylvester! One of the best bands around and look at us sitting here, pictures of misery.'

'I don't think any of us has very much to smile about at the moment,' Jim agreed and nodded to a glass of Coke on the table. 'That's your Coke, but I'm sure it's flat by now.'

Belatedly she remembered him going to the bar. It seemed so long ago. By the look of the Coke it *was* a long time ago. 'I'm sorry, Jim. While you were at the bar Graham asked me to dance, and then I was talking to Alison in the cloakroom. She seems upset about something and I didn't want to leave her alone,' she lied. She looked over at Donald and was surprised to see him wince and squirm in his chair.

'Did she say what had upset her?' he asked.

'No, she just implied that all men were useless, except her Graham of course.'

They lapsed into silence for a while, then Jim rose to his feet. 'Susan, there's no point me hanging around here any longer. I'll get a taxi home. Can I have another dance before I go?'

'Sure.' With a quick glance at Donald, Susan excused herself and followed Jim. 'Are you sure you don't want to come back to the house for a while? You could have a few drinks and stay overnight.'

He smiled wryly. 'If you had said you were coming away with me and I was celebrating, I'd be only too glad to go back with you. As it is, at the moment I feel a bit depressed. Mind you, I haven't given up all hope yet. You might still change your mind. Meanwhile, I'll stay out of the way and see how Donald fares. Okay?'

'If that's what you want.'

'It's better this way. I'm not comfortable when he's around.'

'Does that mean I won't see you at all next week?'

'There'd be no point, Susan. Not while he's here.'

'But I will see you before you go?'

He smiled wryly. 'Mm. I'm still hoping you'll change your mind and come with me.'

'Don't count on it, Jim.'

'Fair enough. Now, let me hold you close one last time, for old times' sake . . . just in case.'

It was about an hour after Jim had bid them all good night that the National Anthem was played. As Susan stood to attention she glanced around her at all the happy, smiling faces. Even Alison looked happy as, arm through his, she pressed close to Graham, who looked his usual sombre self. Donald looked withdrawn and grim. She herself felt down in the dumps.

Both men were sober, having arrived in their own cars. They said good night at the entrance to the car park and headed in the direction of their vehicles. Graham's was parked at one end and Donald's at the other.

Once home, Susan quickly left the car. She was in a quandary. The journey had been travelled in silence. Too short a journey for there to be an atmosphere, but still, surely Donald could have said something? Anything!

'Tea? Coffee?'

'I'll have a beer, if there is any, thank you.'

'There's some in the fridge. Help yourself and would you pour me a brandy, please? I want to get into something more comfortable.' Realising how this might sound, she felt annoyed at herself. Well, she would soon put a stop to it if he tried anything on. He'd been anything but good company all evening.

Donald was sitting on the settee, a glass of beer in his hand. Her brandy was sitting on a small occasional table between the settee and an armchair. Her dressing gown covered her from head to toe and, resisting the urge to sit beside him on the settee, she lifted the brandy and sat down on the chair.

She had looked in on William and the sight of this precious baby of hers convinced her that she had done the right thing in sending Jim away. Whilst changing into her nightwear she had relived the evening in her mind and came to the conclusion that it was all her fault it had been such a big flop. After all, she needn't have told Jim of her decision tonight; Tuesday would have been soon enough. Donald was here on holiday! It was up to her to see that he enjoyed himself. Hadn't he looked after her over in Darlington?

'Donald, I'm sorry.'

He seemed in a stupor and it was some moments before her words penetrated his mind. If she hadn't known this was his first drink, she would have thought him intoxicated.

'I'm sorry. What did you say?'

Concerned, she moved over and joined him on the settee. 'I said I'm sorry I spoilt the night out for us. I could have told Jim some other time.'

He reached for her hand and squeezed it. 'It's not your fault, Susan. I should have been more understanding.' Inwardly he ranted, 'Instead of making a fool of myself over your sister.' How would he be able to face Alison again? He couldn't! He'd have to make some excuse and go home early.

'Donald, let's go away for a couple of days next week, eh? We could go to Donegal. It's beautiful up there at this time of year.' Susan was getting carried away and continued excitedly, 'A friend of Dad's has a cottage there. He rents it out now and again to friends. If it's free this coming week, how about us going there? Now that Alison is home and able to lend a hand with William, I could ask Mam to take over for a few days and we could go on our own. What do you think?'

It was like a lifeline being thrown to him. To get away from this house and not have to face Alison? His prayers had been answered. Putting an arm around her shoulders, he agreed with her plans. 'That sounds a great idea, Susan. I'd like that! I've heard a lot about Donegal.'

His hopes of a clear escape were dashed at her next words. 'Alison and Graham are coming to dinner tomorrow, so I'll ask Alison then if she'll help out with William and, if she agrees, I'll phone Dad's friend. Okay?'

He nodded despondently. So he wasn't off the hook after all. How could he sit through dinner, making inane conversation, while Alison was there? He just couldn't do it! Perhaps he could think up some excuse and take off after Mass tomorrow. He turned to her in desperation. 'I was thinking of taking off after Mass in the morning, Susan. I'm not used to sitting around in someone's house and being tended to hand and foot. I need some time to myself. Just for the day. Would you be offended if I did?'

Grey eyes full of hurt met his. 'Why? Have I done something awful, Donald?'

'No! No, of course you haven't . . .'

'Then why are you acting like this?' She paused, struck by a thought. 'You know, just because I've turned down Jim's offer, don't think I'm about to trap you into marriage. As Alison was quick to point out tonight, two broken hearts are no basis for a happy marriage, so we would have to take our time and see how things go. One step at a time, no strings attached.'

'Why would Alison say that?' he asked, completely bewildered.

'Oh, we were just talking earlier on, and she didn't think it would be fair of me to marry you if I loved Jim. I explained to her that it was your idea and that you were also getting over a broken heart, so you knew just how I felt. And I *do* think we could make a go of it, Donald, I really do.'

'I suppose you told her all about Margaret, and how Jack had run off with her?'

At his tone of voice, her eyes narrowed and, drawing back from him, she slowly withdrew her hand from his clasp. 'Did I do wrong? After all, Alison is family. She won't be telling anyone else.'

Dear God, what must Alison be thinking of him? He rose quickly to his feet. 'I'm tired, Susan. If you don't mind, I think I'll go on up to bed. Good night.'

Open-mouthed, she stared after him. What on earth had got into him? She smiled wryly as she looked down at her dressing gown and a bitter laugh escaped her lips. Had she really thought that she might have to beat him off? Good God, he had practically run away from her. The smell of the brandy was suddenly nauseating. Entering the kitchen, she poured it down the sink and turned on the tap to wash it away. It was as well her father was unaware of such waste or there'd be wigs on the green, she thought, as she made her way to bed.

The journey home to Graham's house had also been conducted in silence. Alison did not find this unusual. She was used to Graham's long silences. Sometimes she thought Graham was more like an older brother than a sweetheart, but this suited her fine. She didn't want an intense affair, if it was going to cause such an upheaval. And it did! Tonight she had experienced that for herself. For one wild moment she had wanted to give herself up to Donald Murphy and let him devour her.

She turned to Graham in the hall. 'Do you mind if I go on up to bed? I've a bit of a headache.'

Concerned, he moved towards her. 'Is it very bad? Shall I get you a couple of aspirin?'

'I have some up in my room. I'll be all right after a good night's sleep.'

Silently she willed him to sweep her into his arms and ravish her. Make her aware that he could also invoke those feelings that Donald had aroused. He kissed her chastely on the brow. 'Happy dreams, love.'

She moved feverishly against him. 'Kiss me properly, Graham.' Again she urged him: make me want you. Bewildered, he took her in his arms and put a lot of feeling into the kiss, but although she pretended to reciprocate it, she felt nothing. Not even the slightest tingle in her toes. This hadn't bothered her before, so why now? Because now she knew how different it could be. When they drew apart she gently brushed his face with her fingers. 'Thank you. Good night, love.'

Disappointed, she climbed the stairs despondently. Why did Donald Murphy have to come into her life at this time, when everything was going so smoothly?

Donald left the house for early Mass in St Patrick's and afterwards crossed over the Queen's Bridge towards County Down. Let Susan make his excuses, he thought. He just couldn't face Alison so soon after making such a fool of himself. What must she be thinking of him? Supposedly nursing a broken heart; willing to take Susan on as a wife, and trying to seduce Alison last night! Because that's how it would look to her. She had practically said so, hadn't she?

He passed through a town named Hollywood and couldn't help smiling as he pictured John Wayne and Maureen O'Hara again. He reached Bangor and stopped for a coffee and a stroll along the promenade, looking at yachtsmen carrying out various tasks of maintenance on their boats. After a while he sat on the sea wall and browsed over Trevor's road map before moving on round the coast.

He made short stops at places like Donaghadee, Portavogie and Ardglass, eventually arriving in Newcastle at the foot of the Mourne mountains in the late afternoon.

He mustn't go home too early or all his manoeuvres would have been in vain. It was a wasted day really. He got no pleasure from all this lovely countryside; his mind was lamenting the loss of Alison. The loss? What was he thinking of? He had never had her in the first place, and now through his own stupidity he never would.

He spent some time at the beach and walking around the souvenir shops, examining the usual ware you'd expect to find in any holiday resort, yet buying nothing. He soon tired of this fruitless browsing and went looking for a café for a bite to eat.

A glance at his watch reminded him that it was time to be moving on, so he took the inland route through Ballynahinch on his way back to Belfast.

It was late evening when he returned. There was no sign of Graham's car in the drive and he gave a sigh of relief. He had been reprieved. It was Trevor who answered his knock.

'I don't know what our Susan's thinking of. She should have given you a key so that you could come and go as you please, not have to stand knocking on the door like a stranger.'

'Or the tick man,' joked Donald. 'Anyway, she knew I wouldn't be too late getting back.' Donald made his excuses. 'I hope you didn't mind me taking off like that, Trevor.'

'Not at all, son. We all need a bit of respite now and again, just to get our heads showered, especially when we are surrounded by strangers. I've done the same myself many a time, I can tell you. And not just with strangers.'

Rachel had quietly followed her husband into the hall and stood nearby. 'I'm just about to make a pot of tea. Are you hungry, Donald?'

'Until you mentioned grub, Rachel, I didn't realise how hungry I was.'

'I'll make some sandwiches then. William is a bit restless. Susan's up there with him, she shouldn't be too long.'

'If you'll excuse me, I'll just nip upstairs and freshen up.'

He paused at the second flight of stairs, wondering if he should go up to see William. Then, hearing a thin wail and Susan's words of endearment as she soothed her son, he decided against it. After a quick wash he changed into a sports shirt and slacks and left his room.

Alison was just coming out of the spare room and he stopped in dismay. With an embarrassed nod he was about to pass her, but with a tentative gesture she stopped him. 'I've been waiting for you. Can we talk?'

He nodded and with a motion of her head she invited him into the spare room. Inside the room, she closed the door and stood with her back to it, apparently at a loss for words.

He waited in bewildered silence and at last twigged what must be wrong. 'You want your room back. Is that it? I'll move my stuff over here now. It won't take too long.'

He moved towards the door, but she remained with her back to it, barring his escape. Her big blue eyes swam with tears. 'I want to apologise for my behaviour towards you. You must think me a right prude, getting on like that about a kiss.'

'It's all right,' he said gently. 'If you're a prude, that's how I'd want you to be.' He stopped in confusion. She wouldn't want to hear this kind of talk from him. 'What's up?'

'I wasn't truthful with you.'

He stood looking perplexed and she found that she couldn't find the right words to explain what she meant. How do you tell a man that he got under your skin so much that you couldn't stop thinking about him? She found she couldn't. Reluctantly moving away from the door, and with a limp wag of her hand, she said, 'Anyway, thanks for listening.'

Aware something was amiss, he hesitated. 'Am I missing something here?'

She raised her head and their eyes locked. The look said it all. Warning himself not to take anything for granted, he slowly reached for her. She willingly entered his arms and they stood, savouring the feel of each other.

It was when he tried to claim her lips that she whispered, 'What are we going to do about Susan and Graham?'

He gazed down in wonder at her. 'I can't take it in! Does this mean that you *do* care for me?'

'Do you think I'd be here if I didn't? I didn't want this to happen! I was happy with my lot till you came along, but it wouldn't be fair my marrying Graham feeling like this about you. And if you married Susan, I'd always be looking at you and wondering . . .' she rambled on.

Joy was flooding through him, making him lightheaded. 'Don't you worry about Graham and Susan. I'll see to them,' he promised and finally kissed her.

They clung together for a long time until at last he gently eased her away from him. Gazing down at her flushed, happy face, he asked, 'Are you sure about this?'

She nodded and smiled sadly. 'Very sure. The effect

you have on me is indescribable. I've been up all night trying to talk myself out of it, but in vain. I believe in my heart we were fated to meet. I think I love you.'

'Well, I don't *think* I love you. I *know* I do. Mind you, I won't be able to support you the way Graham can, but I'll do everything in my power to make you happy, my love.'

'I know you will. I'm a pretty good judge of character.' She gave him a slight push towards the door. 'You had better go downstairs before they start wondering where you've got to. I'll hang back here for a while and get my breath back.' The smile she gave him was breathtaking in its happiness.

Rachel had laid out a variety of cold meats and salad, crusty bread and soft rolls, tea and coffee. They were all gathered around the dining table when at last Susan was free to leave William. When she joined them, her eyes met Donald's and he gave her a huge grin. Surprised at the change in him, she gave him an abrupt nod and took her place at the table.

During the course of the conversation Susan told him that her father had managed to get his friend's cottage for three days. Adding, 'Mam and Alison are more than willing to look after William, so we have three whole days free to enjoy ourselves.'

'According to the forecast the weather is about to break,' Trevor warned. 'And Donegal can be very bleak when it rains, but no doubt you young ones will be able to find something to amuse yourselves,' he muttered, not altogether happy at the idea of what they might get up to.

Alison sat with bowed head. Surely, after her declaration of love, Donald would refuse to go to Donegal for three whole days alone with her sister? It would be unbearable for her to stay behind, picturing them enjoying themselves.

He nodded in agreement. 'Sounds great. I'll see another bit of Ireland before I go home.'

She lifted her head, mouth open at his words. He caught her eye and gave a slight shake of the head, which she took to mean he wouldn't go. Well then, he should tell them here and now and then they would all know where they stood. To her frustration he remained silent.

After the meal the women retired to the kitchen to tidy up and Donald came to a decision.

He and Trevor were in the lounge when he tentatively ventured, 'Don't think me nosy, but are you happy about your daughters' choice of men?'

Unable to hide his surprise at Donald's audacity, Trevor answered honestly enough, 'Graham is a fine, upstanding gentleman and I think Alison will be happy with him. As for Susan? Well now, I can't figure out just who she intends marrying. For a while there I thought you might even be in the picture.' He smiled wryly. 'It shows how much I've changed, when I don't even object to a Catholic as a son-in-law.'

'Then you wouldn't object to me marrying one of your daughters?'

Eyebrows raised, Trevor asked, 'Are you about to ask for Susan's hand in marriage?'

Donald laughed aloud. 'No. I'm just paving the way.'

'I'd be happy if Susan married you.'

'Do you not think that Graham is a bit too settled for Alison?'

'It has never crossed my mind. Although, mind you, Rachel has her doubts about them.'

'Has she indeed?'

'She has, but she won't interfere.'

'What if she's right and Alison changes her mind?'

'I don't think she will, son. Graham is a good catch and Alison will want for nothing. She knows a good thing when she sees it.'

She would want for nothing except excitement and passion, Donald acknowledged to himself.

The evening passed uneventfully. Donald, not wanting to call attention to them, eluded all Alison's attempts to get him alone. It would cause too much speculation and he must talk to Susan first; square things with her. He owed her that much. He was annoyed when Alison, tired of his antics, took matters into her own hands.

'I don't think I'll stay the night after all. I may as well see Graham tonight and come back in the morning.'

'But I've made up the bed in the spare room for you,' Rachel objected.

'I know, Mam.' She flicked a quick glance in Donald's direction and was pleased to see the perturbed look on his face. 'But I'm sure Graham will be glad of my company for a few hours. I'll come back early in the morning.'

'If you're determined to go, I'll run you over,' Trevor offered.

'Let me, Trevor. It will save you getting your car out

of the garage.' Donald rose to his feet and reached for his car keys.

Pleased that her ploy had paid dividends, Alison headed for the stairs. 'I'll fetch my bag. I won't be a minute.'

However, when she returned to the hall, Susan was also waiting. 'I'm coming along for the ride. I need to get out for a bit,' her sister informed her.

Donald was afraid to meet Alison's eye and they trooped out to the car in silence, Susan taking her usual place in the front beside Donald and leaving a disgruntled Alison to climb into the back.

At Graham's house, with an abrupt 'Good night', she left the car and entered the house without so much as a backward glance.

Susan gazed after her in amazement. 'What on earth's got into her? Is it my imagination, or is everyone acting strange this evening?' Donald had turned the car and was heading back. Now she turned to him. 'Well, say something. Why are you all acting so strange?'

Drawing the car into a lay-by, he reached for her hand. 'Susan, I've some explaining to do.'

'Well, thank God for that! I was beginning to think I was going round the bend or something.'

'Do you love me?'

'Huh?'

'Do you love me enough to marry me right away?'

'Ah now, wait a minute. I thought we had decided to take things easy. One step at a time?'

He was roughly caressing her hand and she pulled it away from him. 'Look, whatever's wrong, spit it out.'

'I don't want to hurt you, but things have changed

for me. And I wouldn't for the world let you down if I thought you loved me.'

'But you were so sure we could make a go of it. Why the change of heart? You mean you no longer care for me?'

'I care very dearly for you. I hope we can always remain close friends. But you see, I've fallen in love with someone else.'

Her mind went blank for some seconds, then ran amok as she tried to make sense of his words; tried to make a connection. 'You met someone at the dance last night! That's why you were acting so strange!' She shook her head as if to clear it. 'Still . . . I never saw you with anyone in particular.' She laughed derisively. 'So, some girl looked at you and you fell in love with her. Just like that. Is that what you're saying? Well, I don't believe you! It can't just happen like that.'

'Not quite like that. But as far as I'm concerned, a look was all it took,' he contradicted her. 'At first she wouldn't admit to feeling the same as me. Now she does.'

'You spent the day with her!' she accused. 'That's why you took off! Huh, so much for looking after me.'

'I'll keep my word, if that's what you want.'

'So second best is good enough for me?'

'Isn't that what you'd be offering me?'

She sat silent for a long time. He spoke the truth. He *was* her second choice. Suddenly the truth dawned on her and she swung round in her seat in amazement. 'My God, it's our Alison, isn't it?'

He nodded, shamefaced. 'I'm sorry it had to happen this way.'

'I think you're in for a big disappointment, Donald. Our Alison knows which side her bread is buttered. Graham can give her everything she wants, whereas you . . .' She spread her hands wide to show what she thought of his prospects. 'Sorry to be so blunt, but there it is.'

'She's willing to throw in her lot with me.'

'I don't believe you.'

'It's the truth! She said so.'

She waved her hands about in distress. 'I need to think. Let's go home.'

As he drew the car to a standstill in the drive, he said, 'You understand I can't go to Donegal with you now? It wouldn't be fair on Alison. That's why she was so upset and stormed off like that.'

'Oh, let's on no account upset our Alison. What about me? Don't I deserve some consideration, some sympathy?'

He put a hand on her arm. 'Of course . . .'

She threw his hand off. 'Give over! I don't want to hear any more excuses.'

'What are you going to do?'

'I don't know,' she hissed. 'I need time to think! I'll see you in the lounge after Mam and Dad have gone to bed.'

Throwing herself on top of the bed, Susan beat on her pillows with clenched fists. 'Hell roast the two of them!' she muttered. She didn't deserve to be treated like this. That Donald, of all people, should let her down devastated her. And what about poor Graham? How would he take it? Very well, an inner voice assured her. In fact, she thought he might even be relieved. She felt calmer thinking of Graham. He alone would be composed in this crazy state of affairs. She lay for a long time thinking and at last reached a decision.

She heard her mother and father retiring for the night. Giving them fifteen minutes to get settled, she looked in on William and then quietly descended the stairs. Donald rose to his feet when she entered the lounge.

'Sit down,' she ordered. 'I've a proposition to make.'

He sank down on to the settee again, while she remained standing. 'This shouldn't take too long. As you know, I intend returning to work in a couple of weeks' time. Tomorrow morning I'll pretend to get a phone call asking me to go and see my boss. I'll insist that Alison accompanies you to Donegal to show you around.'

'Are you sure about this?'

'No! But can you come up with anything better?'

'Can't we just tell the truth?'

'That wouldn't suit me at all. I insist we do it my way.'

Thinking that she wanted to save face, he went on, 'What about Graham? Shouldn't he be told the truth?'

'I'll explain to him. When he comes tomorrow night to see Alison, I'll tell him the truth. All of it. Do you agree?' He nodded and she continued, 'Tell Alison to let Graham come here as planned. As if nothing has changed. Okay?'

'Will you be all right breaking the bad news to him?'

She laughed abruptly. 'Do you know something, Donald? I don't think he'll be exactly heartbroken. Good night.'

Getting quickly to his feet, he crossed to her and made to take her in his arms.

'Don't! There is only one man I'll ever let touch me again. I only hope I haven't left it too late. Me and my worrying about other people. That's why I got into this situation in the first place! What do other people matter when your own future is at stake? No one worried how I might feel!'

He gazed at her, uncomprehending. 'I wish I could be more helpful. I feel such a heel.'

'And well you may! I wouldn't have believed you'd act this way. Some mentor you turned out to be.'

'I couldn't help myself, honestly. I fell in love. It happens,' he said abjectly.

'Tell me, Donald, if Alison hadn't returned your love, would you still have pursued me?'

He shrugged. 'How do I know what I'd have done?'

She cried in frustration, 'Agh, away to bed. I'll see you in the morning.'

The realisation of how stupid she'd been ate away at her mind, keeping sleep at bay. She had kept her true feelings under wraps all these months. Had ignored all the signs that she loved *Graham*. And this was the outcome; everyone suiting themselves. Doing what *they* wanted. What if Graham had changed his mind where she was concerned and really believed now that William was not his son? God knows she had denied it often enough. The very idea sent her into a spasm of tears and she sobbed herself into a fitful sleep.

Heavy-eyed, she was passing through the hall next morning just as the phone rang. It was Alison. Not wanting to ask outright if Donald had put her sister in the picture, she dithered.

'I was wondering what time you're leaving for Donegal?'

Keeping her voice low, Susan said, 'You can stop pretending. Donald told me everything last night.'

'Susan, I'm sorry. I couldn't help myself. It just happened.'

'Huh!' Susan gave a disgusted grunt, then sighed. 'I suppose these things do happen. Listen, here's what you must do. You will take my place and go to Donegal with Donald.'

'I can't do that! What will Mam and Dad think?'

'I'll pretend this call is from my boss asking me to go in and see him today. Since he has held my job open so long, they'll understand that I must go.'

'What do I tell Graham?'

'Nothing!' Her voice was sharp. 'You'll tell him nothing. Is that clear? I'll explain to him when he comes round tonight expecting to see you here.'

'That wouldn't be fair, leaving you to do all the dirty work.'

'I want to. I've a lot of explaining to do and I may as well clear the air once and for all. Look, just in case you're tempted to let the cat out of the bag, I'll send Donald over for you now. Tell Graham you'll see him tonight as usual, all right?'

'Are you sure, Susan? I feel guilty as hell about all this.'

'Just do as I say and everything will work out fine. I hope,' she muttered under her breath.

'I didn't catch that last wee bit, Susan.'

'You weren't meant to. See you soon.'

* * *

Later that morning Susan and her mother waved Donald and Alison off and returned to the house. William was letting them know he was awake and Susan took the stairs in a rush. Deep in thought, Rachel went into the kitchen to prepare the child's bottle. There was something going on here, but she couldn't put her finger on just what.

Climbing the stairs, she stood in silence at the door of the nursery and watched her daughter bath and dress her grandson. 'Susan, is anything wrong?'

'Not really.' Seeing that her mother was about to argue, she looked appealingly at her. 'Mam, bear with me. No more questions now, and soon I'll be able to tell you all my secrets – everything.'

'What time are you going to the office?'

Deciding to be truthful, Susan said, 'I'm not.' Rachel's mouth opened, but her daughter forestalled her. 'Please, Mam? Remember, no questions. I would like to go into town this afternoon and get my hair cut and set. Will that be all right with you?'

Her mother nodded dumbly. She would never understand this oldest daughter of hers. She was an enigma.

The morning dragged, but the afternoon flew in. Trevor was surprised when he returned from work and discovered Susan still in the house.

'What happened?' he asked in bewilderment. 'I thought you were all set to go to Donegal today.'

Avoiding her mother's eye, Susan lied convincingly. 'Mr Kennedy rang this morning, about me coming back to work, so I had to go into the office for a short time today to discuss it with him. Alison went with Donald to show him around. Act as courier, as it were.'

'Oh.' Trevor's eyebrows rose as he turned this news

over in his mind for a few moments. Susan could practically hear his thoughts ticking over. 'Can I assume they'll be back tonight, then?' he asked.

'No, they'll stay the three days.'

A frown gathered on her father's brow. 'What has Graham to say about that?'

'He doesn't know yet. He's coming over here after tea tonight. I'll explain everything to him then.'

'That should be interesting!' Trevor remarked, tight-lipped.

Trembling like a leaf, for the third time Susan tried on the ruby dress and fearfully eyed her reflection in the mirror. She felt every bit as glamorous as she looked. The dress hugged her slim figure and the warm colour reflected in her cheeks. Her new hairdo played a big part in her transformation. Cut short and shaped close to the head, it emphasised the delicate planes of her face and her long, slender neck.

She recalled her friend Ruth Vernon's words of praise in the boutique. 'You look absolutely gorgeous in it. You'll never look so lovely again.' Susan smiled to herself in the mirror as she ran her hands over the dress, smoothing invisible creases, glad that Ruth had persuaded her – even bullied her – into buying it. She prayed it would win back Graham's affection.

She stepped into navy court shoes just as the doorbell rang. Quickly leaving the bedroom, she hurried downstairs. The lounge door opened and, before she could stop him, her father was opening the front door.

'Hello, Graham. Come into the lounge. I'm afraid Alison . . .'

'Dad, if I could have a minute alone with Graham, please?' Susan interrupted, her voice slightly louder than usual.

At the sound of her voice both men turned and looked at her. Graham's breath caught in his throat at the sight of her. She was a vision to behold. This beauty should be his wife, he lamented inwardly. He couldn't just stand aside and let her walk off with someone else. What kind of man was he? No! To hell with the promises he had made. He was going to fight tooth and nail to win this beautiful woman over.

Trevor's gaze slowly travelled from head to toe. Why, he thought belatedly, had he always imagined Alison the beauty of the family? Here before his very eyes was a different kind of beauty. 'You're looking well, girl. If I may say so. Is that a new dress?' he blurted out. It was the best he could come up with on the spur of the moment.

'Yes, Dad.' Susan's eyes were fastened on Graham's, 'I bought it for a very special occasion. Now, could I have a quiet word alone with Graham, Dad?'

With a final appraising glance, Trevor nodded at Graham and, entering the lounge, closed the door behind him.

There was still a distance between her and Graham. He was still standing by the front door, she on the bottom stair tread. It felt like a chasm. He stood as if galvanised to the spot. At last she forced her feet into action. Heading for the dining room, she said, 'Can I have a word with you in here, Graham?'

He came to with a start and followed her into the room. Except for the evening light filtering in through the nets on the window, the room was in deep shadow. He reached for the light switch but her voice stopped him.

'Leave it for a moment, Graham. I've a lot of explaining to do and it'll be easier for me in the dark. To be truthful, I'm terribly ashamed of myself.'

Slowly his arm dropped to his side. She was remembering the times she'd had difficulty keeping him at arm's length; practically fighting him off. Now, when she longed for the comfort of his arms, he was standing like a statue. Had she left it too late? Had his love for her finally died after all her rejections of him?

As for Graham, he couldn't make head nor tail of what was going on. Susan had never looked lovelier, but he wasn't daft enough to think she was all dressed up for his benefit. Had she decided to marry Donald and wanted to break the news to him personally? Didn't she realise that, no matter who was the harbinger or what way the news was delivered, it would only break his heart?

'Graham, I don't know where to start. I'm so afraid,' she stuttered.

'If it's bad news, Susan, just get it over with. I'm getting used to hearing bad news from you.'

Big, haunted eyes full of pity gazed at him. Pity was something he didn't want from her. 'Have you decided to marry Donald after all?' he asked abruptly.

'*No!* What made you think that?'

'Well, it looks like Jim's out of the picture now, so I thought marriage to Donald would be the next obvious thing on your agenda. To be truthful, I don't know what to think any more where you're concerned. It's one big hurt after another. I just can't take any more.'

Her heart sank. Had she really been as fickle as that? How could he possibly have any deep feelings left for her, the way she had treated him? 'I've been an awful fool,' she admitted. He remained silent and she continued, 'I worried about what other people would think. Who might get hurt. I was afraid of a scandal and as a result . . .' She paused and licked her lips, suddenly parched '. . . I deprived you of the right to acknowledge William as your own son.'

He abruptly straightened to his full height, his chin jutting out as he absorbed these words. 'Are . . . are you admitting William is *mine*?'

'Yes.'

'Why the sudden change of heart? Are you saying I can have him? Is that it? Does Donald not want to rear him after all? Was it all one big show to let people see what a great fellow he was?'

Exasperated, she cried, 'This has nothing to do with Donald! You're not listening to me.'

'Forgive me, Susan, I'm all at sea here. I don't know what to think. You've lost me completely.'

'Look!' She spoke deliberately. 'Donald and Alison have fallen in love.' Her voice had gone flat. This was not going as she had hoped. And she didn't blame him in the slightest. After the way she had treated him? After all the rejections and denials? She had said some terrible things to him and now she expected him to sweep her into his arms and utter declarations of love, saying that everything would be hunky-dory.

Tears spilled over at the loss of him. She hoped the larkness would hide them, but he saw them glistening n the half-light and was immediately all concern. In hree steps he was beside her, dabbing at the tears with iis handkerchief.

'Don't cry, Susan. I can't bear it when you cry. What :an I do to help?'

She blew her nose loudly and peeped up at him hrough wet lashes. 'You could try holding me and kiss-ng me,' she whispered.

He needed no further bidding and, once in his arms, ıll restraint fled. She devoured his lips, his face and his ips again. 'Oh, I've been such a fool.'

'Hush. Forget it.' Tears were now streaming down his ›wn face. 'Just convince me I'm not dreaming and you eally do love me.'

For some time she did just that, until they were ›oth brought to their senses by cries from William. They ushed into the hall. Rachel had beaten them to it.

Grinning from ear to ear, Graham looked askance, Are we going to let them all know?'

At Susan's nod of assent, he gently put a delaying ıand on Rachel's arm. 'Susan wants to have a quiet word vith you and Trevor, Rachel.'

'And what about William?' Rachel cried with an ınxious glance up the stairs.

'I'll attend to my son.' Graham took the stairs two at ı time, singing at the top of his voice.

'*Your* . . . son?' Rachel shrieked and looked to Susan or confirmation.

Placing an arm gently around her mother's shoulders, Susan said, 'Mam, remember I said I'd tell you everything when the time was right? Well, that time has now come. But I think you'd better sit down first. Besides, I have to break the news to Dad as well, so come into the lounge.'

Mary A. Larkin would like to hear from her readers.
You are very welcome to visit her at:
www.marylarkin.co.uk

For Better, For Worse

Mary A. Larkin

Belfast, 1946. Deserted by the father of her unborn child, Eileen Ross has not married Johnny Cleary for love. Handsome, devoted and eight years her senior, he offers Eileen respectability rather than happiness. Her sister Claire vows to do things differently – and the magic of romance with Michael O'Hara is all she dreamed it would be.

Yet in time married life brings unexpected joy for Eileen as Johnny proves to be the perfect husband and father, but for Claire and Michael tragedy will strike twice and with shocking cruelty. Through all the trauma and heartbreak, it is only Johnny who can hold the family together . . .

For Better, For Worse – a heartwarming family saga of love and fate.